STORMY TIMES FOR THE DOCKYARD GIRLS

TRACY BAINES

First published in Great Britain in 2025 by Boldwood Books Ltd.

Cover Design by Colin Thomas

Cover Images: Colin Thomas

A CIP catalogue record for this book is available from the British Library.

Paperback ISBN 978-1-83656-366-2

Large Print ISBN 978-1-83656-367-9

Hardback ISBN 978-1-83656-365-5

Ebook ISBN 978-1-83656-368-6

Kindle ISBN 978-1-83656-369-3

Audio CD ISBN 978-1-83656-360-0

MP3 CD ISBN 978-1-83656-361-7

Digital audio download ISBN 978-1-83656-362-4

This book is printed on certified sustainable paper. Boldwood Books is dedicated to putting sustainability at the heart of our business. For more information please visit https://www.boldwoodbooks.com/about-us/sustainability/

Boldwood Books Ltd, 23 Bowerdean Street, London, SW6 3TN

www.boldwoodbooks.com

For the fishermen.
And the women they leave behind.

Love bears all things, believes all things, hopes all things, endures all things.

— CORINTHIANS 13.7

1

GREAT GRIMSBY, PEACE DAY, SATURDAY 19 JULY, 1919

A light breeze caught at the flags that decorated the trawlers and sailing smacks sitting idle in the dock and they waved like handkerchiefs in the warmth of the morning sun. Dark ribbons of smoke drifted from the funnels, the boilers the only things at work on this fine July day. In the seven years since she'd moved to Grimsby, Letty Hardy had never seen the docks as they were at this moment, the streets empty save for a few fishermen standing about for want of anything better to do until their ships sailed on tomorrow's tide. No fish would be landed or sold, and the fish market and pontoons were silent. War had not brought it to such a standstill, but it seemed that peace had. Just for the day.

After months of negotiations, the Paris peace talks had concluded three weeks ago with the signing of the Treaty of Versailles, marking the official end to war between the allies and Germany. King George V had proclaimed 19 July as Peace Day, though not everyone saw a national holiday as the way to mark it, insisting the money would be better spent assisting those recently demobbed and without work, and increasing the pensions of those widowed by war. But desire had won out and great military parades were planned in London and elsewhere, to give thanks to those who came home, and remember those who did not. There had been daily instructions in local newspapers all over the country. Gatherings had been planned to celebrate such a hard-won peace. A marker to moving forward. The armistice had been agreed in November, but war had not ended like a full stop. Men were still losing their lives, one way or another. Never was it more clear than in the fishing communities scattered around the coast of the British Isles. Mines still littered the seas, along with the wreckage of ships and U-boats that caught at nets and lines. Many a ship hadn't returned, though the waters were summer calm. No, the war wasn't over yet. Perhaps it never would be. There was always danger where the fishermen were concerned.

Letty pushed the thought away, not wanting to dwell on things that might never happen. It was important to keep her eyes and her thoughts on the future, a better one for all of them. On Gorton Street, she fell into step beside her husband, Alec, who was pushing the empty wheelchair she had borrowed from the Red Cross. Their adopted son, eleven-year-old Alfie, and six-year-old daughter, Stella, skipped ahead of them, the novelty of a ride in the wheelchair long ago losing its shine.

The wheelchair was for Percy Parker, but it was also for Norah, whose life had shrunk with a series of strokes that had led to her husband's incapacitation. The Parkers were family to her, or as good as, her own being in Lowestoft where she had left them on her marriage to Alec. The Parkers' chandlery business had been in decline, the elderly couple keeping things merely ticking along – until she came and 'interfered', as Percy often teased. They had given her a job when she first arrived in Grimsby although Percy would tell that she'd forced herself upon them. And though he'd teased, there was more than a little truth in it. Without them her life here would have been unbearable, the only alternative being to braid nets at home under the instruction of her sour mother-in-law, Dorcas. That relationship too had been a hard-won peace. There seemed to be a battle around every corner – and today would be no exception. Percy was stubborn, but it was Norah who was suffering for his pride. Letty planned to change that.

'I'm wondering whether the wheelchair is a good idea, Let,' Alec said as they came closer to the chandler's shop on Henderson Street, where the Parkers lived and worked. 'Will Percy put up a fight?'

'I would sincerely hope so.' She laughed. 'I'd be worried if he didn't.' There were many men in wheelchairs now, because of the war. It was something they had to adjust to – Percy included. And why couldn't they all have one precious day. Together. She had her argument fixed in her head, had gone through multiple objections that Percy might cast with his limited vocabulary. Letty could have come on her own, she didn't need Alec or the children, but they were her weapons – Alec for his strength, and the children because Percy loved them so, especially Stella, who could wrap him round her little finger. Alec watched her run ahead.

'It's not easy for a man to be seen as weak, Let. Even if he is.' She knew he was talking about himself too. So many of the men had come back from the battlefields of France and Belgium unable to find work – those that were able to do so. Many thousands had returned injured: the limbless, the blind, and the ones whose minds were broken beyond repair. They all had to find a new way of going forward. He gestured to the chair.

'Do you want to sit in it? Rest your legs.'

'I'm pregnant, Alec, not an invalid.' She had dashed off her comment without thought and immediately been aware of his awkwardness. It was hard, allowing him to take care of her, when she was used to fending for herself. 'But thanks for thinking of me,' she soothed. She reached out and linked her arm in his. 'I'm hoping it'll be a good while before I'm waddling like a duck and in need of a carriage.' The baby was due at the end of the year, or early the next if it took its time. She wondered if the child would be impatient to arrive, as Stella had been.

'By! Let, it's odd walking down here in me Sunday best and everyone else the same.'

She caught the wistfulness in his voice, turned her gaze to the trawlers that lined the quay. There were half what there would have been five years ago, but each day more arrived, and with it came work and a sense that life might regain its familiar rhythm. The graving docks were permanently occupied, teams of men working on the trawlers that had been converted to minesweepers in the dry basin, restoring them to their original purpose. But they weren't moving fast enough for Alec. And though she knew he loved her, the call of the sea was too strong to keep him ashore. It had been a bitter lesson to learn – that she would always come second, that his love for her was in constant battle with the yearning to be far away, riding the oceans, hunting the catch and bringing it home. It lit a fire in him that Letty could not counter and over the years of their marriage she had given up trying, accepting her defeat with grace. He was thirty now, more than half his life spent at sea compared to the seven of their marriage. The sea had been there long before she had, and even though her love for him was as constant as a lighthouse, it was not enough to keep him home. The days since he had been recommissioned from his post in the Royal Naval Reserve had started off as joyous, the relief in having him home the answer to her fervent prayers, but as the days went on he'd become irritable, had spent more time at the Clee Park public house trying to shed the long hours of each day with nothing much to do.

'I can't say I like it,' she answered, for it did feel odd, quiet, save for the call of gulls that swooped across the water. The air was free of smoke from trains that were usually in constant movement to and from the docks, free of the steady rumble of the conveyor belt from the ice house as it transported great lumps overhead to the wharf, to be loaded onto waiting trawlers before they set out for the North Sea. Grimsby was a place of innovation and industry, and hard graft. The town was built on fish, and men who took risks not just to catch the fish and bring it home, but also the men who borrowed hard from the bank in the hope of making their fortunes. Many succeeded, many failed, but at least they went home to their beds at night, to their wives – or someone else's. 'It makes me feel uneasy.'

'Aye. We must never be still. It's not natural.' He was talking about himself, and she knew to pay attention, for Alec, like every man she had ever known, was not one to reveal his feelings. He kept them buttoned up like the fastenings on his Sunday suit. Contained. Drink would loosen his buttons as well as his tongue. Oh, the men who had returned all looked unmarked in their best clothing, but at night when the day was cast aside and he fell to fitful sleep she'd begun to learn of the damage he carried within, and though she didn't want him to go back to sea, she knew it was the only thing that would restore him.

Ahead of them Alfie stopped, and Stella clambered onto his back, skinny black stockinged legs dangling, dark curls falling over her shoulders. Letty had fixed her straw hat on with pins, knowing Stella would have lost it in no time at all. 'The little minx,' Letty said, shaking her head. 'She knows full well she can sit in the chair.'

Alec grinned. 'She's not tired; that lass can keep going long after Alfie has given up. She just wants to know he'll carry her if she needs a rest.' He watched them. 'Like us.'

She tensed, his words an acknowledgement of how she was carrying the family while he waited for a ship to command. In the early weeks of the war, she had opened a café that she ran with the help of Dorcas. Over time they had found a way to work together, though they often didn't see eye to eye. Yet, things had improved to what they were. Her mother-in-law had taken an immediate dislike to Letty when Alec told of her his intentions to marry her. She knew now that Dorcas had been worried that Letty knew nothing of the life fishing folk lived. To some extent she'd been right. But it was more than that. Dorcas had favoured Becky Drew, a woman from the beach village in Lowestoft where the Hardys lived. Dorcas was already a widow when Letty made her acquaintance, her husband and younger son, Robbie, lost to the sea. Letty was determined none of her children would go to sea. It was a source of friction between them. Letty no longer talked about it. Words were empty.

Ahead of them, further along the quay, a young woman paced back and forth. She paused, looked down to the water, leaned forward. Letty felt her stomach lurch and gripped Alec's arm. He turned to her, then to the woman, who was now gazing up into the sun. She looked down again, wavered on her heels, and fell into the water.

Alfie dropped Stella from his back. Alec abandoned the wheelchair and raced forward, tearing off his jacket and racing ahead of the boy. At the edge of the wharf, he pulled off his boots and dived into the dock. Letty shouted, 'Help! Anyone, please. Help!' The few men that were around looked to her. She pointed and ran after Alec, Alfie picking up the jacket and boots, Stella at her father's heels, watching too close to the edge at the commotion below. Letty screamed at her to stand back, knowing the child would pay little attention; that was her way. Letty snatched at her arm, pulling her away as other men came to help. One had found a rope and threw it out for Alec to catch; another threw a lifebuoy after him.

Alec disappeared under the dark surface, ripples where he had once been. Letty held her breath. He came up, gasping for air, shaking the water from his head, took another lungful of air and dived again. The surface was still for what seemed a long time before he burst forth again, holding on to a bedraggled wretch of a woman, her small white face ghostlike, and Letty breathed again. Alec slipped the lifebuoy about her, fastened the rope to it and she was hauled towards the iron ladder that was fixed to the wall of the dock. A man went down to him, and Alec slipped the lifebuoy from the woman. Two of the men worked together to bring her to safety, laying her onto the quayside. Alec followed, leaning forward, his hands on his knees, gasping for breath, water running from his clothes and puddling about his stockinged feet. Without being bidden, Alfie had brought up the wheelchair and took hold of Stella's hand, keeping her at his side, leaving Letty to attend to the girl, for she realised as she kneeled beside her that she must have been no more than seventeen. The girl was lifeless, and for a moment Letty thought it too late.

Alec came forward. 'Get back, Let.' Still breathing heavily, he rolled the girl onto her side. A gush of water came from her mouth, setting her coughing and Letty briefly closed her eyes with the relief of it. The girl moved her head, squinting against the light and Letty leaned forward, casting her shadow over a thin face that was bleached of colour.

'Don't worry. We're going to take care of you.' She looked to Alec but could only see his outline against the sun. She said to him, as much as to the other men, 'We'll take her to Parker's. I can let Norah know we'll be a little delayed.' They were almost there as it was. 'It'll give us time to catch our breath. Then I'll get her to the mission at Riby Square. Miss Sheldon will still be at the helm, Peace Day or not.' She thought to put the girl in the chair, but Alec wouldn't hear of it.

'It'll be a rigmarole enough getting old Percy in it without the cushion being wet to begin with.' He swept the girl up in his arms and the party made their way to Henderson Street, the children and wheelchair at his side, while Letty rushed on ahead to alert the Parkers of an unexpected guest.

2

Parker's Chandlery was at the end of Henderson Street closest to Fish Dock Road, the long arterial thoroughfare that beat the lifeblood around the streets and alleyways of Grimsby Docks. It was a town within a town, with its own banks and post office, and a myriad of businesses that had established themselves when the railway came to the docks and turned its fortune. A good portion of the road was taken up by the Coal, Salt and Tanning Company, owned by the Boston Company, who invested in anything that contributed to the wider success of their business. They were not alone, for as a trawler owner built his fleet, he also saw fit to invest in much of the commerce that supported the industry he was a part of. In coal and timber and rope. Many a man had built a small empire around the catching and selling of fish.

They hurried down the narrow street, Letty leading the way, Stella at her father's side, Alfie pushing the wheelchair. Gilbert Crowe, the owner of the shops either side of Parker's, was coming towards them. He stepped back from the Parkers' doorway and grinned slyly at Alec, his thin fingers poking from his waistcoat pocket. He was a slither of a man, mean of spirit – and Letty loathed him. 'Trying to get away from you, was she?' He smirked at Alec as Letty opened her bag for the key.

'No one gets away from me, Mr Crowe. Wait till my hands are free and I'll show you.'

Letty bit back a smile as Crowe hurried into his tobacconist's shop. There would be little trouble from that quarter while Alec was about, and Letty regretted that his days at her side were numbered. The Parkers had withstood Crowe's efforts to squeeze them out of business, but these last few months had been precarious, and Letty didn't know how much longer they'd be able to carry on. She turned to Alfie.

'Run along to Miss Sheldon at the mission and let her know that we'll be bringing a young lady who is in need of her assistance. Come straight back.'

Alfie put the brake on the wheelchair and hurried off on his errand. He was a good lad, and she blessed the day she had taken him in when his mother died.

Letty put the key in the lock and turned it. 'Let me go ahead and let Norah know what to expect. I don't want to unsettle Percy.' Norah would already be agitated, knowing of Letty's plan to get Percy out in the wheelchair, and they were both prepared for the fight that might ensue. The girl had complicated matters, but Letty wasn't going to allow it to spoil what promised to be a lovely day. Alec nodded, water running over his chiselled features and dripping onto his shirt. Stella's attention was fixed firmly on the girl's rust-coloured hair that trickled droplets of seawater onto the cobbled street. Letty pushed open the door, setting the bell above it tinkling, announcing their arrival. Before she was halfway into the shop, Norah emerged from the door marked *Private* at the back of the dark wooden counter, raising the flap and fixing it with the brass catch, and came towards her.

'I don't know if this is a good idea, Letty,' she said, her voice low. 'He's not in the best of moods...' She stopped, catching sight of Alec in the open doorway, the girl in his arms, her head to his chest, seawater dribbling about his feet. She pressed Letty's arm. 'Oh, dear Lord, whatever has happened?'

'The girl fell from the quay,' Letty said quietly.

'Fell?' Norah raised an eyebrow.

Letty shrugged. 'We were some distance. Alec went in after her. We're taking her to the mission as a first port of call, but I wanted to let you know we'd be later than planned.'

The old woman shook her head. 'That doesn't matter. You'd best come through.'

'Norah...' Letty protested.

She gave Letty a look that warned her not to argue and beckoned to Alec and Stella to come inside.

'Let's get you out of those wet clothes, young man. Brave as you are. You'll catch your death.' She gave them no time for argument, and they followed her through to the living quarters at the back of the shop.

* * *

Old age had come cruelly to Percy Parker, a series of strokes gradually eroding his mobility, the last of which had robbed him of his speech so that his communication was limited to little more than a series of grunts and shakes of his fist. His frustration at his incapacity had increased tenfold, and though friends came to sit with him in the small back room behind the shop, he was reduced to being an observer and not the instigator of conversation as he'd been when she'd first come to work for them. Letty couldn't see how they could manage here much longer. But Percy refused to move.

Norah drew out one of the two chairs either side of the drop-leaf table and indicated for Alec to set the girl down on it. An oil lamp was lit on the table that abutted the wall opposite the hearth. Two armchairs were placed either side of it. A fire burned in the grate though it was July, but the room was cold and dark, there being little light or warmth from the one window at the end of the room where the kitchen and stove were situated. Percy, his back to the door, leaned about and grunted, frowned.

'The lass fell in the dock,' Norah explained. 'Alec got her out.'

Percy nodded to indicate that Alec had done a good job, held up a thumb. Letty had come to understand his silent language as well as Norah. Knowing when he was dissatisfied – often – and when he was irritated or annoyed – frequently. In between he slept and she knew there wasn't much for him to be glad about. She worried for him, and she worried for Norah, who needed respite from his constant care.

The girl sat glassy-eyed, shivering violently. Norah told Letty to run upstairs and bring down towels and blankets. When she returned, Norah had the kettle on the stove and Alec was in the yard in his combinations, his trousers hung on the line. Norah was with the girl. Stella had taken the seat opposite Percy and the two of them were watching the goings-on.

'What's your name, lass?' Norah asked gently.

The girl's teeth chattered. When she finally managed to open her mouth, tears came in the place of words, but she managed to spit out her name. 'Pearl. Pearl Wallis.'

'Enough tears, my girl,' Norah said, not unkindly. 'You'll add to the puddle on my floor and there's puddle enough.' She gave a small smile as Letty helped her off with her wet outer garments. While she did so, Norah disappeared and returned with some of her own clothing. 'I haven't worn these in years, but they'll do while we get you sorted.'

Percy looked into the fire and the two women peeled the clothes off the thin body and wrapped her in a blanket. Letty rubbed gently at her hair with a towel. Norah brought over a mug of hot sweet tea. The girl reached out and took it, her hands trembling, and Norah put her own hands on it to steady her. Letty scooped up the clothes and took them out to the line where Alec was smoking a cigarette, his face tilted to the sun. When she came out, he lowered his face, watching her throw the clothes over the line. The fabric was cheap and thin, and the hem had been let down many times. 'How is she?'

'Hard to tell. At least she's alive. Thanks to you.' She put her hand to his face and he twisted his lips to kiss her palm.

'Perhaps she didn't want to be.'

'It didn't look like she jumped, not to me.' Letty rested her hand on the rope fixed between the walls either side of the narrow yard that backed onto the buildings in Wharncliffe Road. As the dock expanded and grew, plots had been sold off, the owners adding a building to their design. There had been an alley that ran along the bottom of the two streets, but all access had been stopped since Gilbert Crowe had bought Webster's, the property to the right of Parker's. He'd built up the walls either side, effectively blocking the Parkers in. The only way in and out of the building was through the front door of the shop. It had made things more troublesome, getting stock in and out – as if the Parkers didn't have enough to contend with – but they had friends and so were never short of help. Their world had shrunk to the premises they had owned for almost forty years.

Letty had tried to buy Webster's, hoping to knock through

and open a café, but Gilbert Crowe had got there first. He'd thwarted her at every turn, but he'd not stopped her. She'd rented premises over by Doig's shipyard and turned it to her advantage. Business was good, but it was inconvenient. She'd wanted to stay close to the Parkers, more so since Percy's stroke. The burden of his care fell to Norah, not that she complained, but she was in her early sixties, and if anything should happen to her Percy would not be long following. Letty felt a lump rise in her throat at the thought of it.

Alec looked about him, at the walls either side and in front. Letty had told him of Crowe blocking them in, but this was the first time he'd seen it for himself. 'He's trying to squeeze 'em out one way or t'other, isn't he? Greasy little bastard.' She felt a swell of injustice at what Crowe had done, and impotency at her inability to do anything to prevent it.

As she stood there, the sun warmed her back, but Percy would feel nothing of it if they didn't get him outside to get the benefit of it. She'd thought today was the perfect day to try. If she could get him out onto the docks this morning maybe she could persuade him to go further tomorrow.

'Perhaps now's the time to persuade them to sell, Let.'

How she wished it was, but even though Percy couldn't articulate it, they'd have one hell of a game getting him to move and the stress of it might well kill him. It was not straightforward. Percy was adamant that they should not give in to Crowe. Norah wouldn't leave without him, so they were trapped.

'One thing at a time,' she said quietly. 'The wheelchair first.'

He finished his cigarette and screwed it out against the wall with his fingers. 'You sort the girl. I'll take Percy out with me.' He began putting on his trousers that had had little time to dry. 'They'll dry in the sun.' He winked at her. 'On the line or on me, makes no difference.'

Back in the house, he roused Percy. 'Nah then, Percy, old lad. What say we get a little sunshine and leave the ladies to their business. You can have a shufty at the trawlers all decked up like Christmas trees.' He leaned down for Percy to take hold of his arm, using a gentle strength to steady the old man to his feet, allowing him his dignity and patting his arm as if they were two pals going out for a stroll. 'Stella, you too,' he said firmly. Stella reluctantly tore her gaze away from the girl and jumped to her feet, dancing her way in front of her father and Percy as they made their way into the shop, and out onto the street.

Norah looked doubtful as they heard them go through the shop. 'I expect he'll be back in a minute.'

They listened. There was a noise of a kerfuffle. Alfie had returned from his errand and Letty heard him speak to Percy. Presently they heard the door close and then silence. Norah gave Letty a small smile. 'Well, I'll be blowed.'

'It seems today is full of surprises.'

They turned their attention to Pearl, who had ceased her shivering. Letty squatted down in front of her and took hold of her hands. The girl had a small, upturned nose and full lips, pale freckled skin. Her thick hair, now that it was drying, took on a brighter orange hue.

'It will be a little more difficult to sort things today. The ladies of the Co-op and the guild will be fully occupied manning the stalls at one park or another.' There had been various fundraising events to pay for the celebrations over the past weeks in order to provide refreshment stalls and other entertainments to occupy both children and adults. Local and military brass bands would be playing in three parks during the afternoon. In the early evening, they would march down to People's Park in preparation for the grand firework finale. Norah poked at the fire to raise the flame and urged the girl to get closer. 'Come and sit in Percy's chair. Keep it warm for him.' The girl did as she was bade.

'I'm sorry to put you out, missus,' she said quietly, as she settled herself. 'I don't want to be any trouble.'

'Why, it's no trouble, lass. It's but a small kindness, a bit of warmth and a cuppa.'

The girl looked down at her hands. 'I've not come across much kindness these past weeks.'

'Do you want to talk about what happened?' Letty asked, folding one of the blankets and placing it on the dining chair the girl had vacated. She would take that and the towels home to launder. A few extra wouldn't hurt on Monday morning, and if the weather stayed fine, they would be back in Norah's blanket box by the afternoon.

'Happened?'

Letty looked to Norah. 'Let me get the lass some bread and dripping.' Norah went to the end of the room that was part kitchen and put out the cutting board, took the bread from the stoneware crock and a jar from the cold slab in the pantry. While she did so, Letty took the other seat.

'You went in the water?'

Pearl slowly gathered her wits. Letty put it down to shock. 'I do believe I must have fainted,' she said, seemingly satisfied that she had worked something out. 'I'd been walking a long time. I was looking out over the water, across to Hull.' She nodded at Letty, as if for reassurance that she was correct, and that Hull was indeed the other side of the Humber Estuary. 'That's where I come from.' She furrowed her brow. 'I looked up at the sun and it was so very bright. It made me dizzy.' She paused. 'I don't recall what happened next.' Norah handed her a plate. The girl was hesitant to take it. 'I mustn't take any more of your generosity.'

Norah dismissed her comment. 'It's bread and dripping, not my best cake. Though I wouldn't begrudge you that, if I had it.'

Pearl smiled, and tore at the bread, gulping it back hungrily.

'When did you last eat?'

She stopped. Shrugged. 'I don't rightly remember.' It seemed the girl had a terrible memory – or was slow of thought. Letty expected the latter.

'You say you're from Hull?' Norah asked. Letty made to get up and give Norah her chair, but Norah stayed her with her hand and pulled out the other dining chair and sat down.

The girl nodded, her mouth full.

'What brings you here?' Letty wondered if the girl would give a straight answer. It was not uncommon that people drifted from port to port in search of work. Letty had half thought she might be one of the herring girls, but she didn't look to have the stamina the lasses had, and her hands were not marked with scars from knives and salt water.

'Sid. My Sidney.' The girl's face was lit with a smile. 'I was told he was here.'

'On the docks?'

'I was led to believe so. He was on the minesweepers. He was discharged. He got work on the *Falstaff*.' Letty and Norah exchanged glances. The *Falstaff* was almost a week overdue and in the summer months that didn't bode too well. Although the seas were calmer, there were many mines and wrecks to catch the unwary. Ships had been seen to hit them and sink thereafter. 'Do you know of it?'

'Aye,' Norah said gently. 'One of Marshall's trawlers. Named for Shakespearean characters.'

'I didn't see it in the dock,' Pearl continued, 'and there was no one to ask. I called to a man on a ship, but he shook his head.' She stared at the scrap of bread in her hands. 'For a moment, I had lost hope, lost the belief that he was still alive.' She looked up, smiled. 'But only for a moment. I'm alright now; it must have been the cold water shocked the sense back to me. I know he'll come back.'

Letty wondered whether the truth was worth telling at this moment. 'Have you family here? Someone we can take you to?'

Pearl shook her head. 'My father died at sea. Mam couldn't manage. She... She hanged herself with a bed sheet.' Norah briefly closed her eyes. The girl showed no emotion, simply stated the facts. 'I don't feel sad. I didn't really know her. I was taken to the Newland Home, the orphanage, along with my brothers.'

'And your brothers? Where are they?'

Her eyes began to pool with tears. 'Gone. In France. All three. Went with their pals, they did. Not one came back.' So much loss and at such a young age. No wonder the poor girl had thought to end it all. 'But my Sidney did.' She pressed her hands together. 'Thank the good Lord above.'

Letty looked to Norah, who shook her head. Neither of them had the heart to deliver any more bad news. Not yet. She reached across and rubbed at Pearl's knee. 'Are you feeling a little better?'

'I am. Thank you very much.' She handed back the mug and plate. 'I'm so sorry to have taken up your time. Will you thank your husband for me? I didn't get the chance to.'

Letty said she would. 'When you feel up to it, we'll walk with you to the mission. Miss Sheldon is a good soul; she'll know where to find help on a day like this.'

A day of peace. How many girls like Pearl would ever know it?

3

When Pearl was delivered safely to Miss Sheldon, Norah and Letty made their way back to Parker's via Fish Dock Road. It seemed merely the blink of an eye since she and Alec had first walked down it, newlywed: a new town, a new home – such as it was back then in Mariners Row. It had been a huge shock to be greeted with such squalor when they arrived at the dwellings Alec had secured for them. Four houses sat either side of a narrow courtyard, a shared pump the only source of fresh water. The house had been neglected, and it had taken Letty and Dorcas more than a week to get it habitable. Their neighbour had been Alfie's mother, Anita, a widow who had fallen on hard times and whose only form of income was selling her body. In the end it had cost her her life. Letty had never known such poverty and that, combined with Dorcas's sourness and animosity, had galvanised Letty to find something other than braiding nets with which to earn a living. As their income increased, she and Alec had rented, then bought a house on the Grimsby side of Park Street. It was further away from the docks, edging ever closer to her dream of one day having a small piece of land to call her own. Norah linked her arm through Letty's. 'Pearl seemed a sweet lass. Do you think she was telling the truth?'

'About what?'

'Being dazzled by the sun.'

Letty knew what Norah was thinking; she was of the same mind. 'She was very thin. I think something might have been apparent if she... well, if she was in trouble.'

'Trouble? That's an odd way of putting it.'

'When you're on your own – and it seems that she is – then trouble is all it is. And sorrow.'

They stopped and admired the bunting and ribboned florets in the windows of the Coal, Salt and Tanning Company. It was situated over three floors and sold everything from a rivet to a boiler. A gilt frame was set on an easel and on it was written a list of the names of those who had worked for the company and given their lives for King and Country, and at the bottom the words 'Their glory shall live for evermore'. Letty talked to Norah through their reflection in the window.

'She didn't look to be in despair, and I know I would in the same position. Especially with no one to turn to.' Letty couldn't bear to think on what her life would be without the Parkers. They had given her hope. And she thought of what the girl had said, that for a moment she had lost hope.

'Well, I'm sure Miss Sheldon will get more out of her than we did. She's in good hands.'

They strolled on to Wiltshire's Chandlery, a quarter of the size of the Coal, Salt and Tanning Company but just as fine. Parker's was no competition to either of them, but there was always room for more. Parker's was down a side street. It would never make a fortune, but it made a living and that's all the Parkers had wanted.

When she first came to work for them, the shop had been

chaotic and shabby. The outside tired, as were the owners. She'd had a passion to transform it, and God bless them, they'd given her free rein to do so – eventually. Norah had been more enthusiastic than Percy, to begin with. In time, they'd offered her shares in the shop, and she'd taken them in lieu of extra pay. These last few years they'd managed to stay afloat thanks to loyalty and goodwill, for there'd been few ships left to bring home a catch while the war was on.

There was a small group by Solly's Café, and they lifted their hands in greeting. One of them called across, 'Percy escaped, then, Norah. Good to see him out and about.' It made both women smile.

'Did you ever dream of branching out and having a larger shop?' Letty asked.

Norah took a step back. 'As you do?' she teased. 'No. I was content with what we had.'

'I didn't mean—'

'Pah. I know you well enough to know what you meant, lass. At least give me credit for that.' They began walking again. 'Things might have been different if we'd had children, like the Wiltshires. You want to give them a better start in life than you had, that's what drives you forward. Leaving something for them – passing on the fruits of your labour. Although, we should all enjoy the fruits of our labour regardless. It can be all too easy to get wrapped up in an invisible future and not enjoy what we have right now.'

Her words were not melancholy, it wasn't Norah's way, but they struck home with Letty. She'd lost count of the times she'd been urged to sell the café, cut back her hours at the shop. But how could she fill the hours otherwise? The children were at school, and she couldn't sit at home, waiting and worrying for Alec's safety when he was away. Her mother never had, always in motion, whether with her children, the farm or her home. She didn't know what it was to sit idle, and she didn't want to. It was all Letty strived for. To give her children, those she had, and those to come, God willing, a good start in life.

'Life has been good to us,' Norah told her. 'We've always been blessed with friends, and then you came along, so we had a family of our own after all. You and the children. No doubt Percy'll be having a high old time of it, now that he's out and about.'

'I'm glad he didn't put up too much of a fight.'

'We don't know that he didn't.' Norah laughed. 'If Alec's sporting a shiner, we'll know that he did.'

* * *

They caught up with Alec, Percy and the children on Wharncliffe Road, Stella riding like Cleopatra in the wheelchair, urging Alfie to go faster, Alec leaning against the wall smoking his pipe and Percy settled on an upturned fish basket.

'Best be getting ourselves to Hope Street,' Alec said as they came close. 'They've put on quite the display by all accounts.' He checked his fob watch, a gift she had given him on his thirtieth birthday. It was not the only gift. She was with child, but there was a long way to go yet. She'd lost a child when Alec had been in the Dardanelles. The combined worry and sorrow had been immense, and she'd longed for his arms about her, his words of comfort.

'I said we'd meet Dorcas outside the Bon Marche,' Letty told him.

Norah looked to Percy, who gave a small nod of his head in agreement. As Letty had hoped, now that he'd got over the hurdle of actually getting into the chair and outside, he was happy to carry on. Pearl had proved a good distraction as any to getting the old man moving – but it was Alec who had made the difference. Percy wouldn't have wanted a woman to push him. When they had broached the subject before he'd likened it to being pushed around like a baby in a pram.

'Right, then,' Norah said. 'Just give me a minute to fetch a few things and we'd be delighted to come with you.'

Alec winked at Letty. She reached across and felt at his shirt while they waited.

'It's still a little damp. Are you sure you don't want to go home and change?' She leaned forward and sniffed. 'You smell of the sea.'

He laughed. 'Let, everyone around here smells of the sea.'

Norah returned with a blanket and put it over the back of the chair, and they made their way down into the town. If they gave the Parkers one good day, it was all Letty could hope for.

* * *

Letty spotted Dorcas outside the Bon Marche and nudged Alec towards her direction.

'Out of sight out of mind, is it?' she said, as they came towards her, her chin tilted upwards.

Alec teased her. 'As if I could, Mother. We had a spot of unexpected business to deal with.'

'Pop pulled a lady out of the water,' Stella told her, rushing forward. 'Pop saved her. She had long wavy hair, just like the mermaid in my book.'

'He wouldn't have to save a mermaid,' Alfie corrected. 'Mermaids can swim.'

'I said she looked like a mermaid. Not that she was one.'

Dorcas put her shoulders back, puffed out her bosom,

ignoring the children, and turning to her son, nudging her friend Bet Chapman from Mariners Row. Letty loathed her, such an old busybody and her daughter no better. She wondered that Dorcas hung on to her. It wasn't friendship, more one-upmanship. Dorcas didn't have to try too hard when she was in her company. Bet's husband was little better than a thief, not that he'd consider it theft, more his due to take what he could from his place of work and sell it on for a small profit.

'A lass fell in the docks. I pulled her out. Nowt much.' Alec nodded to the woman standing with his mother.

'Nowt much!' Dorcas bristled, her handbag dangling between her folded arms. 'Yet another life you've saved.'

Alec gave a small sigh, sucked his cheek and glanced to Letty. 'I did nowt that anyone else wouldn't have done.' He shifted his position, lifted his chin a little to Letty, signalling that he wanted to move on.

'It was lucky that Alec was there at the right time,' Letty said, hoping to end the matter.

'Aye or they'd have been pulling a body out of the water, and we've had enough of those these past years.'

Letty despaired at Bet's insensitivity. Percy grunted, flinging his arm, and Letty could have kissed him there and then. He understood Alec's awkwardness. He was a hero in his own way too.

'We'll walk ahead,' Letty said. 'Leave you to talk with Bet.' She took hold of the handles of the wheelchair, but Percy made a fuss.

Alec took over. 'I'll do that.' He started to walk. Dorcas called out to him, but Alec wouldn't turn back. Letty heard her tell Bet that she would see them later and hurried up to her son.

'What about this lass you've rescued, then?'

'Not now, Mother. We're out to enjoy the day.'

Letty understood his reluctance. It would give his mother something else to brag about and Alec would rather forget. He'd been awarded the Distinguished Service Order for his bravery. 'A bit of brass' he had put away in a drawer.

The minesweeping trawlers had been under fire in the Dardanelles. They'd swept for mines during the night, a tense operation in the daylight let alone in darkness. A new but necessary operation. It was incredibly dangerous and there had been many losses of men, men he knew, men like him. His ship had been hit and caught fire. He got his men to safety in the rescue boat, put out the fire and got them aboard again, the ship limping to harbour where it could be salvaged and repaired. When reports of her son's heroics and subsequent award and visit to London had been in the newspapers, Dorcas had bought three copies of each, sending one back to his uncle in Lowestoft. It would have been passed around the pub many times, and rightly so. Letty had been so proud, but Alec didn't want to talk about it. He wanted to forget.

'I wish she wouldn't go on so,' Alec said, stopping for a minute to pull out his baccy pouch and remove a cigarette he had rolled earlier. She waited while he lit up and shook the match out, tossed it into the gutter. Letty wished Dorcas would rein it in a little. She had little sense of how Alec might feel about it all. His abiding memories were not of bravery but of friends and comrades lost and mutilated.

'She's proud. We all are. People need heroes,' she said quietly. 'It makes them feel a little braver themselves when ordinary folks do brave things. Look what happened with Boy Cornwell.' The sixteen-year-old had stayed at his post during the Battle of Jutland, shrapnel in his chest, his fellow ratings lying about him dying. He'd been taken ashore at Immingham and on to Grimsby hospital, where he'd died of his wounds. He was posthumously awarded the Victoria Cross.

'I'd rather put it all behind me and look to the future.'

'I know. But you can't pretend it never happened. It did.'

He exhaled, blew out his smoke. 'Please God we will never see the like again.'

'That's what this day is for. Peace. Tomorrow is a fresh start for us all.' If only it were so simple.

'Let, I came home in one piece. So many didn't. I want to let it go and I can't if she keeps harping on about it.'

'I'll try and have a word.'

He gave a small laugh. 'Nah, leave it. She'll run out of steam before too long and I'll be off to sea again. Might as well let her have her day.'

They could hear the goings-on in Hope Street long before they turned onto it. People had come from far and wide to see the grand effort exerted by the residents, in memory, and in thanks. Full-size Union Jacks hung from windows, and pennants and squares of sheeting were strung across the street, from upstairs window to window, all the way down to Wellington Street. Halfway down, a piano had been manoeuvred onto the road and a lady with a generous bottom settled herself on a dining chair and began to play. People sang along, some leaning on the back of it, patting the lid with the flat of their hands to beat time. Further still, the Salvation Army band were blasting out 'Onward Christian Soldiers'. A handcart had been decorated with ribbons and rosettes and was being wheeled up and down the long street. Adults and the older children walked alongside it, shaking buckets, jingling the change. Alec put his hand in his pocket and gave Alfie and Stella coppers to throw into them. Farthings, pennies and ha'pennies, sixpences and thruppenny bits bounced into the metal pail and Stella delighted at the sound and of being able to contribute. Whether she knew what she was contributing to was another matter, but the men of St Dunstan's Hostel for Blind Soldiers and Sailors would be grateful for it. Many of the windows in the tightly terraced street sported photographs and drawings, portraits of their own sacrifice, of lost sons. A poignant reminder that many were still grieving and always would be. Not every home was complete, but every one of them was taking part. For the greater good.

When they had seen all they wanted to, they made their way to Freeman Street and stopped to get refreshment from one of the market stalls that were selling drinks and food and make use of the facilities. Percy was tiring and Norah looked weary. 'We can go back at any time,' Letty reminded them. But Percy would not hear of it and vehemently shook his head to say so.

'He'll pay for it tomorrow,' Norah said, smiling. Letty knew she would have gone home long ago if it were not that Percy was having such a marvellous time. People stopped and chatted and shook his hand and it was good to see so many in good spirits. It had been a long time and even now, it wasn't a celebration, more a relief. After a while they settled themselves outside a café, positioning Percy's chair so he could take in the view. A gaggle of sailors came along, arms slung across shoulders, singing their hearts out, caps in hands, and people stepped forward and tossed in their small change, helping to support those who would need it in the coming months. The sun was shining now but it would be winter soon enough and poverty and grief combined did nothing to light the long days. Dorcas kept a beady eye open for anyone she might vaguely know to tell them of how her son had rescued a drowning girl from the docks that very morning. She had taken ownership of the event, delighting in every fresh audience.

Alec shook his head. 'I'm off for a quick pint.' He tilted his head towards the White Bear and went over the road before his mother could parade him before anyone else.

'Alec had enough?' Norah asked.

Letty leaned close. 'Only of Dorcas, for the time being.'

'Well, you can't really blame her. We should all be so proud of our sons.' She watched the parade of lads still in uniform laugh and joke as they tipped their hats to the lively lasses that were catching their eye. It was good to see so many young men enjoying themselves. For a long time there had been so few.

Alec came out of the pub and joined them at the café. Percy had had a grand time of it but for the last quarter of an hour had been asleep in the chair and Norah asked if Alec wouldn't mind taking Percy home. 'He'll stay the rest of the day and half the night, if I let him, but I feel he's overdone it. As have I,' she added. She pressed her hand to Alec's arm. 'Thank you both. It's been a wonderful day. And good to feel a part of it.'

It had been all Letty hoped for. She arranged for the children to remain with Dorcas, and the four of them turned away from the celebrations, quietly making their way back to Henderson Street.

With the Parkers safely returned home, Letty and Alec walked back towards the town, his arm around her waist. 'I reckon that did the pair of them the power of good. Old Percy was having a high old time. It must be hard for him, trapped as he is.'

'It must. I doubt he would have come at all if you hadn't been about. He would never have let Norah push the wheelchair. Truth be told she might not have been able to manage it, but he was out and about in it, and that's the first step.'

'First step of what?' He pulled her close. 'What are you up to, Letty Hardy?'

'I'm not up to anything.'

'Oh, aye?' He grinned. 'Then you're not the lass I thought you were.'

She laughed then. 'They can't go on there, can they, on the docks. And if something happens to Percy...'

'Or Norah. Poor woman looks done in.'

'She soldiers on, for Percy's sake, but I fear they're getting isolated on the docks. No one much else lives there any more, and I know there's always something happening, people and ships coming and going, but it would be easier for them if—'

'And for you. Especially with the baby on the way.'

She stopped.

'They could have the front room.' He grinned at her. 'That's what you kept it for, after all. They'd be safe and warm, and you'd be able to keep an eye on old Percy when he wasn't too good. Norah could still work alongside you.' He paused. 'You'll make it work. I know you will.' He took her hands in his. 'The kids would love it, though I'm not sure about Mother. But she'll come round to it in time.' He'd spoken her thoughts out loud. She knew she'd be taking on more work for herself, but they could take someone on if they needed help in the shop as they'd done before. It would ease her mind no end to have them so close.

'How did you know?'

He put his arm about her shoulder and pulled her to him. 'Let, you're as transparent as a pane of glass. You do what you think is right and I'll back you all the way.'

4

The first aid tent in People's Park had seen a steady stream of patients but thankfully with only minor ailments, mostly lack of water in the heat of the day and too much excitement. There had been the odd child or two with cut knees and grazed hands, from which Ruth Evans had extracted the gravel with a pair of tweezers, and an exuberant child who had fallen into the lake and was none the worse for wear, the mother more in need of comfort than the child. It was mundane and nothing in comparison to what her brother Charles's fiancée, Daphne Willoughby, had faced in Portsmouth and in France. The two of them had taken first aid instruction with Mrs Whittaker of the St John Ambulance in the early months of the war but Ruth had remained at home to make use of her skills, such as they were. Daphne had gone to France with the nursing yeomanry. When news came that Charles was missing in action, feared dead, Daphne had continued searching for news, daring to hope that she might find him, but it had been fruitless. As were all their searches, the many letters, the visits to France looking for the infinitesimal clue that would end their trail. At first, they'd hoped to find him with memory loss, bewildered and confused. Towards the end, they would have taken comfort from having his body and bringing it home. It was not to be.

Daphne had returned home much changed, not only at the loss of her fiancée, but for all she'd witnessed at the hospital station at Saint-Quentin before the men were shipped home. She sometimes shared things with Ruth and together they had wept for their loss. Ruth had been spared the horrors of war close up, though she hadn't escaped them entirely. The wounds were just as deep. Ruth would have gone to nurse in France were it not for her widowed father. How could she leave him alone when both his sons had gone to war? Ruth was with him when news came that Charles was missing in action, and when the port missioner informed them that her younger brother, Henry, had been lost to them also. She would have gone mad if it were not for her work with the mission and the ladies' guild. It had given her a purpose, a way to carry on, to keep living.

Daphne checked her fob watch. 'Your turn for a break. Millie is due any moment.'

'Will you be alright alone?'

Daphne laughed and Ruth squirmed at the ridiculousness of her question. 'I will send for you if we get a sudden surge of patients.'

Ruth removed her apron, laid it across the chair she'd vacated and went to join the throng, glad to be out in the fresh air at last. It had been stuffy in the tent, even though they'd tied back the flaps, and she fought to keep alert when there was no one to tend to and their conversation turned to reflection.

The path around the lake was thick with crowds and she weaved her way over to the refreshment tables that had been set out under a long canopy. Other members of the ladies' guild were there, the middle-aged Hewitt sisters, Rosa and Lucy, who were stalwart in their dedication to good deeds in the community, as well as the others who she knew so well. Women from all walks of life who had come together to help with the war effort in whichever way they were able. It had united them in a way that peace never had, and many divisive lines had crumbled as the losses mounted and the need for more support increased. It had been a dreadful time, but it was well to remember that good had come of it also.

A podium had been erected for the prize-giving later that afternoon, newly constructed from wood donated by Wintringham's, the timber merchant's. Beyond it was the bandstand and band members of the Lincolnshire regiment playing for the occasion, numerous deckchairs set out before it. She threaded her way past it to the large marquee that housed the refreshments for invited guests, namely those who had donated to the afternoon and given their money in place of their time in support of the occasion. Aunt Helen and her husband, Jack Frampton, owner of one of the local newspapers, had sponsored the marquee and provided free advertising as was befitting of the town mayor, and trawler owner Cyril Marshall had donated trophies and prize money for a series of sports races and for children's races and fancy dress.

At the entrance, a man in livery tipped his hat to Ruth and stood aside to let her pass. Inside she searched for her aunt, who, seeing Ruth, hurried forward and took her by the elbow.

'My dear girl, I was beginning to think I'd have to come and look for you.'

Ruth searched among the crowds, returned people's smiles of acknowledgement. 'Is Father here?'

'He is.' Helen took her arm, leaned close. 'I have to say he's been a little of his old self this afternoon. It's good to see a change, small as it is.'

People stepped aside to let them pass, smiling and uttering vague pleasantries as they moved towards the centre. Ruth was pleased to see that her aunt had not been exaggerating when she saw her father amidst the small group Aunt Helen had judiciously assembled. Richard Evans had been reluctant to attend and, before she'd left that morning, she hadn't been entirely sure he would make his way to the park, even though it was but a short walk from their home. There had been much discourse over whether a celebration was appropriate when so many had suffered. Ruth had heard arguments on both sides, but she'd decided it was worthwhile. The cessation of hostilities had not brought any comfort to those whose sons would never return. However, something was better than nothing. She leaned close and kissed his cheek. 'I'm glad you came.'

'Your aunt came to the house and gave me a good talking-to.' He looked about him then to her. 'She was right, of course. Avoiding things doesn't make it hurt any the less. Many here have lost as we have done. Perhaps.'

She followed his gaze. Cyril Marshall was standing close by with his son Arthur, the two of them deep in conversation. Arthur smiled when he saw her, said something to his father and came over to her. He looked much different to when she had seen him last, not just in his appearance, but in the way he held himself – as if he was the most important person in the room. His confidence had never failed to astound her but now he was more so.

'Ruth. When your aunt said you were in the first aid tent, I thought I might have to feign a headache.' He was playful, when she had half thought that he would avoid her. They had not parted on the best of terms and so much had happened since.

'I would have given you an aspirin and sent you off for coming to me with such a trifle.' She couldn't hide the sharp edges of her response, but he seemed not to notice for her comment did nothing to dent his confidence. She wondered that perhaps he had become used to ignoring the slights over the last five years. Cyril Marshall had paid good money to keep his sons at home while others had paid money to get their sons to the front, for honour and for glory. The poet Kipling had done so. And his son had paid the price. If her father had done the same, Charles and Henry would be with them now, shaping the future of the Excel Trawler Company. Without her brothers, there seemed to be no future at all. She had thought Cyril Marshall wrong for what he was rumoured to have done, but no matter what people said, he still had his sons and one day all would be forgotten. It was a bitter thought.

'It would have been worth it.' He softened his voice and to her annoyance she felt herself blush. Aunt Helen came over and guided her father away to speak with the Wintringhams.

'Your father looks quite well,' Arthur said, when they were alone. She wanted to correct his lie, but she couldn't, trapped by the social niceties the situation demanded. She understood why her father found these things so difficult. Putting on a brave face. But weren't they all, Arthur included? He had been presented with white feathers, as had other men who had not taken a uniform. No matter that he had been diagnosed with a weak heart – a sudden and timely diagnosis. No one knew the accuracy of it, but rumours had been rife.

'He is better than he was.' There was truth in her answer this time. 'You enjoyed America?' She knew he had been there on business and his tanned skin was evidence of it. Uncle Jack had spoken of it over dinner often enough. She had listened without interest but knew he'd been successful; Cyril Marshall had been able to build his business operations because his sons were there to work when others were not.

'I did. A land of great opportunity. I think you'd like it.' She had no inclination to discover whether she would, but he smiled so warmly at her that it was churlish not to return it.

'When did you get back?'

'Two days ago.'

She watched her aunt flow through the gathering with ease, taking a lone awkward soul into the bosom of a small group, always smoothing the way. She swooped on a young couple and introduced them to her father. He smiled warmly as they shook hands, and Ruth's shoulders dropped a little. She watched as he became more animated, less interested in what Arthur had to say, glad that her father appeared to be relaxing in their company. Reluctantly she returned her attention to Arthur.

'I'm presenting the trophies later. Marshall's have donated the prize money. Would you do me the honour of assisting me? I'm sure the children would appreciate it.'

'You could choose anyone, Arthur. I'm quite sure the children wouldn't notice.'

'But I'd rather it be you.'

She didn't want to look at him, but he remained quiet until she did, his head slightly tilted to one side, waiting for her answer. Over his shoulder she could see her aunt, watching them intently without appearing to watch them at all. Ruth knew what she was about. She would have suggested to Arthur that he ask Ruth instead of arranging it all beforehand, as was her habit.

'In that case, it would be my pleasure.'

His face broke into a smile, and he took her hand and raised it to his lips. 'You have done me a great honour.' She had to smile herself then, at his overblown charm. Thank goodness he had lost the pompousness that had beset him when he was in his early twenties. Perhaps confidence had rendered it no longer necessary. Whatever had happened in the intervening years had been to his benefit and she found him good company and for the first time that day she allowed herself to relax. 'We should drink to it,' he said, stopping the waiter as he passed by. Arthur handed her a glass of wine and took one for himself, clinked his glass to hers. 'To peace.'

'To peace,' she countered, taking a sip. She turned to check on her father and caught his attention, smiled. He nodded, said something to the couple he was with. They turned to look at her. Another smile. Richard Evans appeared to be enjoying their company. It was the first time he had looked so at ease in years and it lifted her spirit to see him so. Her father came to join them, bringing the young couple with him and standing back to introduce them.

'Ruth, this is Evelyn Howard and her brother Jeremy.' Evelyn was fair-haired and blue-eyed, not much older than Ruth by her appearance, touching thirty perhaps but no more. Her brother was definitely the elder, by five years at least. She held out her hand.

'Your father has been telling us of your work at the mission and the ladies' guild. Your aunt suggested I come to your next meeting.'

'Aunt Helen never misses a chance to recruit to her good causes.' They shook hands. 'You are new to the area?'

Evelyn nodded. 'A few weeks ago. My brother took over Dr Burgess's medical practice on Hainton Avenue.' Nothing more needed to be said. Dr Burgess had shot himself on learning of the death of all three sons in France. The practice had been left empty for some while. 'I came to assist him. I'm nurse, secretary, receptionist and whatever else he needs as he gets established.'

'You're settled?'

'Yes, people have been very generous. Your aunt especially. Our way has been eased beyond measure because of her.'

Ruth wouldn't doubt it. There was no one her aunt didn't know in the town, not of the movers and shakers. And she prided herself on making things happen. Arthur got chatting to Jeremy and led him away to introduce him to his father. Evelyn was deep in conversation with her father when her aunt came to join them, taking Ruth to one side.

'You and Arthur seemed to be getting on well.'

'Did you think we wouldn't?'

'After all this time. You should be flattered he's still interested.'

Ruth smiled. 'I should.'

Her aunt filled the silence that had expanded with her answer. 'You do make a handsome couple.'

'Oh, Aunt Helen. Please, not that again. I'm sure Arthur is not at all interested after the fiasco years ago. He's merely being polite.' She hadn't seen much of him at all since the early days of the war. Their paths had not converged, and Ruth had not sought him out.

'If you'd not turned him down you would be married now, with children of your own.'

Ruth leaned in, whispered. 'I didn't turn him down, Aunt, as well you know. I stopped him before he asked. That's different.'

'Not to him it wasn't.' Her aunt was curt. 'If you had rebuffed him, he would have found someone else, a man of means when there are so few of them left. No, he's still waiting for you. I'm certain.'

Ruth shook her head, looked over to where Arthur stood

with his father and hers, with the Howards, and wondered if there was a glimmer of truth in what her aunt said. He was handsome enough, and wealthy too; any number of young women would be happy to be married to such a man.

'He didn't ask again.' She hadn't given him the opportunity, and it had been the very last thing she'd been thinking of. When her brothers were lost, she'd dedicated herself to her father – and to whatever else she could do to forget her sorrow.

'Would you have wanted him to? You were so fixed on the port missioner. That was a fortunate escape. Your life would have been one of discomfort.'

'You don't know that. We might have lived very comfortably.' She had fallen for the port missioner who served at the Fishermen's Mission before Miss Sheldon arrived to take his place. It had been Colin who had brought news of Henry's death from Lowestoft.

'Though not as comfortable as you have been accustomed.'

Ruth couldn't argue, though she would have done at the time. She'd had a fanciful notion of being at his side. How naïve she had been then. But that was long before the war came along. Her aunt had not deemed him to be a suitable match, and her father, though allowing her to make up her own mind, had not been enamoured with her choice. Then Charles had been lost, and Henry, and she couldn't bear to look too far into the darkness of her future. Her aunt had been right to dissuade her and there was no point in being obstinate. But still, she would rather her aunt not interfere in such matters, hating the feeling of being shoehorned into situations. Her aunt was well aware of her feelings, but she couldn't help herself. She pressed her hand to Ruth's.

'I only want the best for you. It's all I ever have.'

Ruth knew it to be true but these last months she'd felt

burdened with the pressure of her aunt's intentions, more so since she was the only one left subject to them.

'I wouldn't want you to suffer, my darling, and the hardships that come with lack of money are something I would not want for you.' She turned to face her niece. 'It would be foolish to turn him down again – if he asked.' Helen Frampton stared out over the crowd.

'I don't know that I love him.' She had never been sure; that was where the difficulty lay. Could they even take up where they had left off so easily? Would she want to? Would he?

'Love has nothing to do with it. Friendship lasts longer.'

Ruth knew she was talking about her own relationship with Uncle Jack. They were a powerful couple but as far as she aware they didn't share the close relationship her father and mother had had together. He talked of it often, and she wanted the same for herself, elusive though it seemed.

'Look around you, my dear. There are so few young men. Fewer still that are suitable for a woman like yourself. We have lost a generation.' Arthur looked their way again and Aunt Helen raised her glass to him. 'You would work well together. I believe your union will give your father a new lease of life. He needs a reason to keep going. Your marriage might well provide it.' She paused, lifted her hand discreetly to a passing waiter and placed her empty glass on the silver tray. 'With marriage will come grandchildren. It will rejuvenate him – and you. He will be able to see a future again.'

There was a poignancy to her words. Aunt Helen had no children of her own. When Ruth's mother died, Helen had taken on the supervision of her brother's three children. They had become her surrogates while Richard grieved and threw himself into his business, as a way of coping. To forget. She could see what her aunt meant, but that wasn't the best reason to marry.

She had been filled with grief, her father too, their plans and hopes for the future quenched like a flame. It was enough just to carry on each day, to get through each hour. 'He needs something to revive him. Before he loses everything that he has worked so hard for.'

* * *

At four, Arthur came to her and led her outside. He held out his hand and helped her onto the podium. A table had been set with certificates, ribbons and silver trophies. A collection of envelopes contained the cash prizes. The band stopped playing and people began to swarm towards the podium as Ruth stood at Arthur's side, a sea of faces looking up to them. Among them was her father, Daphne and the Howards next to him. How dear he was, and how proud he looked. She smiled at him, and he returned it. It lifted her. She had to live for all three of his children now. For all their futures.

It began to rain, but only a shower, not enough to spoil the day and send people back to their homes. When the prize-giving was over, her uncle came onto the podium and thanked the sponsors and announced that the fireworks would go ahead as planned. The crowd cheered. Arthur helped Ruth down from the platform. 'We work well together, do you agree?'

'I enjoyed it very much.'

'Could I dare to hope it could be something more long-term?'

He had taken her by surprise. 'I hadn't given it a thought.'

'Don't be coy, Ruth. You know there has been no one else.' He bent his arm for her to take. She hesitated. 'Would you think about it? I don't want to make the same mistake twice.'

It was useless to protest. Things hadn't worked out the way either of them had expected.

'I promise.'

It was enough. Once more he crooked his arm, and this time she slipped her hand through it and together they went back in the marquee to join the others.

* * *

After the prize-giving, the crowd thinned, and Letty insisted they went home for a few hours to rest before making their way back to the park for the fireworks that evening. It was a good turnout, and the park was thick with expectant crowds. It felt like more than half the town must have been crammed into the twenty-three acres of parkland and the streets around it. There was a restless excitement as they waited for the first rockets to be lit. Alec had lifted Stella onto his shoulders for a better view and she rested her hands either side of his head, peering about her. With the first spark and explosion and burst of coloured light, there was a gasp of awe and delight, but Letty's attention was taken by a young man directly in front of them who immediately squatted on his haunches, clasping his hands about his head. Alec turned to Letty and shook his head. The woman beside him bent down to him, took him by the elbow and led him away. Alfie looked to Letty, his face writ with worry. She smiled to reassure him and once more he looked to the sky. Stella was rapt, as was Dorcas, but Letty did not look upwards again, aware now of other young men who had turned away, their faces alternately lit by light and covered in shadow. Alec looked silently ahead, his jaw tense, body rigid, and Letty couldn't fathom what might be going through his mind and that of the other men, though she had a fair enough idea. She was glad when it was over and could see the same relief on other faces as people made their way to the exits. Stella grasped for Alfie's hand and Letty reached for Alec's.

'What bloody fool thought a firework display would be a fitting end to the day is beyond me.'

She had no answer, only that of squeezing his hand to let him know she was there for him. She would always be there.

5

The following day, Sunday, Reverend Canon Markham, vicar of St James's, had managed to strike the fine balance with his sermon, being reflective without being maudlin. Instilling hope where in many homes there was none. It was a difficult enough task. Ruth surmised that there had not been a family present who had not lost someone so dear to them. She'd managed to hold back her tears, concentrating her thoughts on how brave the young men had been, how gallant in laying down their lives for King and Country. It did nothing to ease the soreness of her heart. Her father had stared down at his hands for the best part of the service and when her brother's names were given in the roll call of men of the parish, he had reached across and taken her hand in his. It immediately stemmed any idea of tears, wanting to be strong for his sake, united in their sorrow. The choir had finished with 'I Vow to Thee, My Country' and singing with the congregation had filled her with resolve that their sacrifice had not been in vain. Otherwise, nothing made sense at all.

After the service, Ruth and her father had lingered on the green outside with the Framptons and the Marshalls, the conversation mostly of the sermon, and of the success of yesterday's events. There was news of rioting in Luton, where the town hall had been burned down in protest. Not everyone had been agreeable to money being spent on the activities of Peace Day. Many had rather the money go to helping the ex-servicemen, many without jobs, many who would never have one again, being too badly wounded, both physically and mentally, to hold on to any meaningful employment. But to dwell on the disagreement was to ignore the valiant efforts of ordinary folks to contribute.

'The collection at Hope Street raised more than eighty pounds,' Ruth informed her aunt. 'From people who had little to spare.'

'There has to be balance,' Uncle Jack stated firmly. 'We cannot live in darkness for the rest of our lives.'

'That might be easier for some than others,' her father said.

Her uncle was sympathetic. 'I haven't suffered your loss first-hand, Richard, but those boys were like any sons I might have had, you know that.'

Her father's mouth turned upwards slightly but it could hardly be called a smile. Her uncle was not unkindly; both he and Aunt Helen had been there in their many hours of need. Ruth had gained great strength from Aunt Helen but now she sensed their frustration as how best to help her father. Richard Evans had stepped out of the very flow of life, as if he were in a stream and the water was flowing around him, unaware as to whether the water rose or fell. Ruth had been able to busy herself with the guild and the mission and, latterly, when the wounded arrived home, helping at Brocklesby Hall, which had been converted into a VAD hospital for the duration of the war and some time afterwards. But her father had lost his stomach for his business. She understood only too well. What was the point? Why build a business when there was no one to hand it on to? Her aunt excused herself and went to stand with the Marshalls, who had commandeered the vicar. From time to time, Arthur caught her eye and smiled. He was different to how she had remembered him but then they all were. War had left its mark at every turn.

In the corner of the churchyard, a small group of children had clustered together, an elder girl making the younger one stay still while she fastened the buttons on her shoes. Three boys were tossing a coin, calling heads or tails as it spun in the air and before it fell onto the grass. The sun was high overhead and Ruth squinted as three figures came towards them, not certain who it was until they were close. Daphne Willoughby and Evelyn Howard came to stand with her, while Jeremy joined the larger group, shook hands and began talking with her father. They had exchanged no more than a few words when Aunt Helen interrupted them. 'Richard, Cyril Marshall is thinking of setting up a fund to help the widows of our men who gallantly served on the minesweepers. I think you should be involved.' She took his arm to let him know he had no choice. 'Come along, young man,' she said to Jeremy. 'We could use your young brain.'

Jeremy grinned at the three women as he did as he was told.

'Your aunt is quite magnificent,' Evelyn observed.

Ruth could not help but laugh. 'I agree. A force to be reckoned with.'

'I was sorry we didn't get the opportunity to talk more yesterday; you were so busy.'

'That was down to my *magnificent* aunt. She likes to make sure we are all suitably occupied.'

Evelyn smiled. There was a warmth to her though her colouring was cool, blonde hair neat at the back of her head. 'I have to say I agree. It's all too easy to let the days slide by. And the days we have are so precious.'

'Evelyn was over in France,' Daphne offered. 'Nursing. Her fiancé was killed at Loos.'

Ruth didn't wonder that they had got on so well. They shared much in common.

'As was my brother. Jeremy was in the medical corps.' Evelyn glanced over to where he stood. 'He couldn't settle back to the country practice as he had planned. Not after his experiences on the battlefield.'

'I thought he might have craved it?' Ruth had an idea that after the slaughter, men would seek the quiet. Peace.

'It didn't feel right, somehow.' She paused. 'It was too quiet.'

Ruth understood. It was the very reason she kept herself busy. Most days the worse feeling of all was returning to the empty house. A house that had once been filled with such love and laughter when the boys were home. Her father spent many hours in his study, though she doubted he got through much work. Many times she had taken in a coffee or a sandwich and found him staring into space. He'd lost his only sense of purpose when his sons were so cruelly taken from him.

'It was somehow easier to make a brave step when we might not have taken it before,' Evelyn continued.

Her father was now deep in conversation with Jeremy. Evelyn sighed. 'I am so sorry, Ruth. I fear Jeremy will talk your father's ears off if he gives him the opportunity. Perhaps we should interrupt them?'

Her father caught her eye, nodded.

'Let's not,' she said, glad that her father seemed at ease. 'It will give us chance to get to know each other.'

* * *

The clock chimed the half hour as they entered Meadowvale House. Ruth stopped for a moment and gazed on the portrait of her mother that hung at the half turn of the stairs, watching them when they left, waiting for them on their return. Her father looked up at it. 'Your mother would have enjoyed the company this morning. Most especially the Howards I think, don't you? That young man has many ideas for innovations for Dr Burgess's old practice. A breath of fresh air.'

'His sister too. Daphne looked happier than I've seen her in a long time.'

She helped him off with his jacket and hung it on the hall stand. He removed his hat and placed it on the hall table, swept his hand over his thinning hair. 'Maybe that's what we need. Fresh faces.' He picked up the Sunday newspaper that the housekeeper, Mrs Murray, had left on the table and held it to his chest. 'I found the sermon helpful. It was a comfort to be with people who have lost someone dear to them. They understand as no one else does.'

'They do,' she agreed. 'I'll go and find Mrs Murray and let her know we're home.'

They settled in the sitting room and Ruth opened the doors onto the garden. It was walled to give privacy and not so far from the park where yesterday they had celebrated peace. Far enough away from the town to give a sense that they were on the edge of the countryside, and all the convenience of being able to walk into the town if they so wished. Leaving her father to his newspaper, she picked up her secateurs and went out into the garden, selected some roses and placed them in her trug. After a while her father came to join her and took a seat on the bench, stared out over the shrubs and flowers. He tilted his face to the sunshine for a time then opened his eyes.

'It went well yesterday. All over the country by all accounts.

Apart from pockets here and there. Luton being one of them. But we mustn't let that distract us from the huge amount of money that was raised. It will help so many.'

'Aunt Helen will be pleased.' Ruth put down her trug. 'It will fill more than a few column inches tomorrow.'

Her father shook his head. 'I don't know where she finds her energy. I have so little left.'

Ruth took a seat beside him. 'She is not carrying sorrow on her shoulders.'

He rested his hand on her leg. 'She is, my darling. She loved the boys dearly. It was such a tragedy that she did not have children of her own. She would have been a wonderful mother.'

He followed a damselfly that danced over the small pond, a weeping willow draping its arms over the water. They had loved to lean over it, as children, waiting for tadpoles to turn into frogs. There was no one left to remember the scenes of her childhood with, now that Henry and Charles were gone.

'She has been a wonderful aunt.' Ruth placed her trug at her feet and dropped the secateurs into it.

Her father agreed. 'A mother when you lost your own. We have been lucky to have her in our lives. I don't know what I would have done without her.'

Ruth didn't either. Aunt Helen was the one constant in their lives and Ruth was grateful for it. Especially at times like this, when she could not look to her father for her own strength. The last few years they had navigated stormy waters. Ruth hoped there might be the glimmer of a little calm for the future.

They sat together in quiet companionship, as they had done so many times lately. There were no words that could ease his pain, or hers. Being beside him was the only support she could offer.

6

Her father remained in the garden while she dealt with the flowers, arranging them in a variety of vases while Mrs Murray prepared a cold lunch. They ate it at the small iron table under the shade of the apple tree. Afterwards, her father went into his study, and she gathered together her sketchpad and pencils and went back outside. She had spent a pleasant hour sketching when Mrs Murray called out to her.

'You have a visitor, Miss Ruth.'

Arthur was waiting for her in the sitting room, standing before the empty grate, staring down at his gloves. He looked up when she came in.

'Arthur. This is a surprise.' She went to greet him, and he kissed her cheek.

'A lovely one, I hope.'

'Of course.'

He looked about him, then to her. 'The last time I was in this room I was to be disappointed.' He was smiling when he spoke but even so, the memories it brought back were not happy ones. For either of them.

'Please don't remind me of that. It was an awful time.' She had stopped him before he uttered the words. He'd had the ring in his pocket. Did he have it still?

'It was.'

She'd had not an inkling then of what her future would be. It was a strange time. Many people had been taken up with euphoria when war was declared. It seemed to override the fear until the reality of it sank in: when boys didn't come home, when it wasn't all over before Christmas, or the next, or the one after that. The last few years had been a blur. She could only recall significant days, and they were the unhappy ones. The day Charles left with his regiment; when Henry joined his ship. The letter informing them that Charles was missing. Henry's death. Other days had come and gone, birthdays, Christmas – they were nothing of significance.

'It's the past,' she said. 'Can we leave it there?' She wanted to move on, to embrace the future as Evelyn and her brother had done.

'Of course. I won't mention it again.'

She waited, wondering what had brought him here.

'I wondered if we could take a walk. I leave for London tomorrow evening and I didn't want to go without having first spoken with you.'

She felt her heart race, guessing what he wanted to say to her that couldn't be said here. It seemed to her that he caught her thoughts.

'I wanted to be free of the constraints you might feel here, or that I might feel. Neutral ground?'

She understood only too well. There had never been a moment when she'd not felt the weight of expectation when Arthur was about. 'Let me tell Father I'm going, then I'll get my hat.'

Ruth knocked on the study door and when her father didn't answer, she quietly opened it. As she'd expected, he'd fallen asleep in the chair by the window. She closed the door behind her and picked up her hat, fastened it in place and left the house with Arthur. As they stepped out onto the pavement, he shut the gate behind them and held out his arm for her to take. This time she took it readily. It was still beautifully warm and just for once, she wanted to forget her sorrows. He placed his hand on her arm. 'Thank you for agreeing to come with me.'

He was considerate in ways he had not been before. Or had she forgotten? Had the intervening years clouded her memories of him? Good and bad. It did not matter. Today was a fresh start and she would take it as such.

They walked to the park where only yesterday there had been crowds. The bandstand was empty now and even though couples and families walked in the sunshine, it was calmer than it had been only hours before.

'Tell me of America. What were you doing there?'

'Mostly salvage. Buying American-built ships from elsewhere and selling them back to the Americans. All very patriotic.' He told her a little of what he'd been doing, of the connections he'd made and the sights he'd seen. They turned to walk along the lake and stood for a while watching a cluster of ducks waddle towards two young children who threw breadcrumbs from a brown paper bag. 'I've missed you, Ruth,' he said, turning to her.

She didn't want to look at him, afraid of her feelings. Unsure as she had been almost five years ago, in the sitting room of Meadowvale House. She kept her voice light.

'I'm sure you've been far too busy to think of me at all.' She knew he'd not been engaged, but he had been seen out with pretty girls. And more than one or two. Brief flirtations and nothing more, according to her aunt, who kept her niece informed of Arthur's movements, whether Ruth wanted to know or not. But yesterday she'd been curious as to why he hadn't settled down to marriage, though she hadn't mentioned it to her aunt. There had been no time, and her aunt would have taken her interest as intent. This time she wanted things to move at her pace.

'I can assure you I have thought of no one else.'

She turned and he gazed into her eyes. She wanted to look away, but she couldn't. He was in earnest; she could see that. And she'd hurt him, not intentionally, but it must have been a shock when she'd reacted so harshly. She'd had many months to think on it afterwards. But she couldn't turn back the clock, much as she wanted to. For so many reasons.

'I stupidly thought that you would accept my proposal. It makes me a little afraid to ask again.'

She laughed, ignoring the implications of his confession. 'Arthur Marshall, you are not afraid of me.'

'Of your rejection?' He raised his eyebrow. 'Yes. Yes, I am. We were always friends, Ruth. I had always hoped it would be more than that.'

She did not answer him and, in her reluctance to converse on the matter, he held out his hand for hers and they walked back towards Meadowvale House, talking again of trifles. It was comfortable that way, and because of it she enjoyed his company once more. There was no pressure on his part, and she was almost sorry when he returned her to her door and took his leave of her.

Her father was in the sitting room smoking his pipe. He looked rested, happier. He smiled when she walked in. 'Did you enjoy your walk? Mrs Murray said Arthur had called?'

She took the chair opposite him. 'I did. I didn't think I would. He seems much changed.'

'More considerate?'

'Yes.' That was precisely it. He'd been more aware of her feelings than his own.

'He has no doubt learned to think a little before he acts,' her father said. 'That comes with age, and experience.' He got up, checked his watch, went over to the drinks cabinet and poured two fingers of brandy and took a small sip from the glass. 'And how do you feel about him now?'

She looked to her father. 'I'm not sure. I've never been certain of my feelings towards Arthur.'

He took another sip from his glass, went back to his chair. 'Maybe pressure from your aunt contributed to that. That it was more her choice than yours?'

Ruth nodded, though it hadn't seemed that way at the time. She'd been determined to get the port missioner to notice her, her head filled with fanciful ideas of a life of service at his side. How foolish she had been. It was so obvious to her now. 'She thought she was doing the right thing by me.'

He nodded, smiled. 'As I said earlier, she only ever has the best of intentions towards you. As she did for Henry and Charles.'

Ruth could not argue. She would keep that in mind from now on.

7

When Letty went into the shop on Monday morning, Percy was still asleep in his armchair in front of the fireplace. Norah had wrapped him in blankets and his feet were raised on a footstool. Letty was concerned.

'Maybe it wasn't such a good idea to get the wheelchair. We were out too long.'

Norah brushed away her comment as she would a fly. 'Don't be daft. He had the time of his life.'

Letty took off her hat and placed it on the table along with her handbag. The flesh sagged on Percy's face and his skin had a grey tinge to it, more so than normal. A small bowl was on the table to the side of him, a shaving brush and soap, a small towel.

'His happy moments are few and far between these days. It's a price he won't mind paying.'

'And you?'

'Letty, I wouldn't have it any other way. It's not as if we've got a lot to do in the shop, is it. You keep it all ticking over.'

It was easy enough to do so at the moment, but Letty worried that they would be without help when she was nearer her time.

It had been easier to carry on when she was pregnant with Stella; she'd seemed to have all the energy and more, just as the child did, always on the go. The other pregnancy she'd not fared so well and had not carried the baby to term, losing it at four months. The doctor had warned her not to overdo it this time. She'd blamed herself. Dorcas had warned her she'd taken too much on, but Letty thought it was not so much that as the fear for Alec's safety. There had been too many young widows. She didn't want to be one of them. She would be more cautious this time around, although she had no intention of abandoning the Parkers. If she could persuade them to give up living on the premises, it would be easier for all of them. It seemed the opportune moment to broach the subject. She took Norah to one side and lowered her voice.

'Do you think Percy would reconsider selling the shop?' He appeared so very frail and vulnerable as he slept. He had dribbled a little and Norah took her handkerchief from her sleeve and mopped his mouth, then went back to Letty.

'He would sooner die than let the shop go. And never to Gilbert Crowe. The time has passed when he might have done.'

'More to spite Gilbert?' Their neighbour had offered numerous times to buy them out.

'But now spiting himself,' Norah added.

'And you. Oh, Norah. Life would be easier for you if you were in the town. You'd not be so isolated as you are here, especially during the night.'

'I doubt it, lass. The dock never sleeps; there's always someone about. Our life is here, where it's always been.'

'Always?'

'Most of what I remember. There was no life before Percy. We've had a good life.'

'You speak as if it's over.'

'We can look back farther than we look forward at our age. I'm not complaining, lass, simply stating the facts.'

'You wouldn't have to stay with me, although you would be very welcome. I could find lodgings in town for you. You could keep the shop and we'd take on extra staff if we should be in need of it. I don't need to take my share.' She would gladly relinquish it to have them somewhere more comfortable. Alec would be back to earning good money once he had a ship again. It would take a bit of juggling, but it wasn't impossible. 'Things have improved now that the men are mostly home. The ships are returning, and the men are back to sea. Things will soon return to what they were.'

'Things will never be as they were, Letty. Times are changing. We must try to change with them.'

'But not Percy?'

Norah laughed. 'Not Percy.' On good days he still went into the shop and seated himself on a chair on the shop floor. He could comprehend but not converse as such. His pals came to see him when they left their shifts and so he was still a part of life, the comings and goings. 'It may seem odd to some folk, but it suits him, so it suits me.' They were interrupted when the bell rang out over the door.

'I'll go,' Letty told her. She hurried through the door to the counter. A young woman was waiting quietly by the window; her long wavy hair cascaded down her back, fastened at her neck with a navy-blue ribbon. Now that her hair was dry, she did indeed look like the mermaid Stella had imagined. Pearl turned when she heard Letty enter and hurried forward, smiling brightly.

'I came to give my thanks.'

She was bonnier than Letty remembered, her eyes brighter, and her cheeks had a glow to them. Not a beauty but Letty assessed a gentle soul. Letty came from behind the counter. 'If it hadn't been for your hair, I might not have recognised you.'

Pearl beamed at her. 'Miss Sheldon has been very generous.' She pressed her bag to her stomach. 'She found me lodgings and loaned me money enough for it. I'm to pay her back when I find work.'

Letty had expected nothing less. The port missioner was as resourceful as she was kind. 'I'm glad that she was able to assist you. And your lodgings, are they suitable?'

'Oh, yes, Mrs Hardy. Very suitable indeed. There are other young ladies there too. It is quite respectable.' She stepped closer to Letty. 'I thought to make an early start. And Miss Sheldon said you might know of anyone in need of help on the docks.'

Letty began to lift the metal pails and rubber boots that were displayed outside the shop. 'You might fare better if you tried down Freeman Street, or the shops on Cleethorpe Road.'

'You know I worked in a shop?' The girl's eyes widened.

Letty moved her head. 'Your hands are not marked by braiding. It gave me to believe that you had worked in something of a gentle manner.'

Pearl looked at her hands as if Letty had made a revelation and Letty had to bite back a smile. 'I worked in a department store. I've worked in lots of shops, but I'll do anything.' She smiled again, her face full of her innocence. 'I'd rather be on the docks. I'm sure to find Sidney that way.'

'Sidney?'

'My young man, Mrs Hardy.'

Letty had forgotten the name of the young man in question. 'He wasn't on the *Falstaff*?' The ship had docked on the early tide that morning. Had the girl not been aware of it?

'No.' She frowned. 'He was taken badly. The skipper put him

ashore in the Faroes. I suppose he'll get another ship when he's well. Until then I need to fend for myself.' She stared dreamily at the metal pans hanging from the ceiling beam then jolted herself, as if she'd suddenly remembered where she was. 'I thought to call next door at Crowe's.'

Letty shook her head. 'I wouldn't advise it.' She paused, wondering how best to express her misgivings without alarming the girl. Working on the docks was fraught with challenges for a young woman, and the girl seemed terribly naïve. Letty was more than capable of looking after herself and gave as good as she got to their taunts, having learned from her brothers how best to defend herself. 'Mr Crowe is not a suitable employer for a young woman.'

'I suppose most places are looking for experience,' she said. 'I've only done shop work – but I can clean, and I can sew. I'd be happy to turn my hand to anything.' Her eagerness reminded Letty of herself when she first arrived in Grimsby, willing to do anything rather than spend her days with Dorcas. Ironically, when Letty bought the café, it was Dorcas who had been her greatest ally and they'd spent a lot of time together in the beginning, working to get it established.

'Would you be willing to work in a café? Making teas and rolls, wiping tables, cleaning floors, washing up. Generally, I'm looking for someone who's willing to muck in and give a hand where it's needed.'

While she spoke, Pearl nodded vigorously, then just as suddenly stopped. 'Is it on the docks?'

'It is. By the graving dock. Where they work on the ship repairs,' she explained when Pearl looked blankly at her. 'I'd take you over there myself, but I need to stay here for an hour or two. It's called Hardy's. Wait a moment while I get a scrap of paper. I'll draw you a map.'

While she waited, the girl looked about her, taking in the boots and sweaters, the fearnoughts and oilskins, the racks of hooks, of twine and ropes, and all manner of other things that were needed by a ship's crew, from a saucepan to an oven.

Letty showed her the map. 'This is us here, Parker's.' She pointed with her finger. 'And this is where you need to be.'

Pearl nodded her understanding, taking hold of Letty's quick sketch and studying it as if it were a map of the entire world.

'Hilda and her daughter will be there. Tell them I sent you. I'll take you on two weeks' trial.'

The girl looked quick to tears. 'Oh, Mrs Hardy. What can I ever do to thank you?'

'No need to thank me. I was given a chance once; I like to pass a kindness on where I can. Life is a little more bearable that way.' It was the only thing that made it bearable, most especially these last four years. It was perhaps needed even more as people gathered together the pieces of their broken lives. Letty turned to look at the clock over the counter. 'Off you go. If you hurry, they'll have time to show you a few things before it gets too busy.'

Pearl looked again at the map, smiled broadly. 'Thank you, Mrs Hardy. I won't let you down.' She hurried out of the shop, came back seconds later to check she had closed the door properly, and disappeared from view.

When Puggy and Wolfie arrived to sit with Percy for a chinwag and Norah was up to being in the shop for an hour or two, Letty went over to the café to check how Pearl was getting on.

It was still busy, thank the good Lord. The little business had kept them going when Alec's pay dropped drastically when he signed with the naval reserve. Pearl was gathering empty mugs and plates from tables and relaying them to the counter. Over in one corner, Stella was standing on a chair singing to some of the regulars, counting the coppers they gave her before dropping them into her pocket. At home she had amassed a pretty penny in a glass jar that she kept for sweets and comics and treats. Alfie was at the sink, his sleeves rolled up to his elbows washing dishes. Dorcas was bustling about behind the counter her back to the door. Beside her was Hilda, whose expression told Letty to tread carefully as she approached. Letty took a breath and walked briskly behind the counter and into the small store cupboard where they left their belongings. Dorcas followed her, as Letty knew she would.

'You didn't tell me we were taking on more staff.'

Letty put her gloves in her bag, pushed it under the stool they used to reach the higher shelves. 'It was a spur-of-the-moment thing. The girl came for work, and I gave her a two-week trial. Percy's not so good these days. I didn't feel I could leave Norah to run the shop and be with him.' He would only get worse when the poorer weather arrived, and she would be heavy with child when winter came around. Far better to put things in place now.

'She's not from round here. Says she's from Hull. Stella's had some daft notion she was a mermaid. Alfie says she's the lass my Alec saved from drowning.'

'She is.' Letty made her way back to the counter. 'How has she been?'

Dorcas wiped her hands on her apron. 'A drip. I've had to show her the same thing twice over. Stella could do better.'

Pearl looked over and when Dorcas caught her eye, she quickly turned away and picked up the tray of mugs. She began carrying them back to the counter and tripped, managed to steady herself, and avoided dropping any of them. The mugs rattled on the tray. 'Breakages will come out of your pay packet, my girl,' Dorcas called across the shop.

Letty intervened. 'Give the girl a chance; you're terrifying her.'

'Well, she's clumsy. We'll go out of business quick enough if she breaks more than she saves.'

Letty went over to Pearl.

'I'm sorry, Mrs Hardy, but Mrs Hardy, the other Mrs Hardy, I don't think she likes me.'

Letty whispered, 'She doesn't like anyone to begin with. She'll thaw.' She winked at her and picked up the tray. 'I'll take these.' She nodded towards the counter. 'Looks like there's an order ready.'

Hilda pushed two bacon butties towards her. 'Table to the left of the front door.'

Pearl stretched out her left hand and looked to Hilda, who confirmed the direction. The older woman grinned at Letty and turned back to her customer. Poor girl was terrified and no wonder. Letty herself had not taken to Dorcas but she knew her odd ways now, and, more importantly, how to soften them.

Letty worked at the café for a couple of hours during the busy period and went back to the Parkers. Dorcas would lock up the café and take home the takings, Alfie and Stella as escorts during the school holiday. There would be more to juggle when the pair of them went back to school, but she'd cross that bridge when she came to it.

The children were doing chores when Letty got back home. Dorcas came in from the yard with a basket filled with the washing that had been on the line all day. Alfie pulled out the chair and the children began pairing socks and folding the smalls while Dorcas tackled Alec's shirts, pulling the sleeves sharply and folding them ready to iron that evening. Letty had not time to get herself a glass of water when Dorcas started her chirruping.

'You can't keep that lass on. She's not right sharp. Got herself in a pickle, I'll bet.'

Stella giggled and Alfie gave her a look.

Dorcas picked up another shirt. 'Waiting for some fly-by-night to come and make an honest woman of her.' Again, she tugged the sleeves. 'She'll be waiting a long time.'

'She seems pleasant enough. A little timid perhaps but her confidence will come.'

'We can't afford more staff,' Dorcas said flatly.

'I won't be able to be at the café so much as I get nearer my time. I'm thinking ahead. Percy is not so good. He'll be a whole lot worse when the weather takes a turn. I can't be here, there and everywhere, and neither can you.' She winked at Alfie. 'Unless Alec wants to serve and wash dishes while he's out of a ship.'

'*My boy?* He's a skipper, not a skivvy.'

Letty bit the inside of her cheek. Dorcas was such an easy bait. Alfie tried to suppress a smile but failed.

Dorcas sucked her cheek, knowing she'd bitten too early. 'You don't know anything about the lass. How do you know she isn't spinning you a yarn?' The clothes were neatly folded on the table and Dorcas put them back in the basket, pushed a chair forward, and put them in the cupboard under the stairs.

'I don't. But there are plenty of people with references who I wouldn't employ. My instinct tells me that she's to be trusted.'

'I'd rather have it in black and white,' Dorcas said. 'I'd be careful where you place that trust of yours.'

Letty didn't answer. If she gave Dorcas the last word, it would put an end to the conversation and some battles weren't worth fighting.

8

On Friday, Letty was behind the counter at Parker's when Pearl came in, tearful. Letty opened the flap and hurried towards her.

'I'm really sorry, Mrs Hardy, but I can't work with Mrs Hardy – the other Mrs Hardy, Mrs Hardy.'

Letty gave her a handkerchief, stifling the urge to laugh. 'Call me Letty; that will save the confusion.'

'Thank you, Mrs Hardy. Letty.'

Letty reached out and put her hand over Pearl's. 'What's the problem?' She knew without asking that Dorcas would be at the root of it.

'I told her I fell in the water, but she keeps telling folk I tried to drown myself.' Pearl swallowed down a sob. 'But if I wanted to do myself in there's easier ways to do it than drowning. I could drink a bottle of poison and go to sleep like Vicky Belstaff.' She began to cry.

Norah went to the door and turned the sign to *Closed*.

'Poor Vicky,' Pearl sobbed. 'She shouldn't have done it and left her kiddies, but what else could she do?' She looked up at the two women, eyes red, nose running. Letty put her arm about her shoulder and drew her to her. The girl rubbed at her eyes with the handkerchief then blew her nose. 'I'm sorry to cause you so much trouble when you've been so kind to me. But though Mr Hardy was very good to come in the water after me, I wasn't trying to do myself in.'

Letty held her. No wonder Dorcas had snapped. Her mother-in-law would hate to think that Alec wasn't the hero of that particular hour. Saving the lives of thirteen men was clearly not enough. But it wasn't right to say such things when they weren't true. Dorcas hadn't been there. Looking back, the sun had been bright, the girl dazzled by it. It was far too easy to make it something that it wasn't. And Pearl had stuck to her story through thick and thin.

'I'll have a word with her,' Letty consoled, knowing it would be fruitless. Once Dorcas got something fixed in her head, she didn't give it up lightly. It would be best to help Pearl find other employment.

'Why not have the girl work in the shop?' Norah suggested when Letty went to get Pearl a glass of water. 'It will free you, and me, and we'll have a lot less trouble. Both of us. It will be as well to train someone up now.' They had trained other girls over the years, but they had left when they found better paid work in the munitions factories on Freeman Street.

'I don't know,' Letty said, dabbing the droplets of water around the glass.

'Let's give her another trial, then. With us. By the time the baby comes, she should have found her feet.' The two of them exchanged looks and smiled.

Letty took the glass. 'I'll tell her the good news.'

* * *

Letty was exhausted by the time she got home later that day. It had been hard work talking Pearl through the stock, and in the end, she'd broken it down into sections, Pearl writing it all down in a small notebook so that she wouldn't forget. She was not a quick learner, but she was very careful, and Letty was sure she'd catch on eventually. When she returned home, she told Dorcas that Pearl would no longer be at Hardy's but would be with the Parkers at the chandlery.

'Have you taken leave of your senses? There are dozens of local girls you could have given work to.'

'She doesn't know anyone. She was alone.'

'That's not your problem.'

Letty pressed her lips together. 'I remember what it was like to be in her position.' Dorcas opened her mouth to interrupt, but Letty was too quick. 'Or something very similar. The Parkers took me on when they knew nothing about me.'

'Aye, but you're different.' Dorcas turned her back, muttering under her breath, and Letty knew that was the closest she was going to get as a compliment from her mother-in-law. Dorcas was like a squall, quick to rise and soon to blow itself out. 'She's gormless. Waiting for some lad who's spun her a line. If he exists at all.'

'I'm sure Sidney exists. There are plenty of young men that go from ship to ship.'

Dorcas huffed and Letty tried not to snap. 'Throwing herself in the water like that, trying to end it all.'

'She fell.'

'Huh. My eye she did. Only one reason a lass wants to end it all. We'll know soon enough when it starts to show. Then what will you do? You can't save everyone.' She glanced to Alfie to make her point and Letty bit at her cheek. Alfie hadn't been quite four years old when his mother died. She'd promised

Anita she'd take care of him and had never regretted it. 'She'll string your pity to its end.' Dorcas was in full flow, enjoying giving voice to her thoughts whether anyone listened or not. 'But you know your business best; far be it for me to interfere.'

Letty suppressed her answer. *If only.*

They bustled about getting the evening meal ready, then waiting for Alec. When he did not return at seven, or even half past, Letty fed the children and herself. Dorcas wouldn't eat until Alec came back. Letty didn't have the patience. 'He's well aware of what time we eat. If he chooses not to grace us with his presence, then we eat without him. The Lord knows his time with us is precious, and so should he.'

'Even more reason to wait,' Dorcas said. Alec was still out of a ship. He was unused to being ashore for long periods and while he waited, he drifted through the days. He had fixed all the outstanding repairs in the house, did what was asked of him, and spent the rest of his day down at the docks, or in the pub, trying to fill the hours. He had rolled in drunk every night this week and Letty was getting weary of it. The children quietly took their places at the table. Stella was about to open her mouth to ask why her gran wasn't joining them when Letty glared at her. Dorcas sat in the chair, her knitting needles clattering a tune as angry as she was, muttering all the while that she didn't know what the world was coming to.

* * *

They had cleared everything away and the children were washed and in their nightclothes when Alec staggered in. Letty heard him fumble at the front door, bumping into the hall stand and knocking it over, steadying it as well as himself, apologising to inanimate objects as if they were human. Dorcas sprang out of her chair and went to the stove. Letty watched her plate it up, the pie dry, the potatoes shrivelled along with the peas. She warmed the gravy and poured it over the top, setting it on the table as he came to stand in the door frame, swaying from side to side.

'My little darlings. How bonny you look in your nighties. Are you going to give your father a kiss?' He opened his arms, and they went to him, Alfie looking first at Letty, who nodded for him to do as he was asked. Stella screwed her face up at the smell of her father's breath and pushed him away with her hands.

'Up to bed, you two,' Letty ordered, too angry to remain in the room, following the children upstairs. When she returned, Dorcas was sitting at the table. Alec was trying to spear a potato and not having much luck but, somehow, he managed to finish his meal. When Dorcas took his empty plate, he rested his head on his arm and went to sleep.

Letty took up her mending basket, picked up her darning mushroom and pulled one of Alfie's socks over it.

'A wife should eat with her husband,' Dorcas said.

'I agree,' Letty said. 'When he's sober. When they can converse about their day. When their husband comes back when he says he will.'

'He has a lot of time on his hands now his ship's been delayed again.'

'There's plenty he could be doing.'

'He's a skipper. What do you want him to do? Put a cloth in his hand and wipe down tables? You'll know, when you have a boy of your own.'

'I already have a boy of my own.' She loved Alfie as much as she loved Stella, even though she hadn't given birth to him.

'But it's not the same, is it? He's not of your flesh.'

Letty rested her sewing in her lap. 'He might not be of my womb, but he is of my heart and *that's* what matters most.'

Dorcas didn't reply, and they sat in silence, punctuated by Alec's slobbers and snores until he roused himself. When he did, Letty got up and placed a glass of water in front of him. He slaked it back and she poured him another. He drank it too, rubbed at his face with his hands. She didn't want to argue here, not in front of his mother, who would take his side. She held her tongue until they could be alone.

* * *

When Alec went into the bedroom, he pushed up the sash and looked down onto the street. There were still folk out, a couple of blokes staggering home. They'd be in for an earful, no doubt about it. He'd meant to come back on time to eat with them all, but he'd got talking and he hated himself for it. His mother had stayed downstairs with him and her griping had sobered him up, moaning about Alec having to eat alone. But Letty was right. He should have come home. He got undressed, pulled back the sheet and lay beside her.

She was lying on her side, her back to him, and he leaned close and kissed her shoulder, moved his hand to her softly swollen belly. 'I'm sorry, Let,' he whispered.

'You're always sorry. But your words don't make me feel any better.'

He sat back, propped himself up against the pillows. 'I can't seem to help meself. I get talking and it passes the time. I'd be on the ship in a heartbeat, you know that.' She turned to him and he moved his arm, grateful that she still wanted to curl into it. 'I must stink of sweat and ale.'

'You do.'

'And you still want to be with me?'

She placed her hand on his chest and tilted her head to look at him. There was enough light through the window to see her beautiful face, the kindness that radiated from every pore of her skin, and he was suddenly vulnerable, waiting for her answer.

'I'd never want to be with anyone else – though you drive me to distraction, Alec Hardy.'

He kissed the top of her head, and she stayed in his arms. Outside they could hear a dog barking and the sound of horses braying in the yard on Mansel Street. She nestled her head into his chest.

'I never meant it to be like this. I promised you the world when we came here. I thought you'd have it by now.'

'If it hadn't been for the war, we would have done. I'd have my land; you'd have your ship. It wasn't for the lack in us.'

'The lack in me.'

'The drink has made you maudlin.'

He shook his head. 'It's not the drink. Well, not just the drink. I met Baxter today. He's the same age as I am, and he kept fishing. He made a few bob as well, the fish scarce, the prices high. Mebbe I was a bloody fool to sign up so quick.'

'You did what you had to do. I'm proud that you did.'

'Aye, but they all seem to be mistakes to me now.' He'd had too much time on his hands to dwell on these things. The days endless, waiting for his turn, for someone to call him forth for his own ship again. 'I saw Richard Evans down dock. A shadow of a man he was before he lost his sons.'

She smoothed her hand over his stomach and every fibre in his body set alight. He took her hand, kissed her palm. She looked up at him, her eyes soft.

'He'll find a way of going on; we all do. Somehow. Look how well your mother has done.'

'Because of you and the kids.'

'No, because of us. We made the move and left her no choice. It could have gone wrong, but we all made sure it didn't.' She was being generous. It wasn't down to him; he was hardly ever home. Letty had made things work, relentlessly driving forward, refusing to accept defeat, even when it stared her in the face. She lifted herself on her elbow and kissed him. 'Let's get some sleep. I've an early start in the morning.'

He bent his head and kissed hers. God, how he loved her, her spirit, her strength. He'd known the moment he set eyes on her that she was special. A woman far above any he'd ever known.

'I love you, Letty Hardy. More than life itself.' She turned her back again and settled herself to sleep. He lay for a while looking at the shadows pass across the wall as the curtain flapped in the breeze. He didn't want to close his eyes, didn't want to dream, or relive the numerous occasions he'd been helpless, watching men suffer, men he couldn't save. In his torment, and to his eternal shame, he'd betrayed Letty. That tortured him most of all. May God forgive him for it, for Letty never would.

9

The nets at the window kept the room at the front of the house in Park Street cool and Letty often escaped there, to have time alone, to think. It was here that she kept her precious things, the china tea set her godmother had given her on her marriage, and her photographs. Dorcas rarely came in there, and as such Letty felt it was her room. Sanctuary. When Ruth or any of the ladies from the guild were visiting, they were shown directly into this room. It was a far cry from their first home they'd had in Mariners Row. It had been such a disappointment, but they'd worked hard and done well for themselves, more so when Alec became skipper. He'd been earning well, taking a good wage and one and three-eighths of a percentage of the profits, as was his due. His income had reduced drastically when he signed for the Royal Naval Reserve and went on service pay. But between Parker's and the café they had managed to stay afloat when so many looked to be drowning. It had been hard graft but they had survived. She'd not wanted to fall out with Alec, but she had to stop him throwing good money over the bar each night. There had to be a better way for him to spend his time until he was allocated a ship. And she thought she knew what that was.

She glanced at the photograph they had taken when Alec was ashore in the first months of the war. Letty had had a large print made and set in a mahogany frame. It hung on the wall facing the hearth, over which was a large over-mantel mirror, positioned so that she could sit on the sofa and look at it in reflection. Alec looked so fine. He'd been on leave, and she'd been afraid, overcoming it by capturing him in sepia, praying it would keep him alive. The signs of strain were already visible on his handsome face. He'd already lost pals while on the minesweepers. And there was worse still to come after that when he was sent to the Dardanelles. He spoke little of it to her, but his nightmares told her more. On the mantelpiece was a silver framed photograph of Alec in his uniform taken when he received his medal. His mother had an identical one in the back room that she had placed in the middle of her own family photos, of her late husband, Will, and her son Robbie, both of them lost to the sea. Letty was glad to have Alec safely ashore, even for a short time, but it wasn't doing him any good.

In the mirror she saw the door open. Alec popped his head around it. He came into the room.

'I'm sorry, for last night, Let. And the night before.' He grinned. 'And the night before that.'

He came closer, tentative. She turned to him and smiled, letting him know it was safe ground. In truth she pitied him, for without a ship he was lost as surely as if the stars had fallen from the sky, and he could no longer get his bearings for safe harbour.

'I know it's hard, Alec, but you could be waiting a long time yet for a ship.' The navy had staggered releasing men from their commissions, service pay being better than none. Trawlers that had been converted for minesweeping duties had been returned to their owners as soon as they became available, but there was a huge backlog, men working around the clock to convert them back to fishing vessels. And while they worked, the fishermen had nought else to do but wait.

'Hammond reckons another week or so.' He sank down on the sofa. 'I'll be out of my brains if it's longer than that.'

She took a seat beside him. 'We'll be out of money too if you drink your time away.'

He was contrite. 'It can't be easy with Mother either, stuck in her ways. I don't know how you put up with the pair of us.'

'I can cope with her odd ways; I've got used to them. But the sun doesn't shine out of my backside as it does yours.'

He gave a half laugh.

She gripped his hand tightly. 'I was thinking. You ought to take her back to Lowestoft for a few days. She deserves a break – and I reckon she'd like to show you off.'

'Oh, I don't know about that.' He shifted uncomfortably. 'I've had enough of the fuss to last me a lifetime.'

'But she hasn't, love. Your uncle Eric and aunt Minnie would love to see you, I'm sure.'

He wasn't as enthusiastic as she thought he'd be. 'We'll all go,' he said, jiggling her hand. 'The kiddies are out of school. We'll make a holiday of it.'

'No. Not this time.' Letty had thought he might suggest it. 'I think it will do Dorcas the power of good to go back to the old places. With you. She'll enjoy having you all to herself – without any competition.'

'You're not competition.'

'Sometimes it feels like that, Alec.'

'But what about the café?'

'Hilda and her daughter will do more hours; they'll be glad

of it. Her husband hasn't been able to find work since he was released.' He'd been in the prisoner-of-war camp at Ruhleben most of the war. 'He can't work as he did. And Pearl is with me at Parker's.'

'How's she getting on?' His mother had told him what she thought of Letty's decision, and more than once.

'Well enough. She's more suited to the shop. I don't know why I ever thought she could work in the café.'

He squeezed her hand. 'If you ask me, Pearl fell on her feet when you took her on.'

'When you saved her, you mean,' Letty teased.

He smiled, kissed her. 'Now you sound like me mother.'

'Go and tell her the good news. And don't say it was my idea.' They got up. Letty glanced at the photographs, checked her hair in the mirror. Alec came to stand behind her, placed his hands on her shoulders. 'I sometimes think she's lonely for familiar streets and familiar faces.'

'What about you, the kiddies?'

'We'll go when the baby arrives. My mother will enjoy it far more. And then Dorcas can hold the fort while we go together. Let her go first. I can wait.'

* * *

His mother was delighted at his suggestion, as he'd known she would be, and Letty stood back and let him take the credit for it. He would have owned up but for the delight on his mother's face when he told her of his plan. He couldn't take that from her, and once again he gave thanks for Letty's thoughtfulness. There was not a woman to match her. In no time at all his mother became like a gale, swirling about the laundry, snatching up her belongings and his when he told her they would leave first thing in the morning. Later, he sat on the bed while Letty folded his shirts and packed a small bag. 'I thought you'd be glad to go back to Lowestoft too,' she said.

He was in two minds about it and she sensed his reluctance. 'I saw enough of it these last few years, Let.' The Royal Naval Reserve had been based out of Lowestoft and he'd been many times. He and what had remained of his crew had been put ashore there when the *Black Prince* was hit. Henry Evans had died there.

She fastened the bag and sat down beside him. 'I think it's time you went back and found the happy memories you left there, Alec. Lay ghosts to rest.' She knew of his nightmares, things he couldn't get out of his head, burned as they were into his brain. Sometimes there were no words.

He nodded, reached out for her hand. 'I'll do my best.'

10

Aunt Helen had been delighted to discover that Arthur had walked out with Ruth on Sunday afternoon. She'd called at Meadowvale House on Monday lunchtime, stopping off on her way to the newspaper office to deliver her report of Peace Day for her society column. A huge bouquet of flowers arrived for Ruth shortly after. 'From Arthur?' her aunt enquired. Ruth read the card, nodded. 'He's eager, I'll give him that.' She leaned in and sniffed at the abundance of roses and lilies, froths of green fern dotted among them. 'You must have given him a little encouragement?'

'It was a pleasant hour. Two old friends catching up, that's all.' It had felt like something much more, as if she stood on the brink of something between joy and fear. She hadn't been quite sure which. Part of her felt as if she was reaching back to grasp at something she'd lost and pull it firmly into the present. It had left her confused.

Her aunt raised an eyebrow. 'He was testing the water. No one likes to jump into icy seas.'

'I was never icy to Arthur.' Ruth set the bouquet down on the sideboard.

'He didn't see it that way.'

Ruth twisted to her aunt. 'Aunt Helen, you haven't—'

'We chatted at the church service,' her aunt said quickly. 'He asked my advice.'

'And you told him to call?'

'Not as such,' her aunt said, deliberately vague. 'He asked if you and your father would be at Saxon Hall for luncheon and I told him we were otherwise engaged.' She fiddled with her pearls. 'Oh, Ruth. You can't spend the rest of your life running after your father...' She paused. 'Where is he?'

'At his office.'

Her aunt rested her hand on the sideboard, then picked at the roses. 'He's buried himself away – as he did when your mother died. As have you.' Ruth made to protest. Her aunt stopped her. 'You can't save him, Ruth, and you can't hide away from life, my darling.' She considered for a moment, looked directly at her niece. 'You're twenty-six; if you want a family, children, you can't afford to dally.'

For a long time, Ruth hadn't wanted anything – only what she couldn't have. Her brothers, for life to go back to how it was. Her aunt picked up the card that had come with the flowers, and smiled. 'It would be rather sad if you let life slip by. Left *things* too late.' She glanced to the grandfather clock. 'I must go.' She made for the door, stopped, turned. 'I was thinking of throwing a dinner party on Friday. Just a few friends. The Howards, Willoughbys. The Marshalls.' She studied Ruth's expression. 'Would you and your father join us?'

Ruth shook her head, exasperated by her aunt's terrible stab at nonchalance and gave a small laugh.

'I'll leave it in your good hands.'

* * *

Richard Evans waited downstairs, looking handsome in his dress suit. When she had mentioned Aunt Helen's invitation to dinner, he'd accepted with enthusiasm. It had both delighted and surprised her. Over the past three years his sister had issued invitations for numerous fundraising functions and dinners, and had received just as many rejections. There were only one or two that he felt able to attend. Ones that were close to his heart, usually connected to the search for the lost. Like Charles, many young men had no graves. A commission of men were carrying out gruesome duties in the fields of France and Belgium, exhuming bodies from the churned earth to give them a Christian burial. If they were found with means of identification, however slim, they were buried in one of the war graves close to the battlefields; otherwise, their graves were marked *Known only to God*. Ruth had wondered many times whether one of them could be her brother; they would never know for certain. Those – she refrained from calling them lucky – who had graves to visit couldn't always afford the journey. Richard Evans would readily put his hand in his pocket and had donated large sums of money to the YMCA for the purpose. He looked up at her as she descended the stairs and smiled.

'You look rather lovely tonight, my dear. Is that the brooch Arthur sent to you yesterday?'

'It is.' A gift had arrived each day he had been in London: flowers, chocolates and now jewellery. She went to her father and adjusted his bow tie, brushed at his shoulders.

'Do I pass muster?'

'You certainly do.' It was wonderful to have him in such good spirits. He seemed to have shed the reluctance that these occasions had ignited of late. He stared at her brooch as she stood back to assess him.

'Arthur appears to be in earnest if this week is anything to go by. I suppose he doesn't want you to slip through his fingers again.'

Ruth pinched her cheeks, checked her lipstick in the hall mirror, tucked a wisp of blonde hair about her ear. She had begun to look forward the daily deliveries. 'It's not as if men are beating their path to our door.'

'That's more because you've pulled up the drawbridge on any attention such men might give to you.' He helped her on with her stole. 'And because you have given all your attention to taking care of me. It has to stop.' He glanced up at the portrait of his wife, then at Ruth and smiled. 'Life has to go on. It must.'

He made his way to the front door, opened it and stood back to let her pass. 'I'm pleased that Helen has invited the Howards. And Daphne,' he said, as they stepped outside. It was warm, and the scent of honeysuckle that wrapped itself around the porch floated in the still air. 'I've had my fill of sitting with the fuddy-duddies.' He locked the door, pocketed the key. 'It's good to have fresh faces, new conversation, perspectives.' Her father opened the passenger door. 'I think Jeremy might be glad of Daphne's company too.'

Ruth rested her hand on the door frame. 'You think they like each other?' It hurt a little, to think of what might have been. They would have been sisters-in-law, had Charles returned. Almost a year after her brother had been declared missing, a letter had arrived from a private in Charles's battalion. He'd seen him fall before being injured himself and languishing in a field hospital, unable to remember. As he'd healed, so had his memory. His mother had written the letter, for the young man had lost his hand in the blast. She had wanted him to be mistaken but Daphne had been more pragmatic. Someone had witnessed his death. It was enough.

'They would make a good match,' her father said.

'Like Arthur and I?'

He made a movement with his head to indicate she should get in the car, and she did so, sliding into the seat. He leaned forward as he closed the door.

'We have to take our happiness wherever we might find it, my dear. We never know how long it might last.'

* * *

They were not the first to arrive at Saxon Hall and Ruth was glad of it. The Marshalls and the Howards had congregated in the drawing room. The French windows were open into the garden and though there was still ample light, large lamps that were set about the room gave off an amber glow from under their gold silk shades, rendering the room warm and welcoming while keeping the temperature cool. Uncle Jack was deep in conversation with Arthur and his father, Cyril, the three of them straight-backed, no doubt trying to outdo each other, though Uncle Jack would have no difficulty in that quarter. The two older men were long-standing rivals, though they sat side by side on the board of the Trawler Owners' Association, as did her father. That Jack Frampton had trumped Cyril on his attempt to become mayor of Grimsby had not gone down well. But as Uncle Jack had said at the time, 'The best man won.' It had been a light-hearted joke and though Cyril had laughed he'd not taken his defeat lightly and was no doubt making plans to topple his rival. Evelyn Howard was standing with her brother, Jeremy, and Mildred Marshall, and she visibly brightened when Ruth and her father came to join them.

'Ruth, so good to see you again.' Mildred offered her cheek and Ruth touched her own to it. 'You look well, Ruth. Your father too. It's good to see you so after... Well, after.' There was an awkwardness that was quickly dispelled when Evelyn admired Ruth's brooch.

'How pretty.'

'A gift from Arthur.' She lifted the silver and diamond flower and caught Mildred's smile of satisfaction.

'The boy has remarkable taste.'

Evelyn bit back a smile and Ruth immediately sensed an ally. Her father was right; fresh faces and new perspectives might shake things up a little. The front bell rang again, and Aunt Helen went into the hall. The Willoughbys had arrived, and Jeremy shifted, watching the door, waiting for Daphne to make her entrance.

When they went through to dinner, her father was delighted to find himself seated with the Howards, Evelyn on his left, Daphne on his right, Jeremy next to her. Nothing missed her aunt's attention and that the evening was seamless was down to Helen Frampton's great skill at bringing the right people together at the right time – and seating them accordingly.

'I hear your trip to London was successful, Arthur,' Richard said across the table. Mildred preened. 'Your father mentioned a deal you had concluded this week.'

'My son has developed a keen instinct for business,' Cyril interjected. 'His latest endeavours should turn a handsome profit. He has learned to take a risk where risks need to be taken.'

'Not too many, I hope,' her father countered.

'Calculated risks,' Arthur qualified, steering the conversation away from his father.

'The best kind to make, young man.'

'We find we're making more from salvage than fishing at present,' Cyril added. 'That's where the money is.'

'There's plenty sloshing about, if you look in the right places,' Jack Frampton commented from his end of the long table. 'I'd like to see a bit more of it go to the right places.'

'I hear many companies have not fared so well,' Jeremy Howard said, finding his moment to join in. 'I know I've only been in the area a short time but there has been a lot of talk of trawler companies going under.'

Ruth gave a quick glance to her father. Things had been touch and go after Henry died. Her father had gone to the office each day only to sit there among his paperwork doing nothing more than stare into space. It had been the office manager who had kept things going and Ruth herself had gone in to help bring it to order, leaving only when she felt things were back on an even keel and her father able to cope. With the loss of his sons, Richard had lost his purpose, seeing no future for the Excel Trawler Company. Uncle Jack and Aunt Helen had coaxed, then cajoled and finally bullied him back to taking the reins, telling him Ruth was the future, that there would be grandchildren to hand it on to. There was hope yet. He caught her eye, gave her a reassuring smile.

'Some have not been so fortunate.' Richard addressed himself to Jeremy. 'At the outbreak of war, the navy requisitioned the best of the trawling fleet to convert for minesweeping duties.'

'For which we received remuneration for tonnage and loss of profit,' Uncle Jack added. 'It was a fair deal, in the circumstances. For both sides. And we all wanted to play our part.'

Arthur shifted uncomfortably and Ruth felt a sliver of sympathy for him.

'Many of the trawlers were lost at sea. Caught by torpedo or mine,' Uncle Jack continued. 'Or captured by the enemy and destroyed with explosives. Those that survived are being reconverted but it's not a quick job, nor an easy one.'

'And the bank loans still have to be paid whether the ship's in dry dock or on the fish,' Richard added. 'It's been very difficult. Very difficult.'

Cyril Marshall sprinkled his beef liberally with salt. 'It's a challenging business. Over in Hull, the fishermen are on strike. We've avoided it here.'

'So far,' Uncle Jack interjected. Cyril nodded and turned back to Jeremy. 'It's estimated that three hundred fishermen have come over the Humber to Grimsby in search of work. Arthur has taken some of them on.'

'That's commendable,' Jeremy offered.

Richard gave a small snort. 'Not when it takes jobs from local men.' He eyed Cyril. Ruth could sense the friction between them. Aunt Helen intervened.

'Gentlemen, I didn't invite guests to a business meeting.' She beamed at them all, her expression leaving the men in no doubt that that particular conversation was at an end.

The guests talked to their immediate companions while the plates were removed, Arthur asking Ruth how she'd spent her time while he'd been away. He was attentive and considerate in ways he hadn't been previously and once again, Ruth doubted she'd ever really got to know him before. He was telling her of his time in London when she heard Cyril mention Philip Proctor's name and she turned away from Arthur, eager to hear news of her friend.

'He's a well-respected marine artist. Made quite a name for himself. I've commissioned him to paint the ships of the fleet for the new boardroom,' Cyril was telling Jeremy. 'We're expanding our offices on Wharncliffe Road since buying into premises at the rear, on Henderson Street.' He caught her father's attention. 'Gradually working our way down to your offices at Excel, Richard.' He waited while the maid removed the vegetable tureen. 'Who knows, there could be an amalgamation on the cards.' All eyes were on Arthur and Ruth, and she felt her cheeks flame.

'I believe Proctor's a friend of the family?' Mildred said. 'Apparently, we met him briefly at your garden party a few years ago, Helen. I had quite forgotten. Cyril reminded me that he was with the naval contingent that day, though I can't quite place him.'

Ruth wasn't surprised by her admission. Mildred seemed only to remember people who would be of importance to her husband and sons.

'He served with Henry on the *Black Prince* when it went down,' her father said quietly. 'He was with him at the end. He and Alec Hardy brought him home.'

Ruth twisted her napkin in her hands.

'Henry was very fond of him. He stayed with us once or twice.' He looked to his daughter. 'He still writes to us both. More regularly to Ruth.'

Ruth felt Arthur's eyes on her.

'It will be good to see him again,' Richard added.

'He was in Malta, I believe?' Cyril picked up his spoon in anticipation of dessert, the silver glinting in the candlelight.

'There for two years.' Her father looked to her for confirmation and Ruth nodded. 'He stayed on until the navy left and remained to tidy up things, before they shipped out for good.'

'Left it shipshape.' Cyril smiled at his own wit.

'Knowing Philip, yes, he would. I can think of no finer man for the job.'

'Did his wife go over with him?' Arthur asked casually.

'Not married. Confirmed bachelor,' her father replied, giving Ruth a quick glance.

'I think I remember him,' Arthur said, touching his glass for more wine. The butler stepped forward and filled it. Ruth remembered it well enough. Henry had been mischievous that day, and Arthur had been grumpy and demanding. She felt a sudden longing for her impish brother. Had he lived, no doubt he too would have changed. He would have had to settle down eventually, there being no place for mischievousness in the Excel boardroom. She smiled to herself. He would have hated it.

After dinner the ladies retired to the drawing room and the men remained at the table to drink port and smoke cigars. Evelyn took a seat next to Ruth and Daphne came to join them while Aunt Helen fussed around Mildred and Daphne's mother. The hours seemed to slide by, and Ruth was delighted to see her father so lively when the men came to join them. For a while she had shed her sadness, though a shaft of guilt pierced her when she remembered she'd not thought of her brothers for the last hour or more.

Ruth and her father were last to leave.

'An enjoyable evening, Helen. Thank you.'

Aunt Helen took her brother's hands in hers. 'And more to come, my dear.'

He nodded and went out to start the car, Jack Frampton following. Ruth pulled on her gloves, leaned forward to kiss her aunt's cheek.

'Arthur was very charming. I thought you two were getting on like old times. Rather better, I fancy?'

'It was not fancy. I enjoyed his company, perhaps more than I did on previous occasions.' He had asked more of her work during the war, of her work at the mission and with the guild. More importantly, he'd listened when before he might have been dismissive. He had made her laugh with his stories of mishaps on his travels. How had she not noticed before? Maybe the fault was with her. 'I think Father enjoyed the evening more than I did.' She'd actually heard him laugh at something Evelyn had said.

Her aunt put her hands to Ruth's shoulders and drew her close. 'He looks at you and sees possibilities. That's exactly what he needed to see. That life goes on. That there is a future – and you are that future.'

11

The day after the dinner party, Richard Evans had once again gone to Saxon Hall. Arthur had arrived at Meadowvale House that morning to ask for Ruth's hand in marriage – and Richard had no reason to object, not one he could readily think of. Troubled whether he had done the right thing, he sought his sister's counsel on the matter. The maid showed him through the house and onto the terrace, where he found Helen reading through a file of papers.

'No rest for the wicked,' he teased.

'Mother would have approved,' she said, closing the file. 'Old habits die hard.' She got up and went over to him, kissed his cheek. 'Jack's on the golf course.'

'It was you I came to see.' She would have been expecting him to call, of course she would. Arthur would have made sure of the lie of the land with Ruth's aunt before making any attempt to speak to him. It was to be expected. Things hadn't gone to plan the first time; he wouldn't want anything to derail his proposal a second time.

'Coffee?'

He nodded. She gave her instruction to the maid, who hurried off to the kitchen. Helen motioned for him to take a seat.

'I had a visit from Arthur this morning.' He pulled a chair away from the teak table. 'Don't pretend to be surprised. You above anyone would know it was on the cards.' He placed his hat on the table between them, touched the crown of it and sat down.

'You gave him your blessing?'

He paused, made her wait. 'Not so much my blessing. I said it was up to Ruth.'

He saw her shoulders soften.

'So what's troubling you? Ruth will say yes.'

He admired her certainty. He wished he had a little of it himself, but Ruth was his only child and there was much at stake. Most of all her happiness. He sensed she would say yes more for his happiness than her own. 'It's not so much Arthur. More his father.'

Helen gave a small laugh. 'Ruth isn't marrying Cyril.'

'The apple doesn't fall far from the tree.'

The maid came and placed a tray between. Helen dismissed her, began pouring the coffee.

'He's nothing like his father.'

'I hope not.' Cyril Marshall wasn't well liked but he was successful. Mostly because he was ruthless as far as business was concerned. He countered it by donating large sums to worthy causes, more to bolster his image than for the good his money would do.

'His mother exerts her own influence on Arthur, as will we. And Ruth has a sensible head on her.'

'I don't feel we are in as strong a position as we were.' He worried for his daughter, who stood to inherit everything, not just his wealth but that of his sister and her husband. It amounted to a great fortune. 'If the war hadn't come along—'

Helen interrupted. 'If the war hadn't come along, they would have been married long ago, and you know it. Heavens, you might have had one or two grandchildren by now. I'm sorry to be so harsh, Richard, but we have to concentrate our energies on Ruth, on steering her through until the next generation are ready to take over.' She handed him a cup. 'It's fruitless to think otherwise.' She was right; she usually was. All they could do now was make the best of the hand they had been dealt. 'There are ways of keeping her close and we will take every advantage of them. I have already talked it over with Jack.'

He raised his eyebrows. 'Told him?'

She ignored his remark. 'We shall give them a piece of land on which to build a house. As a wedding gift. The girl won't want to be shut away with Mildred and Cyril at Garth Hall for longer than necessary. I suggest you give them a sum of money with which to build it. Cyril will want to outdo you, so make it a substantial amount.' Her eyes glittered wickedly, and he had to laugh at her scheming. 'Ruth will be mistress of her own household and they'll be able to live their life on their terms.'

'You have it all mapped out.'

'Thinking ahead. Best not to leave these things to chance. Not where Cyril Marshall is concerned. Whatever my opinion of Arthur might be, his father likes to be the one who calls the shots. I'd rather we were the ones holding the gun.'

He took the cup and sipped at the coffee, staring out over the immaculate lawns in front of them. Images of his children danced across them, when they were young and carefree, and life was opening out before them. He closed his eyes and had a fancy he heard their laughter from long ago as they raced down towards the woodland beyond and disappeared in a game of hide-and-seek. Shadows now. It was all that was left. Brother and sister sat in quiet contentment, until the coffee was cold, and he made a move to leave.

'I'm going to tell Ruth of his intention,' he said as he got up. 'I'd rather give her time to consider her answer.'

'Don't you think that might spoil the moment?' For all her pretence otherwise, his sister was at heart a romantic.

He picked up his hat, placed it on his head. 'I doubt it. It's not as if it's the first time. On this occasion I'd like her to be prepared.'

* * *

Arthur proposed on the Sunday. Thanks to a quiet conversation with her father, it had not been unexpected – but it had been sooner than Ruth anticipated.

They had been in the restaurant of the Yarborough Hotel and he had gone down on one knee. 'Would you do me the great honour of becoming my wife?'

She was aware that all eyes were on her and her cheeks flushed with warmth at being the centre of attention. As he slipped the ring on her finger, the diamond cluster glittered under the light of the chandeliers and the diners burst into a round of applause. He kissed her hand, and as he got up, leaned close and kissed her cheek. 'You have made me the happiest man on this earth.' There had been no mention of love, and she felt a whisper of disappointment as he took his seat and gave a nod to the waiter. The relief that his evening had gone to plan was evident and he was immediately more relaxed, more talkative. He ordered champagne, which no doubt had cost a pretty penny, the reserves low and the vineyards in Épernay not back to full production. He smiled at her as the waiter poured, the bubbles racing to the top of the crystal coupes. He raised his glass to her.

'To the future. Our future.'

She touched her glass to his, still quite dazed from how quickly things had moved on between them. But, as he had said, he'd already waited long enough.

12

In Lowestoft, down in the beach village that locals called the Grit, Dorcas Hardy made her way towards the cottage that she'd once called home. It seemed much smaller than when she'd left it, the windows squat and the door low. There was a barrel to the left of it, the top still covered with shells and stones the boys had gathered from the beach below them over the years. She should have taken them with her, but it had seemed wrong to do so. They belonged here. She belonged here, and if Letty hadn't come along and turned her boy's head she would have remained here until her dying day. But Alec was all she had left, and she had clung to her boy as a barnacle to a rock.

The row of cottages sloped down towards the shore and she had followed the path, the tide washing along the sand, staining it darker. Here and there along beach the fishermen were about their boats, mending nets and making small repairs, the day's catch landed and sold. Many more were still out on the water, the distinctive red barked sails rising and falling with the waves. She'd forgotten how many times she'd stood on that same shore, waiting for Will and the boys to return, and before that, standing with her mother waiting for her father, her brother. Her heart ached for those she'd lost, for happier times, hard as they were. As she gazed out across the water, Alec came by her side, told her to put out her hand and pressed something into it. She knew without looking what it was. He'd done the same thing as a boy. 'Brought you a present, Mother, a gift from the sea.' She opened her hand and stared down at the coral and cream ridged cockle, more precious than any ruby or diamond, felt the smooth underside with her thumb, wrapped her fingers about it and put it in her pocket.

'We should never have left,' she told him quietly. 'We belong here. It's where our roots are.'

'Our roots are where we choose to put them down. Those who came before us weren't from here. Grandfather was from Barking. He followed the fish as we have done. It's what we do. It's who we are.'

Dorcas shook her head. 'Not my father, nor my grandfather.' She had betrayed them, all they'd worked so hard for. They'd survived good times and bad, here on the Suffolk coast. Other folk had stayed put and made a living. She should have made him stay but her heart told her he didn't feel the same. He stared out over the water. The sun was low in the sky, but it was still warm.

'Let's not be maudlin, Mother. It's not what we came here for.' He turned and looked down at her, a warm smile on his fine handsome face. He was so like his father, with his bright blue eyes and square jaw, that it made her shiver, and she said a silent prayer for the Lord to see fit to spare him. She nodded in answer and threaded her arm through his as he led her back up the beach towards the pathway. 'Is there anywhere special you'd like to go tomorrow?' he asked her. 'The pier? We could go Gorleston way.' As they got to the roadway, he stopped and wrapped his hand over hers. 'I want to take you places that make you smile.'

It was the first time they'd been together, mother and son, for many a year. A precious time, with no one else to have to share him with. She'd thought that coming here would bring back happy memories. She'd forgotten that she couldn't have the good without the bad.

'I should like to go to the harbour. To see the *Stella Maris*.' He and his uncle had sold the boat when Alec decided to move to Grimsby and Eric had settled for life ashore. She knew Alec would never do that; the sea was in his blood.

'She might have been lost to a mine, Mother. She might well have a new name.'

'It doesn't matter that you change her name. We'll know her when we see her. Your uncle will know if she's been lost.'

They made their way up the street to her brother-in-law's house, where they would be staying. She'd not been back since before the war. Between working at the café and looking after the house and children while Letty worked all hours, there had not been time, and she'd had no inclination to come without Alec. Whatever she might think of the lass, she was grateful that Letty had suggested their visit, for no matter that Alec had made out it was his idea, she knew it was nothing of the sort. Her boy's thoughts were of his next ship. His next catch, his crew.

The house was on Lighthouse Score, a row of cottages set back a little from the path, with a small garden to the front and rear. With every step she felt herself drawn to the earth, rooted as she never did elsewhere. The door was open, and Alec ducked as he went over the threshold. Inside it was as it ever was, neat as a pin, dried flowers in the grate, two comfortable chairs either side, the long oak cupboard bathed in sunlight from the open door and the small window. Eric was settled in his chair, his unlit pipe between his teeth, reading the *Lowestoft Gazette*. He got up when Alec walked in, dropping the newspaper onto the small table at his side. Will Hardy had been thickset and tall, his brother more wiry, more like their mother's side of the family, but the family features were unmistakeable. The same thick sandy hair, the same disarming smile. He kissed her cheek and took hold of her hands in his, his grip firm, his hands calloused from his years at sea, man and boy. 'Good to see you, Dorcas. And looking so well. It's been a long time.' He brushed the chair he had vacated, gestured for her to take it, and Alec put down their bag and shook hands with his uncle.

Before she could take a seat, Minnie came scurrying from the scullery, wiping her hands on her apron. Alec bent down to kiss her cheek, and she wrapped her arms around him.

'Looking better than when we saw you last, boy,' she said as she released him. 'Thank the good Lord all that business of war is behind us.' She pecked Dorcas on the cheek. 'Settle yourselves. You'll be tired after travelling. I've got just the thing to perk you up.' She disappeared into the small kitchen, soon returning, carrying a large teapot that she put on the sideboard that had already been set with her best china cups and saucers, tea plates and a generous Victoria sponge in anticipation of their arrival. 'I was going to write and let you know that Betsy had her baby, another girl.' She handed Dorcas a cup of tea, having already added the milk and two sugars. 'Poor Norman. A house full of lasses.'

Dorcas drew back her shoulders, proud that she had given Will two sons. 'Mebbe she'll be blessed next time.'

'She's already blessed,' Minnie said gently. 'A healthy child is a healthy child.'

'Of course,' Dorcas said quickly. 'I hadn't meant to offend. You must be delighted.' Dorcas sipped her tea, hoping that

Minnie's chatter would smooth away her thoughtless comment. The couple had no sons and Alec and Robbie had taken their father's share of the *Stella Maris* when Will died. At least Minnie had held on to her daughters and knew they were close by. Perhaps Dorcas had not been so lucky after all. Alec was away for weeks on end and Letty was the nearest to a daughter she was ever going to get. Though they'd gradually forged a better relationship, it was not as Minnie had with her girls. The talk was of their journey; Eric and Minnie asked of Letty and the children.

'We thought she might have come with you. It would've been lovely to see the kiddies. They must be quite grown up now.'

Alec beamed when he told them of Alfie and Stella.

'It was a shame that she lost the child, but she'll be blessed with more, God willing.'

'God has seen fit to bless us already, Aunt Minnie. The lass is four months into her pregnancy.'

Minnie clapped her hands in delight. 'Oh, that's wonderful news. She must be thrilled. You all must be?'

Alec nodded, as did Dorcas.

'And is her business doing well? The café? The shop?'

'They are,' Alec said, his voice heavy with pride. 'She kept 'em going through the war, Lord knows how, but she's a canny lass.'

Minnie's smile of admiration was too much for Dorcas. She put her cup on the sideboard and went to her bag, brought out a buff envelope and a small blue box.

'I thought you'd like to see Alec's medal.' She handed it to Minnie, who opened it and smiled at her nephew.

'Take it out, feel how heavy it is.' Dorcas withdrew the newspaper cuttings from the envelope.

'Uncle Eric and Aunt Minnie don't want to look at all that, Mother,' Alec protested gently. 'They'll have seen it.'

Dorcas was insulted. 'Your mother is proud of you. And quite rightly so.' She handed over clippings she'd saved from numerous local and national newspapers that had reported Alec's bravery. Minnie read them, speaking aloud when it came to any mention of Alec, and Dorcas felt herself grow a little.

'I wasn't the only one, Mother,' Alec said, folding his arms and tucking his legs under his chair as he'd done as a child. He might well have performed heroic deeds, but he was still her boy and he'd made her prouder than any son could make a mother. His father would have puffed out his chest to know his boy had done so well.

'You must be very proud,' Minnie told her, as she handed back the clippings.

'I am,' Dorcas said, carefully placing them back in the envelope. Her gaze lingered on the medal before she closed the lid. His uncle got up.

'I'll bet you've got a thirst on, lad. How about we walk down to the Lord Nelson for a jar or two.' Her boy was quick to his feet and as Minnie helped Eric on with his jacket, Dorcas caught her giving a sly wink to Alec. 'Ladies,' Eric said, taking his cap from the hook, and the two men left.

'Perhaps I went on too much for his liking,' Dorcas said, when they'd gone.

'You did what any mother would.' Minnie started clearing away the cups and saucers. 'Thank God for men like him, those poor boys who were prepared to lay their lives on the line.'

'Thank the good Lord he came back,' Dorcas said quietly. If she had lost him, she would have lost everything.

13

The following morning, Dorcas and Alec walked along Whapload Road on the way to the harbour to see if the *Stella Maris* was in the port. Uncle Eric had been happy to inform them that the sailing smack had weathered the war and fished close to shore during the hostilities, managing to avoid any of the skirmishes that had seen many a vessel sent to Davy Jones's locker. Alec pointed out places he had stayed in lodgings when his ship had docked in Lowestoft in 1914, before he'd been sent down to the English Channel for a time. Some of it had been damaged, Lowestoft being the easternmost point of the British Isles, closest to the German coast. The German ships had been able to bomb the town from their position in the North Sea. There had been bombardment and damage that Dorcas knew of, she'd read of it in the newspapers, but seeing it first-hand was different. To see the rubble of fine buildings that she'd walked past, that she'd seen built was sobering. 'It must have been dreadful.'

'It was.' Alec didn't talk much of his experiences. She knew little of his work but knew of the losses and how it had affected him. He was not the boy he had been. He'd lost some of his joy and ebullience; war had stolen that from him. They had not seen much damage in Grimsby. There had been zeppelins of course, and men had been killed when the Baptist church was bombed in Cleethorpes. That had been dreadful enough. Thirty-three men of the Manchester regiment had been killed and forty-eight injured. But, overall, they had been lucky; she saw that now.

'It's changed a lot, hasn't it, Mother?'

'Not so much that I can tell.' She knew what he meant. Nothing stayed still, there was always an ebb and flow, but she hadn't wanted to be taken along with it. 'Why do you always have to be racing forward? Like the steam trawlers. Why couldn't you be content with sail? We could've stayed where we were.' She felt out of place now, just as she did in Grimsby. A divide had been crossed, and she belonged in neither place; but this was where her roots were. She walked beside him, and he pointed out different ships that had escaped the war. Some bearing the scars. There was no sign of the *Stella Maris* and when Alec asked of her was told that she was out fishing on the Dogger Bank. Dorcas was disappointed. They watched the herring lasses, dressed in their long oilskin aprons, hands deep in the wooden troughs, fingers wrapped in rags as they slit fish bellies and tossed guts aside with alacrity, the lasses cheerful and calling to each other as they worked. One of them started singing, her voice pure and clear, and they stopped a while to listen. The sound drew her back through the years, and she felt a pang of melancholy as they stood there.

'Come on, Mother. Let's get a bite.' He offered to take her into town, but she wanted to sit in the café on the quay and drink, listen to the sing-song softness of their accents. She missed the sounds, the smells. This had been her home. She felt a swell of emotion.

'Perhaps you could get a ship quicker here,' she suggested, hopeful. 'Or buy a smack like your father and uncle did.'

'Things have changed, Mother. I couldn't afford it if I wanted to. Ships are scarce. The price too high. I couldn't buy a half share in the *Stella* now, even if she were for sale. I missed the boat.' He gave a grim smile. 'It's never good to look back and dwell on what was. It allus seems better when we do, but we have to look forward. That's the way we're going. Likely to bump into things walking backwards.'

She said no more about it, and they spent a pleasant hour together on the quay. He was right. They had a lot to be thankful for.

They walked back along the High Street, up towards the lighthouse, and made their way down the curve of Lighthouse Score. Dorcas stood for a moment or two and stared down along the coastline, closing her eyes for a few seconds, remembering all the times she'd walked down it to her own small home. Her boys racing before her. Happy times. The sun had warmed her face, and when she opened her eyes she saw her boy running towards her, dear Robbie, as plain as day. She was overcome, aware that her legs would no longer hold her weight, and placed a hand on the stone wall to steady herself, softly speaking his name. 'Robbie.' The boy was running towards her, his smile impish, his eyes as blue as the sea, as blue as her Hardy boys' eyes.

A voice called out from the path below, a voice she recognised. 'Slow down, Johnny Trent. You'll do your mother a mischief.'

A young woman appeared beneath them, breathless with laughter, her eyes on the path, an older woman lumbering a few steps behind, the pair of them in widow's weeds. When she looked up, Dorcas was shocked to her core. It had not been a dream, nor her imagination, but he was her boy again, her Robbie, his sandy hair, his eyes. So like Will, like Alec... She felt herself sink, then Alec came behind her, his strong arm about her waist, holding her up, taking hold of her hand.

'Mother...' He fell silent as the boy came close.

The young woman stopped when she saw them and Dorcas saw her own shock reflected. Becky Drew, the lass Alec had been walking out with before Letty came along. The lass had not changed in the intervening years; she still looked much like the lass who was sweet on Alec, though better dressed than he could have provided for. She swiftly regained her composure, though she glanced back to see how far the older woman was behind her. 'Why, Mrs Hardy. Alec. It's been so long since we met.'

Dorcas managed to find her voice, somehow found a smile. 'Becky. I heard you'd married.'

'And widowed.'

'Your boy.'

She looked at Dorcas. 'My blessing. Especially since I lost John.'

'To war?'

'Verdun.' She moved to one side as the other woman caught up with her, standing close, blocking the path. 'You remember Mrs Trent. John's mother. She and her husband have the hardware store on the High Street.'

'I do.' Dorcas nodded her acquaintance. 'I am sorry to hear of your loss. It's hard to lose a child.' She knew only too well the pain of it, but today it was numbed with seeing the boy. The woman thanked her, but Dorcas could not move, watching the boy as Becky caught his hand and held on to it.

'Little scamp. Like his father,' Becky said. Again, she glanced to Alec. Dorcas caught the meaning of it, wishing she'd never seen it. They stood aside to allow people to pass by them. The steps began to swim before her, and she leaned to the wall to steady herself once more.

'You are unwell?' Becky was concerned. Dorcas forced herself to stand upright.

'Unsteady. I'm not used to the pathways any more. Grimsby is very flat,' she explained to Mrs Trent.

Alec took hold of her elbow. 'We should move on. Let the good people pass. We're blocking the way.' He doffed his cap. 'It was good to make your acquaintance again, Becky. Mrs Trent.' He kept his arm on his mother's as he guided her safely down the remaining steps and she was in sore need of it. At the bottom she leaned against the wall. He spoke to her all the while, but she couldn't make sense of what he said, her brain trying to work through what she had seen.

'Do you want to go inside to Eric and Minnie?'

She shook her head, remained there, staring down at the path, attempting to reconcile the images that jangled and knotted in her head. When she looked up at him, she knew. There was no need for words.

She couldn't talk at her brother-in-law's house. She didn't want to go inside, not yet.

'We'll go to a café. I need to sit down. *We* need to talk.'

He found her a table and, once she was settled, ordered tea. He insisted they both have something to eat but she was in no mood for sweetness. The waitress brought a teapot and cups and when she left, Dorcas splashed a little milk into the cups and poured the tea, put down the teapot. Only then did she speak to him. 'The boy. Does he look like his father?' She watched his face, aware of every small movement. 'I don't remember his father being fair. John Trent was dark.'

'Children change all the time.' He was awkward. She nodded. He was trying too hard. He was her child, and she knew every muscle, every sinew.

'He was Robbie's double.' Alec stared over the café, avoiding her scrutiny. 'Tell me I'm wrong.' He didn't reply so she repeated her question, this time raising her voice. People looked and he turned back to her.

'I can't deny he looks like…' He stumbled over his own words, each one an obstacle.

'You,' his mother snapped. 'He looks like you.' He didn't deny it; she knew he wouldn't dare. Not if it was the truth. Her throat thickened with disappointment. He looked as he had looked when he came to tell her Robbie had been lost at sea. That he wouldn't be coming home. That there was just the two of them, just as there was now. 'No need to ask when, for you were here often enough during the war. But why? Dear God above, why?' She picked up her cup and held it in her hands. She drew it to her lips but couldn't drink. He had a son. Alec had a son. Had the mother noticed it too? 'Mrs Trent. Senior,' she added to qualify. 'She looked curiously at you.'

'She looked as any woman might look at me.'

Dorcas leaned forward, spat her quiet words over the table. 'She looked at you as I looked at the boy. A recognition.' She sat back in her chair, looked out of the window. The sky had darkened, and the clouds were low and heavy. A summer storm, quick to come and quick to go. The rain came hard on the window and folk ran for shelter, their coats over their heads. It beat down like bullets and bounced dust from the road. 'Did you know?'

'No.'

She studied his face.

'No, Mother,' he repeated. 'I was as surprised as you were.'

'Surprised! Shocked, more like!' She shook her head, wishing she could shake away her anger as easily.

'It was one night, ten minutes, less.'

She couldn't hide her disgust, but she wanted to know. Had to know. Her thoughts went to Letty. If the lass should ever find out, Dorcas, God forgive her, wanted to know the whole grisly truth of it should she have to defend him.

'I'd had a few beers.'

She huffed.

'Mother, I'd just seen the *Artemis* blown to smithereens. Not hours before I'd been chatting with the skipper and crew. He had leave for Christmas, was going to see his wife and kiddies. I couldn't get the image out of my head.'

'So you thought lying down with Becky would cure that?'

'It wasn't like that.' He paused, looked to her and she was so sorrowful it must have been plain on her face. 'I went to the beach. It was dark. I wanted to forget. I... I lay down, looking at the stars. I didn't want to look at the sea. I wasn't paying attention to owt.' He stared down at his cup, his hands too big to hold it by the handle. 'She must have followed me. I was barely aware of what I was doing. She came...' His voice tailed off. 'I was drunk.'

'Don't give me that old flannel, boy. I wasn't born yesterday.' A rage burned in her breast, and it hurt something terrible. To think her boy had betrayed his wife. Worse still, had a child born of it. 'You knew well enough what you were doing.' She wanted to scream at him, furious at his stupidity. 'Dear God. It will break Letty's heart. You've broken mine. By God, I never... I...' She put down her cup. He was her sun and her moon, the reason the world kept turning. If it hadn't been for Alec, she would have drowned herself to be with Will and her boy. She'd been so proud to see Alec on his ship, a skipper. She felt her eyes water and she pressed her lips together to keep tears at bay. He couldn't hide it from her, and he would never be able to hide it from Letty.

'You'd better hope Letty can forgive you.'

'She might not have to.'

Dorcas looked at him.

'You won't say anything?'

Dorcas shook her head. 'I won't have to, my lad. There's always someone who wants to bring a man down.'

* * *

His mother didn't say much when they got back to Uncle Eric's and mostly he'd been glad of it, for what was there to say? Seeing the boy had been as much a shock to him as to his mother. It had been a fumble in the darkness. Nothing. And now it was something.

He had known the child was his, as soon as he laid eyes on him. Being here, in Lowestoft, there was more chance that other people would put two and two together – if they hadn't already.

His mother feigned tiredness when they went back to Eric and Minnie's, but it wasn't much of a lie, for she had not regained her colour and had collapsed in a chair while Minnie fussed about her. There was little conversation between them and presently his uncle picked up his pipe and got to his feet. 'Perhaps a beer or two would be in order, boy?'

He glanced to his mother, who briefly closed her eyes, and got up. They left and walked down the cobbled street, side by side. Alec took out a cigarette and they stopped while he lit it.

'It's been good to see you. Your mother too. She looks well. The Grimsby life must be doing her the power of good.' Eric chewed on his pipe stem. 'Your father would be proud of how you've looked after her. I know she wasn't agreeable to going.'

'No.' He gave a half-hearted laugh. 'But she's got used to it.'

'We all have to make hard decisions.' There was weight in his words that Alec couldn't ignore. 'You don't regret it?'

'I did what I thought was right.' It was all he'd ever tried to do, except for what he thought had been one small mistake, a pebble tossed to the sea, the ripples of which could now become a huge wave that might sweep away all he loved and dash it upon the rocks.

He was wary in the pub this time, searching for the slightest word or glance that might suggest something, that he might have to defend himself. But nothing was said out of turn and after a couple of beers he relaxed and enjoyed the time with his uncle though his thoughts were elsewhere. They walked back to the house in silence and Alec paused on the path.

'I'll walk a while if you don't mind, Uncle.' He had half a mind to find Becky, to ask her outright.

'I'll come with you.' Eric held the bowl of his pipe and drew on it, then let go of the smoke. It drifted away on the night air and when he looked up, he held Alec's gaze but didn't say anything. No words passed between them as they walked. Alec couldn't talk about it, and he knew his uncle would never ask, but he didn't have to. If he knew, others might have thought it too. Down on the shingle, they stood together as they had stood on the *Stella Maris*, side by side. Somehow, standing shoulder to shoulder with his uncle made him feel he might be able to weather the storm that was undoubtedly heading his way.

After a time, his uncle spoke. 'I gather you saw Becky?'

Alec turned to him.

'Nothing else would have that effect on your mother. She

looked like she'd seen a ghost. Perhaps she wished she had.' His uncle chewed on the stem of his pipe.

Alec thrust his hands into his pockets. 'There's been gossip?'

'Not that I know of, and the lass won't want it known. Not now she's got herself in with the Trents.'

'You don't think they'd see the likeness?'

'They'll not be looking for it. And if they did, they would blank it from their mind. It is less painful to believe he is their grandson, a part of their boy that remains. They will cling to anything.'

Alec wanted to believe it was that simple. He'd read in the newspapers of families searching for loved ones, willing to claim any poor soul who had lost their memory as their own, such was their grief. The two of them made their way back to the path.

'She'll be this way soon enough, coming back from her father's.' He stopped and looked down the road and saw a figure coming towards them. 'He was widowed a year back and she allus goes to make sure he's settled. You'd best have a word.' He knocked out his pipe in his hand, tossed it to the ground. 'I'll take a slow walk home, but don't be long after or you'll have your mother out after you.'

Alec leaned against the low wall and waited, and just as his uncle had told him, Becky came hurrying towards him, a small lamp in her hand. As she came close, he stepped away from the wall and into her path. She startled when she saw him, quickly looking to see who was about, then stepped to one side. He moved in front of her, blocking her way.

'Leave me be, Alec,' she hissed. 'I don't want to be seen with you.' He didn't much want to be seen with her either, but he had to know. She made to move and he grabbed hold of her wrist. 'Let go of me,' she snapped, as she tried to free herself. 'I'll be missed.'

'The boy. Is he mine?'

She laughed. 'Don't flatter yourself.'

'Liar.'

She twisted and cried out when he didn't release her. He loosened his grip a little and she stopped pulling and went close to him. 'My boy is set to inherit the hardware store. It's a fine business. I'll not have you spoil it for us.' He knew she'd set her sights on John Trent for that very purpose. She put her hand to his jaw. 'Although, if you were offering an alternative...'

He pushed her away and she sneered at him. 'Don't cause trouble for me, Alec Hardy, and I won't cause it for you. You got what you wanted and so did I.' She turned from him and hurried on her way.

His insides churned, and his head felt as if his brain was trying to burst out of it as the reality of the day took root. He had another child, a son. He had a son. His mother was right; it would break Letty's heart if she ever found out.

Uncle Ernie was lingering outside his cottage and, seeing Alec, he opened the door and went inside, Alec following soon after. He saw the flicker of suspicion on his mother's face and had to look away. Her disappointment was too much to bear.

14

Ruth felt as if the days were being stolen from her as preparations for the wedding got underway. She fought to grasp hold of any one of them, but they'd been torn from her as the pages were torn from the paper calendar on her aunt's desk. Helen Frampton had launched into her plans for her niece's wedding the moment she had been informed that Ruth had at last accepted Arthur Marshall's hand in marriage. Arthur was leaving for business in Paris and America at the end of October and he wanted to take Ruth with him – as his wife. When Ruth suggested they wait, he wouldn't hear of it, playfully suggesting she might change her mind. Ruth had only smiled; there was much truth in what he said. As it was, she delighted in the happiness it gave her aunt as she commandeered the arrangements and set forth to give the society wedding of the century. The ceremony was set for 11 October and they would leave for Paris the following day, spending five days in the French capital before going on to America, where they would reside in Boston for two weeks, returning home in the middle of November.

'We have had so little to celebrate, my dear. This is exactly what *we* need. What your father needs. You shall have the finest wedding day this town has ever seen.' It was no use protesting that she'd rather have a quiet wedding. A simple family affair, a small wedding breakfast, a few days in the Lake District. Aunt Helen had already swung into action as if she were going into battle and planning a major offensive.

Her dress was to be made in London. They'd already made one journey there for the tailoress to take measurements, and for Ruth and her aunt to choose the fabric for her gown and trousseau. Helen Frampton had called in at Asprey and given her niece a leather monogrammed notebook. In it, Ruth was to record the details and preparations of her nuptials. Afterwards it would be a treasured keepsake. The vellum pages had soon filled with details of the couturiers, the florists and caterers, the jewellers, the printers and a host of others involved. Ruth opened it now and withdrew the silver pencil from her bag and followed her aunt into the dining room. The table had been cleared of the silver, which had been moved to the long Chinese sideboard, and large foolscap sheets of paper, taken from the newspaper office, were spread out across it. A table plan had been drawn to scale and here Helen Frampton had marked who would be seated where. Ruth had read the names on the plans and made a small star by each name in her book, checking off all who had been invited. Her aunt had made no omissions; there had been no mistakes. Every guest would have been weighed for their social worth and placed accordingly.

'It can easily be rearranged if you decided I haven't quite got it as you would wish,' her aunt commented as she worked her way through the names.

Ruth would have wished that Alec and Letty Hardy were seated closer to the head table. That they were there at all was down to Ruth's insistence.

The door opened and the butler stepped into the room to announce Arthur's arrival. He strode in and took hold of Ruth's hand and pressed it to his lips.

'Your meeting is over?'

'I made sure it was.' He indicated to the table. 'What is more important?'

He leaned over the table and nodded his agreement. All seemed in order until he cast his eye over Letty, Alec and Miss Sheldon. He pointed to the plan, and frowned.

'I thought we had agreed that there was no room on the list for the Hardys. Nor Miss Sheldon.' He looked to her aunt. Helen looked ruffled and Ruth was confused.

'I remember no such agreement. We had discussed it, and I had said that I wanted Letty there; she was a good friend to me when Henry was lost. Alec was with him when he died.'

Arthur softened. 'I understand. but it would be beneficial to have Mr and Mrs Taylor and Mr Taylor Senior in their place.'

'Beneficial to whom?' Ruth questioned. 'This is our wedding day, Arthur. And the Hardys are my guests too.' She had thought this battle already won.

'But they have no influence.'

'Are we only inviting people of influence? I have so little family, Arthur; my friends are few.' Many of the young men, her brothers' friends, had been lost in the last years. And when the relief of the armistice had barely been acknowledged, the numbers of deaths from the Spanish influenza took many more. 'Once upon a time my father had no influence. What he has accrued in life he has done by his own hard work and sacrifice. I see the same efforts from the Hardys.'

'And Miss Sheldon?'

'Is a dear friend and mentor. I wish her to be there. I would have thought your father would too – being as he recently donated such a large sum towards the building of the new mission.'

Her aunt interrupted. 'I'm sure we can find a way to accommodate the Taylors if they are so important to you, Arthur?' There was a raised eyebrow.

Ruth smiled inwardly. How cunning her aunt was, to neither agree nor disagree between the couple.

'You are a diplomat of the highest order,' Arthur conceded. 'You should be down to London and sort them out in Whitehall.'

'Marriage is about compromise, Arthur. If it is about anything more than that, I don't know what it is.'

'I would hope it is about a great deal more,' he said, casting his gaze to Ruth. 'But my future wife's happiness is all that matters.' He took her hand. 'I apologise, my love. Let's leave things as they are. No need for compromise at all. I bow to your superior skills, Mrs Frampton.'

There were no further challenges and when he left, her aunt caught her eye. 'You will need to stand your ground with that young man. He is used to having his own way.'

Ruth did not disagree. Her aunt put her hand to Ruth's shoulder. 'I have discovered all men are pretty much the same. They have been used to the indulgence of their mothers. Mildred dotes on that boy. Had I had sons of my own, I would have done the same.'

'You were a mother to Henry and Charles. They thought of you as such.'

Her aunt reached out for her hand and clasped it to her. 'And to you as well, I hope.' She held herself for a moment, gathering her emotions. Ruth had never seen her angry, or sad, come to think of it. Her emotions were tightly reined in, at least in company. How she felt when alone, Ruth had no idea.

'Tea in the drawing room. We shall go through the invitations together. Two months is rather short to plan a wedding of this scale, but we will do you and your father proud, my dear.'

While her aunt attended to the plans and gave instructions to the butler, Ruth went into the drawing room. Warm light streamed through windows, catching at the gold lamps and furnishings, dancing over the paintings that decorated every wall. Ruth went to the French doors. Two of the gardeners were mowing the vast lawns, the lines as straight as if they had been measured with a ruler. Two more men were digging over the flower beds and enriching the soil with rotted manure and a wheelbarrow was high with prunings. They had spent so many happy days here as children, their aunt indulging their every whim. They'd had a freedom and happiness she'd not known since, and felt as if she never would again. Her aunt came beside her. Ruth reached out and took hold of her hand, gave it a squeeze more to comfort herself than for anything else. As she turned, her aunt put up a hand to her face.

'You look very pale.'

'I'm tired.'

Her aunt nodded. 'There is a lot to be considered. A wedding is not something to be taken lightly.'

Was she speaking of the plans, or had she sensed Ruth's reluctance? At first, she'd been sure she'd made the right decision; seeing her father's happiness had confirmed it. But as the preparations consumed most of her days, she began to feel uncertain.

'A wedding – or a marriage?'

'Both.' Her aunt held her gaze. 'Don't worry, child. It can be overwhelming, all the preparations and people to please. I seek only to be of help and not to take charge.'

'It is taken as such. Dearest Aunt Helen, I wouldn't have been able to do any of this without you. And Father would be as lost as I am.'

Helen looked out of the window. 'It's a pity it's not a summer wedding. The garden would have been at its best.' Was she giving Ruth the opportunity to slow things down?

'We could postpone it.' She would prefer it.

'I wouldn't dream of it. No, Arthur wants you with him in America. It will make for a spectacular honeymoon. And Paris too. I can't deny you that opportunity. Garden or not.' She took Ruth's hand. 'No one will notice anyway. All eyes will be on you.'

The thought did not thrill her.

15

When Ruth returned to Meadowvale House, Mrs Murray was cheerful and the voices coming from the sitting room appeared to be the reason for it. Her father's had a vibrancy to it and whoever it was had affected the house with a feeling reminiscent of old times. She felt a flutter of excitement. 'Father has guests?' Ruth removed her hat and placed it on the hall table along with her gloves.

'He has,' the housekeeper replied, going towards the kitchen without breathing a word of who it was. Ruth was intrigued. She walked into the sitting room to find her father chatting to someone who was sitting in the chair opposite to him, their back to the door. Her father smiled up at her when she walked in and got to his feet. His guest did likewise.

'Lieutenant Proctor. Philip.' She hurried towards him, and he held out his hand to her. She shook it, then impulsively kissed his cheek. He appeared surprised, as did she at her own actions. But so many letters had passed between them that she felt inordinately close to him. They had given her the greatest of comfort during such a dreadful time. 'How good it is to see you after all these years.' She'd not seen him since Henry's funeral in the first year of the war. They had served on the same ship, along with Alec Hardy. Philip was a naval man while Alec Hardy and Henry had served with the naval reserve.

'I hear congratulations are in order?'

She nodded. 'I would have written to tell you, but I see that Father has beaten me to it.'

'I would expect nothing less of a proud and loving father.'

She took the chair next to him and the two men sat down.

'You arrived today?'

'A few hours ago. I've been securing lodgings.'

'How long have you been back in England?' He looked well. His face was tanned, which made his eyes appear more green. His hair, once so dark, now had streaks of grey but it suited him. He was a handsome man, touching forty, and she had no idea why he hadn't been caught by any number of women.

'A few weeks. I've been with my mother and aunt, helping with their affairs. Things had, shall we say, slipped a little while I was away.' He smiled and she felt a connection to him that she didn't feel with anyone else. It was almost as if Henry had joined them in the room; she sensed his spirit close.

'I was telling Philip that he must come to the wedding.' Her father looked to her for her approval and it was easily given by a smile of agreement. 'I will ask Helen to add another place.'

'I could not put you to the trouble.'

'I insist. You're practically family, dear boy.'

Ruth agreed. 'It would mean so much to us to have you there. Father and I.'

He seemed uncomfortable but her father insisted, and in the end, he said he would be honoured.

They spent a pleasant hour talking of his work in Malta, of

her father's business, Ruth's impending wedding, of Henry and Charles.

When Philip got up to take his leave of them, they walked with him to the door.

'Where should I send an invitation?' Ruth asked. He gave her the name of his hotel. He put on his hat and walked down the path, turned as he closed the gate behind him, smiled. She recalled Henry walking away, the day he left, a spring in his step. She suddenly felt the ghost of him at her side. It was strangely comforting, as if Philip's presence had brought him home. Her father put his hand to her shoulder.

'It was good to speak of Henry and Charles. So many people seem to avoid it.'

Arthur never asked of them. He'd told her many times it would only upset her, raking over a past that could not be changed. But they had given their lives in sacrifice, and she wanted them to be remembered as they were, when they were full of life and the future offered an abundance of possibilities.

16

When Alec and Dorcas returned from Lowestoft in the first week of August, they were changed. Something had gone on between mother and son, though both of them denied it. Dorcas only said that she'd been disappointed. That it wasn't as she remembered, and she doubted she would ever go back. Letty was incredulous.

'I had thought it would make her happy.'

'It did.' Alec was uncomfortable. 'It's not always a good thing to go back. Sometimes it's better to keep the good memories than discover the reality is not what you thought it was.'

She frowned at him. 'I never feel that when I go home to the farm. There's comfort in it.'

'That's because your family are there. Mother found the place filled with sad memories, more than happy ones.'

Letty picked up a towel and folded it over, hung it from the range rail. Dorcas had insisted she open up the café that morning, taking the children with her, Stella protesting that she wanted to stay with her mam. It was kind of her to give them time alone and

Letty appreciated it. 'Perhaps it was a good thing. Sometimes things are not as we thought they were.' She'd been thinking on it while they were away, when the children were in bed and the evenings were quiet. She told him how much she'd missed Dorcas; she was used to her, the pair of them sitting in front of the fire, Dorcas grumbling. She laughed. 'I can't believe I'm saying it.'

He slipped his arms around her waist, as much as he could, now that her belly was swelling, and pulled her towards him. 'You're a good woman, Letty Hardy. I don't deserve you.' A knock at the door interrupted them and Letty went to answer it. She returned with the ship's runner from Hammond's. Alec's expression changed.

'News?'

'Aye.' The runner handed over a paper slip. 'You sail the day after tomorrow.'

Alec was delighted. He went to Letty, lifted her off her feet and kissed her. 'I have a ship. At last, I have a ship.'

When Dorcas returned, Letty was already preparing Alec's kit bag for going away.

'You got news, then?' she said brusquely, nodding towards his bag. There was still an awkwardness between them, though neither would admit to it.

'I did, Mother. I sail tomorrow.'

'Can I come with you, Pop?'

Alec looked to Letty. Alfie's words had taken her by surprise even though she'd expected him to ask at some point or another. Boys as young as four had been with their fathers and uncles during the summer holidays when the seas were calm and the trips shorter. Alfie was eleven. She knew Alec would have taken him long before if it were not for the war. The pair of them looked at her, faces expectant. How could she say no, much as she wanted to? Reluctantly, she gave her assent. Alfie wrapped his arms about her waist.

'Thank you, Mother.'

When he released her, she cupped her hand about his chin and gazed upon his dear face. If anything should happen... No, she shook the thought from her head. Alec would keep him safe; he loved the boy as his own. She let go of him. 'Stella will have to behave. She'll have no one to take the blame for her mischief while you're away.'

His delight was obvious and much as it hurt her, she knew she was fighting the tide. He had curiosity like all boys. Going to sea might seem like an adventure, but the reality might cure him of it. She hoped so. He was a clever lad with his books. His late mother, Anita, had been a stickler for it. When he left school he could work alongside her. They could build the business into something bigger, something that kept them all in work for years to come.

'Time to get your sea legs, son,' Alec said, ruffling the lad's dark hair. She and Alec exchanged a look. He'd not tried to put her off when she took Alfie in, another mouth to feed when they were only just trying to make their way in Grimsby. His mother had been against it, but he had stood with her. It was her turn to stand with him now.

* * *

Letty put together a small bag for Alfie, pulled out one of Alec's old roll-up mattresses, and found a sweater. He was tall but wiry and Letty had found a pair of old trousers from the jumble sale that were a good enough fit, loath as she was to spoil his good trousers, his only other pair those he wore for school. He wouldn't be in need of much else.

She went with Alec to Parker's to buy the lad some boots. Pearl selected a pair in his size and handed them to Alfie as if he were the Prince of Wales trying on fine slippers. She exchanged a smile with Letty. She'd been no bother in the shop and Letty wondered at Dorcas's short temper with the girl. Pearl was not quick, but she had a lovely way with the customers. She was on hand to help the Parkers and ran up and down the stairs to the store, which was a blessing to them all, for Letty was getting slower now that she was in the middle months of the pregnancy. There'd been no news of Sidney, and no letter arrived from the Faroes, but Pearl was steadfast in her belief that it would come. Letty prayed her hope was not misguided. Messages were often sent from trawler to trawler. It was odd to hear nothing at all.

Alfie pulled the boots on, and Alec tested them for fit, instructing Alfie to walk up and down the shop for inspection. Satisfied, the boots were bought and paid for and Alec announced he was taking Alfie to Solly's Café.

'And not the café where your own mother waits on you?'

'Not today, Let. The lad needs to be with the other fishermen. Most of the lads down Hardy's are shipyard men and fitters. He needs to be with his shipmates.'

When they'd gone, Letty began clearing out the shelves behind the counter where she kept all manner of things: string, pencils, scissors. She had no inclination to go home. Not yet. Norah put her hand over Letty's. 'His father will look after him. God will look after them both.'

Letty nodded, stilled her hand. God had not looked after Will Hardy, nor his son. The sea had taken them, as it had so many others.

* * *

There were two kit bags in the hall the following day. Letty and Dorcas stayed at home for the hour, wanting to bid them farewell. Letty could not see her men off at the dock; superstition had put paid to that. If you waved a man off, you would wave him overboard. Letty had been annoyed by the many superstitions Dorcas presented her with as she learned the ways of the fishing folk, but fear had taught her to do whatever it took to keep Alec safe. Who knew whether it worked or not; no wife or mother would ever take that risk.

As they gathered in the back room where they spent most of their time, Dorcas handed Alfie a red and white neckerchief. 'My Robbie and Alec had the same when they went to sea with their father. It's our tradition.'

Alec gave him a gutting knife. 'It was my brother's. I know you'll take good care of it. It's yours now.' He turned to Letty and kissed her, held her more tightly than he'd ever done, and whispered into her hair. 'Don't fret, Letty. I'll take the very best care of him.'

She could only nod her acknowledgement, her throat tight with fear. Stella began to whine now that the time for their leaving was near.

'I don't want Alfie to go. I want him to stay.'

He gave her a hug. 'We'll be back soon, Stella, me and Father. You must look after Mother and Granny Dorcas while we're away.'

Stella pushed her bottom lip forward and though Letty laughed she wanted to pout too. It was hard to let them go.

Alec kissed his mother then came to Letty again, wrapped his arm about her waist one last time and drew her close, kissed her, whispered that he loved her, and released her. It took all her will not to follow him.

'Off we go, Alfie boy.' Her two men picked up their bags

together and left. She did not go into the street and held Stella back, her hands tight on her shoulders, for she knew it wouldn't take much for the child to run after her brother. She would miss Alfie more than any of them. When Letty calculated that she'd left enough time for them to be safely away, she relaxed her grip and Stella ran upstairs, slamming the door behind her.

17

The *Clarissa* had steamed out on the afternoon tide. Alec had been in the wheelhouse and had left Alfie on deck with his crew. They were a good lot, some he'd sailed with before; a couple of the lads had sailed with other companies and had been glad to get with Hammond's this time around. Men had come and gone, many lost to the war. During his time with the RNR he'd worked with men who had never been on a ship before, other than rowing their sweethearts across a boating lake. His second hand, or mate as was the common term, was Wally Bristow. He had a competent chief engineer and, importantly, a good cook. He hoped to keep him going forward, for a good cook was the difference between a happy crew and an unruly one.

It was good to have the old feelings, out to hunt fish and not the enemy. He'd told the lads to keep an eye out for mines. They all knew the seascape had changed for there was a huge amount of wreckage in the sea and close to the shore. Many a crew had come back cursing that their nets had been torn. In some cases they had to be cut away and lost altogether. It affected Alec's share of the profit, for lost gear had to be paid for and it came out of their own pockets. The skipper and mate were on a percentage and had to pay for their own food and kit. All the men brought their own mattresses to sleep on. And many a trawler owner found a way for the crew to pay more than their fair share of the losses. Marshall's had a reputation for it and could get away with it. Men needed work and there were more men than ships.

He watched Alfie below him as the men put him to work. It was meant to be a pleasure trip, for young lads to get a taste of the life at sea. He'd done the same as a boy. It had been the only life he wanted. But not everyone took to it, or had the stomach for it, their time spent below, hurling into a bucket as they lay on their bunk. The lad was a quick learner and paid attention. If he wanted it, he would do well.

When they were safely out of the river and into the open sea steaming forward, Alec checked his charts and made adjustments accordingly. It would take three or four days to get to the fishing grounds and he had plenty of time to think as he sat in the wheelhouse watching the endless waves once they lost sight of land. Would he still be able to make good money? Had he lost that inner sense, of knowing where the fish were to be found? He tried to focus but his thoughts kept turning to the boy he'd seen in Lowestoft. His boy. Anyone who saw him could not fail to see the resemblance, and those who knew him and Robbie as boys would not take long to put two and two together. But he had a son, and though he loved Alfie as his own, this boy Johnny Trent was his own flesh and blood. The boy was part of him. The boy was a Hardy and Trent in name only.

Alfie came up the ladder and brought him a brew. Alec looked in the tin mug and smiled. 'You've lost half of it over the side.'

'The ship was unsteady... and the ladder,' the boy explained.

Alec grinned, nudged him with his elbow. 'It's allus unsteady. This is calm.'

Alfie raised his eyebrows.

'Aye, wait 'til you're out in a gale then you'll know what unsteady is.' Alfie stood beside him, looking out over the endless sea while Alec supped. 'The men alright with you?'

'Yes, Pop. I can take their joshing. They're not too unkind.' His voice faltered.

Alec looked sideways at him. 'Take the banter with good heart; they'll get their fill of it soon enough.' He emptied his mug. 'And don't go tellin' 'em anything they might use against you – or me. And if they offer you beer, sup it slowly. They'll delight in getting you drunk and you'll pay for it in hanging over the side.' He stared down onto the deck where three of the men were leaning with their backs to the rail, puffing on Woodbines, the smoke trailing in the wind. 'It's long days when they're not busy and there'll be mischief. But I'll not have cruelty. Let me know if they give you any bother.'

'I like listening to their stories, Pop. They've taught me a lot.'

'Aye and not all of it good, I'll wager. Don't use any of the words you learn from 'em in front of your mother.'

Alfie grinned.

His father handed back his mug and Alfie took it and shimmied down the ladder a lot faster than he'd come up it. Alec watched him cross the deck. One of the men called out to him and Alfie nodded. A few minutes later he returned, three mugs in his hands for the crew.

They came to the fishing grounds three days later and Alec told the men to cast the net over the side. Hours later he watched as it was hauled aboard, the rope of the cod end untied and the fish showered on the deck. Alfie got to gutting with them, slow and sure, staggering a little as the ship rolled and pitched on the waves. Alec felt his chest swell with pride. Alfie had been confident enough to make a start; not every lad would have done. He looked up to the wheelhouse and Alec tipped his head in acknowledgement. The boy had it in him to be a good fisherman. Letty would not be best pleased. And that displeasure would pale into insignificance if she ever found out about Johnny Trent. Alec pushed the thought from his head and concentrated on his charts.

Days later, the holds full of mostly prime fish – good-size haddocks and plaice, a fair few cod and skate – Alec turned the *Clarissa* and began steaming home. In the days that followed, the crew made small repairs to the nets, and cleaned down the ship of fish guts, tossing them out to the gulls that followed them home. Alfie's face was sore and dry with the mix of sun and salt water. He looked every inch of him a fisherman, moving about the deck as if he had been doing it all his life. Instinct. But it was not from Alec. The lad's own father had been a merchant seaman, had travelled to places Alec had only ever seen pictures of in the periodicals that Letty handed over for him to read at sea. He passed most of them on to the deckies, who needed to fill their time when they were not putting in the gruelling hours when they were on the fish. He preferred his thoughts, though lately they had tormented him, and he couldn't shake the darkness of them from his brain. He thought too much of Becky and the trap he'd fallen into.

They arrived in the Humber Estuary too early for the lock gates to open and waited there with the other trawlers, a long line of them sitting in the river. Home, but not quite. As they moved closer and the gates opened, he was eager for his turn at the lock pit. On the wharf he could see Letty and Stella, waiting with other women and children. For two pins he would have left the mate at the wheel and jumped ashore himself, just to have her in his arms. He'd missed her like never before, and the sight of her made his heart twist at how he had betrayed her.

18

Ruth couldn't remember the last time the drawing room at Meadowvale House had felt so inviting. It was reminiscent of happier times, when the boys had been home from school at the end of term and filled the place with noise and laughter. The house had felt full then, even though it was only the four of them. It softened her heart to think on it and she realised she had shed a little of the burden that lingered about her shoulders and cloaked her in gloom. Hope had entered the house again and found its way to her.

Her father had invited Philip Proctor and the Howards over for Sunday lunch after the church service. The last few weeks had seen a great change in him. He was opening up to life again, and the house was opening with him. Mrs Murray had mentioned more than once that her father seemed a little more like his old self. His business, which had taken such a battering during the war, had stabilised and, so it seemed, had he. It gave Ruth the greatest of happiness to see him slowly return to the man she always knew him to be. Jeremy and Evelyn Howard had been the first to arrive, Philip Proctor soon after. Arthur was late and Mrs Murray had been holding back lunch for the last fifteen minutes.

'Are you looking forward to America, Ruth?' Evelyn asked as they waited for his arrival.

'I think I shall enjoy Paris more. I'm looking forward to visiting the Louvre and seeing the Eiffel Tower. Although I do wonder at what it will be like. The war will have left its mark at every turn.'

'It will be interesting, nonetheless,' Philip commented. She was glad he was there. The house took on a different feeling when he was present. She had no idea why, and couldn't explain it if asked, but his very presence calmed her. He withdrew a cardboard folder from the side of his chair and held it out to Ruth and her father. Her father nodded for her to take it, then open it. 'I didn't want to confuse them with a wedding gift. But I thought you might like them.'

She pulled out a sheaf of etchings and was stilled, unable to comment while she took in the details. Henry with his cap askew, laughing, another intense as he worked at his letters – which were few – at his gun, with the men on deck, sitting on a capstan, laughing, smiling, always smiling. She passed them to her father, who stared at the likeness of his son and for a long time did not speak. Ruth could not fill the silence.

'What are they?' Evelyn enquired. Ruth looked up, her eyes brimming with tears. Her father handed her a sketch and Evelyn leaned towards him, her smile comforting.

'Philip stayed with us when he and Henry had leave. These are some of the sketches he did then, and thereafter.' She looked at Philip. 'Words seem inadequate.'

'What a wonderful gift,' Evelyn said, filling the silence that followed. 'You seem to have captured his personality so well from what I have heard Richard and Ruth speak of him. I cannot say of the likeness, but the personality, yes. It is in his eyes, the joy, the spirit.'

Philip had captured him perfectly and Ruth drew her fingers over the pencil marks. How she missed his dear face, his smile, his rebellious spirt. Had she an ounce of it, she would have lived a different life. Her father excused himself and left the room. Ruth did not go after him, knowing he would need a moment to recover himself.

'I've upset your father,' Philip said, his face wreathed in concern.

'No, not in the least,' Ruth said, her voice wavering. 'He...'

'I think it's the most perfect gift you could have given them,' Evelyn said, saving her, studying the sketch Philip had done of Ruth. 'I do so love this one of you. Such an earnest expression.'

Ruth looked over her shoulder. 'I was sketching at the time. He has captured my concentration.'

She looked to Philip. 'I think he has captured your very essence,' she said quietly. They exchanged a glance as Evelyn passed the sketches to her brother, one by one.

'You are like your brother, Ruth. Your mouth... your smile certainly,' Jeremy said, looking first at the sketch then at her. 'You were like Charles too. I can see from the photographs the family resemblance.'

'Charles favoured Father, his height, his build.'

'And my temperament,' Richard said as he came back into the room. 'Henry was a—'

'Whirlwind,' Ruth said, remembering, smiling. 'You couldn't quite know what he was going to do, or where he was going to go next.' Her father nodded and she squeezed his arm and went over to Philip and kissed his cheek. He held her gaze and she found herself not wanting to look away from him. 'We will treasure them, Philip. Thank you.'

'Thank you for what?' Arthur said as he came into the room, looking intently at Ruth. She felt her cheeks burn and moved away from Philip as if she had been given an electric shock.

Evelyn handed over the sketches. 'Lieutenant Proctor came bearing gifts. Hasn't he captured Henry's likeness?'

Arthur gave them a cursory glance and handed them to Ruth, directing his reply to Evelyn and her brother. 'He has. My father wouldn't have commissioned him otherwise. Good to see you, Proctor. I didn't know you'd be here.' He kissed Ruth's cheek, shook hands with the rest of the guests, and inserted himself in the gap that had appeared between Ruth and the lieutenant when he arrived. Ruth felt a spasm of guilt, though she had no idea why, and the atmosphere seemed to prickle with energy that hadn't existed before.

'I'll put them in your study, Father.'

In her father's room, she opened the folder and stared at her brother's dear, dear face. Always a boy. Always. She looked at herself as Philip had seen her that day, remembering Henry's gentle teasing. They were so young, with no idea of what lay ahead. Closing the folder, she placed them on her father's desk and looked about her. There was more order, more light, and it didn't feel so full of sorrow as it once did. He was at last moving on. And so must she.

19

Towards the end of September, the women of the Grimsby and District Ladies' Guild were a hive of industry. Trestle tables had been set around the hall at the rear of the Bethel Mission on the corner of Tiverton Street. Donations of clothing and bric-a-brac had been arriving throughout the last three weeks and were being distributed according to Mrs Barton's directives, a table each for men's and women's clothing, a table for children (the largest), and others for household items and baby paraphernalia. All was arranged neatly but would soon become the jumble of the event. Though Ruth had done her best to attend meetings, this was the only one she'd been able to make in the last four weeks. She'd made the extra effort today, not wanting them to think she had abandoned them – and because wedding nerves were getting the better of her as October approached. Therefore, she'd been greatly moved when they'd set aside the small room beforehand and presented her with a wedding gift. Lucy Hewitt had written a few lines in verse and recited them while her sister smiled approvingly.

'We have all contributed,' Rosa Hewitt told her. 'We wish you many years of happiness.'

Ruth had been touched at their kindness and the thought and effort they'd put into choosing the Waterford crystal vase. She replaced it carefully into its box and tucked it at the back of the store cupboard, loath that any mix-up might occur, however inadvertently, on a day like today. Mrs Barton had brought their little ceremony to an end with a bracing rally to the tables. The ladies took their allotted positions and prepared themselves for the onslaught. Each of them had a wooden box containing a small float of change that Mrs Barton had counted and marked in her notebook.

Letty peeked out of the window. 'I think they might be ready to hammer the doors in, Mrs Barton.' There had already been a line of women and children snaking down the pavement when Ruth had arrived more than an hour ago – mostly the same women they saw every time they held a sale. Women standing for hours, whatever the weather, to get the pick of what was on offer. Good-quality clothes the middle classes had no use for would be adapted to fit the new wearer, crockery and knick-knacks with chips that the women would cheerfully ignore if it were still serviceable. Children's prams and highchairs would soon be taken, as would umbrellas, hats and shoes. What was left would be sold to rags and scrap and salvage, all monies raised for the benefit of those who were in need. That need was greater than ever.

Mrs Barton went to the door, and turned to them all. 'Brace yourselves, ladies.' She reached up and dropped the bolts at the top and bottom of the doors and barely had a chance to step back before a swarm of women surged forward, making beelines for the tables according to their needs. The clothing and boots were always in demand and Letty and Ruth had been assigned it, being the youngest members, and more suited to stand the furore as clothes were tussled and fought for. Mrs Barton stayed in the thick of the crowd watching for thieves. Ruth had thought this unnecessary, as the items had been donated, and on one occasion had said as much. Lydia Barton had soon put her straight.

'That's not the point, Miss Evans. Every penny raised provides funds for those even worse off.' It was not hard to imagine who those people were, for sadly there had been much call on their services of late. Many men could not find work; many more had lost limbs. The blind were reduced to standing on street corners selling matches, and she had passed men with no legs, whose only means of getting about was a small wooden platform on wheels. Such was their reward for serving King and Country.

The surge of people advanced like an unruly army and Letty and Ruth were quick to react, Letty helping the women find what they were in need of, Ruth taking and giving change. They worked easily together, and Ruth realised how much she had missed their easy camaraderie. Ruth would never forget how kind Letty had been to her when she was in despair at the loss of her brothers. She had a strength that was not uncommon among the women, but her kindness set her above many of them. She grinned at Ruth as she handed over a thruppenny bit. 'Only one more hour to go.' A woman sporting a black eye handed over a halfpenny in exchange for a blue blouse. The bruising was heavy around her cheekbone, and it must have been a mighty blow that had caused it. Ruth had learned not to stare. When she'd questioned why they stayed with men who could do such violence, Letty had put her straight.

'Where would they go? They are trapped by poverty and a misplaced sense of love – and duty. But mostly poverty. There is nowhere else to go but the workhouse. What would you choose?' It was a bitter cycle of poverty and want, despair and frustration. 'They have too many children and not enough money. The men, as well as women, drink to forget. We might well do the same in their position.'

Ruth could only wonder at how they managed to survive.

When they were down to the last pickings and few stragglers hung around, Letty and Ruth began folding what remained. The garments that couldn't be made use of would be sold for rags. Her own grandmother had made her fortune that way, building up a fine business on the Freeman Street Market, standing out in all weathers in order to give her children a better start in life. She was thoughtful as Letty cleared the last garments from the table and Ruth totted up the money they had collected and handed it over to Mrs Barton.

'Thank you, Miss Evans,' she said as Ruth added the coins to the large tin and handed over a small piece of paper with the amounts of coinage and total taken. 'Though the days are few when we shall be calling you Miss Evans.' It didn't fill Ruth with happiness, and she knew it should.

Letty noticed. 'You aren't excited?'

Ruth shook her head. 'I'm not sure how I should feel.'

'There's no "should" about anything.' Letty folded a jacket over her arm. 'I imagine there's quite a lot going on at home and with your aunt. It has to be with such a big wedding to organise and important people travelling such distances. It's a lot of pressure.' She paused, lost in her thoughts. 'My own wedding was small in comparison, and I was full of nerves. You'll feel differently on the day.'

'What if I don't?' It had kept her awake at night, this dull feeling that she couldn't shake off.

Letty smiled. 'What you feel is what all brides feel as the day of their wedding grows ever closer. It's far away and then all of a sudden, it's rushing up to meet you.' They stood side by side, watching Mrs Green sweep the floor. The Hewitt sisters were piling the remains of the bric-a-brac into a crate that the caretaker would store in the basement.

'I'm not sure that I love Arthur enough to spend my life with him,' Ruth whispered, relieved to give voice to her fears, knowing she could rely on Letty's discretion and her plain speaking. She couldn't talk of her misgivings to anyone else, wasn't sure Aunt Helen would take her doubts seriously – and she didn't want to worry her father, who was somewhat revived by all the preparations. But everything was moving too fast. Far too fast for her to think clearly, her days full of meetings, fittings, tastings, her aunt at the helm, enjoying every moment. It was all beginning to feel more like a business merger, as Cyril had joked at dinner a few weeks ago.

Letty was sympathetic. 'I'm not always in love with Alec, when he slurps his tea and forgets he is at home and not on his ship with his men, when he smells of ale and keeps me awake half the night with his snoring. Whatever his faults, large and small, he is a good man. I can't imagine my life with anyone else.' She pressed her hand to Ruth's arm. 'It's a big step, giving yourself to another. But it will be alright, Ruth, keep faith in that.'

20

Alfie had returned from his summer trip with Alec and if it hadn't been time to go back to school he might well have gone to sea again. The *Clarissa* had had a successful trip, and Alec had paid him for the work he had done – a small fortune to a boy of eleven.

'A fair share for the lad – he worked alongside the men, and he was quick to learn.'

Alfie had drawn back his shoulders in pride. Letty had tried to be enthusiastic, fearing her battle to keep her family on solid ground already lost. She had no such fears for Stella, who had missed Alfie terribly and was glad when he too had to return to school.

In many respects, things were getting easier. Dorcas had bridged the gap between the home and the café, and the staff at Hardy's were reliable. Pearl was proving to be a good little worker, and it eased Letty's mind to think that she would be about when Letty eventually gave birth. But they were not without their troubles. Percy had had a series of small turns and as the weather turned colder she knew they would be more frequent, as they had been the last winter. It would mean that the Parkers' world would shrink once more to the small room at the back of the counter. For one last time, she broached the idea of them coming to stay with her at Park Street during the worst of the winter months, when the damp and fog seeped into every brick and stone of the building and leaked in through gaps in the windows and doorways. Norah was as stubborn as she ever was. 'Our needs are very small, Letty, and we've managed on far less than we have now. Don't fret yourself, lass.'

While Percy slept, the two women went into the shop for a time. They watched Pearl as she went over to the shelving and brought across the ladder, climbed up to the top where the larger sizes were kept. 'That lad's a forty-inch chest by my reckoning. He just wants to look at her ankles as she gets him a forty-eight.' Letty grinned. 'She's either daft or she knows exactly what he's up to and she likes the attention.'

'Daft,' Norah whispered without missing a beat. The two of them left her to deal with the customer and went through to the back room to discover that Percy had got up from his chair and was standing by the table. 'I told you not to get up unless me or Letty were with you,' Norah chided. 'What if you fell, you silly blighter?' She shook her head as she went to him, but he wouldn't move and lifted his arm as if to ward her off.

'Fussin'. No.'

Norah lifted her hands in despair.

'You can't stop her fussing, Percy.' Letty laughed. 'She's done it all her life. She isn't going to stop now.'

He gave her a small nod of his head, his crooked familiar smile. They understood each other. She watched him as he slowly returned to his chair. He'd lost much of the strength in his right arm, and he listed to one side as he lowered himself into it.

'What if something happens to Percy in the night, or you?' Letty whispered.

Norah would have none of it. 'There are people about the docks, night and day, as you well know. And I would only have to go next door, to Gilbert's storage. There is always someone or other there banging about.'

The mention of his name set Letty's teeth on edge. 'I wouldn't want to call on him for help.'

'We'll never have to.'

That afternoon, Norah had to call into the chemist for Percy's medication. Letty kept checking the clock for her return. Each afternoon she would take the bulk of the café's takings to the bank, there being no safe on the premises. If she didn't get back in the next fifteen minutes, Letty would run short of time herself. She checked the clock. Percy was asleep. Pearl would only be alone a matter of minutes. She picked up her bag. 'I'm sure Mrs Parker won't be much longer, Pearl, but I have to go out myself. I'll leave the door ajar for Percy – listen out for any sounds, but I'm sure you'll not be bothered as he's fast off.'

'I'll be fine, Mrs Hardy. Don't you worry about that.'

Outside Parker's, Letty checked the window display. She liked to change it at the turn of the season. There were plans to mark the anniversary of the armistice and she thought to have some photos in frames of local men who had been lost. She would think about it as she walked. As she was standing there, Gilbert Crowe came out from the premises next door with a board under his arm and set it down in among a line of five similar ones propped against the window that carried the headlines of different newspapers. 'How's Percy these days? I haven't seen him about much.'

She raised an eyebrow. 'Am I to think you are concerned?'

'Now, now. No need to be so sharp, Mrs Hardy.' He leered at her, and she gritted her teeth.

'What has brought on this wonderful change of heart? Not that I thought for one minute you had one.'

'Just being neighbourly. I heard the old man wasn't too good these days.'

'He'll be touched by your concern, Mr Crowe,' she said sarcastically, turning her back and walking away.

* * *

Gilbert Crowe watched his nemesis hurry towards Fish Dock Road. Only when she turned the corner did he move to look through the glass of Parker's door. He'd heard old man Parker had had another turn and doubted either of the Parkers would last much longer. If Letty Hardy hadn't come along, they'd have packed up a lot sooner. The woman had caused him no end of trouble, but the pressure was on to get them out of the premises. Arthur Marshall had insisted they be out before the end of the year, forcing his hand. He'd made no bones about what would happen to Crowe if he didn't succeed, and Gilbert had no reason to doubt him. Not that Marshall, father or son, would get their hands dirty. They were far too wily for that. Marshall's offices faced onto Wharncliffe Road and backed onto the shops and other premises on Henderson Street. Gilbert owned two of them, the Parkers the one in the middle. Five years ago he'd borrowed heavily to buy Webster's, on the other side of Parker's, more to thwart Letty Hardy than for any desire to expand, though he'd got a sniff of Marshall's plans to buy up the properties and knock through. He'd thought to make a handsome profit selling all three premises on to them, but he was no match for Cyril Marshall. The interest on the loan was crippling and Gilbert had left himself wide open when the Marshalls made their approach, offering to service the loan in exchange for taking Webster's for their own use. Throughout the war they had run a racket diverting stores when the navy was in charge and Gilbert was involved by association, not that he'd seen any of the profits. Now they wanted Parker's and Arthur Marshall had made no bones about what his father would do if Gilbert failed. Gilbert had driven himself into a corner. He had his own family to think of now.

The shop was empty, and the girl Pearl was alone. She wouldn't prove much trouble. He'd softened her up over the days, slowly making her acquaintance, a word or two when she passed of a morning and when she left. He knew the comings and goings of the shop as well as his own. The lass was not sharp enough to think he was anything other than what he wanted her to think of him. He opened the door slowly so that the bell the other side of it didn't ring out too loud, putting his hand up to still the clapper. He didn't want Norah to come running. Pearl had her back to him, carefully straightening a row of boots, singing a popular tune.

'What a sweet voice you have.'

She spun around. 'Mr Crowe.' She looked to the door, puzzled. 'I didn't hear the bell.'

'You could be on the stage with a voice like that,' he said, avoiding answering her question. She flushed. Flattery worked on most women, Letty Hardy being the exception.

'You've just missed Mrs Hardy. What can I do for you?'

She could do plenty for him if that was what he was after. She was a nice-looking lass, in her own way, neat and tidy, lovely hands, pert bosom and those lips – but that wasn't why he was here.

'Mrs Parker?'

'She'll be back shortly. She's gone out for Mr Parker's medication.'

It might be easier than he anticipated. He knew the keys were kept on a hook behind the counter and he felt the block of soft clay in his pocket that he would use for a mould.

'And you're looking after the shop and Mr Parker?'

She beamed proudly, nodded.

He walked to the counter, smiling at her. 'I was expecting a delivery. Could you check that it wasn't left here?'

She began looking under the counter, moving things aside.

'The delivery boy is sloppy. He doesn't pay attention to detail, not like you.' He nodded his head towards the display of boots she'd been sorting.

She preened with pleasure. 'No. There's nothing here.'

'Could you check Mrs Parker hasn't taken it through the back way?'

The girl hesitated. 'I'd rather not disturb Mr Parker. Could you come back when Mrs Parker returns?'

He could feel his palms beginning to sweat. 'It's rather important. I wouldn't have disturbed you otherwise.'

She looked at the front door as if she could summon Norah Parker to it.

He persevered. 'It would be such a help. You don't have to wake old Percy. I wouldn't want you to do that. But if you were very quiet...?' To his relief she agreed. The instant she turned her back, he glanced at the door of the shop and, seeing no one was close, he took his chance. Hands shaking, he lifted the key from the hook at the back of the counter and pressed it into the mould, pocketing it, then wiping the key with his handkerchief before replacing it on the hook, just as Pearl tiptoed through the door.

'I can't see nothing,' she whispered, coming closer.

He wiped his forehead with his handkerchief. 'I'm sorry to have bothered you.' At the door he turned and gave her a lingering smile before hurrying out into the street, away from the docks and down towards the alleyways of the east marsh where he could get a copy of the key, no questions asked.

21

One day had run seamlessly into another, with little time to think, to come up for air, or so it seemed to Ruth, as she waited in the hall at Meadowvale House with her father on the morning of her wedding. The carriage had arrived a few moments ago, signalling the time for her aunt to take her leave of them. After checking the carriage was as she had ordered it to be, she'd left Ruth with a parting peck on her cheek, telling her what a beauty she looked and how lucky Arthur Marshall was. Her words only served to make her feel as if she were a prize at the county show, that Arthur Marshall had somehow won her by default.

She had slept little, watching the shadows play over the bedroom wall. The drapes had been left open, Ruth not wanting to shut out the world and fully embrace the darkness. Her thoughts had raced forward then doubled back. Thinking of love, of Arthur. If Arthur had told her he loved her, she couldn't recall it. They had not spoken of love, only marriage – and they were two different things. Her father had asked her if she was happy and she had assured him she was, uncomfortable in the lie. But he looked so wonderful this bright October morning that she couldn't regret her decision. It would be strange for a while, as it had been when Charles and Henry went off to fight. The two of them had adjusted and found a way to live without them. She could do it again, for his sake. He took her hand in his and kissed it.

'You look as beautiful as your mother looked on her wedding day, my darling daughter.'

The two of them looked up to the portrait of her mother. When she returned to this house after her honeymoon, she would be a married woman. Ruth Marshall. No longer an Evans, not in name. It felt as uneasy as a dress that was too small. But she would get used to it. She could get used to anything if it made her father happy. He put out his elbow and she linked her arm through his. As they made their way down the hall, she pictured him returning at the end of the day, alone, save for Mrs Murray. The thought made her shiver. Was she doing the right thing in leaving him? As they stepped over the threshold, she took one last lingering look over her shoulder and bit back her tears.

* * *

The coach-and-four was outside, the horses decked in ribbons, the coach adorned with flowers. Neighbours she'd known for most of her life had gathered on the pavement and called out their good wishes as she walked towards it. A little girl came forward with a posy, a boy carried a horseshoe tied to a white ribbon and both were handed to her. Her father held out his hand for Ruth to take as she stepped up and settled herself in the carriage, Mrs Murray arranging the silk of her dress. Ruth looked up to the windows over the landing where all three siblings had stood to wait for Father to come home. She longed to turn back the years, but she could only go forward and make the best of her life from now on. Crowds lined the streets as they made their way to St James Church in the centre of the town, peering to catch sight of the bride in all her finery, her father in his morning suit and top hat. Many of them would have been standing a long time, watching the great and good of the town and counties beyond arrive in their splendour. Cheers went up as they passed, people waving handkerchiefs, calling their good wishes, and Ruth and her father exchanged smiles and waved back as they moved slowly along the road. After many years of sadness it was good to feel her wedding might have brought a little light and happiness to the day and Letty's words came back to her. '*You will feel different on the day.*' As the coach came to stop at the church her father alighted and came round to take her hand. He smiled so proudly up at her and she knew she had worried needlessly. It was going to be a wonderful day.

The wedding service went smoothly, as did the wedding breakfast at Saxon Hall. She was tearful at her father's speech and so was he. Arthur squeezed her hand to reassure her, smiling at her as she turned to him, and she suddenly relaxed, now that it was all over. She scanned the marquee and found Letty and Alec seated some distance away with Miss Sheldon and Philip Proctor, glad that Alec had been able to be at his wife's side. They raised their glasses to her happiness and she nodded her head in thanks.

After she'd changed into her suit for the journey to London and onward to Paris, Ruth walked down the staircase into the hall where their guests had gathered to see them off. Arthur walked up to meet her halfway, took hold of her hand and pressed it to his lips. 'You look radiant, Mrs Marshall.' Her name was new and fresh; she wondered how long it would take to become familiar. He stood beside her on the stairs, smiling down to those assembled below.

'Time to throw your bouquet.' He held out his arm and she linked her own through his and together they made their way down to the floor. He released her and she turned her back. The single women gathered behind her and when she thought they were ready, she tossed the flowers over her shoulder. When she turned, she saw Evelyn had caught it. She looked delighted, and Ruth was pleased for her, though she had hoped it might be Daphne. Just to give Jeremy Howard a nudge in case he was in need of it. It suddenly made her aware of how few young men were present. Not just the absence of Henry and Charles, but the other friends they had lost.

Out on the drive, people lined the way to Arthur's new Wolseley. Tin cans and a sign bearing the words *Just Married* had been tied to the rear bumper. He opened the door for her to get in. Her father came and kissed her. 'Have the most wonderful time, my dear. I shall miss you.' She smiled, a lump in her throat, and climbed into the car. Guests gathered on the drive to see them off and she searched among the happy faces, noticing Philip Proctor standing head and shoulders above many of them. Daphne came to his side and slipped her arm through his and Ruth felt a strange little stab to her heart, unsure of what it was, or why. As Arthur released the brake and pulled away, she turned, staring longingly at those she loved and was leaving behind.

Arthur patted her thigh. 'No looking back, Mrs Marshall.'

She turned back to him. 'No. No looking back.'

22

As autumn took hold, there was a familiar rhythm to Letty's days, the children at school, Alec back with Hammond's. He was happier when he came home, glad to be back fishing, though his earnings were not what they had been before the war. The catch brought a lower price, now that fish was more readily available, which meant Alec's share of the profit was smaller. Still, they managed well enough. To every up there was a down. Dorcas was more agreeable than she had ever been, and Letty was filled with hope for the future. She'd carried her unborn child for seven months. There had been a few minor niggles over the last couple of weeks but now there was a problem.

On the Monday after the wedding, she'd carried out an end-of-quarter stocktake with Norah, going through each item and tallying with sales. It was clear things were adrift. Either stock was going missing, or Norah had made a mistake with the books. Letty had been reluctant to ask her, but Norah had been only too glad for Letty to go over things.

'Your eyes are sharper than mine. And your brain.'

'You're still sharp, Norah but you are...' She was going to say 'tired', but one look at Norah and she changed her mind. '... exhausted.' Her eyes had lost their sparkle and the skin under them was dark and sunken. 'We all make mistakes when we're tired.' She pressed her hand to Letty's shoulder.

'Ah, Letty. I'm too old in the tooth to believe it's tiredness. I've made a mistake. You'll pick it up and it will be right as rain again.' But Letty hadn't picked it up. She'd gone through the receipts one by one – and twice over. The neat figures were all in order.

'Things have gone missing, then?' Norah looked to Letty for confirmation. 'It's not the accounting?'

'All shipshape, as they always have been.'

'How much is it, then? A little bit here and there? The odd pair of boots? A pan?'

'More than that.' She knew Norah was hoping that she'd made the mistake herself. That Letty would ferret out the error. She liked Pearl; they both did. They couldn't fault her about the shop. She was slow but she was careful. Or had it all been an act? Letty couldn't quite believe that it was. 'It amounts to a pretty penny. And now we've found it, we can't allow it to go on.'

Norah sat back, glanced to Percy, who had been listening, his disappointment clear. 'She's been such a good lass. I can't quite believe it of her.'

'Neither can I. But the figures don't lie. I've gone over them religiously. I can't find an error in your numbers Norah. Or mine.'

'And if we took another look?' Norah didn't want to believe it, but they couldn't avoid the glaringly obvious.

'We'd find the same result. I'll go over them again if you want me to?'

Norah looked down at her hand. 'No, lass. You must be weary going over them.'

'I'd do it again if I thought it would bring another answer.'

'I'm sure if anything's missing she didn't do it on purpose.' Norah sat down in the chair. 'I can't see the lass taking anything. Whatever would she do with it?'

'Sell it on?' Letty closed the books.

'I can't believe she'd do such a thing, not on purpose.' Had she deceived them with her simple ways, pulling the wool over their eyes? Norah shook her head. 'She doesn't have the guile.'

Letty had to agree. 'Maybe not, but she's costing us money, whether by accident or design – it's there in black and white and everything tallied before she came to work here.'

Norah turned away and Letty could have wept. She'd trusted the girl, had thought she was too slow-thinking to outwit her, but outwit her she had. 'I'll give her her cards when she comes in this morning. Best to cut our losses.' It grieved her to be back to square one. She was tired, not as quick as she'd been when carrying Stella, but then she hadn't had the café and Percy had been fit and well and working in the shop each day. Percy had turned to stare into the fire. She knew how frustrated he felt, how useless, and now she'd added to it. More would fall to Letty and Norah, and he could do nothing to help. 'We'll just have to get someone else. There are plenty of people looking for work,' she said brightly.

Norah gave her a half smile. What Letty said was true, but they needed to find the right person – and that was never easy. Percy, more than any of them, had to approve. Requesting that Norah remain with Percy, Letty picked up the books and took them through to the shop, placed them on the counter and waited for Pearl.

* * *

The girl came in, smiling as always. Letty stopped her before she took off her coat. Pearl frowned. 'Is Mr Parker alright?' Her concern for Percy almost weakened Letty. Could she be wrong after all?

'Mr and Mrs Parker are quite well,' she said firmly. 'But things in the shop are not.'

Pearl's expression changed. Letty took out the receipt book, placing it on top of the books containing the accounts and stock records. Pearl looked at the pile, puzzled. Letty tapped them with the flat of her hand. 'Have you given a receipt for everything you've sold?'

Letty scrutinised Pearl's slightest movement, trying to work out whether Pearl knew she had been caught out, but the girl looked Letty straight in the eye.

'I have,' she said quietly. 'I take great care when I do it.' She clasped her hands. 'I know I'm not very bright, Mrs Hardy. That's why I'm slow. I don't want to make a mistake—'

'But mistakes have been made, Pearl. If that's indeed what they are?'

Pearl stared at her, confused, until she came to a slow understanding of what Letty's words meant. She sprang back.

'I would never take anything, Mrs Hardy. The money is always there for the things sold.'

Letty could not disagree. But she'd spent too much time away from the shop and Norah was too caught up with Percy. Whatever had gone missing was down to Pearl's lack of attention if nothing else, and they couldn't afford for it to go on.

'And you've not given anything away to anyone – or told them to pay later?'

'Never.' The girl's cheeks reddened. 'Mrs Hardy, is something wrong?'

It all felt dreadfully wrong. Letty couldn't imagine that Pearl had the nous to deceive.

'Things have gone missing. It amounts to a lot of money. And the profits—'

'It isn't me, Mrs Hardy.' Pearl shook her head vehemently. She was beginning to tremble, which only served to make Letty think her guilt was the cause of it.

'Mr and Mrs Parker would hardly rob themselves, would they? Are you taking it to sell on?'

Pearl stared at her. 'I would never... I wouldn't... you've been so kind... I...' Tears began to fall and she fumbled in her pocket for her handkerchief, drew it out and pushed it to her eyes to stop the flow. Was it all an act? Letty didn't want to weaken.

'It can't be explained, Pearl. And it can't go on. Do you understand?'

The girl nodded, rubbing at her eyes then her nose. 'You're going to give me my cards, aren't you?' She looked to Letty, her eyes red, her face swollen with tears. Letty withdrew the letter she had already prepared from between the pages of the accounts book.

'There's a reference and pay to the end of the week.' Norah had insisted that it was only fair. They'd both been uncomfortable about the decision they'd come to but decided that it was the best way for all concerned. Norah told her that she wouldn't have rested if they'd dismissed her without giving her a chance to get further work. If it was purely down to carelessness there would be no end to the problems that could be caused. 'I can't have Norah and Percy distressed.' They were vulnerable enough without the added uncertainty that Pearl may very well be robbing them left, right and centre and under their noses.

'I understand.' She tugged at her coat buttons, tears still rolling down her cheeks. 'I wouldn't have them distressed either. They've been very good to me. You all have.' She took the envelope Letty proffered and put it in her pocket. Letty fought the urge to change her mind. But where there was doubt... Pearl walked away, head bowed and stopped at the door. She turned to Letty. 'If my Sidney should happen to come, you will you tell him I'm still waiting?'

'I will.' There had been no news of the young man, no letters, and it had been almost three full months since Pearl had arrived in Grimsby. Letty and Norah had both agreed it was highly unlikely he existed at all. Had she spun them a yarn, as Dorcas had suggested? The girl turned away, opened the door.

'Pearl,' Letty called after her. The girl turned once more. 'Try the Royal Hotel. I know they're looking for staff.'

Pearl gave a half smile, nodded and closed the door behind her. Letty stared at the door. Something didn't feel right but faced with the evidence it couldn't be laid at anyone else's door. Norah came through to stand in the shop.

'Did she deny it?'

Letty shook her head. 'No. Nor did she admit it.'

'She didn't put up a fight?'

'No. It was as if she couldn't quite believe what was happening. That we could think that she would do such a thing.' It troubled her. 'What if we're wrong, Norah?'

Norah picked up the receipt book from the counter. 'We couldn't do anything else. If it isn't Pearl, then the place must be haunted.'

'I'd rather that be the truth.'

'So would I, Letty. So would I.'

* * *

Dorcas had been delighted to be proved right when she learned of Pearl's dismissal.

'You're a soft touch, Letty, and people know it. She was sly, that one. All that meek and mild was an act. I could see it a mile off. Twisting the truth and all the while—'

'If only she'd admitted it,' Letty interrupted. 'If she was in trouble, we could have helped her.'

'What! Then you'd have forgiven her thieving ways. Good God, Letty, have you lost leave of your senses?'

'No,' Letty snapped. 'But I might have understood, then I would have forgiven her.' Dorcas opened her mouth, closed it and turned away. 'It will mean I'll have to do more hours at the shop for a while.' She hated to ask. 'I can open the café, but I wondered if you could do a few hours there and close up? So that I can stay with the Parkers. Until we find someone else to cover the hours.'

Letty had been grateful when Dorcas agreed without making a song and dance about it. More so when she made her sit down in front of the fire and handed her a mug of hot milk. 'For the baby,' she said, taking the chair opposite and picking up her knitting.

* * *

Letty's daily checking became another burden, but things still went missing. Not just clothing but pencils and buckets and other paraphernalia they kept behind the counter. A pile of sweaters had been pulled about and things moved around the shelves. Norah thought it was her own doing, that she was becoming forgetful. Letty had a mind to agree until one morning when she came into the shop and discovered boots taken out of their boxes and scattered around the floor. She went through to the back of the shop and found Norah, pan in hand, spooning porridge into two bowls.

'What happened?' she asked Norah, taking off her hat and hanging it on the hook on the back of the door before removing her coat. It was bitter outside and when she leaned over Percy to kiss his cheek, he shuddered at the touch of her skin.

'Cold. Brr.'

'Happened to what?' Norah frowned.

'Have you been in the shop?'

Norah returned the pan to the hot plate. 'Is everything alright?'

Letty shrugged.

Norah placed the bowl on the small table at Percy's side. 'Two ticks and I'll be back.' She followed Letty into the shop and stopped when she saw the mess. 'What on earth...'

The pair of them stared at the boots.

'Did you hear anything in the night?'

Norah shook her head, not taking her eyes off the pile of boots. Then she started pairing them, Letty squatting down to help her, her belly uncomfortable. Norah begged her to leave them, but she couldn't. 'I can do this. Give Percy his breakfast. It will only take me a minute or two.' Norah relented, and Letty replaced the boots and quickly checked the rest of the stock. Nothing else had been disturbed. It was all very puzzling but there had to be a rational explanation. She went through to the back room.

'Do you think you might have been sleepwalking, Norah?'

Norah shrugged. 'I wouldn't know if I was. And I doubt Percy would notice.'

It disturbed Letty. There was no way it was Percy and if the stress was getting too much for Norah... if it went on much longer, she would have to insist they leave. For their own safety.

'Perhaps someone is getting in and causing mischief. Children?' Norah suggested. Percy nodded.

'The only way in is through the front door. Whoever it is would have to come over the back and you'd see them – and they'd have to get in through Gilbert's first and climb over that high wall. It hardly seems worth the trouble.'

Letty went upstairs and checked the windows. No glass was broken, and the snecks were fastened across. She leaned on the sill and looked over the small yard at the back of the buildings that faced onto Wharncliffe Road. Had Pearl taken a key? Was she doing this to spite them? No, Letty tossed the thought away. The girl would never do that. She didn't have it in her. Letty might have made a mistake but there was no malice in Pearl. There had to be some other explanation, but she was baffled as to what it was.

23

When the newly wedded Marshalls stepped onto the boat, Ruth finally felt able to cast off the tension of the last few days. They had travelled by sleeper to London then on to Dover, a journey she had made many times, both before the war and after it. Latterly in search of news of Charles. None had been forthcoming. It was hard to comprehend that the armistice had been signed almost a year ago, difficult to cast all thought of it aside and think the happy thoughts of a new bride. Memories of her brothers engulfed her as she stepped onto French soil, thinking of them and all the other pour souls who had never returned home. Somewhere, in the fields that had seen so much carnage, her brother lay. Daphne had been here, nursing the wounded and the dying, as had Evelyn, and their bond of shared experience had left Ruth firmly on the outside. She stood aside as Arthur instructed the porter to transfer their bags to the Paris train. There would be no detours to the east or to Belgium. No moving from town to town in search of small details that might lead to her brother's resting place. She was here for pleasure only, and it was alien to her.

Arthur looked very dashing, wearing a new dark brown coat and matching bowler, his dark moustache shining with wax. He strode back to her, a man at ease with his surroundings.

'I am pleased to report that the train is on time.' There had been strikes and protests during the summer months. The newspapers had carried the daily details. Paris had become the centre of the peace process, and the allied powers had gathered to argue over the way forward and decide on German reparations for the war. Britain's prime minister, Lloyd George, had argued for a 'just peace' that would avoid future conflict with Germany. Peace was never a straightforward process. It ended in July with the signing of the Treaty of Versailles. It had taken six months to come to some sort of agreement but there were no winners. Germany was not happy with the outcome and any peace made was fragile.

As the train moved out of the port and into the countryside, she could see the signs of recovery. There were people in the fields and evidence that a small harvest had been gathered in. She couldn't even begin to imagine how the French and Belgian people had fared during the hostilities. Buildings were in a state of disrepair but here and there a man would be on a roof, fastening tiles, and others working on walls.

'We should be in Paris in under four hours.'

She nodded. They had been on the ferry for three. It would be early evening when they arrived.

He took up a newspaper and read. She turned to ask him about politics.

'There's no need for you to worry about anything. I'll take care of you.'

'I'm not worried, Arthur.' How silly of him to think she would be. 'I want to know how things are in the world. Father and I always discussed world affairs. I like to have an informed opinion on such matters.'

He closed the newspaper, folded it and set it to one side. She sensed a slight irritation.

'I shouldn't have picked it up.' He acted as if he were indulging a child. She opened her mouth to protest but he took her fingers and kissed them, placed them on her lips. 'You have my full attention from now on.'

They arrived at the Hotel George V just after five in the afternoon. There was a telegram waiting for Arthur when they checked in. He read it and smiled. 'That is good news.'

She tilted her head to one side.

'Monsieur Clémentel, the minister of commerce. He wants to have lunch tomorrow.' He pulled a face to show his disappointment. 'I should ask him to come another day but...' He shrugged, glanced again at the telegram. 'It might not be possible.' He returned the telegram to the envelope.

'No, don't cancel it, Arthur. It's only lunch.' What difference would one day make?

'But lunch can turn into dinner.' He leaned into her, lowering his voice. 'You know what a reputation these people have.'

'I do.' She smiled. 'I will go to the Louvre.'

'But I wanted to take you.' He pouted.

'Then I will find something else to occupy me. We can go to the Louvre the day after.'

They were taken to their suite and Ruth tried to suppress her excitement until the porter had unloaded their trunks. She stepped out onto the balcony and gasped with delight at the view they had across the city. The Eiffel Tower was lit like a Christmas tree and felt so incredibly close that she might reach out and touch it. She leaned on the iron balustrade and scanned the horizon. It did the heart good to see so many beautiful properties still intact. The towns and countryside to the east had not fared so well; much of it had become a vast wasteland. It would take years to rebuild. Where did one start when confronted with so much devastation? Behind her she heard Arthur repeating '*Merci*' to the porter, the rustle of paper as he handed over the tip. When the door closed, he came to stand behind her, slipping his hand about her waist. He turned her to him, his hand still about her waist. 'Happy, Mrs Marshall?'

'Very.'

He took her hand, led her back into the room and kissed her face then her neck. He had refreshed his cologne and she inhaled the smell of wood and musk, feeling heady with nervousness at what was to come. Her aunt had briefly spoken to her of such matters but it had been decidedly awkward and her aunt had concluded by telling her to close her eyes, and let Arthur do what he needed to. She had no idea what was expected of her as he removed her blouse and other garments, dropping each item on the floor, drawing her towards the bedroom as he did so, kissing each part of her skin as it became exposed. She had no doubt that he knew what he was doing. He led her to the bed, his kisses more earnest. Her heart was pounding as he laid her down on it. She closed her eyes, and he lay beside her. She could sense the smile on his lips, the hardness of his body as he came on top of her, and she gasped in shock.

'Oh, what a good and virtuous woman you are, Ruthie.'

She froze. Only Henry had ever called her Ruthie. No one else. She didn't want to think of him, not now; she mustn't. As Arthur thrust himself inside her she couldn't hold back the tears, fighting the urge to sob as Arthur moved up and down on her, grunting like an animal. It hurt and she cried out, but he didn't stop, writhing and thrusting deeper and deeper until he cried out himself, and with one final thrust fell onto her, his breath heavy and deep. She opened her eyes and stared up at the ceiling. This wasn't what she had imagined at all.

While he slept, she picked up her clothes and then bathed herself. Her insides felt sore and bruised. It made sitting uncomfortable but at least it was over. When he awoke, he came to her and kissed the top of her head as she sat at the dressing table, slipping his hands over her breasts. She tried to be relaxed but it felt odd to have a man touch her, even though he was her husband.

After dinner they walked by the Seine. Being out in the fresh air settled her. Hopefully, things in the bedroom would get better – and if not, she would have to bear it, as was her duty.

While he had his meeting, she walked along the avenue George V and the streets in the 8th arrondissement, to pass the time. There were many things she would have liked to do but she didn't want to do them alone. When Arthur's meeting was over, they would be free to do as they pleased.

They were having dinner when a waiter came and informed him of a telephone call. He wiped his mouth with his napkin, excused himself and went to answer it. 'That was unexpected but rather fortuitous,' he explained on his return. 'That was Monsieur Boucher. You remember I told you of him? He has a merchant shipping business in Marseille?'

Ruth nodded, knowing what would come next.

'He happens to be in Paris for two days.' He slipped his napkin over his lap. 'I really can't pass over a meeting with him.'

She couldn't hide her disappointment. The two days had been kept entirely free for them to spend time together. He reached for her hand across the table, but she wasn't inclined to give it. He withdrew his hand. 'You knew well enough that I had business to do while we were here. You can't expect me to pass over these wonderful opportunities on a whim to go shopping.'

'I wasn't thinking of shopping. Only to spend time together. We've had little time these last few months.' Surely she wasn't being unreasonable?

'And we will, we will.' He laughed. 'You made me wait long enough, Ruth. You can't begrudge me a couple of days.'

In the morning, Monsieur Boucher was waiting for them in the lobby. She held out her hand and he kissed it, bowed to her. She spoke to him in his own language, and he responded enthusiastically. 'Will you be joining us, Madame Marshall?'

Arthur smiled at her. 'No, my wife intends to go to the Louvre today.'

She could not keep the surprise from her face. Not when he had made such bones about wanting to go with her only two days ago.

'Ah, such a pity. Another time perhaps.'

'Yes, another time,' Ruth replied.

Arthur handed her some money, which she placed inside her bag. 'Have a wonderful time, dearest,' he said, kissing her cheek.

After the Louvre, she strolled back through the Jardin des Tuileries and on to the Champs-Élysées. It was late afternoon when she returned. Arthur was waiting for her in the bedroom. She caught the waft of cognac as she placed her bag on the dressing table.

'Monsieur wanted to see you before he left.' His face was dark.

'You didn't express a time I should be back.'

'Where have you been?' He got up, grabbed hold of her wrist.

'You know where I've been, Arthur. You told me to go alone.'

He pushed her onto the bed. 'Liar.'

'Arthur!' She was shocked. 'You're hurting me.'

He wasn't listening. He wanted his way with her. He unfastened his trousers.

'Arthur, please. Not now.'

This time he was rough and clumsy, with no care for her at all. When she cried out, he put his hand across her mouth until he was finished with her.

She didn't go down to dinner, and cried herself to sleep, was silent at breakfast. He was contrite. When they returned to their suite, she found it full of flowers. There seemed to be a bouquet on every surface. Their beauty took her breath away.

He came close to her. 'Am I forgiven?' She was quiet. He took her hand and pressed it to his lips. 'It was the drink. I hated not being with you. Father had contacted these people. I knew nothing of it. I called him last night. It won't happen again.'

She struggled, knowing her forgiveness was being bought. He looked at her expectantly and she relented. He drew her to him and kissed her, tenderly this time. He put his hand to her face. 'Thank you, dear Ruth. I promise it won't ever happen again.' It felt like an uneasy peace but what else could she do?

24

They had sailed from le Havre of the SS *Rochambeau*, arriving in New York eight days later, travelling onwards to Boston, where they remained for two weeks. Arthur had been as good as his word and there had been no further unseemly incidents. He'd introduced her to many of the friends he'd made during his time there, and they'd been invited to dinner and to parties, and spent numerous nights attending concerts, and at the theatre. It had all been rather wonderful, though she was uncomfortable with Arthur's willingness to lay a wager at any opportunity. He was such a sore loser. It would put him in the foulest of moods and she would have to soothe him back to good humour or they would both be miserable. They spent the last few days in New York, taking in shows on Broadway before sailing home on the RMS *Aquitania*. After dinner, Arthur would retire to the smoking room most evenings and join in a hand of poker with two Texans who had newly made his acquaintance. Ruth became practised at knowing how well his hand had played each night, depending on how much drink he had consumed. When she'd challenged him, concerned about how much money he was losing, he'd turned on her, telling her it was none of her business what he did with *his* money and it had been a relief when the ship docked at Southampton. Although the men were charm personified, she hoped never to see them again.

There was a loud sigh as the brakes gripped the rails when the train finally pulled into Grimsby station. It had been a long journey from the south coast, and she was glad to at last be on familiar soil. Arthur got up and escorted her from the carriage. She waited while Arthur gave instructions to the porter to transfer their baggage to his parents' home at Garth Hall, where they would reside until their own was built. The wind was howling and icy and she put her hand to her hat in fear of losing it. He hurried her to the waiting car, a protective hand to the small of her back. The chauffeur closed the door firmly behind her and Arthur dashed around to the other side and got in beside her. It was bitterly cold, but she was warmed by the thought of being home. She'd missed her father more than she'd anticipated and longed to see him again. She'd written every day, sometimes a small note on a postcard, illustrations and photographs of the sights she'd seen on their travels, and though it was her honeymoon she would have liked to have been able to share it with him. The chauffeur pulled away and Arthur sat back and closed his eyes.

'Could we call in to say hello to Father? The car will go past Welholme Road. Just for a minute or two.'

Arthur opened his eyes, gave her a lazy smile. 'It's very late. I need to get back. Father will be eager to hear my news before he retires for the night.'

'But a few minutes won't hurt, Arthur.'

He put up a hand. 'I'm exhausted. It can wait until tomorrow. You're not a child.' He was curt. It was useless to press him. They had been married precisely thirty-nine days and in those few weeks she had learned more about his small idiosyncrasies than she had in all the years she'd known him. He was good company in parties, driven and ambitious, but he had a short temper, and she had quickly learned when to push and when to hold back. This moment was one of them. She was too tired to argue.

Garth Hall was on Humberstone Avenue, on the outskirts of Grimsby, and the car turned down a long drive lined with sycamores. It was ostentatious, built for grandeur, but Mrs Marshall did not have the flamboyance to carry it off as well as her aunt Helen. She'd been here a few times as a guest, played tennis on the courts and swum in the indoor swimming pool that was as hot as the orangery. There was a grand colonnade of Doric columns and a series of shallow stone steps that led up to grand entrance doors that were half glazed. The arched windows overlooked lawns laid out in intricate patterns. It was all very regimented and formal, having none of the easy flow that she associated with Jack and Helen Frampton's house, Saxon Hall. Lights glowed out from many of the downstairs rooms and as the car pulled to a stop, the large entrance door was opened. The Marshalls' butler, Chambers, came down to greet them, standing to attention in the bitter cold dressed in only his suit. He gave a slight bow when Arthur got out of the car and once again when Ruth stood before him. 'Welcome home, Mrs Marshall, Mr Marshall, sir.' He was an older man, a similar age to her father, steeped in service. She had heard Mildred repeatedly boast to her guests that he had worked for landed gentry in the past. The chauffeur unloaded their light cases and Chambers picked them up and followed them into the house.

Cyril and Mildred Marshall were waiting in the formal room to receive them. They were delighted to see their son and she tried to bite back her irritation that she had not been able to see her own father. Mildred proffered her cheek to Ruth, who kissed it.

'It was good of you to wait up for us, Mother,' Arthur said.

Mildred put out her hand to indicate Ruth to sit down opposite her. Cyril handed Arthur a whisky. 'What would you care to drink, Ruth?'

'Would tea be too much trouble at this hour?'

Mildred got up and rang the bell at the side of the chimney breast and their maid came to the room and bobbed a small curtsey. Many of the young women had found work during the war, taking up positions that the men had vacated; they had been used to better wages and better hours with time off other than the half-day given when in service. Things had changed so fast. Women over thirty who were in possession of property had been given the vote last year. There was still a long way to go before all women were given the same voting rights as men, but it was a step in the right direction. They all needed to pull together and be valued. She sensed that it would not be so here. That the Marshalls were very firmly entrenched in the Edwardian manner of doing things. While they waited for the tea to arrive, Mildred asked Ruth if she had enjoyed their travels. Ruth told her of the museums and galleries she'd visited.

'On your own?'

'Yes. Arthur was engaged in many meetings.' She smiled. 'It wasn't as I had expected it to be.'

'Business before pleasure,' Mildred interrupted, taking a sip from her sherry glass. After an hour or more of questioning, Ruth was growing weary. Thankfully, Mildred noticed and got up. 'I think the ladies must leave the men to their brandy and their conversation.'

Relieved, Ruth got up. Arthur and his father bade them goodnight and Ruth was shown to her room by the maid.

Her bag had been unpacked and the soiled clothes removed. A new cream silk nightdress and gown was laid on the bed, along with a small card. She opened the envelope and read it. Another gift from Arthur.

She went to the dressing table and touched in turn her comb and the silver-backed brush that had belonged to her mother, wishing that she could speak with her, just once, suddenly feeling very alone. While the maid turned down the bed, she moved to the window, looking out into the darkness. Although they had a large plot at Meadowvale House, there was a glimpse of other houses from the upstairs windows, indicating the presence of people close by. Here, there was only darkness. Not even the moon was showing itself.

When the maid left, she wandered around the room, opening drawers and looking in wardrobes. A door to her left led to an en suite bathroom with the latest bathroom china. A door to the right led to Arthur's room. She tiptoed into it like a thief, looking at the paintings on the walls and the bareness of it, the masculinity. She quietly closed the door, hoping that he would not disturb her tonight, and got into bed, listening to unfamiliar sounds before falling asleep.

She woke in the morning to discover the maid making the fire in her room and drawing back the curtains. 'It's a beautiful morning, Mrs Marshall. Everyone is already down for breakfast.'

She dressed quickly and hurried downstairs to find the Marshalls at the table. Cyril stood up as she came into the room. 'I trust you slept well?'

'Wonderfully well, thank you.' Arthur was helping himself to food from the silver salvers set out on the sideboard and she went beside him and took up a plate. He leaned and kissed her cheek, smiled at her. She relaxed a little. Perhaps things wouldn't be so bad after all. She took a seat next to him.

Mildred put down her fork. 'Ruth, my dear. I have invited my ladies around for luncheon. I'm quite certain you may have already met some of them but not as Arthur's wife.'

'That's very kind of you. At what time should I return?'

'Return?' Arthur asked.

'From Father's. I could go before the luncheon. When Arthur goes into the office.'

'I'd rather you didn't, Ruth. I will be going into the office with Father this morning. We have an important board meeting at eleven. The directors will need a comprehensive update of my dealings while I've been away. And I will have a full day thereafter, catching up with all I have neglected while we have been travelling.'

'I suppose I could go after the luncheon. If you could send the car back for me?'

Mildred smiled. 'I would much prefer that, if you didn't mind. My ladies have been so looking forward to hearing about your trip, to America especially.' She indicated for the maid to refresh the teapot. 'The ladies will be arriving at twelve prompt. Except for Mrs Bridges, who has a dreadful habit of arriving late.'

Arthur smirked. 'And still you invite her.'

'I must. Her husband is the principal shareholder in the Marine Insurance Company. Everything is tolerable for the good of the family.' She addressed Ruth. 'I trust that fits with your plans, my dear?'

Ruth knew she was meant to accept. It would mean less time with her father, but for the sake of a peaceful life, she agreed.

25

As the chauffeur turned the car onto Hainton Avenue and made its way towards Welholme Road, Ruth viewed the streets and houses afresh. Inwardly she was changed but the familiarity of the streets and houses settled her, and the tension of the last few weeks fell from her shoulders. She had done her best to please Arthur, to make him happy, but he seemed to find fault at every turn.

When the car drew up in front of Meadowvale House, Ruth was impatient for the chauffeur to open the door and set her free. After thanking him, she stood for a moment looking at the house where she had known such happiness. She stopped in the porch, considering whether to ring the doorbell and bring Mrs Murray to greet her, and decided against it. It was her father she longed for. But at the sound of the door opening and closing and her heels on the hallway, Mrs Murray appeared in the corridor from the kitchen. The housekeeper opened her mouth to greet her, but Ruth put a finger to her lips. Mrs Murray nodded her understanding and Ruth pointed to her father's study, hoping she would find him there. The housekeeper nodded her confirmation, and Ruth quietly removed her hat and gloves, placed them on the hall stand as she had so many times. She looked up at her mother's portrait, smiled at the familiar welcome home, knocked lightly on her father's door and opened it. He looked up from his desk, his smile wide, and removed his glasses, laid them on the desk as he got up to greet her, his arms open. She hurried into his embrace, and all the jagged and sharp edges of her that had been carved since her marriage suddenly softened.

He stood back and held her hands. 'How wonderful you look.' He looked her up and down. 'A little peaky perhaps but nothing I wouldn't expect from a woman who had travelled two continents these past months.' She kissed his cheek, and he indicated for her to take a seat opposite his desk. 'Let me tell Mrs Murray that we'll take tea in the drawing room.' He gave a quick glance to the clock and went to the door. Ruth was gratified to see the change in her father's surroundings, the change in him. Where once there had been chaos, there was now order. It appeared that her father had restored himself along with his study. 'I finally took myself in hand,' he said as he came back into the room. 'Fresh starts for both of us.'

It had been hard to leave, to make the commitment to Arthur, but here was evidence that it had all been worthwhile. Her father looked in far better health than he'd done in the years since the boys had been lost to them. His face had filled out a little and he'd shed that gaunt and haunted look. He'd gained a little weight, and it suited him. But as he moved, it was clear that it wasn't just the weight. A general air of happiness exuded from him that had been missing for such a long time.

The sketches Philip had gifted to them had been framed and hung on the wall opposite the window that looked out over the front of the house and the drive. He saw her looking. 'We will never forget but we must also go on.' He came to her side and they studied the portraits in companionable silence until he said, 'Come. Tell me of America.'

'I would have come to see you yesterday,' she said, turning away, 'but we were late arriving at the station and Arthur needed to get back.' Again, the little flush of irritation, that he couldn't have spared a few minutes to make her happy.

'You're here now, and that's all that matters.'

Mrs Murray came to tell them that tea was in the sitting room and Ruth got up to give her a hug.

'It's good to have her home again, isn't it, Mrs Murray?' The housekeeper had been integral to their life here and was as much a part of the family as her aunt or uncle.

'You look like you need a good meal inside you,' Mrs Murray commented. 'All that travelling has surely worn you down. But,' she said, her face lighting up, 'it must have been very exciting.' She left them in the sitting room, removing the guard from the fire before doing so. Ruth sank back into the chair and closed her eyes. It was heaven.

'How are the Marshalls?' her father asked.

She sat up, poured the tea, handed him a cup and took one for herself. 'Pleasant enough.'

'Mildred a bit of a martyr?' he teased. It made her laugh.

'I'm sure we'll get used to each other.' She didn't think it was going to be easy. 'I would have come earlier but she had organised a luncheon.'

'That was kind of her.' He supped from his cup, curious as to her answer.

'It was. But I'd rather she'd waited until I was more settled. She has a list of things lined up for me. I shan't have a minute to myself if she has her way.'

'You're used to your aunt having her way and you know how to handle her.'

'But I don't know Mildred well enough. I didn't feel that I had an option. It was awkward.'

'She'll want to show you off,' her father suggested. 'You have to allow her that, I suppose. These things take time; living under someone else's roof isn't easy. Arthur will be able to start working on getting the new house built now that you're both home. Things will gradually become more comfortable. I'm sure that you can tolerate Mildred and her ways until then.'

Ruth pursed her lips. 'I see that I'll have to organise my excursions as I never had to do here.'

'You'll have to learn to drive.'

'Or get a bicycle.'

He laughed. 'I don't think Arthur would take to that, would he? What, have people think he couldn't afford to buy his wife a car?' He gave her a wicked smile. 'You might have to shame him to it.' He winked at her. 'But you'll find a way.'

She sighed. 'I hope so. Arthur can be rather old-fashioned about what is expected of a woman.'

'That will be Mildred's influence. She's yet to embrace the Evans women's way of doing things. Lord, help her.' He stood in front of the fire. 'Your uncle Jack still believes he's in charge. You can learn a lot from how your aunt gets her way with him.'

They were interrupted when the doorbell rang.

'Are you expecting someone?'

He put his cup and saucer on the mantelpiece. 'I am.' He took a breath as if to speak then changed his mind, a little agitated, waiting for whoever it was to join them. She was surprised when Mrs Murray showed Evelyn Howard into the room, closing the door behind her.

'Evelyn. How lovely to see you.' Ruth went to her, kissed her cheek. 'Is Jeremy not with you?' There was a slight hesitation as Evelyn looked to her father. Ruth turned, puzzled. Her father took Evelyn by the hand and Ruth could not fail to notice the squeeze of reassurance he gave to her. She stared at them. Evelyn was uncertain, but her father was not.

'Ruth, my darling. We wanted you to be the first to know.' He cleared his throat. 'I have asked Evelyn to marry me.' He turned to her, his smile broad. 'And she has agreed.'

For a moment she was stunned to silence, forcing back the storm of emotions that his words had erupted. Her father was two years away from sixty and Evelyn not yet thirty. Evelyn smiled nervously and Ruth was startled to life. She kissed Evelyn's cheek once more, then her father's, delighted, though a ball of confusion had swamped her brain.

'That's the most wonderful news to come home to.'

Her father couldn't hide his pleasure, or his relief now that he had shared his news. 'We wanted to wait until your return. Evelyn hasn't told Jeremy.' He ushered Evelyn and Ruth to take a seat.

'Your brother will be thrilled for you.'

Evelyn smiled at her father and the scales fell from Ruth's eyes. All this time she had thought it was her own marriage that had made her father feel he wanted to step into the swim of life again. But it had been Evelyn. How had she not noticed?

'I fell in love with her the moment I laid eyes on her. Do you remember, Ruth? It was Peace Day.'

'I do.' How could she forget it? Her aunt's words came back to her. '*Love has nothing to do with it. Friendship lasts longer.*' She saw something between her father and Evelyn that she found wanting in her own relationship with Arthur. They sat down, and her father went to get another cup and saucer, leaving the women to talk, Ruth trying to overcome her shock at such news.

'Will you still carry on at the surgery?'

'For a while. Until Jeremy can find someone to take my

place.' Ruth didn't think he would have to look far. 'I have yet to tell him. I insisted we wait until your return. Oh, Ruth, do we have your blessing?'

'Of course, how could you not?' She was grateful for Evelyn's sensitivity of the situation, though she might have agreed to almost anything if it made her father happy.

Her father returned and they talked until the clock chimed the quarter hour.

'Arthur is sending the car for me at five,' Ruth told them reluctantly. Was this to be the pattern of her life now? Leaving when Arthur instructed.

When Mrs Marshall came to tell her that the car had arrived, Evelyn remained in the sitting room while her father went with her to the door. She put on her hat and pulled on her gloves. How swiftly everything had changed. She intuitively sensed that it would never be the same again, that when she returned there would be a woman other than herself, other than her mother's presence, in the house. She made her way to the door then stopped, turned to look to her mother's portrait. Her father did the same.

'Do you think she would approve?' They stood, side by side, gazing upon the woman who had loved them so dearly, and been taken all too soon. She had died when she was only a few years older than Evelyn was now. Was her father trying to recapture something of the life he had lost? She studied his dear face as he stared up at the portrait, the lines that worry and laughter had threaded across it, and latterly the greatest of sorrows.

'Mother would want you to be happy. That's all we ever want for those we love.' Her voice wobbled with emotion. 'And she loved us all.'

Ruth was glad to be alone in the car. It was dark now and lamps gave homes a rosy glow. Here and there candles still burned in upstairs windows, lighting loved ones home. She had done the same when Charles was lost, the candle a symbol of faith that he would return. How naïve she had been. Her throat thickened with a feeling of sorrow that she couldn't explain, and she turned away from the window, forcing back tears, suddenly overcome by the feeling of being a small child who had been abandoned.

26

Though Pearl had been dismissed more than six weeks ago, things still went missing. The stocktake had revealed a loss of items that were unusual, too big not to be noticed if anyone took them during the day when both Letty and Norah had been in the shop. A large chair had been brought onto the shop floor and on good days Percy sat watching the comings and goings, enjoying the banter with friends who called in on their way to and from work, on the ships, on the fish market and the smoke houses. People they'd known most of their lives. Some of them hadn't even been born when the Parkers set up shop on Henderson Street. There were too many of them not to notice someone helping themselves, Letty and Norah were certain of it. Percy would have noticed. He couldn't speak up but there was nothing wrong with his sight or his sharpness. Another pair of eyes made no difference, and Letty was at a loss. It kept her awake at nights, along with the baby, who was as restless as she was herself.

Alec's ship was due in shortly after eleven, when the lock gates were due to open. Both children had gone to bed and

Dorcas was sitting by the fire, the newspaper on her lap. The room was filled with the aroma of beef stew simmering on the stove, Dorcas occasionally getting up and giving it a stir, adding a drop or two of water if it were needed. Alec would never come home to an empty grate or an empty table. In a few hours he would be with them, sinking into his chair, his skin and clothes reeking of fish, but oh, what it was to have him home, even if for only the briefest of times.

Tonight, she was unable to settle, wrestling with where to sit out the night and deciding it wasn't here with Dorcas. 'I'm going down to the dock,' she announced to her mother-in-law as she got to her feet. 'I'll wait for him there.'

'You'll not be going to wait on the wharf in this weather, Letty Hardy, not in your condition,' Dorcas said, her mouth pursed like a cat's backside. 'Have you taken leave of your senses?' She put aside her knitting, not that she'd added to it; it had merely rested on her lap. For most of the night she had been deep in thought.

'I meant to the Parkers'. I'll wait there and go to the dock when his ship is fast in the fish dock. It's the perfect opportunity without them thinking I'm mollycoddling.' She stood in front of the fire, warming herself, turned and rubbed her hands together, hoping to store as much warmth in her body as she could before stepping out into the cold. 'If there's something going on, I'll find out what it is. Someone's up to mischief and by God, when I get hold of them...'

'You'll do no such thing! A woman in your condition.' Dorcas shook her head, leaned across and put the newspaper on the table. 'Like as not it's Norah, poor soul. She's sleepwalking, doing things and not aware of it.' She smoothed her hands over her skirt. 'And no wonder with all she's got on her plate. They shouldn't be living in that damp place this time of year. Or any time of the year.'

'They won't move.'

'No, they're stubborn. A lot of folks are,' she said pointedly.

'Is that remark aimed at me?' Letty challenged.

Dorcas shook her head, stared into the fire. 'Perhaps I can understand the pair of them better than most. Letting go of all you've known isn't easy. It was a wrench to leave my little cottage.'

'I'm sorry,' Letty said quietly. She'd been young, eager to please Alec, prepared to follow wherever he yearned to go.

Dorcas looked away from the flames and to Letty. 'It wasn't you, though, was it? It was my boy.' Her admission almost took Letty's breath away. Dorcas had taken every chance she could to lay the blame at Letty's feet, sniping and jibing whenever she found the opportunity. 'You wouldn't have left your mother and father, I know it.' The glow from the fire coloured her face. 'You must love my boy to have left it all behind.' She turned to Letty. 'I hope you always love him so.' Letty frowned and Dorcas looked away. She pressed her hand to her knee and got up. 'Best get yourself wrapped up against the weather.'

Letty went to get her coat and hat. When she returned, Dorcas was coming out of the pantry with the pork pie she had brought back from the café. She cut it in half and wrapped it in a waxed cloth, then handed it to Letty. 'Give them my regards when you see them.'

Their hands touched and Letty looked to her. They'd not always seen eye to eye but somehow, they'd managed to find a way to get along. Tonight, Dorcas's words had been heavy with regret, her sadness palpable. Letty had not considered how things might have been for her mother-in-law when they moved to Grimsby, how frightened she might have been by such a huge change. She had thought her a misery, determined to come between her and Alec. Alec, who could do no wrong, and Letty, who could do no right. Tonight, they could put all that behind them.

'I will.'

Dorcas picked up the newspaper and pulled out a few sheets. 'Put that across your chest. Keep the wind off.' Letty did so and Dorcas picked up her shawl and put it around Letty's neck, tucked it between the lapels of her coat. On impulse, Letty leaned forward and kissed her soft cheek. In seven years she'd never once been so close, and when she drew back she noticed that tears pooled in the old woman's eyes. Letty's instinct was to hug her, but Dorcas suddenly tensed and quickly turned from her, concentrating her attention on the clock on the mantel.

'It'll be a few hours afore Alec lands,' she said, tapping the mantel. 'Make the most of your time with the Parkers. They'll be glad of your company.' With a swift movement she turned, picked up the plate from the table and went back to the pantry.

It was bitterly cold outside, and frost sparkled on the tops of the low front walls of the terraced houses. At the end of the road, lights burned bright in the Clee Park on the corner of Park Street and Grimsby Road. The pub had become Alec's local when they moved to Park Street. He would no doubt be in there tomorrow to celebrate his catch or drown his sorrows, but she allowed him that, as long as he was home with her and the kiddies for the rest of his time ashore. Three and four weeks in rough seas, in a cramped bunk with no home comforts, only hardship and long hours. It was the skipper who carried the responsibility for his crew, and the ship, and the company profits, let alone a good haul. The most dangerous job in the world – and that was in peacetime. There wasn't a month that passed when news didn't come that a ship was lost somewhere along the coast, and even when a ship made it safely home not all the crew did. It was the same in Hull and Fleetwood, in Aberdeen and Boston and every port in existence. There wasn't a fisherman's wife the world over who didn't know the price of fish. It was paid for in men's lives.

The trains were still, the wagons empty, waiting for fish to be landed in the early hours, sold and then transported all over the country. She made her way past the police box on Humber Street and down Fish Dock Road, electric lights enabling her to see her way clearly.

There had been much innovation during the war; many of the trawlers now had wireless onboard that enabled them to keep in contact. The navy had left behind many of those benefits when they withdrew from the docks.

Ahead of her, she made out the dark shapes of men making their way to their vessels and beyond them the long dark outline of the dock tower, visible from land and sea, a marker that meant home for all who looked for it. As she turned in the direction of the water, she adjusted her shawl so that it covered her mouth and cheeks and was warmed by her own breath. It was a bright night, and the stars were scattered across the heavens, some brighter than others. Alec had taught her the constellations. Though she'd known a few as a girl, she did not know them all. He had learned to steer by the stars, knowing his position only by the placement of Orion and Ursa Major, Ursa Minor and numerous other guiding lights. She had come here knowing very little of the fishing life and now her knowledge was equal to that of the land, when to plant by the quarters of the moon, when best to harvest. Her two worlds had somehow combined. She thought of Dorcas and her admission that it had been Alec's choice to come here. It had caused so much heartache, Letty made guilty for something that was not of her making.

As she turned into Henderson Street, she saw two men going into the premises next door to Parker's. It was hard to tell in the light and from a distance, but she was certain that one of them was Arthur Marshall. But what on earth would a man like him be doing here at this time of night? Whoever it was had obviously seen her, for he stepped smartly into the building and disappeared. She walked down to the chandlery and took the key from her coat pocket, opened the door and called out to the Parkers. The door behind the counter that led to their rooms was closed tight, and as she neared it she called again, not wanting to startle them. She quietly opened the door. Percy was asleep and by the look of things, Norah had dozed off. The fire had been backed up with slack to burn through the night. Percy had a blanket over his legs, a pillow behind his head, and he did not move as Letty came into the room. Norah stirred, smiled at her, made to get up. Letty put up a hand to stop her. 'Let me warm myself and I'll make us a cuppa.' Noah roused herself. Letty unwrapped the pork pie and put it on a plate, cut two generous slices and handed them over, made them a hot drink and pulled up a chair.

'What time do you expect Alec?'

Letty glanced to the clock. A couple of hours, no more than that. His ship was in the estuary, and by all accounts close to the front. They had been waiting in the river for a few hours, the long line of trawlers a familiar sight along the horizon. She often wondered how it must feel to be so close to home, waiting for the tide to turn.

As Letty gradually thawed, she removed her outdoor clothing and they chatted quietly, Letty leaning forward and adjusting the coals as the slack burned through and gave off more heat. When

Percy moved, Letty got up and made him comfortable, handed him a hot drink and a biscuit. When he wanted to use the chamber pot, she picked up the coal bucket and went outside to fill it. The air was crisp and sharp and her breath curled in front of her. She heard noises from next door – men's laughter and a banging of tables, scraping of chairs – and wondered what they were at to be there so late. There were limited comings and goings to the building during the day; many times she'd thought that Gilbert Crowe had bought it to spite her. Buying it from under her nose had been repayment for thwarting him over the Parkers. But if all he wanted it for in the end was storage, why would it matter? And what was Arthur Marshall doing there this late at night? What was anyone? She glanced to the clock. It was long after eleven. The lock gates would be open, the trawlers making their way to the wharf.

She went back into the room, keeping her voice low, and pressed her ear against the dividing wall. She could hear muffled voices, nothing of any clarity. They took no care whether the Parkers heard or not – they knew they wouldn't complain.

'What are they up to, do you think, Letty?'

'No good. Why else would they be there?'

'I did inform the dock police but there's not much they can do – or are willing to do. Gilbert owns the shop and it's up to him what he does with it. They've knocked and walked around inside but it's only boxes according to PC Hall.'

'Bugger,' Percy managed to say.

'Aye, Percy. It is.' She felt impotent. If she knocked to tell them to keep the noise down, she knew she'd only get a mouthful of abuse. She turned her attention to the dishes and began to wash them quietly. The door to the shop had not clicked shut fully and as she went to close it, she heard a noise from inside the shop. She looked to Norah and pressed a finger to her lips. She knew every creak of every floorboard. She slipped off her boots, and Norah came and placed them side by side. Letty held her hand to keep her back. Norah pointed to her swollen belly, but Letty dismissed it with a shake of her head. She wasn't going to do anything; she just wanted to know what was going on. She took hold of the doorknob and gently drew it towards her, letting the light spill out a little, waiting for her eyes to adjust to the semi-darkness before creeping out behind the counter.

It was hard to be light on her feet, her centre of gravity out of kilter. Light from a small lamp lit a shadowy figure and she knew at once who it was. She stood up, hands to her hips as she went out to confront him.

'Well, well, well. If it isn't Mr Crowe.'

Her voice boomed out and startled him, so much so that he dropped the clothing in his hands and it fell to his feet. She heard Norah come to join her. As Gilbert twisted to face her, he knocked the lamp that he had left precariously balanced on a pile of trousers. Paraffin spilled onto the clothing, and he leaped back as it caught fire. Letty screamed.

'You bloody fool, Letty Hardy,' he snarled at her. She dashed forward, trying to beat it out with a wax coat, but it had already spread. Norah called out to her. Letty turned. There was no way out by the rear of the shop. She had to get them out and she couldn't manage Percy on her own. The paraffin had spread across the floor and pieces of paper curled and rose in the air, falling on other items. A stash of paraffin tins were locked in a cupboard and it wouldn't take long before the fire reached it. It would block their way entirely if they didn't get out. Gilbert made for the door.

Letty screeched at him. 'They can't get out the back! We have to get Percy.'

He hesitated. She screamed again and ran into the back room. Norah had got Percy out of the chair. Letty pulled the chenille cloth from the table and dropped it in the sink among the pots. She threw a tea towel in with it and pulled it out again, dripping with water, and thrust it into Norah's hands. 'Put it over your head and get out, Norah.' To her relief, Gilbert appeared at her side.

'But...'

'Go,' Letty urged. 'We'll get Percy out.' That the day had come when she had to put her faith in Gilbert Crowe sickened her, but getting out alive, no matter who helped, was all she could think of. Gilbert had pulled Percy's arm about his shoulder and was moving forward with a strength and stamina that belied his wiry frame. Letty hauled the tablecloth, dripping with water, and spread it over the old man's shoulders, put her shoulder under Percy's armpit and used all the strength she had to lift his weight, tugging at the tablecloth and covering her hair.

'Stay close,' Gilbert shouted to her as they made their way into the shop. Norah was in front of them and Letty saw her making for the door. She was shocked how quickly the fire had spread. Flames leaped from every quarter, and she heard the window shatter and splinter. There was no going back; they had to go into the fire. The flames had caught hold and were travelling towards the tallow. If that went there was nothing to do but go back into the yard and hope that someone would come and put the fire out before they burned to death.

She would not contemplate it. Beyond the flames and smoke, people were shouting, and she heard the sound of water coming into the shop. Gilbert led the way, taking most of Percy's weight as he dragged them forward. Her groin ached and the smoke stung her eyes as they blundered blindly on, towards people calling out to them. A burly man came towards them, a scarf across his nose and mouth, taking Percy from her, pushing her forward. Someone caught hold of her arm and hauled her out and she stumbled, almost fell but the arm that held her was strong. Her feet barely touched the ground when someone else grabbed her and she was carried forward. It was the last thing she saw before being showered with water, the coldness making her shudder before a blanket was thrown about her and she was lifted up and away from danger. Gilbert fell to his knees.

'Norah! Norah!' she gasped, tears blinding her. Her mouth and nostrils were dry, her hair dripping with seawater. She saw Percy on the pavement, lying on his side, Norah bending over him, crying and coughing. She was carried beyond them until she suddenly felt the cool air on her face as the wind blew down off the sea. The window that had cracked with the heat, the gold letters of *Percy Parker – Ship's Outfitters* blackened and blistered. She watched the flames light up the street as they went up into the roof and into the buildings either side. A bell rang out in the distance, getting closer by the second. People gathered to help, some to watch helplessly. She could see the crowd parting, someone pushing through, shouting her name. Alec stopped at the shop, his face wrought with fear, and tried to enter it, but he was held back, and a man pointed to Letty. He ran to her, pulling her into his arms and held her so tightly that it hurt. She wanted to cry but couldn't; she wanted to scream and rage, but she could do nothing, only stay in his arms, limp and useless. A lifetime, a whole lifetime and it was her fault.

'Oh, God, Letty.' He crushed her to him, his hand on her head, messing her hair. 'When they said there was a fire on Henderson Street...' His voice broke. 'I thought I'd lost you.'

She tried to pull away from him. 'Percy?' Her voice was

barely audible against the noise of the commotion of people tackling the fire. He held her face, brushing her hair away from it.

'He's safe. Norah too.'

She didn't believe him. She'd seen him on the floor.

'Percy. Norah, Norah,' she called out. 'Let me go to them, Alec. Where are they? Where are they?' She writhed to free herself, but he held on to her. She saw the fear in his face. It frightened her and he knew it. Alec craned his neck, looking over their heads, searching, searching until he found what he was looking for. He gripped her arm with one hand and made people move back with the other, guiding her through the crowd of men who had come to help. 'Don't fret, my lovely lass. I can see the old boy; they're putting him in a wagon.'

'Is Norah there? Is someone with him?' Suddenly she didn't need to ask for she could see the cart and Norah being helped up onto to it, taking a seat at her husband's side. Letty pulled away and this time Alec let her go, keeping close. 'Norah?'

Norah turned and Letty wanted to sob; she looked so suddenly old and frail. She managed a smile for Letty and nodded, raised her hand. Letty stood at the wagon, saw someone checking Percy's pulse. The old man was coughing and spluttering and a sob caught in her throat to hear it. She pushed her face into the wood of the wagon, not wanting to cry, not yet. For Norah's sake.

The wagon moved off and Alec held her up until she could see it no more. When it was gone from sight, her knees give way; she would have sunk to the floor were it not for Alec. People moved past them, the fire under control, and she caught phrases here and there:

'Hope the old boy's alright.'

'I bought me first pair o' seaboots from ol' Percy.'

'Poor old sod. What a way for it all to end.'

She pressed her hands to her ears, wanting to block it out, looking to Alec to tell her that it was a dream, a nightmare, that it wasn't real, even though she knew it was. He gently took her in his arms and pulled her to his chest. Above them smoke filled the sky, obscuring the stars.

* * *

Gilbert Crowe had scrabbled from his knees, tearing himself away from men who gripped his shoulders, slapping him on the back for being the hero of the hour, and pushed his way through the crowd of men intent on limiting the damage. The door to Webster's was wide open and he hesitated, staggered past it, wanting to distance himself from the fire, the chaos. At the bottom of the street, he stopped to catch his breath. Flames licked across all three buildings, the wind taking the flames towards the premises on Wharncliffe Road. Marshall's offices. He stared helplessly. If they caught fire... His stomach twisted. Another fire wagon came behind him; men rushed past, jostling him out of the way. He staggered against the wall. Marshall would blame him. He wouldn't see it as an accident and Letty Hardy wouldn't keep her mouth shut. He needed time to think. To plan. He needed to disappear.

27

When the wagon left with Percy and Norah, Letty insisted she go back to see what was left of the shop, but Alec wouldn't let her. The fire no longer lit up the sky and a dense cloud of black smoke hung over Henderson Street.

'What's left of it will still be there in the morning.'

'While people help themselves to the Parkers' belongings.'

'They have enough friends to guard it, Let. I need to get you home.' He sent a lad to fetch a taxi and put her in it, while she complained of the expense.

'What about the landing? You'll miss the market.'

He placed his hands to her lips. 'The mate will see to it. I sent word.'

The colour drained from Dorcas's face when they walked into the back room in the early hours. 'What on earth...' She leaped from her chair as Alec gently made Letty sit down in the one opposite and briefly told his mother what had happened. Letty's face was black with soot and streaked with white where her tears had fallen. Her hair and clothes reeked of smoke, and she did not fight Dorcas when she quietly removed them and covered her with blankets. Dorcas filled a bowl with warm water and fetched a flannel, a towel and a bar of sweet-smelling soap and tenderly washed her face. Letty inhaled the scent of roses as Dorcas moved to her hands, her arms then the rest of her body as if she were a small child. While his mother tended to her, Alec explained in more detail what had happened. She caught the odd word but all she could see and hear were the flames and the sight of Percy and Norah leaving for the hospital.

'We'll leave your hair until tomorrow, lass.' Dorcas had wiped it as best she could with a scrap of flannel, trying to remove the smell that was deep inside Letty's nostrils and caught in her throat. She watched as Dorcas bustled about, spent of energy, not caring of her modesty nor anything else she might have once hidden from her mother-in-law, utterly defeated. Her clothes were scooped into a pile and there was a cold blast when Dorcas opened the back door and put them outside. It was not the homecoming they had expected. Alec squatted on his haunches by the chair, holding her hand and planting long kisses on it, looking into her eyes, putting his hand to her face, sweeping back her hair as it fell about her and tucking it to her left shoulder. 'Give her this,' Dorcas said, pushing a mug of hot milk into his hands. He held it out to her, urged her to sip, but the taste turned her stomach, and she retched. A glass of water replaced it, then a welcoming cup of tea, strong and dark and sweet, Dorcas making it all without so much as a murmur of complaint.

'Perhaps we should get the doctor out.'

Letty shook her head. 'I'm alright,' she insisted. 'I'll be fine.'

Dorcas sucked her cheeks, looked to Alec.

'I'll watch over her, Mother.' There was no argument, no talk of his trip and what price it might fetch, the familiar conversation as he ate his meal. His mother sat opposite him at the table and while they talked Letty stared into the fire, contained in the grate, thinking of the damage it had done on Henderson Street. Percy and Norah had lost their home and their livelihood in one fell swoop.

* * *

In their bed, Alec had held her in his arms, her head wild with thoughts of the happenings of the last few hours. To think of Gilbert sneaking into the shop night after night, making Norah think she was losing her mind. She'd blamed Pearl when instinct had told her otherwise. Why had she not listened? How had she not realised what had been going on right under their noses? Images of Percy swam into her head, the fear on Norah's face. Gilbert hesitating. The lamp. The fire. Her eyes grew heavy and finally she succumbed to sleep.

Alec was not beside her when she awoke, and she glanced at the small alarm clock on the bedside table and saw that it was after eleven. She'd not heard the children, nor Dorcas, as she usually did. The water in the wash bowl on the chest of drawers was cold. She splashed herself and got dressed. Alec must have heard her moving about for he came up to her.

'You should have woken me.'

'You needed to sleep.'

'You'll be gone. I've wasted time.' She remembered the fire and sank down onto the bed. 'I had hoped it was a bad dream.'

He sat down beside her. 'Would that it was.' He clasped her hand.

'I must go to the shop.' It might not be as bad as it had looked. Help had come quickly, and she thanked the good Lord that there had been people about, grateful that it had been a late tide. That they had all got out alive.

'There's not much left of it,' Alec said, quietly, stroking her hand.

'You've been there?'

'Not yet. Didn't have to. Puggy came and told us.'

'Percy? Norah?'

'Still at the hospital.'

'I must go.'

'You'll have something to eat first. Mother's got some porridge on the go. She sent Alfie out for cream from the Maypole before he went to school.'

Reluctantly, Letty did as she was told. The kitchen was warm and there was no sense of the horrors of the night before. She was grateful that the children had been in bed and known nothing of it. She bent over at the kitchen sink and Alec washed her hair, his strong hands gentle as he rubbed at her scalp, then rinsed it, wrapping a towel about her shoulders. She took a seat at the table and Dorcas placed a bowl of porridge in front of her.

'I'm not hungry.'

'I don't imagine you are,' Dorcas said kindly, 'but if you can't think of yourself, you must think of the baby.'

Letty picked up the spoon and dipped it into the porridge. As she put it into her mouth, tears came; she couldn't hold them back, though she did not make a sound.

Dorcas rubbed at her arm. 'Don't worry about the kiddies, or the café. Hilda will take care of things.'

'Everything's in hand,' Alec told her. 'Puggy and the boys are watching over the shop and trying to salvage what they can. They're all worried about you and the baby. Please, Letty, don't upset yourself.'

'I need to see Percy and Norah. To know for myself that they're alright.'

'We'll get a taxi. I'll find one outside the Clee Park while you get yourself ready.' They were always outside the pub, and numerous others. Fishermen with money to spend and little time to spend it would think the expense worthwhile.

'We can't afford to throw money about. Not now.' The shop had provided both families with a good income.

'Money will come and go, like the tide. You can't walk there, and you'll not be waiting for a tram. Not today.'

* * *

At the hospital, Alec was her voice and found the ward. As they entered, she saw Norah sitting at Percy's bedside, her hand placed on his. Her grey hair was in a mess, her clothes burned and blackened, and Letty inhaled the bitter smoke again. Norah turned and Letty stared at Percy's lifeless body, his eyes closed, his cheeks sunken, all colour drained from it. She searched for the rise and fall of his chest and saw none. Norah shook her head. 'He's gone, Letty. Not five minutes ago.'

A sob caught in Letty's throat, and she put her hand to it in an effort to hold it all back. Norah got up and Letty hurried to her, wrapped her arms about her, Norah suddenly shrunken in her embrace. When she released her, her grief came with such a force that she bent forward as if it had leaped on her back. Behind her, Alec caught at her arms and pressed her into the chair next to Norah. Somehow, she managed to stem her tears, the ugly sounds that had come from her, and she felt ashamed. Norah had lost her husband, her only love. How dare Letty succumb to such selfish sorrow. She took a deep breath, composed herself.

'It wasn't the fire, Letty,' Norah explained. 'It was another stroke. I had expected it to come at any moment. Every extra day I had with him was a blessing.'

'If I hadn't gone into the shop, startled Gilbert...'

Norah took a firm hold of her hand. 'It is *not* your fault. None of it is. Gilbert should not have been there. If we lay the blame anywhere, it is at his feet.'

Rage surged around her body. Alec pressed his hands on her shoulders as if to keep her feet to the ground, for she was suddenly overcome with an energy that would have propelled her all the way to Henderson Street to hunt him down. She pushed again to get up and once more Alec pushed her down with gentle pressure. Eventually she gave up and sat with Norah, holding her hand. Alec left them and returned a few moments later, a doctor to one side of him, a nurse to the other.

'Now then, Mrs Hardy. We can't have you upsetting yourself like this. It's not good for baby.'

She protested, unwilling to leave Norah, but the old woman touched her arm.

'It will set my mind at rest if you go with them.'

Letty pressed her lips together, nodded, and looked to Percy, so still. All the life gone from him.

'He's not in pain any more, Letty. Think on that. I'll still be here when you get back.'

When the doctor had checked her over and found her to be well, and the baby none the worse for the experience, she went back to Norah. 'Please come home with us, Norah. You can't stay here.'

Norah got up and touched Percy's hand, kissed his pale lips. 'I've nowhere else to go. And there's nowhere else I'd rather be. Not now.'

Norah leaned over and kissed Percy's forehead, whispered

something to his ear, patted his hand for one last time. She spent a few minutes more standing at his side while Letty and Alec waited for her by the door until she was ready to leave. She took a deep breath, pulled back her shoulders and turned away. As she walked towards them, Letty stepped forward, linked her arm through Norah's and left the ward. Norah didn't look back.

* * *

When they left the hospital, Norah told them she wanted to go to Henderson Street. Alec tried to dissuade her.

'I appreciate your concern, Alec. But I'd like to see for myself.'

He couldn't deny her and though Letty was afraid, it was better faced if Alec was at her side. On the Boulevard, they stopped a wagon, which dropped them on Fish Dock Road. Alec helped Norah down and she waited on the pavement for Letty to join her. The two women linked arms and made their way down to Parker's Chandlery. The debris of blackened wood and broken glass had been swept up and shovelled into oversize buckets then loaded onto a wagon. A handful of men, their shirts and trousers protected by long aprons, came and went, clearing what was of no use, creating a pile of what could be salvaged. From this distance the pile was very small. Norah stopped, then took a deep breath and carried on down the street. Men stopped their work and removed their caps.

'Careful, Norah love,' one of them said as she stopped in front of what was her and Percy's livelihood and home. The window was gone and the interior blackened. The counter remained and the floor to the room above still held. Above the gold letters that bore the name *Percy Parker – Ship's Outfitters* was bubbled and covered with soot. Panes were missing from the oriel window that jutted out on the first floor. The fire had spread to the premises either side and Gilbert Crowe's newsagent and tobacconist had suffered a similar fate. Letty followed Norah into the shop. Two men wielding large brooms were clearing the floor of mangled saucepans, burned boots and other items that were once on sale at Parker's. Some might be salvaged but couldn't be sold. What was left was useless. Norah stepped carefully and found her way to the counter, no doubt remembering all the hours she'd stood behind it, Percy wedging himself in the gap between counter and shop floor, a pencil behind his ear, reading the local newspaper. Letty wanted to weep, not for herself but for Norah, as she walked among the blackened ruins of what had been their entire life.

'Thank God he never lived to see it,' Norah said quietly. 'He couldn't have come back to this.' She gave Letty a sad smile. 'We never had a day apart. I can't remember life without him.' Out of respect, the men had stopped sweeping.

'It's a good job Gilbert Crowe was passing,' one of them said. 'I heard he got everyone out safely, like.'

Letty pounced on him.

'Gilbert Crowe!' she screamed. 'Don't you dare make him out to be anything but the thieving scum he is. This was all down to him, the fire – if he hadn't been sneaking about...'

Alec had been talking to one of the men outside and he ran over the rubble and caught her arm. 'Let, don't upset yourself.'

She wrested her arm from his grip. 'Upset myself! I'll scream it from the top of the ruddy dock tower, creeping about in the middle of the night, stealing things, moving things. Trying to make out Norah was losing her mind. I'll kill him myself if he ever dares show his face again.'

Norah came out from behind the counter and she was ashamed of herself. But the very idea that people could think he was some kind of hero… The man held on to the broom, unsure of how to react. Alec came close again and said in a low voice, 'Let, folk don't know the details. They're just trying to help.'

'They can help by getting the facts straight.' Her voice trembled and she didn't want to cry, not when Norah was being so stoic. But they couldn't hold on to a lie and have Gilbert as some hero who had saved them all from a fire he was responsible for. She took a breath and spoke to all the men about. 'You let everyone know that Gilbert Crowe started the fire with his own hand. He wanted the Parkers out for years and he's succeeded – and I hope he rots in hell.' Norah went back behind the counter and Letty followed her. The two chairs were still facing the grate, blackened, as was the table.

Puggy came down the staircase and looked to Norah with great pity. 'How's Percy?'

Norah's small shake of her head told him everything he needed to know. His face changed and he responded with a small nod of acknowledgement. He went to Norah and pressed her hand in his. No words were exchanged until Puggy found his voice. 'Best not to go up, Norah. We don't know if the floor's safe. We'll get everything out and clean it up. Mr Evans has offered a room at the Excel offices to store it in.'

She put her hand to his wrist. 'Thank you. I appreciate that, Puggy.'

PC Hall came into the shop. He came to Letty, glanced at her swollen belly. 'When you're ready, Mrs Hardy, could we have a word about what happened? Mr Crowe's name has been mentioned as being present, but no one has seen him since.'

'He'll be hiding in some dark alley. This is down to him.'

Letty threw up her hand and looked about her, the Parkers' life reduced to ash. Tears coursed down her cheeks.

'The insurance money will help,' Puggy offered.

Norah looked about her. 'Money won't replace a lifetime of memories. The hardships, the friends. To some people it's just a small shop in a small street, but to Percy Parker it was the centre of the world.'

28

The report of the fire at Parker's had been in the evening's newspaper. Cyril folded it and placed it on the table to the side of him. 'It could have been disastrous for us if it had spread any further. The damage to our offices would have been extensive.' He drew on his cigar, blew out the smoke and eased back into the leather chair. 'Where's Crowe now?'

Arthur poured himself a large whisky. 'I haven't the damnedest idea.' He drank, swallowed, enjoyed the bite in his throat as the fire hit. He walked over to the fireplace and stood by the hearth, resting his glass on the mantel.

'Bloody fool of a man. There'll be no end of delays while the police investigate and the insurance company poke and prod around the place. I was hoping to have things all wrapped up by the end of the year.' Cyril smoothed his moustache with his thumb and forefinger, deep in thought. 'There'll be rebuild costs to consider but we might get the job lot for a good price. It could work in our favour.' He puffed again on his cigar, tipped back his head and exhaled. 'Better tell Crowe to get his story straight.'

Arthur turned to face the fire, his back to his father. 'I've told him to disappear.' He'd wanted to disappear himself. When the reporter had stopped him, he'd made sure to mention that he'd been working late at the office and had been alerted by the smell of smoke and the sound of breaking glass.

'You bloody fool. Every man and his dog will be looking for him.'

But Arthur couldn't afford for Gilbert to be around to shoot his mouth off. He knew too much.

'I don't know that he can be trusted.' The man had been devoid of his wits when he spoke to him, Arthur dragging him away in the pretence that he was getting him to a doctor. He had prayed Webster's would go up and everything in it, hiding all traces of what had been going on there for the last few years. They had stolen naval supplies and sold them on. They had double-ordered their own stock to set against the tax and sent their ships to sea with short rations. No one dared question it – they didn't want to lose what little work there was – and if they did, the paperwork was always in order. Arthur made sure of it. There was always someone short of cash and willing to turn a blind eye for a grease of their palm. The chandlery would have made a good front for it, making it easy enough to load things through the frontage on Wharncliffe Road and sell it on Henderson Street. But his father knew nothing of his gambling, or that he used Webster's for illegal sessions. It wouldn't take long for the police to see what had been going on. The card game had been abandoned when they heard the cries for help, and the smell of smoke was hard to ignore. He'd been losing heavily and had succumbed to writing IOUs before they had an inkling at what was going on next door. He had made to grab his promissory note from the table, but Shackleton had beaten him to it. Hopefully, all other evidence of their underhand dealings would have been lost to the fire.

'Suspicion will fall on Mrs Hardy. Why was she there so late at night if not to commit arson? There are a lot of questions to be asked... and if Crowe isn't about...?'

'Then why was Crowe about at all at that hour?' his father snapped. 'You haven't thought this through.'

Arthur walked back to the drinks table and refreshed his glass. The fire hadn't meant to happen. The old boy was on his last legs. Hardy was the problem. He'd loathed having her at the wedding and had tried to sever the relationship she had with Ruth. She was smart as a tack. But if suspicion fell on Letty Hardy, it would divert all attention from Marshall's and buy him a little more time.

* * *

Alec had left on the evening tide. There had not been time to make plans or even to know if he'd had a good trip. Dorcas had washed his gear and got it ready for his sailing. To her shame, Letty had not given it a thought. When it came time for him to leave, she had been numb, her thoughts with Norah, with Percy. They had gathered what they could from the shop and brought it home. It was enough that Norah had a change of clothes.

Dorcas had taken care of everything. Stella's room had been made available to Norah for as long as she needed it. Letty had always intended to convert the best room at the front of the house for Percy and Norah. It was too late.

Alec had held her close, his bag at his feet, dressed in his going-away gear, his cap in his pocket. She had leaned into his chest, drawing on his strength. 'I hate to leave you, Let. But if I don't go, I'll miss the sailing.'

She had nodded, though it took all her willpower to let him go.

'I could stay?'

She shook her head. 'What good would that do us? We have no income from the shop now, and to lose yours on top of it would add to the worry.' If Alec didn't turn up to take command of his ship, there would be plenty willing to take his place. The ship would not be held in dock a minute longer than it had to be; the turnaround time before it went out to sea again was tight. A ship in dock was costing the firm money, with no consideration that a man who had been away from his family for weeks on end might want to spend a few more hours with them. Especially at times like this.

'I haven't had the chance to tell you afore, but I don't know when I'll be back. Hammond put me back on the fleets.'

It was what Letty had feared all along. Alec was a good skipper, he was successful for the firm and as such he would sail out on one vessel, fill the holds with fish, then be transported to another empty vessel to do the same again. Alec had the rare knack of being able to smell the fish – it was born in him. It meant he could be away for months. He kissed his hand and pressed it to her belly.

'Stay safe, little one.'

She placed her hand over his. 'Make sure you stay safe too.'

* * *

On the morning after Alec sailed, Letty got up early, ready to open the café. Dorcas was already downstairs, the fire lit and the bread in the oven, a pan of porridge bubbling on the stove.

'Did you sleep?'

'A little.' Letty put grips in her mouth, twisted her hair into a knot and fixed it in place.

'Why don't you go back to bed?'

'I'm going to open up the café.'

'You are not. Hilda will do it. I'll go in later to see to things.'

'You've already done enough. I need to do my share. It's Hardy's, remember – the two of us.' Her voice broke at the thought there was no longer Parker's to go to. No Percy. There would never be two of the Parkers again.

'Letty—'

'I have to.' She pressed her hands to the table, stared at grain of the wood, the scars, the stains. 'I can't bear to sit in the house doing nothing.'

She chose to walk, wanting the breeze to blow away the images that filled her head, wanting to feel connected to the earth, to be anchored instead of the constant sensation that she was adrift. On Gorton Street she hesitated, tempted to make for Henderson Street, and decided against it. This time she didn't have Alec to lean on. Men lifted their caps, their faces sorrowful, and women gave her gentle nods in acknowledgement of her grief, her loss.

She was glad to open up, to hear the key turn pleasantly in the lock, aware of every noise, every sensation, the world suddenly thrown into sharpness. As she pushed the door open, she was gratified that it was all still there, with the mugs and plates, the tables scrubbed, the chairs tucked neatly beneath them. She put on her apron and set pans on to boil for hot water, then checked the cutlery was clean and in order. It was wasted effort; she knew it would be. Dorcas and Hilda had kept everything running smoothly. When Hilda and her daughter Polly came in, she kept them at arm's length. She wasn't looking for sympathy, only to grasp at the normality of life. A while later a familiar face appeared at the window and Letty went outside.

'Pearl.'

'I heard about Mr Parker. I came to offer my condolences. I didn't know where to find Mrs Parker.'

Letty could barely look at the girl she had wronged. 'She'll be staying with me for a while. I'll tell her I've seen you.' A bitter taste rose in her mouth. 'I'm so sorry we dismissed you, Pearl. It wasn't your fault.' She hadn't the energy to explain, didn't want to speak of Crowe again, not today. Not when she was only just managing to keep the lid on the pot of her anger.

Pearl gingerly reached out and touched a gentle hand to Letty's arm. 'Please don't upset yourself, Mrs Hardy. You did what you thought was right.'

'Can you forgive me?'

'Nothing to forgive.' She smiled. 'I'm very happy at the Royal Hotel. I have some lovely friends now and I'm settled. I save what I can.'

Letty hardly dared ask. 'And Sidney?'

'I got a postcard. He's on a merchant ship. Gone to Argentina. He'll be back next year.' The girl was possessed of a cast-iron belief that he'd return, even if evidence told her otherwise. Letty wished she had some of her certainty.

'Make sure you bring him to see us when he does.'

Pearl said that she would and when she turned away, Letty went back inside the café. They were busier than usual and there wasn't time to stop and talk. It was what she had wanted. As things were slowing down, she went out from behind the counter to clear the tables, tray in hand. She set it down and began to add the dirty crockery to it. A man was reading the early edition of the *Grimsby News*.

'More about the fire at Parker's.' He pressed a dirty finger to the print. Letty leaned over, then took it from him, began to read aloud. '"Thanks to the quick thinking of Mr Gilbert Crowe, who had been working late at his own premises, Mr and Mrs Parker were rescued before the flames took hold."'

Letty was incandescent with rage. She banged a tin mug on the table until everyone looked around and stopped. 'I don't care what you read in the paper – any one of them. Gilbert Crowe started the fire. He was causing mischief, and I caught him at it. He startled and the lamp fell. He was saving his own skin, a rat leaving a sinking ship.'

'But he did help,' the owner of the newspaper said.

'But he wasn't going to.' She looked about her. 'If you hear anyone saying any different, send them to me.'

Hilda hurried from behind the counter, took her by the arm and sat her down. Polly came with a mug of tea, ignoring the customers who waited to give their orders.

'Don't upset yourself so, Letty. Everyone knows it's just gossip.'

Letty didn't have any more words. She took the mug Polly held in front of her and supped from it. If they believed Crowe to be the hero, what else would they believe?

29

Two weeks after fire had destroyed the chandlery, Percy Parker's funeral was held at the Bethel Mission on Tiverton Street. The church was non-denominational and though both Percy and Norah were God-fearing people, they were not regular church-goers, especially in the latter years when Percy had been far too ill to get out and about. The sheer amount of people who stood out in the rain as the small cortege made its way down Cleethorpe Road gave Norah and Letty great comfort at a time where there was little to be found elsewhere. Norah remained stoic throughout, not shedding her tears in public, though Letty knew that many were shed in private, her soft weeping sometimes sliding through the gap in her bedroom door when Letty made her way to bed.

There had been a lot of speculation over the last weeks as they moved towards Christmas. Letty and Norah had filled in endless forms for the insurance company but the investigation had been held up and it had unsettled them all, making them feel as if they had done something wrong. Neither hide nor hair had been seen of Gilbert Crowe since the fire, which only complicated matters. He was the only one who could corroborate Letty's report of what had happened. Arson had not been ruled out and Crowe was now a suspect, as was Letty. She'd been interviewed by the police on more than one occasion, as had Norah, which only added to her anger. Dorcas had tried to soothe her. 'It will all come out in the wash. It always does.'

'But how long is that going to take? And all the time we have it hanging over us.'

She was close to her time and had been no match for the two older women as they bossed her about. Norah had proved a great ally to Dorcas in that regard. Letty had no alternative but to sit back and watch as they decorated the house, hoping that by some good fortune, Alec would be home to share at least some of the Christmas season with them. Dorcas had taken Alfie with her to Freeman Street Market and bought the vegetables, and a goose from the butcher's on Cleethorpe Road. They'd been cautious with what they spent. Not that they were on their uppers, not yet at least. Alec's pay had been sent after each fish auction, which managed to keep them all ticking along. He was doing well, but sometimes Letty wished he wasn't so successful and would come home.

On Christmas Eve, the three women were sitting by the fire, filling the children's stockings. 'Another stocking next year,' Norah said, passing Letty an apple to push into the toe. She'd been wary the entire length of her pregnancy, but she had held on to the baby. The good Lord only knew how. Dorcas had been afraid she'd lose it, but Letty had kept faith, and been rewarded for it. Earlier that day she'd felt a twinge and her back had begun to ache a little. The stockings filled, she sat back and watched Dorcas and Norah prepare the veg for the morning, Norah peeling, Dorcas chopping. She got up to put another log on the fire.

'Stay where you are; I'll sort it,' Dorcas said, putting down her knife. As she moved towards Letty there was a sudden gush and water spattered about Letty's feet.

'Well, what a time for that to happen,' Norah exclaimed, wiping her hands on her apron. 'I'd better get some hot water going.'

There was little time to get her upstairs and into the bed. Dorcas lifted a sleeping Stella up from her mother's bed and put her in her own, checked that Alfie had not been disturbed, then nipped next door and asked Mr Benson to send for the midwife. Norah remained with Letty, holding one hand tightly, her other stroking Letty's hot forehead.

The midwife had not long put down her bag when Letty felt the urge to push. Letty held on to the bed rail, biting on a rag so as not to make too much noise. In the end it all happened so quickly that Letty gasped with surprise when the baby almost slid out into the midwife's hands.

Norah had not released her grip of Letty's hand, wincing only slightly when Letty had gripped it fit to break her bones. 'Well, how wonderful,' the midwife said as she turned to place the baby on the end of the bed. 'Who's a lucky boy.' She twisted to Letty. 'He's been born with a caul.'

Letty sat up on her elbows, peering at the midwife as she removed the protective veil, a part of the amniotic sac, from the baby's face.

'Oh, praise the good Lord above,' Dorcas said, peering down at the child, her hand to her throat, then moving it to cover her mouth. She was smiling and crying at the same time. 'It's a good omen, Letty. Oh, if only my boy were here to see it. Now take it carefully.'

The midwife sucked in her cheeks. 'Mrs Hardy. I know it's a rare occurrence, but I also know how precious these things are, especially in a town like this. Why don't you get me a sheet of clean brown paper to place it on. Then we can be sure we have preserved it and given it its due respect.'

Dorcas needed no further encouragement and scurried off to the kitchen. Norah got up to leave but Letty asked her to stay. The midwife made to hand the baby over to the mother. Letty shook her head, indicated that she wanted Norah to hold her son. Norah made to protest but Letty insisted she take him first. The old woman cradled him as if he were made of glass.

While the midwife washed her hands, Dorcas returned with the paper and carefully stretched out the caul. 'He'll never drown with this, Letty,' Dorcas said, carefully laying out the caul on the paper. He wouldn't go to sea at all if Letty had her way, but she would take the superstition as insurance. It would bring him luck either way.

'Do you have a name for baby Hardy?' the midwife asked, rubbing a towel over her hands and up to her elbows. Letty looked at the bundle in Norah's arms. She hoped the baby gave her some comfort.

'William,' she said, looking to Dorcas. 'But we'll call him Billy. William... Percy... Hardy.'

Norah looked at her and back at the baby, and beamed down at him. 'He would have been very proud to know his name lived on through a child of yours, Letty. He loved you so.'

Letty had never doubted it. Percy had not been one for sentiment but he showed his affection for her in so many ways, in their easy banter, in the small words of praise. She felt her throat tighten with emotion and swallowed back her tears.

When the midwife was happy with the health of both baby and mother, she packed her black leather bag and Dorcas showed her out. When Dorcas returned, Letty was feeding the baby.

'You must wireless Alec,' Letty told her. 'Let him know he has a son. His firstborn son.' She loved Alfie with all her heart, as did Alec, but this boy was made from each of them, flesh and bone. She stared at the babe in her arms. 'How proud he will be.'

It was too much for Dorcas and she couldn't look at her daughter-in-law lest her face betray her. She went to Letty and bent her head over the child, touched his dear little face. He was a big baby, as Alec had been. He would be strong, like his father, and his father before him. Letty's face shone with pride and Dorcas's heart broke to see it. Her fool son had taken so much away from her. 'I'll send a wire first thing in the morning.'

30

Christmas passed in a blur of visitors and friends who came to wish Letty well and press a silver coin into the baby's hand. Dorcas paraded the caul for anyone who cared to look, holding out the fold of brown paper while people smiled – or grimaced before quickly turning back to the baby. Ruth visited the day after Boxing Day, bringing a small gift for Stella and Alfie to celebrate their new sibling, flowers for Letty, and an expensive layette for Billy, the likes of which Letty had never seen, the soft cotton gown decorated with fine lace. She stayed for an hour, cradling Billy for the duration of her visit and Letty hoped it would not be too long before she was blessed with her own child, knowing of the happiness it would undoubtedly bring her. It seemed to Letty that a great cloud of love had arrived on the night of Billy's birth and filled every nook and cranny of the terraced house, and the constant comings and goings left little time to dwell on all the things that were left unresolved because of the fire. If she tried to speak of it, both Norah and Dorcas told her not to upset herself, to concentrate on her beautiful child. She longed for Alec, wondering when he would come home – if he would come home. The winter months at sea were always more treacherous and she forced away the black thoughts as best she could, though they seeped into her brain in the small hours while Billy slept and she lay awake, remembering.

In the first week of the new year, Letty's mother arrived and stayed for a week, the children all sleeping in with Letty to free up a bed for her mother. It lifted Letty to have her there. The euphoria of giving birth had long deserted her, and she felt as though she were being carried through the days. There was nothing to do but rest and enjoy her company.

'Things have changed since we last met,' her mother confided. 'Dorcas has been quite magnificent in the way she's kept everything going.'

'I don't know how I would have managed without her,' Letty said truthfully. She hadn't had to think of anything without discovering it had already been done. 'When we first came here, she hated the sight of me.'

'I'm sure that's not true, Letty.' Her mother didn't know the half of it. Many times she'd started to write to her mother to complain and thought better of it. Her mother would not want to think her daughter was miserable.

'It is. I wasn't what she wanted me to be.'

Her mother placed Billy down in his crib. 'No, you were something far better, and it's taken her time to realise that. She knew of nothing but hardship and sorrow, and suddenly you breezed into her life and showed her something better. You showed her kindness.'

'Only because kindness was shown to me.' She thought back to her first days here: a hovel for a home, Alec leaving after only two days and not back again for almost a month. It had been incredibly hard. 'If it hadn't been for the Parkers, I might very well have given up.'

'They felt the same; Norah told me so.' She picked up one of Billy's woollen bootees that had slipped onto the floor and searched for the other to the pair, smoothing them together. 'I know Dorcas was, shall we say, a challenge.' They shared a smile. 'Your letters were always so full of your fondness for the Parkers. Then your love for them. It eased my heart to know you had found them.'

The time with her mother passed all too quickly. Letty was bereft when she left and though she was cared for by Dorcas and Norah, it was as if a dark cloud had descended and clung to her shoulders.

Alec arrived home at the end of January. Word had come from Puggy that his ship was in the river. Dorcas fussed about making the fire and a meal, much to Norah's fascination, telling the children to be on their best behaviour when their father arrived. 'None of your endless questions when your father gets home, you Stella. Hold that tongue of yours until he gets himself sorted. We're all excited to see him. Your mother most of all.'

* * *

In spite of her grandmother's instructions, Stella rushed towards her father when she saw him and clung to his legs. 'Let me get in the door, lass,' he said, laughing.

Letty's heart was full to see him again, safe. Tired. But safe. Thank God, he was safe. Never had the smell of fish that emanated from every pore of him smelled so welcoming. He held her, kissed her head. She wanted him to lift her and hold her so she didn't have to stand, could finally let go.

'Where's my boy, my son?'

She saw a look pass between Alec and his mother.

'He was born with a caul,' Dorcas said. 'The boy is blessed.'

Letty bent into his crib and laid their child in his arms. 'Nah, then, our Billy.' He looked to Letty to confirm she'd given him the name they'd agreed on.

'William Percy Hardy,' Letty said, coming to stand beside him. She put her hand close, and the child grabbed at her finger. She would never let him go to sea; she would hold on to him as long as she could, caul or no caul.

Stella was on Alec's lap the minute he handed Billy over to his mother. Alfie was never far from Letty's side, handing her small squares of muslin to wipe the dribbles from Billy's mouth, making sure Stella wasn't getting too excitable. Alec caught his eye, gave him a nod as if to tell him what a grand job he was doing. After a time, Alec sat down to eat, his mother fussing over him as she always did, Alec talking of the sights he had seen, the narrow escapes, the good hauls. Norah and Letty smiled at each other to watch Dorcas as she topped up his mug and ladled more beef stew on his plate. He asked the children of school, all the time glancing to Letty and his boy. Their boy.

'How long before you have to go again?' Norah asked.

'Forty-eight hours. The gaffers want me back as soon as the ship's ready.'

'You'd think the more successful, the more they would want to give you a break,' Norah said. 'To rest. To spend time with your family.'

'If only it worked like that. They always want more. To be fair, so do I. If I get enough under my belt now, I can perhaps have more time home in the summer.' He pushed his empty plate away. 'Any news on the insurance?'

'Not until they find Gilbert Crowe.'

'He's not returned?'

'Gone to ground like a fox,' Norah said. 'No doubt he'll raise his head before long. Then we can get things sorted out once and for all.'

Letty didn't hold out much hope of him ever turning up, just to spite them further. She had called on his wife, two small children clinging to her as she answered the door. She denied any knowledge of his whereabouts – or any that she would tell Letty – and looked to be in a sorry state herself, her face pinched and white. What if he were dead? Things would never get resolved and all that the Parkers had invested in the shop would never be returned to them. Letty was young enough to wait but Norah was elderly; the insurance payout would leave her comfortable for what time she had left. Letty would never forgive Gilbert for putting them through this; she would never forgive herself.

One by one the children went up to bed, Norah going with them, Letty and Alec soon after, leaving Dorcas alone in front of the fire.

* * *

Dorcas raked over the coals and stirred a flame. She was not surprised when Alec came down and joined her. He stood beside her. 'How has she been?'

'Can't you tell by looking at her? The fire hit her hard, Percy's death more so. She blames herself.'

'But it's not her fault.'

'There's a lot not her fault, my lad, but it will break her heart all the same.' She picked up the coal bucket and he took it from her, threw the slack over the fire to bank it up. 'If you'd have seen how happy she was that she'd given you the son you've always wanted…'

'Nothing will change that.'

'She won't see it like that, boy.' She put the guard in front of the fire and leaned her hands on the mantelpiece. 'I pray to God she never finds out.'

* * *

When Alec left again, Letty seemed to fall further into the abyss. Some days she was brighter than others, but she'd lost the spark that drove her forward when times were difficult.

'I feel so helpless,' Dorcas confided to Norah as they cleared up after dinner. 'I've no inkling how to bring back the fight in her.' Each day it was clear she was merely going through the motions; her mind was elsewhere.

'We can only show her that we are here for her,' Norah replied. 'That's all anyone can do.'

In April, things came to a head. Alec had been away for two months and had missed their wedding anniversary. A few days after, it was her birthday. Letty arrived home from the café to find that the children had decorated the back sitting room with ribbons. The table was set with daffodils and tulips and Letty's best china tea set that had been a gift from her godmother on her marriage. Stella excitedly made her sit down and Dorcas brought out cake she had made that morning. When they gathered around the table and sang 'Happy Birthday', Norah could see that Letty was barely holding herself together. She put her hand on the cake but didn't eat it. Tears pooled in her eyes then fell onto her plate. She wiped them away.

'I think I need to...' She looked to Stella and Alfie, their faces full of their concern.

'Don't you like it, Mam?' Stella asked, taking hold of her hand. Letty wiped away more tears. Norah offered a handkerchief and Letty took it gratefully, dabbed at her eyes, her cheeks.

'It's wonderful. Truly it is.' She reached out and drew Alfie to her. Billy began to grizzle. Dorcas picked him up, soothed him. The tears kept falling.

'Let me sit in the best room for a little while. I feel a little unwell.'

Stella's face was a picture of disappointment.

Letty touched her cheek. 'I'll be right back. You've made things so lovely but I…' The child was not comforted and looked to her grandmother.

Dorcas took her hand. 'Your mother is overtired. She needs a little peace and quiet.'

Norah picked up the coal scuttle. 'Let me make the fire up. It's chilly in there.' Alfie dashed forward and took it from her. He was gone in the blink of her eye. His mother would be proud to see the wonderful young man he'd become, thanks to Letty's love and care. She'd fought for that boy, for all of them, but she had lost the fight for herself when she needed it most. Stella picked up Billy's rattle and handed it to her grandmother to settle her brother. The simple things they anticipated reminded Norah of her own childhood with her siblings. Did Dorcas appreciate all she had? If she did, Norah was quite sure that she didn't fully appreciate how important Letty was to them all. To her and Percy, the lass burned like the brightest star, and in the darkest of skies. It saddened Norah more than she could bear to see her light so dimmed.

When Norah went through to the front room, Letty was sitting in the chair, staring at the photos on the mantel. 'You miss them more than you ever say,' Norah said, taking a seat beside her.

Letty did not respond. Alfie came in with the coal bucket, set it to the hearth. Silently, he took down the matches and lit the kindling then slid from the room as quietly as he had come, gently closing the door behind him.

'Talk to me, Letty,' Norah said, leaning close. 'You used to share so much with us. Percy and I loved to hear your stories. Of your family. Of the farm. The times you helped your mother at the market.' She leaned close, teasing. 'Of Dorcas and her funny ways.' Letty's mouth stretched in a thin line. 'You can't go on like this, Letty. Percy wouldn't want you to.' Norah reached across and took her hand in hers. 'The Lord knows I didn't want to lose him, Letty, but he was frail. He was trapped inside a body that was failing him. He couldn't be all he wanted to be, and he'd given up. Don't you give up too. I need you.'

Letty nodded. Tears dropped onto their linked hands, and she lifted the other to her cheek to brush them away. 'I don't know why I'm feeling sorry for myself when I have so much to be grateful for.'

Norah freed her hand and stroked Letty's hair. 'Remember the good times, Letty, for there were so many.'

They sat together in silence and presently Letty began to talk a little. They spoke of her home, of Percy and happier times they'd shared. All so precious. Something to hold on to. When she felt Letty was calmed enough, she went to get her a drink.

Stella gave her a worried look when she walked into the kitchen. Norah smiled to reassure her. 'Your mother is in need of a cup of warm milk.'

Dorcas went to the pantry and took out a saucepan. 'How is she?'

'Melancholy as I have never seen her.' Norah took a seat at the table, held the cup of a daffodil in her hand. 'I think it would be a good idea if she went to stay with her mother for a while. We can take care of everything here, you and I.'

'Alec has already said they'll go in the summer months, when his ship is due a refit,' Dorcas said, adamant that Norah's suggestion was a bad idea, that Letty needed her husband at her side. That was the only tonic she needed. 'They won't give him time off or any allowance for circumstance. Wouldn't give a man time off for his own father's funeral.'

'I don't know if she can wait that long,' Norah said quietly. Dorcas's reluctance surprised Norah, for she was willing to do anything for the comfort and well-being of her daughter-in-law. Surely she could see that the girl was in need of mothering herself. Her own mother. Norah pressed her case and in the end Dorcas conceded.

'I'll send another wire.'

Later, when Letty joined them all in the back room and Norah suggested that Letty go home to Lowestoft for a time, it appeared to lift the girl's spirits. It gladdened Norah's heart to see it, though Dorcas still appeared reserved about it. 'Time with your mother will restore you as only a mother can.'

31

The wedding ceremony was quiet and understated, just as Evelyn had requested. She had worn a simple linen suit and a cloche hat. Arthur had been critical, and Ruth had done her best to ignore it.

'You'd think the old man would have splashed out a bit,' Arthur commented. 'Anyone would think he couldn't afford a big do.'

'It's what they wanted,' Ruth said quietly, hoping no one had heard Arthur's crass comments. Her father and Evelyn had eschewed all Aunt Helen's attempts to make it more of an occasion. And that was more down to Evelyn's strength than her father's. Ruth admired her for it. Evelyn had a self-assuredness that Ruth had never possessed. Was that down to her experiences in France? Or had she always been like that? She liked the Howards; they were kind, and that mattered more in a town where there was much ambition. Few had been invited to the wedding breakfast. It was a small and intimate gathering, close family only. Philip Proctor was the only guest present who had no connection other than his friendship with Henry. Evelyn had been radiant and her father so proud, standing before the registrar in the town hall, Jeremy and Daphne as witnesses to their signatures. Ruth thought back to her own wedding day, when she had thrown her bouquet and Evelyn had caught it, not for once imagining that it would be her own father who would fall in love with the young woman who now stood at his side. Life was full of surprises, Ruth considered as her father placed a gold band on Evelyn's finger, and she in turn on his, many of them lovely – but not all of them. The registrar pronounced them man and wife, and a few minutes later the wedding party gathered on the town hall steps for photographs, Ruth next to Arthur, the distance between them widening by the hour, before they all walked on to a private dining room at the Yarborough Hotel.

After the meal, Arthur seemed to disappear. Her aunt came to stand with her.

'We haven't seen you at the ladies' guild this year?'

'I am mired in Mildred's good deeds. She likes me to be involved in the village.' It had been hard to extricate herself from her many lunches and coffee mornings, helping with the flowers in the church, and serving teas during fundraisers at the village hall. She found the other women pleasant enough, but village life was not what she was used to. She missed the many long-standing friends she'd made at the guild, and she missed the people they served. Somehow, the car was always unavailable for Thursday afternoons and many requests had been fraught in argument. Arthur had baulked at her wanting to visit Letty after the fire, made getting there difficult until she'd suggested she take the bus. Mildred had been almost apoplectic, and the car had been made available – as it had when she'd wanted to see Letty's new baby. 'I've missed the guild. I miss Letty and the Hewitt sisters, Mrs Barton.' Unlike the women Mildred kept company with, the women of the guild were not afraid to roll up their sleeves and get on with the less pleasant chores of helping people. During the war they had scrubbed floors and washed dressings and done whatever needed doing, no matter how lowly it would have seemed to them before. It was all far removed from how she lived now.

'They all ask after you.'

'Please give them my regards.'

Her aunt narrowed her eyes. 'You're looking a little peaky, my girl. Are you eating enough – or is something else making you unwell these last few weeks? Arthur will be eager to be delivered of a son and heir.'

'It's hardly the time or place to discuss such matters.' She felt her cheeks flame. 'And the answer is no, not yet.'

'Early days,' her aunt said, quietly encouraging. 'These things take time.' She patted Ruth's arm and Ruth regretted that she had answered her so sharply. Helen Frampton was not as confident as she appeared, perhaps thinking that her niece, like herself, might never bear her own children. Helen moved, cast a glance at her brother and his bride. 'She makes your father happy.'

'She does.' The years had fallen from his face. She was fascinated by the way he looked at Evelyn as she chatted to Daphne and Jeremy. She couldn't recall Arthur once looking at her with such love. He never made her feel the way her father so obviously made Evelyn feel – like she was the most beautiful and interesting woman in the room – and Ruth wondered, not for the first time, if Arthur loved her at all, or she him. Her aunt had said love would grow but it was taking its time – on her part as well as Arthur's.

'It's not difficult to guess who the next couple will be,' Helen commented, as they watched the two couples. Daphne glanced her way and Ruth smiled. She came over to join them.

'How are you, Ruth? I haven't seen you in such a long time.'

'I am well. Keeping busy.'

'You have kept up with your sketching? Your art?'

'As much as I can.' It was her solace, her escape from the tedium of life at Garth Hall.

Jeremy went to speak with his sister. Daphne did not take her eyes off him.

'You're enjoying the surgery?' They had not seen so much of each other since Ruth's marriage, but then she hadn't seen much of anyone. Her father had told her that Daphne had taken Evelyn's position.

'Very much so. It is interesting work. Jeremy has taken it upon himself to give his time to the families of the East Marsh.' She was suddenly awkward. 'Life isn't how we thought it would be, is it?'

'Charles would want you to be happy.'

Daphne nodded, bit at her lip. 'You don't mind?'

'Why on earth would I?'

'I thought you may think that I had forgotten.'

Ruth knew what she meant, that by stepping into the flow of life again you were dishonouring their memory.

'We will never forget what we have lost,' Ruth told her. 'But we have to live on for them. Find happiness. For them. It's what they gave their lives for.'

* * *

Arthur returned and together they went over to stand with Ruth's father and Evelyn. Jeremy came to stand with Daphne and brought Philip Proctor with him.

'How was Ruth? She didn't look her usual self.'

Daphne turned, looked over to her. Ruth smiled at them and Philip's heart beat harder. 'I have to confess I haven't seen so much of her of late.'

'No, neither have I.' She seemed to be incarcerated at the house. He'd visited a few times with paintings to deliver and collect payment. Any attempt to talk with her seemed to be thwarted by Arthur.

'Not all women bloom in pregnancy.'

'Oh.' The thought hadn't crossed his mind. 'I had no idea.'

'I don't know for certain,' Daphne qualified. 'It's merely a notion. She's looking a little pale. I thought morning sickness?' She became a little flustered. 'Ruth wouldn't want to announce anything, would she? She wouldn't want to spoil the day.'

'No. Of course.' He'd felt she was concealing something. It would be easy to suppose that she was unhappy at her father's marriage. It would be hard to accept that after all these years someone would take her mother's place. But she wasn't a child, and he knew she was genuinely fond of Evelyn. What a fool he was to think it was anything else.

* * *

'Well, that's your father sorted. You won't have to worry about him being lonely any more,' Arthur said as he drove them back to Garth Hall. She hated the long drive out of Grimsby, feeling herself shrink with every mile put between them. 'I shan't have the bother of dropping you off there on a whim.'

'It was hardly a whim, Arthur.' It had been anything but, having to carefully schedule her visits to coordinate around the availability of the car. He seemed to delight in making her feel that each visit was a huge inconvenience.

'Well, the two of them won't take kindly to frequent visits from you. Evelyn will want to make the house her own. Quite right too.'

'As will I. In our own home.' She couldn't wait to get out of Garth Hall but progress on their own home had been slow, despite having all the available funds for the build, thanks to generous wedding gifts from her father and Arthur's. The money had been deposited in Arthur's bank account, as was the custom. She'd seen the plans but not been given any say in them. It had all been presented to her as a gift, as if Arthur had been the sole benefactor. Arthur had been proud of the design. She thought it far too large and proposed they scale it down. Arthur had been hurt by her suggestions. 'I understand why your father didn't want more than Meadowvale House when he lost your mother, but we will have children. And we will entertain. We can't scale down; we have to scale up. It will be expected.' He didn't enlarge on by whom.

'Have you finalised a start date with the builders?'

'Good God, Ruth. Don't harp on about it. You're a terrible nag.'

Ruth was taken aback. 'I was hardly going on. It was a simple enough question. I should like to run my home in my own way.'

'My mother's way is not good enough for you?'

'I wasn't implying...'

He pressed his foot hard on the accelerator. It was dark, the roads unmade, and they bumped along at a pace. She could see the milometer rising and she pressed herself back in the seat and away from the windscreen. 'Arthur! Slow down. Someone might step out in front of you.' The road was not straight. Only last week someone had been hit and injured.

He ignored her, pressing harder.

'Arthur!'

He slowed down, laughing. 'What's the point of having a car if you can't push it to the limits?' He turned to her. 'It's alright, my lamb. Just a bit of fun.'

She couldn't speak. The way he had so quickly terrified her and thought it all a lark. When they arrived at Garth Hall, she went straight to her room.

* * *

In the drawing room, Arthur poured himself a large whisky, knocked it back and poured another. It had been a tedious afternoon. Ruth's old man had asked far too many questions. It had been hard work deflecting them and he'd taken the first opportunity to excuse them both and leave. He'd obviously been questioning Ruth to some extent, for she too had prattled on about the progress of their house and he'd had more than his fill for one day. He sank back into the leather armchair, appreciating the peace and quiet with only the crackle of the fire to disturb him, when his father came to join him. He clenched his jaw and braced himself for another barrage of interrogation. When would he ever get time to think?

'Ruth gone to bed?' Cyril pulled the stopper from the decanter and poured himself a brandy.

'It's been a long day.'

Cyril took the chair facing his son. 'I thought you'd have been back long ago.'

'These things always last longer than you hope they will.'

'All rather unexpected. Who'd have thought old Evans had it in him.' He gave his son a wry smile. 'Let's hope the new Mrs Evans doesn't fall pregnant before Ruth does. That will rather scupper things.'

Arthur had been thinking the same himself. On her brothers' deaths, Ruth had become the sole heir to her father's fortune, as well as her aunt and uncle's. Cyril Marshall had fought hard to hide his unseemly delight that things had panned out as well as they had. He had pushed Arthur towards Ruth from the off, calculating the advantage of what such a union would mean. It had all worked out far better than expected. God forbid that she was barren like her aunt. It wasn't for want of trying on his part.

'As long as it's another daughter, I've nothing to worry about.'

He had worry enough as it was. Ruth had hit a nerve when she asked about the house. The money was gone. The fire at Parker's had seen to that, and there was no opportunity to win it back. Not yet.

'Better get a move on then, my boy. Your mother fell pregnant with you on our wedding night. What has it been now? Six months, more?'

Arthur wasn't counting. There were more pressing matters on his mind. But if his wife were pregnant, it might prove a welcome distraction.

* * *

Ruth was still reading when she heard Arthur haul himself upstairs and enter his own room. From the manner in which he was banging about, he'd had rather too many glasses of whisky. She closed her eyes, listening, waiting for it all to be quiet, felt her stomach twist when he opened the door that joined both rooms and walked into her room, half undressed, his tie loose about his shirt, his trousers missing. She put her book down when he staggered towards her and breathed into her face. She drew back.

'Arthur. Please. I feel nauseous.'

'Have you any reason to feel nauseous?' he leered at her.

'Your breath. The alcohol.'

He placed his hand to her breast, and she tried not to flinch. She'd learned these past months what made him strike out. While he moved his hand, she bit down on her lip, praying that the drink would take hold and render him useless. She turned her face away from him, the smell making her heave. He grabbed at her jaw and gripped it hard.

'You're a cold fish. Nothing like the warm-blooded women I've had before.' He kissed her hard and the smell of stale whisky made her want to vomit. She freed herself from his grip, pushed him away as best she could.

'Why you little bitch…' He slapped her hard across her face, pushed her back, forced her legs apart and got on top of her. She closed her eyes, knowing it was easier to let him have his way. In the end he gave up, incapable, flopped on his back and fell asleep.

When she was certain he wouldn't wake, she got up and went to the bathroom. She studied her reflection in the mirror, the deep red mark of his hand imprinted on it. There was no love between them; she knew there never had been – and it was as much her fault as his.

32

The wireless his mother had sent had been vague, but Alec had instantly known something was wrong. He had another month fishing before he could get back and he was agitated for the best part of it. Short-tempered and quick to snap if things weren't going the way he wanted. The crew had kept out of his way and he couldn't blame them. He had none to blame but himself and he knew his time was running out.

He'd hurried home when his ship docked in the second week of May, leaving the mate to deal with the paperwork and the unloading. The ghost train would be at work unless someone kept watch. He knew exactly how many kits of fish were in the store and wanted each and every one carried out to be logged and checked. A few baskets disappearing would be taken from his profit and he wanted every penny from his back-breaking work to be accounted for. The lads had worked their guts out, on the fish day and night, and they all deserved what was owed to them.

It had made his heart glad to be with Letty and the kiddies at last. Norah looked well, as did his mother, but Letty was like a wraith. The weight had dropped from her and her face was gaunt and grey. She'd lost every bit of her lustre, the light of her spirit barely present. He would do anything to spark that light again.

There had been little chance to talk to his mother alone and he was relieved when he came downstairs in the early morning to find her sitting at the kitchen table. She told him of Letty's yearning to go home to her mother.

'Can't her mother come here?'

Dorcas shook her head. 'She has too much on at the farm. And she has the market and her other children to care for. She can't simply drop everything. I know she would if she could, especially if she could see just how bad Letty is.' She nibbled at the corner of thumbnail. 'I'm sure I don't know what to do for the best. I don't want to leave the café but it's the ideal time to go, it being Whitsun and the kiddies on half term.'

'What about Norah?'

'She can't manage things here, not at her age. It's not fair to expect it of her. The café's too busy. Hilda's lumbago is playing up. She can't run the place without one of us being there.'

'Can't you hold out a few more weeks? Till the ship is in for its refit.'

'You've seen how she is. And she's set her heart on it. I do believe it's the only thing keeping her going.' Dorcas wrapped her apron about her clothes, tied the bow with speed born of repetition. 'I don't know what I fear most. Letty going to Lowestoft, or not going.' She dropped her voice. 'What if she sees Becky and her boy?' She went into the pantry and brought out a bowl of eggs and set them on the table, alongside an empty dish. Alec watched her ram them on the rim of the bowl and drop the eggs into the dish, discard the shells. She picked up a fork and began to beat them.

'What are the chances of it? And she'd have to put two and two together—'

Dorcas batted him across the head with the flat of her hand. 'Have you lost leave of your senses, lad? This is Letty we're talking about. The lass is as quick as lightning.'

His mother was right; if Letty didn't see Becky this time, she would see her the next, or the one after. Letty would always want to visit her family, and he'd never be able to stop her. She had looked so brittle last night when he came home that he'd feared she would break. He couldn't let her go alone, not as she was. And he would have to tell her sometime. And break her dear heart. The thought sickened him. He stared through the window, onto the brick wall that divided them from next door. He'd had one hell of a game this last trip, but the catch had been good, and he'd made the market in good time. It was sure to fetch a good price. The gaffer should be pleased. And surely to God he was owed a break. 'I'll ask Hammond for a few days.'

Dorcas huffed.

'I can ask. He can only say no.'

* * *

The queue was the length of the stairs at Hammond's with men waiting in line for their pay. But he was a skipper and afforded a seat in the office. And he liked to see his pay packet and the calculations while he was there. Though, he had to admit, John Hammond was a fair boss and he'd never found a ha'penny's error.

He walked past the line of men waiting at the wicket and was shown into Hammond's office. The gaffer got up, all smiles, when Alec walked in, and offered him a seat in the leather chair opposite his desk. The window was open and sounds of the docks filtered through it: muffled shouts, the movement of horses, wagons, of trains. Hammond's desk was bare save for a leather blotting pad, a silver ink stand and a photo of his wife. They were a good couple. Much like the Evanses. Family was important. He would understand. One of the staff came in and handed Hammond a sheaf of papers. He looked through them, his smile wider. 'Looks like you've smashed the market record, Hardy. *Again*.'

'Good time to ask for a few days off then.'

Hammond put down the papers, staring at him. 'Far from it, Alec. You're on a winning streak. You've broken your own records. No one can match you. Not in Hull or across at Fleetwood. You're the talk of the industry. A few more trips under your belt and they'll be naming a street after you.'

It was meant to flatter him. At any other time, it would have done. This was what he'd worked so hard for. And he couldn't knock Hammond's delight at the firm's success. He took a breath.

'The thing is...' He looked to the photograph then to his boss. 'Letty's not good.'

The smile went from Hammond's face. 'Nothing too serious?'

'Not far off.'

'The baby? Billy, isn't it?'

Alec appreciated that he remembered his son's name. 'Aye, Billy. He's thriving. But his mother isn't.' He drew his shoulders back. 'I know the ship's not due a refit for a month or two but I need to take her away for a few days.'

Hammond frowned, still sympathetic. 'I understand. I do,' he said to reaffirm. 'But not yet. Two more trips and you can have two weeks.'

'That's nigh on two months, John. I don't think my lass can wait that long.'

'It's business, Hardy. A fortnight is a very generous offer on our part.'

'Aye, it is. And I appreciate it, but it's not what I asked for.'

Hammond sat back in his chair. 'Then the answer has to be no.'

Alec got up. They shook hands. 'Two trips, Alec. I promise. Then two weeks off.' Alec made his way to the door. 'I expect a quick turnaround. Tomorrow on the evening tide. The quicker you get those trips under your belt, the better.' Alec didn't reply. Hammond slapped him on the back. 'Good man.'

Outside, on the street, he leaned against the wall and checked his pay slip. He'd banked enough these last few months to keep them going for a while. He'd promised to call in at Solly's Café and see his mates, but he couldn't stomach that right now. There were choices to make, and he alone could make them. He didn't need anyone else's opinion to cloud his head.

He walked down to Wharncliffe Road and looked out over fish dock number one. Men moved about the trawler decks, and ladders were being taken away as the last of the crew went aboard. The ships were low in the water, laden with coal and ready to sail. The *Clarissa* was over by the coaling berth. In less than twenty-four hours it would be readying to move towards the lock gates and set sail. He'd already made up his mind that he would not be on it. He knew no other life but the sea. But Letty mattered more, and he was prepared to risk everything to hold on to her love.

33

Arthur was remorseful the next morning, as he always was. Ruth had been sitting in the chair overlooking the garden. He sat up on the bed, rubbing his face with his hands. 'I'm sorry I frightened you.'

'On which occasion?' There had been so many lately.

'In the car, driving at speed.'

'Speed had nothing to do with it, Arthur, as you well know. It was dangerous in the dark.'

'I'm sorry for last night too; I think I had had more than my fill that day.'

'What's wrong with us, Arthur?'

He seemed to be so wrapped in Marshall's business. Always at his father's beck and call. Mildred was no help. Fawning over him like a child. The sooner they got into their own home, the better. It might give them half a chance to make a go of things. He got up and came to her, kissed her forehead.

'I apologise. Am I forgiven?'

'No, you are not.'

He pulled away.

'You shouldn't drink so much, Arthur. It makes you...' She held back on the words she wanted to say. 'You are not yourself.'

He held out his hand for hers. She waited for a moment before holding out her own. He clasped it, a small boy wanting absolution. She thought of Henry, how he'd infuriated her father with his escapades, but he'd always been kind, had never frightened her. Arthur seemed to delight in it.

'I think it was seeing your father so contented. After all his troubles and sadness.' He let go of Ruth's hand and stared out of the window. 'Do you like Evelyn?'

'Why would I not? She makes Father happy. That's all I ever wished for.'

He turned back to her. 'And us?'

She didn't understand.

'Our happiness?'

'Of course.' She stared at him.

Arthur inhaled, let out a long breath. 'I've run into a bit of trouble.'

'What sort of trouble?'

'I want to give you everything, Ruth. I always have.' He walked over to the bed, picked up the nightdress he'd bought her in Paris, looked down at it. 'When you turned me down, all those years ago...' He let it fall back onto the bed. 'I didn't think life would ever be the same again.' His eyes glittered with emotion. 'You wanted me to wait, and I waited. I didn't want anyone but you.' His intensity made her uncomfortable.

'What kind of trouble, Arthur?' she repeated. He sat on the bed.

'I am in need of a little cash.' He looked to her, forlorn. 'I've made some investments, but the money is locked in. It will be some time before it comes to fruition; that's why the build of the house has stalled. I need to get my hands on some ready cash before the end of the month. It's only for a matter of days, that's all. Just to get me out of a difficult situation.'

'Couldn't you ask your father to help?'

'Not on this occasion.'

'Why ever not? Surely he would want to help you.'

Arthur came beside her once more, stroked her hair. She wanted him to take his hand away but did not speak up. 'My father is not like your father, darling. You have no idea.'

'Oh, Arthur. What have you done?' It had to be a gambling debt. She'd been astounded by his wagers when they had been abroad, had begged him not to go to the smoking room with the two Texan gamblers on their journey home, certain he was being duped. She had an inkling that things had escalated as his behaviour became more erratic. But surely there was little Arthur could do that his father wouldn't know of?

'I've been threatened. The next body in the dock might well turn out to be mine.'

She gasped. 'How much?'

'Three hundred pounds.'

She was aghast. 'I don't have that kind of money, Arthur. You know what is in the bank account better than I.' She had no idea of the status of their funds. Arthur had told her it was the man's duty to handle such matters. Mildred had concurred, and Ruth had let the matter drop, knowing it useless to argue here, resolving to change things when they were in possession of their own home. But how long would that be? 'Couldn't you borrow it from the funds set aside for the house?'

'I can't. I've invested it. Didn't you listen—' He stopped himself, changed his tone. 'I thought you could ask your father? I would have asked before, but the wedding was coming up... I didn't want things to be awkward.'

'Awkward? Between who? You and Father? Or me?'

He began to pace the floor, wringing his hands. He stopped in front of her. 'These men are dangerous. They won't stop at me. They've threatened to hurt you. And I couldn't bear that. Oh, Ruth, I've been such a fool.' He looked almost as if he would cry. It was distasteful. She felt suddenly hot, trapped.

'But what should I say it is for?'

He got up. Moved his hand over the dressing table. Picked up her brush and put it down again. She knew he would have thought about it. He could have answered her straight away. She hated being played like this. The tension was unbearable. 'A car? Three hundred would buy a car. He would want you to have it. It would mean you could visit them more often. And the guild – and everything you like to do. You wouldn't be reliant on Mother or me.'

'But it's not for a car, Arthur.' Was he so deluded?

'But it will be. When I get paid out on my investment.' He took her hands in his. 'I promise I will buy you a car. I hadn't given a thought to how difficult it would be for you here. The sooner I can get the house built, the sooner we remove ourselves from Father's control.'

She could see the sense in that at least. 'I believe that would be better for both of us, Arthur.'

He waited, never taking his eyes from her face. In the end she relented. It was for a few days, and at the end of it she would have her own means of getting away from this insufferable house.

'I'll ask my father. Though I shouldn't have to.'

He pulled her to her feet and kissed her, gently, as he'd done when they married.

'Thank you, darling. You won't regret it.'

34

The carriage had been relatively empty, and Letty had been able to lay Billy in a nest of blankets on a vacant seat. Stella had kneeled at the window, fascinated as the train moved through the towns and villages, the landscape brick then green. Letty had felt the knots in her unravel with every field and copse they passed. Alfie had chosen to stay with Dorcas and Norah, declaring he would be the man about the house. Dorcas and Norah were moved by his chivalry, though neither of them needed looking after.

Alec appeared tense, though he denied it, but he looked as though he carried the world on his shoulders. Throughout the war she'd feared for his safety. His ships had been hit by mines on many occasions but somehow, by God's blessing, he had come home when so many had not. She tried to count her many blessings, yet still this inertia dragged her back. Sometimes she felt as if she were drowning and only just able to keep her head above water.

Her father was waiting for them when the train pulled into the station at Oulton Broad. Alec lifted the pram from the guard's van and her father helped him load it onto the cart. Another time and she would have opted to walk the two miles to the farm but knew she didn't have the stamina she'd once had.

When they reached Home Farm, Alec dropped from the cart and opened the gate. He lifted Stella down and she sprinted ahead of him, her pigtails bouncing as she ran. 'She's your double in every way, that one.' Her father laughed as the horses made their way along the dirt drive that led to the farmhouse. The door was open, hens pecking in the dirt and as her father called the horses to a halt, her mother came out, drying her hands on her apron, the broadest smile on her face at the sight of them. She held up her arms for the baby and Letty placed her latest grandchild into them. Alec reached up to help her down, his hands about her waist, and settled her firmly on home ground. Her elder sister, Clemmie, and two of her girls had come to greet them and they took Stella by the hand and led her inside.

'What a blessing it is that you both came together,' her mother said, cooing over Billy. 'It will be more like a holiday for the pair of you.' Her sister took their bags while Alec took down the pram. 'You'll not be needing that for a time, Letty. There's arms enough to hold that child.'

The table was laden with food for their arrival, and Letty picked up a tomato and held it to her nose to smell the flesh. Her mother sliced the bread thickly and Letty slathered it with butter, bit into it. 'I've not tasted anything so wonderful in a long time.'

'You've had butter surely?' Clemmie's youngest girl, Josie, was wide-eyed. It made them all laugh.

'I have,' Letty said, smiling. 'But nothing tastes as good as this butter. It doesn't taste of home.'

It was good to sit at the old table, children at their feet, the cat curled up in front of the stove, hens wandering in and out pecking at the stone floor, her father shooing them out again. The children disappeared, Letty knew not where, and her mother and Clemmie cleared the table, insisting she see to the baby then settle herself in a chair.

Her father and Alec were talking but Alec seemed ill at ease. He'd been the same on the train, distracted, though he'd taken great care of her. She caught his eye and he smiled. She relaxed. A few days and they'd both feel the benefit. They didn't see Stella until it was time for bed. She came back with Josie and Jane, looking coy. Josie whispered to her mother. Clemmie nodded. 'It seems we'll be having one extra mouth for breakfast, if that's alright with you, Letty. The girls would like Stella to come home with us.' Stella looked to her mother. How could Letty say no?

When they'd gone, Letty was suddenly exhausted. It was not long before her eyes grew heavy. Her mother told her to get to bed. She grinned at Alec. They were children in her mother's house, and she must do as she was told.

'Sleep in. Don't get up, the pair of you. You're here to rest.'

They awoke to sunshine. God had given them the most glorious weather. Her father was out in the fields with her brothers, and she did not see them until their work was done.

On Friday, Letty was up with the cock crow and went down to her mother, leaving Alec in bed. 'What on earth do you think you're doing?'

'I'm coming to market with you. I look forward to it.'

'No, you're not, my girl. Kathy will be here in a minute or two. She gives me a hand on Fridays.'

'But not this Friday. Kathy can look after Billy.' She knew her middle sister would jump at the chance. Her mother sucked in her cheeks.

Alec came downstairs, fastening his belt, his feet bare. 'I was worried.'

'No need,' Letty said. 'I'm going to market with Mother. My sister will look after Billy while I'm gone.'

'I don't think that's a good idea, Let. You're not well enough.' He looked to her mother knowing the two of them were no match when Letty set her mind to something.

Letty went to him, pressed her hand to his chest. 'I want to be with Mother, like the old days.' She looked to him to make sure he understood.

He put his hand on hers, lifted it to his mouth, kissed her fingers, his worry for her evident. 'Let, you're not strong enough.'

She shook his words away. 'Let me go, Alec. It's the medicine I need.' He tried all manner of times to persuade her otherwise, but she wouldn't give in, and eventually he relented, as did her mother. Alec went into the yard and helped them load the cart, made to get up into it and Letty stopped him. 'What are you doing?'

'I'll come with you. Unload the cart.'

She folded her arms. 'Can't a girl have time alone with her mother? You'd deny me that?'

Reluctantly, he climbed down, taking her gently by the arms. 'Don't overdo it.' He hesitated, wanting to say something more. She saw the fear in his eyes but it was needless. She could already feel her spirits reviving. She pressed her hand to his cheek and he looked away, buried his mouth in her palm. 'You're more precious to me than life itself, Letty. I hope you know that.'

She gave a small laugh. 'I'm going to market, Alec, not the end of the world.'

He nodded, worry etched across his face, and released her, helped her up onto the cart. She settled herself beside her mother and took the reins. The sun was rising and the warmth on her shoulders infused her with long-forgotten strength. It was good to be home, and she wanted to squeeze every drop of happiness from it while she was here.

It was hard work setting up the stall, but she enjoyed it. Doing something different yet familiar. She reached on the cart to bring down a crate of potatoes. Her mother put her arm across and stopped her. 'We'll lift it together.' Her strength was not what it had been. 'It will come back,' her mother told her. 'You've had a bit of a battering, but you'll mend.'

It was good to be with her mother, just the two of them, chatting with shoppers and shouting out their wares. Many of the old customers remembered her from when she was a single woman and asked for news of her children, of Alec. She'd a thought that Becky Trent might come again to taunt her, sore as she was at losing Alec. It had been on her mind these last weeks, when she'd been in her despair, ruminating over the last few years of her life, the things she'd done wrong, the bad choices, the mistakes – the times she'd let people down. Failed them. It was a look, that was all, and a few spiteful words, but in her darkest moments, it had risen like a serpent from the long grass. She'd been silly to let it bother her so. It was all water under the bridge. But all the same, she'd have liked to have shown Becky that her words didn't matter. Never had.

She was tired when the market came to an end and the stall-holders began to pack down their stalls and clear away. Her mother made her sit on the cart.

'You've done too much. I should have put my foot down and made you stay at home.'

'I would have walked here.'

Her mother laughed. 'I know. Why did you think I gave in?'

On the way home, her mother took the reins and Letty sat

back and enjoyed the sun on her face. 'I thought I might have seen Becky.'

'She won't know you're here.' Her mother shook the reins and clicked her tongue for the horse to move on. 'You would hardly recognise her. She put on a lot of weight after her husband died. And Mr and Mrs Trent keep her busy at the store. I've seen her once or twice but she's not the lass she was.' She leaned to Letty's shoulder. 'You've nothing to worry about there. You never had.'

'I didn't always know it.'

'No. We can't always see what others see in us. More's the pity.'

* * *

Alec looked anxious himself when she returned. 'You've not overdone it?' he said as he lifted her down. He stepped back as she brushed the dust from her skirts.

'Mother has taken good care of me.'

Alec looked to his mother-in-law.

'For once I'm pleased to tell you she did as she was told.' Her mother went to take the empty wooden crates from the cart, but Alec stopped her.

'I'll do that.'

Her mother stood back and watched him, her hands on her hips. 'We should have him on the farm.'

Letty shook her head. 'He's man of the sea, Mother, not the land. I know he loves me, but he loves the sea more.'

He put down the last of the crates. 'That's not true, Letty. If only you knew...' He brushed his hands of dirt, staring at her so forlornly, and she went to him, linked her arm in his.

'Yes, it is. I made my peace with it long ago.' She smiled at him, sorry that she had caused those she loved so much concern these past months, resolving to be more cheerful and shake away the darkness that had settled upon her since the fire.

Billy's pram had been left outside the farmhouse door and Letty bent over him. He was fast asleep, his cheeks red, his chubby little legs splayed. She touched his skin, loving the soft pudginess of it. Inside the kitchen, Kathy was at the range, eggs were spitting fat and bacon sizzled alongside them. The bread had been sliced and spread with butter. For the first time in months, Letty felt ravenous.

Afterwards she and Alec sat side by side in the sunshine and held hands. Stella came back with her cousins and without giving her parents a second glance followed them as they ran into the house in search of something to eat. She heard the clatter of dishes and scraping of chairs. She lay back, closed her eyes against the sun. A breeze rustled the birch leaves. It sounded not unlike the sea, a gentle sea, washing along the shore, and she gladly succumbed to sleep.

35

On Sunday morning, they all went to St Michael's church in Oulton, where Letty and Alec had married. Her father took the cart home while they all walked to the station. Her mother had suggested they go to Lowestoft, to spend the day on the seafront and stroll along the piers. Letty had thought Alec might have wanted to visit his aunt and uncle at the beach village but he wasn't interested. 'This is your time with your family. It's what we came for.' It meant a lot, that he was so unselfish. Stella and her cousins had run on ahead and waited on the platform for the adults to catch up. A large wicker basket had been filled with fruit and sandwiches and Letty had balanced it on the pram.

'Stella is having the time of her life,' she said to Alec, as Clemmie and the girls boarded the train. 'It's a pity Alfie didn't come with us.'

'Ah, he's too grown up for all that now. He'd have been leaving school this summer if they hadn't raised the age limit.'

Letty punched his arm playfully. 'You're never too grown up for the seaside.'

* * *

When the sun shone, as it did today, it was difficult to believe they'd lived through four years of war. The crowds milled along the promenade and they strolled leisurely along the two piers, the South Pier and the Claremont. People had smiles on their faces, though many a heart had been broken or bruised by loss, and she was grateful to be here with her family, to be alive, for in her darkest moments she'd thought they might all be better off without her. Days like today filled her with hope, that things would be bright once more.

After a while they stopped at a kiosk and bought a jug of tea for the adults and ice creams for the children. They sat at a table to enjoy it, her mother taking Billy to her shoulder. Gazing across to the harbour, Letty understood Alec's reluctance to come back. This was where they had brought Henry Evans and other members of his crew ashore when the *Black Prince* had been hit by a mine in 1915. Were all the bad memories fresh in his mind, as hers were of the fire? It had taken the entire week for Alec to loosen up and unwind. Tomorrow they would take the early train back to Grimsby. It was a pity they couldn't stay any longer, but she was grateful that he'd been with her at all.

'I'll get your father a tin of baccy,' he said when they got up to move again. 'As a thank you for his kindness. You walk on; I'll catch up.'

'But the crowds, Alec. We'll be lost among them.'

'You think I wouldn't find you? Even if there were a million people here.' He glanced about him. 'I would find you anywhere.' He squeezed her hand and let go, disappeared into the tobacconist's.

Letty and her mother walked on, people moving aside for

the pram. Letty leaned forward, bringing over the hood to shade Billy from the sun.

'Mr and Mrs Trent, how lovely to see you.' It was her mother's voice. Letty looked up, and, as the couple came to look at the baby, stood back as they peered into the pram.

Mrs Trent smiled at her. 'Children are such a blessing, aren't they?'

Letty agreed wholeheartedly. 'I was sorry to hear about John. You must miss him terribly.' Letty's parents had bought from the Trents when they first started with a small shop down a side street more than thirty years ago. They now occupied three adjoining shops along the High Street. Letty knew they'd lost their only son. She also knew that he'd married Becky Drew. There was no sign of their daughter-in-law today.

'We do.' Mrs Trent twisted to her husband and gave him a sad smile. 'But we have been blessed with his son. It means we still have a small part of him. Thank the good Lord.' As they talked, Stella pulled at her skirt, restless, too excited to be standing still when there were swing boats and the helter-skelter to ride. Letty glanced back in search of Alec, and froze as a young woman and her child came towards them. There was no mistaking Becky, big as she was, a small boy with hair the colour of sand at her side. He was eating an ice cream and Becky had bent down, mopping his face and fingers as his summer treat dribbled down his hands. When she straightened up she saw Letty, and her expression changed, awkward when her in-laws beckoned her over. As mother and son came closer, Letty understood why. She gripped the pram handle, glad it was there to hold on to, for the world had tilted to one side and she felt the ground slide from under her. She stared at the boy.

'Here they are now.' Mrs Trent beamed. 'Johnny, come and

say hello.' Letty's mother made a fuss of them, as did Clemmie. Letty forced herself to smile.

'He looks so much like his father,' Mrs Trent said proudly. 'He has his eyes.'

He had Alec's eyes. Letty wondered how they couldn't see it. She looked at the boy. Ice cream was around his mouth and Becky stooped again to wipe it. Letty twisted to look for Alec, saw him weaving towards them. He smiled, lifted his hand in a wave. She felt her anger swelling like a huge wave. She forced it down, held on to the pram to keep her fists from striking out at him – and as he came closer and saw the Trents, she knew. In the subtle movement of his body, the slight change of his expression, imperceptible to anyone but her, she knew. Becky had won after all.

* * *

Letty had suffered a thousand agonies while she tried to retain her composure, not giving way to the anger that had burned her insides raw. She'd tried not to show that her whole word had been torn apart. Alec came and stood beside her.

'You alright, our Letty?' Clemmie said, concerned. 'You've gone very pale.'

Her mother touched her shoulder, turned her towards her, shook her head. 'You've done too much. I should have put my foot down on Friday and not let you come to market with me.'

'I'm fine,' Letty replied. Smiling had been an effort. She'd wanted to weep, to release the rage that was building inside her, but not here, not now. How she managed to keep her tongue and exchange banal pleasantries with Becky Trent, to make something of her son, she had no idea, and when the Trents said their goodbyes and moved on, her mother found a bench and made Letty sit down. 'I don't want to sit down.'

Her mother frowned. 'What's wrong?' Clemmie had taken the children onto the beach. Letty watched them wait in line for the swing boats. Alec didn't know what to do with himself. She was sure her mother would guess something had passed between them. She swallowed down her bitterness, smiled. 'It was standing too long in the heat. I'm alright now.'

Her mother nodded, though Letty knew she didn't believe her. 'Alec, go and find her some water. I'll sit with her.' The two of them watched him go to a kiosk.

'Everything alright, lovey?' Her mother was watching Alec.

'Yes. Yes,' Letty said brightly. 'Everything is absolutely fine.'

* * *

She was silent that night as they lay side by side in bed. Alec wanted to talk but she had no words. 'Not here. Don't spoil what I have here, in this house.' She felt the tears on her cheeks. It was already too late.

In the morning as they readied to leave, she put on a bright show for her parents as they loaded them with vegetables, with eggs, and jars of her mother's honey to take home to Grimsby. And when they parted at the station, she wept as she always did, but this time her weeping was not that she was leaving, but that she didn't know how she could ever return.

36

Letty ignored Alec for the entire journey home. Stella was a handful, no doubt picking up on the tension between her parents. Letty snapped at her and immediately regretted it. Billy grizzled for hours, and in the end she got up and walked up and down the aisles between carriages to soothe him. When he at last fell asleep in her arms, she did not go back to the carriage to sit with Alec. He came looking for her. She gritted her teeth and told him to go. The man on the seat opposite looked up from his newspaper, and when she scowled, quickly lifted it over his face.

They got off at New Clee station, Letty marching ahead with the pram as if the station were on fire, Stella walking behind with her father.

'What's wrong with Mother?'

'She had to leave her mother and father behind, and her sisters. It makes her sad.'

It wasn't just her family she had left behind; she'd left something else. Trust. How could she ever believe a word he said? The look of fear on Becky's face was imprinted on her brain. It had replaced the gloat of satisfaction that Letty remembered. It was of no comfort.

Letty had no words. No words for Alec or for anyone. She pushed the pram over Cleethorpe Road and walked along streets that seemed duller and greyer than ever, aware of the soot and the reek of fish that hung in the air. Home. This was home – except it wasn't. She'd done her best to make a life for them all here, but what for? She was adrift now, no sight of land.

'She's not sad, Father. She's angry. I made her angry.'

Letty slowed. It wasn't Stella's fault. She turned, smiled at her. 'I'm not angry with you, Stella. I'm just eager to get home. I want to see Alfie, don't you?' She looked at Alec, the man she'd given her heart to. The man she'd put above all others, her family, her friends. He hadn't been worth the sacrifice.

The smell of roast chicken wafted through the house and Alfie hurried downstairs when he heard the door open. He squeezed through the gap and took the pram from her, manoeuvring it into the front room. 'I'll bring Billy through, Mother. You sit down; you'll be tired.'

She was tired but she was loath to go through to the other room. She left her hat and coat and waited while Stella removed hers and hung them up. 'Go and wash your hands and face, Stella. Granny will have your dinner ready.' Alec took her hand, and she slapped it away. 'Don't touch me. Don't ever touch me.' She took a deep breath, bracing herself before she went through to the rooms at the back of the house. Dorcas's gaze flicked to Letty, to Alec, and back to her daughter-in-law, unable to conceal the shame from her face.

There had been plenty of time to think on the train while she walked up and down the aisles, Billy in her arms. Their first-born son, or so she'd believed. She thought of the birth, upstairs. When Dorcas had been so kind when she went out to wait for

Alec at the Parkers', the night it had burned down. They had come together and now the gap between them was wider than it had ever been. Dorcas and her precious son had known, and they'd said nothing. No wonder Dorcas had been reluctant for her to go to Lowestoft without Alec. All the kindnesses were nothing, nothing at all. Norah got up from the chair and embraced her.

'You have a little more colour in your cheeks,' she said quietly. The room crackled with tension. Stella was chattering with excitement and Norah, sensing trouble, indulged her to fill the awkward silence.

'I didn't think you'd have a chance to eat,' Dorcas ventured. 'We waited—'

'How kind,' Letty said through gritted teeth. 'How thoughtful.'

Norah looked up. If it were not for her presence, Letty would have sent the children out of the room and given Alec and his mother the full force of her anger.

The dishes were set on the table, but Letty couldn't eat. There were too many unsaid words in her throat choking her. Sitting around the table was the family she had yearned for. Not a family in the ordinary sense but one of her making, with Alfie and Norah. The good Lord must know she loved them, but right at this moment she couldn't sit there. Dorcas couldn't look at her and neither could Alec. She picked up her fork, pushed some chicken on it, but couldn't put it to her mouth. She couldn't pretend. She laid it on her plate and pushed her chair away from the table, and went to sit in the other room. Alec followed her as she knew he would. 'Let, I can explain...'

She put up her finger. 'Don't, don't.' She couldn't look at him. He walked towards her and again she put up her hand. If he touched her, everything she had held in for two days would erupt and she was afraid of what she might do. If they had been alone, she wouldn't have cared, but the children were next door, as was Norah. Dorcas she had no care for. Rage bubbled inside her. The family portrait they'd had taken at the studio hung on the opposite wall and was reflected through the over-mantel mirror. Alec in his uniform standing behind her, Stella on her lap and Alfie at her side. Dorcas. A family. Her family. It had been taken when he was home on leave. He'd been based in Lowestoft, operational home of the minesweeper section. She'd not given a thought to Becky then, fearing only that he wouldn't survive.

'It meant nothing.'

She placed her hands on the mantelpiece and stared at the empty grate. 'That's alright then. We can go back to how we were now that I know that.'

He took a step closer.

'Don't.'

'I was drunk.'

'Not drunk enough,' she spat.

'If you'd let me explain...'

She stepped away from the fireplace, threw her hands in the air. 'Explain? Explain? What in God's name is there to explain?' Her voice was shrill. She balled her fists, gritted her teeth. 'I don't want to hear. I don't want to know. Nothing you say or do can make it any less than it is. She has a child. Your child.' She could drown in her own misery. 'Your *firstborn* son.' She spat the words at him. 'I wish I'd never laid eyes on you, Alec Hardy.' Her heart hurt so much she could hardly breathe, the cracked pieces of it pressing against her ribs.

'Letty. Please?' He grabbed hold of her wrists, and she wrestled them free, crying with frustration, trying to force down the anger that raged inside, not wanting to frighten the children, not wanting Norah to know what he'd done. But it was only a matter of time. Norah would have to know. And who else? Her mother, her father. The entire village.

'No wonder you wanted to come with me to market. No wonder you didn't want to go to the beach village to see your uncle. You couldn't take that risk, could you? But your dirty little secret came out anyway – as dirty little secrets do.'

He let his hands drop.

She walked to the window; through the net curtains she could see silhouettes of people on the other side of the road. 'Leave me. I want to be on my own.'

'But we need to talk.'

'There's nothing to say.'

He stood for a long while, not saying anything, not moving. Just standing there. It got on her nerves. She sat down on the chair. The light was fading, and the room was cold without the warmth of the sun. After a while he left, closing the door behind him. Only then did she let go of the tears she'd held back for so long.

She had stopped crying when Norah brought her a cup of tea. Letty couldn't look at her, knowing her face would be puffy and red, her eyes swollen and stinging. It would be a while before she could let the children see her like this, let alone Norah. Norah took a seat on the sofa to the side of her.

'I don't know what's gone on, Letty. Don't be afraid of that. I haven't asked and I doubt neither Alec nor Dorcas would tell me. But I do know that whatever it is, they love you, Letty. And they hurt for you, not for themselves.' Her words made the tears fall again and Norah handed her a handkerchief.

'I'm overwrought. I'm tired.'

'Yes, you are both of those things. But you have been tired

and overwrought before now and I have never seen you like this, my lovely girl. Try and drink something.'

Letty's hand shook as she lifted the cup to her lips, and though she opened her mouth she couldn't drink it down. She returned the cup to the saucer. Norah stepped up and took it from her, placed it on the mantel. Letty caught her face reflected in the mirror and tears fell, though she'd thought she had no more left, only an emptiness that she'd never felt before.

Norah turned away from the fire and opened her arms and Letty got up and came to her, buried her face in her shoulder. Norah rubbed her back. Billy began to cry and she heard the door open and close as someone took her boy away.

'I can't think what has brought you to this, my dearest girl. But you can overcome it.'

Letty shook her head. 'I don't know that I will.'

Norah took Letty's face in her hands. 'Love bears all things, believes all things, hopes all things, endures all things.' Letty knew the verse from Corinthians was meant to comfort her.

'But what if this is more than I can bear?'

'The good Lord sends these things to test us. If anyone can endure, Letty, you can.'

* * *

Dorcas told Alfie to take Stella upstairs. Billy was propped up against her shoulder. When they were alone, she turned on Alec. 'You saw her?'

'The last day. Letty knew, just as you did.'

'I'm surprised her mother didn't say anything.'

'She might have thought something amiss, but she didn't pass comment. I don't know that she made any connection.'

'She wouldn't have known what you looked like as kiddies.

Letty had the photos.' She glanced to the mantel where she kept the photographs of her boy and husband. Lost to the sea. She thought her days could never be as dark again. 'That's not your only problem, my lad.'

He knew what was coming next.

'The runner came from Hammond's.'

Alec stared down at his hands.

'You told me and Letty you had leave.'

He didn't answer. There was no point.

'Hammond came himself.'

'Bugger.' He looked to his mother. 'What did he have to say?'

'The short of it? Not to bother yourself going back. He wipes his hands of you.' She sat down, Billy on her lap. 'God, boy, if you weren't all I had left, I'd do the same.'

He knew she meant it.

'You were doing so well and you've thrown it all away. And what for? You thought you could spare the lass pain? Well, that little plan didn't work, did it? God only knows what Letty will do when she finds out.'

He didn't want to think on it; his head was already too full of knots he didn't know how to undo. 'I'll get another ship. There's plenty of firms will want me. I'm a good earner.'

His mother stared at him. 'Have you taken leave of your senses? Do you think that matters? They'll have to make an example of you.'

He'd taken the risk knowing full well what the consequences might be. The gaffers had the power, whether you made money or not. Alec had done the worst thing of all. He might never get work in Grimsby again. 'There's other places to get work.'

'Aye, perhaps you'll be going alone.'

37

Arthur dropped Ruth off at Meadowvale House on his way to Blundell Park. He and his father were directors of Grimsby Town, the local football team, and this Saturday they were playing Bristol Rovers. She rang the bell and waited for Mrs Murray to admit her, but it was Evelyn who came to the door.

'Ruth, you must always come right in. This is your home.' She kissed her on both cheeks and ushered her into the hall. Two men in overalls were on the hall landing. The staircase was draped in protective cloths and the paintings removed from the walls. For the first time in years, her mother's portrait was not there to greet her. Perhaps she never would again.

'I'm so glad you're here,' Evelyn enthused. 'You can help me choose the fabric for the windows. Your father is not in the least interested. He pretends he is, to indulge me.' She led the way to the sitting room. Books of wallpaper samples and fabric swatches were laid about the chairs and sofas. Evelyn moved them to one side and motioned Ruth to sit down. 'Your father has stepped out for a newspaper. He'll be home soon enough. He'll be delighted to see you. As am I.' She walked over to the armchair, picked up a book. 'Would you care to look at the samples? You might find something you like for your own home.' She passed it to Ruth. 'How is your house coming along?'

'It isn't,' Ruth said, running her hand over the washed silk in one of the books.

'Problems?'

Ruth knew she was only expressing concern but didn't want to reveal too much. It wasn't Evelyn's problem, or her father's. She was still reeling from the shock herself. Arthur had repeatedly stressed how much danger he was in, how much danger *she* was in. 'Arthur has it all in hand.'

Evelyn peeled back a swatch, showed it to Ruth for her opinion. Ruth shook her head and Evelyn laughed. 'I thought so too.' She put the book down and picked up another. 'It must be difficult to live so far out of town,' Evelyn said, looking up from samples, alert to the changes in Ruth's expression.

'Mildred doesn't seem to have a problem with it.'

'But you're not Mildred.' A smile played upon Evelyn's lips and Ruth could only return it, her shoulders sinking a little.

'I can't say it's been easy. If Arthur had scaled things down a little, the house would be near to finished now. The plans for the house were far too...'

'Large?' Evelyn offered.

'Ostentatious,' Ruth said, relieved to be honest for once.

'You'll have to put your foot down.' Evelyn snapped the book shut. 'Don't let Arthur have his own way too much. It's not good for him. Or you,' she added pointedly.

Her father joined them, dropping his newspaper on the swatches. Evelyn picked it up and placed it on the side table. His delight at seeing his daughter was evident and she immediately felt safe. He wrapped his arms about her.

'You're not eating enough, my girl. Are they not feeding you at the hall?'

'Too much.' There was too much of everything, aside from comfort and laughter. But that could change. If she helped Arthur, it might very well be the thing to unite them.

Evelyn moved the wallpaper book from his chair, and he sat down.

'Not often we see you on a Saturday, darling. Not that I'm complaining. It's always a pleasure.'

She smoothed her hand over her skirt, stared at her wedding ring. It was more uncomfortable than she'd thought it would be. The ring and the request. 'I came to ask a favour of you.'

'Would you like me to leave?' Evelyn asked.

Ruth shook her head. Having her there made her feel more confident. 'I wondered if you could see your way to advancing me a loan. For a car?' Her father furrowed his brow. She had an idea what he was thinking. She'd spent the morning anticipating any questions he might have. 'Arthur's money is tied up in investments. He can't get his hands on it for another month or so. He sees how I struggle.'

Her father nodded, still concerned. 'Your aunt mentioned you can't always make the guild, and I know how much it has meant to you over the years. Quite aside from how much Evelyn and I miss your company. Helen suggested you have a car but it's not our place.' He laughed. 'It must be the only time your aunt hasn't interfered.'

Evelyn rested on the arm of his chair, put her hand to his shoulder. Ruth thought how happy they looked together. How content. They had an easiness in each other's company, something Ruth and Arthur had never managed to acquire.

'And it's just for a car?' her father asked. 'Nothing else?'

'No.' She became flustered. 'It's only for a month, two at the most. It would make such a difference to me.'

Evelyn came to her rescue. 'I think it's a splendid idea. You will have so much more freedom. I'm thinking of getting a little car for myself.'

Her father raised his eyebrows.

'Lots of women are driving these days, Richard. I drove ambulances in France. Lots of the girls did.'

Her father patted her knee. 'I know when I'm beaten.' He turned to Ruth. 'I don't keep that sort of cash in the house, but I will make sure you have it on Monday morning.'

With that awful business out of the way, she gradually relaxed and spent the rest of the afternoon with them, knowing Arthur would not grumble. He came to collect her at five. He was overly ebullient, but when her father and Evelyn asked them to stay for dinner, he made an excuse, and they left.

* * *

Evelyn had been unsettled by her stepdaughter's visit. After she and Richard had waved her off at the gate and were walking back to the house, she expressed her concerns. 'I don't think you should give Ruth a loan.'

'Why ever not?' He stopped on the path.

'I don't think she'll use it for a car. I think it's for something else.'

'Something or someone?'

'It could be something to do with Arthur's gambling. I don't know. A woman's instinct?' He'd spoken to her of the rumours when she'd raised her concern for Ruth on a previous occasion. Richard had insisted it was hearsay, but Evelyn adhered the old adage that there was no smoke without fire. And Ruth had said it was Arthur's money when it belonged to them both. Richard and Cyril Marshall had gifted the couple handsomely on their wedding day. There had been more than enough to build the house – and furnish it. 'Wouldn't it be better if you bought her the car – as a gift. Then she wouldn't be beholden to the Marshalls. It would give her some independence. I think she is in dire need of it.'

'I will be guided by you.' He opened the door for her and stepped back to let her pass.

'I get the feeling that Ruth is unhappy, though she tries hard enough to deny it.'

'She would tell me if she was not happy,' Richard said with confidence as they went back into the sitting room. Evelyn was not so sure. Ruth only sought to please other people. It had been evident at her wedding. She'd been swept away, first by her aunt, and then by Arthur's family. Thinking of others' happiness. It was about time she thought of her own.

38

Letty slept, giving in to exhaustion. Alec did not come upstairs. Stella had woken in the night and climbed into bed next to her and Billy, perhaps sensing her mother's sadness. In the morning, Stella had gone in search of Alfie and she'd lain there for a while, staring at the ceiling, not knowing what to do. When she went downstairs, Alec had gone. Dorcas came in from the yard with the empty wash basket and set it on the kitchen floor. Without a word, she made scrambled eggs and put them on the table. 'I don't want anything,' Letty told her.

'You need to eat.'

'I'll eat when I'm hungry.'

Her mother-in-law looked haggard, as well she might, thanks to her son. The thought was another stab at Letty's heart. Dorcas tapped lightly on the table for Letty to eat, held out her arms to take Billy. 'I could wring his neck myself.'

Letty didn't answer.

'He's sorrier than you'll ever know.'

Letty nodded. 'I can imagine. Getting caught out like that.' She was bitter.

'Becky—'

'Don't try laying the blame at her door. Alec was, is, a married man.'

'I wasn't going to.'

Letty put Billy in the playpen, peered into the kitchen, looked out of the window into the narrow yard, the high wall that separated them from the house next door. She wondered what their neighbour had heard of their argument. 'Where's Norah?'

'She took Stella for a walk. She thought you and Alec might need a little privacy, to sort things out.' She clasped her hands together. 'He didn't know, Letty. Not until we went to Lowestoft.'

'Ah, so if Becky hadn't had the evidence he would have got away with it, you mean. His betrayal. And yours.'

Dorcas sank down onto the chair. Her hands were red from washing and scrubbing. 'I hope you can find it in your heart to forgive both of us.'

Letty looked at her mother-in-law, hating what Alec had done, what they had both done, but it was hardly down to Dorcas. She had walked into a trap. 'Alec could have said something.'

'He could. So could I. But where would we start? Oh, child. If I could've saved you this pain, I would. I didn't know how.'

Letty knew she was speaking the truth. 'What is done is done. I can't unknow what I know. Much as I wish I could.' The pain stabbed at her heart again and she turned away. 'I don't want to talk about it. I want to forget.'

* * *

Alec asked his mother not to say anything to Letty while he got the lie of the land. If he didn't tell her, someone else would take great pleasure in it, wanting to bring him down a peg or two. The men were waiting in line for their pay as he made his way up the stairs. They stepped aside as he moved past them and went to John Hammond's office. One of the skippers he knew came out of it, nodded to Alec, gave a small flick of his head as if he knew what was in store for him. Word would've got round. He'd had the looks and the calls as he walked down the road. Brazen.

'I'd like to see Mr Hammond.'

The clerk looked up. 'He's not seeing anyone today.'

'Ted Jones has just seen him.'

'I have my instructions.'

Alec nodded, understanding, and barged past. The clerk got up to stop him, but he had no weight on him and Alec pushed him aside. He rapped once on the door and walked in, closing it behind him.

Hammond glanced up. He did not offer him a seat as he usually did, only carried on writing in his ledger. The clerk came in to apologise and Hammond asked him to leave. Alec waited as if in front of the headmaster.

'I'd like to say it's good to see you, Hardy. It would have made a difference last week.'

'I know I let you down.'

Hammond put down his pen, took off his reading glasses and leaned back in his chair.

'You let your crew down. They've sailed with Lenny Carter. I fear they will not get the payouts they've been used to. He is not your match.'

Alec was glad Lenny had got the ship. He'd not had much luck of late. Two of his sons had gone down on the minesweepers and Lenny himself had taken a battering.

'How long have we worked together?'

It had hardly been working together. Alec was never in any doubt that he worked for Hammond; there was no *we* about it. And never more so than this moment. 'Eight years. You gave me my first job.'

Hammond nodded to himself, looked at the oil painting on the wall behind him. 'And your first ship as skipper, the *Black Prince*.'

The *Black Prince* had been requisitioned by the navy and had gone down when hit by a mine. He'd been lucky to escape; not all of them had. Richard Evans's boy was badly injured and died before they could get him home. The images swam into his head. Boys, they were just boys.

'You'll not work for me again, Hardy. You'll have to go elsewhere.' It was an empty suggestion and they both knew it. The gaffers had an agreement. Upset one, you upset them all. Who knew how long he'd be walking around.

'Mr Hammond. John. I've broken all records for you, nationwide. Does it count for nothing?'

Hammond picked up his pen, moved papers in front of him. 'Close the door on the way out, Hardy.'

Alec ignored the looks, the nudges and the mutterings as he made his way out again. He went from office to office, but no one would give him the time of day. He'd expected as much. He walked along Wharncliffe Road, his hands in his pockets, and stopped outside Excel. Old man Evans might give him a job, for old time's sake if nothing else, Alec having brought home the body of his son, Henry. But Alec couldn't put him in the position of having to say no; he had too much respect for the man than to ask.

Having exhausted all avenues, he made his way out of the docks and onto Cleethorpe Road. He called in at the Albion, trying to decide on what he could tell Letty. A few of the blokes looked up but no one passed comment, and he was grateful for it. He sat down in the corner, nursing his pint. He'd need more than one, but he needed to keep a clear head. He drank it back and pushed the glass away. After a few minutes he got up and walked towards the door.

'How the mighty are fallen,' someone commented. He stopped, his fists clenched, deciding whether to give the man what for. The bigger the success, the more a target for folk to take a pop at. He took a breath and walked on, and went home to deal Letty another blow.

* * *

Dorcas had quickly removed her apron and left the house when Alec made an appearance. He wasn't sure whether he was glad or not. Letty might have held back in her presence, but he thought back to the previous evening and decided it didn't matter. It was Norah and the children that had tempered her anger, not them. Letty was surprised by Dorcas's swift exit but she carried on taking the dry clothes from the wash basket and folding them, smoothing out the creases with the flat of her hand. He swallowed. 'I have something to tell you.'

She carried on with her folding, not turning to face him. He knew she wouldn't. 'I... When I...' The shame choked him. 'I was meant to sail the day we went to Lowestoft.'

She stared at him, one of Billy's bonnets in her hands.

'When I said Hammond had given me time off... I lied.'

Letty's eyebrows narrowed. 'You seem to be rather good at it.'

Well, he deserved that. Now he'd started the conversation, he wanted it all to be over. 'He told me if I didn't take the ship, he would see I didn't work again.'

She shook her head, no doubt wanting to shake away the

words he threw at her. He saw her face darken, her lips set in a thin line.

'I tried all day to get work. I knocked on every door. I...'

She put down the small bonnet.

'Say something.'

She splayed her hands. 'What is there to say?'

'I can sort it out.'

She turned on him, her hands on her hips. 'Can you? Can you, Mr High and Mighty? You think they'll take you back?'

'I'm good at my job. They know it.'

She laughed. 'I thought your brains were in your trousers, Alec Hardy. But I was wrong. You have no brains at all.'

He grabbed hold of her arm. 'I did it for you.'

'Don't you dare. Don't you ruddy dare.' She pulled away, pushed at him with her hand. 'You did it to save your own skin, not mine. Do you think your being there made it any better?' She turned her back to him. 'Go back to the pub, Alec, and drown your sorrows with your fair-weather friends. You'll soon find out how many you have when your pockets are empty.'

39

Alec remained at the Clee Park drowning his sorrows with whoever would listen in exchange for a pint of bitter. Long after time was called, the landlord took him by the elbow and guided him to the door. 'Best go home and face the music, Alec. I'm for my bed and you should be for yours.'

The fresh air hit him as he stood on the pavement. There were cycles and the odd man on the street, in the same state of inebriation as he was himself. He crossed over the road and stumbled down Park Street. The light in their room above the front bay burned low. He wondered whether Letty was awake. He didn't attempt to climb the stairs when he went inside, staggering through to the back way, banging into the walls to keep him upright and trying not to trip on the rug. A lamp was lit on the table and his mother was waiting for him. He fell into the armchair at one side of the fireplace.

'You think this is how to solve your problems, lad?'

'My problems are past solving, Mother.'

She thrust a glass of water into his hand. 'Nothing is past

repair. You've got yourself in worse messes than this, my lad. And I'll not let you give up now.'

He looked at her, his vision clouded by ale, and could still see the hurt in her eyes. He was a bloody fool; she was right about that. But he could see no way to right his wrongs. He drank the water, and they sat in silence until he fell asleep and could remember no more.

* * *

He woke hours later. His mother was still there, the smell of fresh bread baking, the window open, letting in the cool air. She put a bowl on the table and made him wash. His throat was dry, and he drank two glasses of water to slake his thirst.

'Smarten yourself up and get back down the docks,' she told him, handing him the soap brush and his razor.

'It's a waste of time.'

She slapped him with the towel, pressed it into his hands. 'Go back to the beginning. Start again. They need to know you'll not let them down again.'

'There's no point, Mother. The gaffers will be united in teaching me a lesson.'

'Then you teach them one. Don't you dare give up, my lad. Not if you want to win Letty's love back.'

'You think I can?' Was it worth hoping?

'If she thinks you deserve it. Which I don't think you do,' she added quickly. 'But then I'm not as kind as Letty.'

* * *

Alec made his way to the pit area with the other men, waiting to be picked for any work that might be available, no matter what it was. He stood, cap in hand with men less skilled, waiting for someone to point and call him forward. He looked about him. There were too many men and not enough work for them all.

'What yer here after?' one of them called to him.

'Work, like everyone else.'

'Yer a skipper,' the man sneered.

'Only when I have a ship,' Alec replied. It was the first time in his life he'd been without one. He'd first gone to sea with his father when he was but four years old in the summer months. As old as Becky's lad – his lad. He couldn't get the boy's face out of his head. One drunken mistake and his life had fallen apart.

'Tekkin' work from men who can't do owt else.'

'I can gut fish as well as the next man.' The chap was getting his goat.

'But the next man can't skipper a trawler,' he jeered. Alec saw the men around him grinning. Lads, most of them. They had no idea.

'Can't take a big cut of the profits either.' That was what he'd worked for. Had gone without pay while he studied for his certificate, or skipper's ticket as it was called. He carried it in his breast pocket now, but it was no use to him. Not as things stood. All those years working his way up from deckie learner to deck-hand, then third hand, to mate and skipper. He couldn't let it go to waste. He had to find a way back.

'What do you want to be doing here, Hardy, with yer missus putting bread on the table?' someone called from a distance. Alec lurched forward, pushing his way through the men, who shuffled aside, happy to see some action. The foreman forged through the crowd, calling out for them to stop, but Alec ignored him, his anger having nowhere to go except his fists. He grabbed hold of the man by the throat, saw the veins pulse in hands, the man laughing at him. 'Go on then, Hardy. Give us what you've got.'

He'd soon wipe that smile off the gobby bastard's face. He drew back his arm ready to throw a punch, but someone caught hold of it, and he was dragged back by his collar. He twisted to see young Ben Harris, his father beside him.

'Come away, Hardy,' Sam said. 'Save your fight for something worthwhile.' By the time the foreman had got there, they'd already turned to go, and Alec caught his eye. He would've loved nothing more than to take him down a peg or two.

In Solly's Café, Sam pushed him into a chair while Ben went for mugs of tea and bacon and egg butties. Sam slid into the seat beside Alec. 'What was yer thinking of, lad?'

Alec slumped in the chair. Anger raged through him, not at anyone else, but himself. 'He got my goat.'

'Not him. You. What was yer doing there to begin with?'

Alec leaned forward, elbows on the table, and ran his hands through his hair. 'I can't stand hanging around. Too much time to think.'

'No more time than on the bridge when you're at sea.'

'That's different.'

'Thinkin's thinkin', no matter where you do it.'

The lass pushed mugs of steaming hot tea in front of them and Ben came with the butties. He was a big lad; Alec remembered him sailing with him his first time out of Grimsby on the *Black Prince*. He'd been fifteen then, had wanted to fight in the army. Thank God he'd lived to come home. His father had been skipper and Alec had served as mate. They were pals of long standing.

Sam dropped three sugars in his mug and gave it a slow stir. 'It'll be a long time afore Hammond forgives yer. If he ever does.'

'I need to get back at sea, Sam. I know of nothing else.' He had no map, no course set.

Sam slapped him on the back. 'You'll survive. Think on it as sitting in the harbour to see out the storm.'

But the storm had already hit, and Alec knew he was on the rocks.

40

Alec's mother was civil with him. Letty mostly had nothing to say. Only Norah treated him as she always did, with a kindness that he didn't deserve. On Wednesday, he spent another fruitless morning waiting in the pit for work, ignoring the jibes, standing though he knew he would never be chosen. But they would give in before he did. When the work available was allotted, he wandered the docks doing anything he could find, heavy lifting, sweeping floors, anything that a boy of twelve could do, although he couldn't take work if someone needed it more. Some of the lads were the only ones bringing in a wage and every farthing counted. He knew it well enough. It had been the same for his mother when Father died.

The newspaper boy was on the corner as usual, a sheaf of papers over his arm, crying, 'Read all about it. Trawler sunk by mine.' Alec tossed him a copper and took the paper. He felt bile rise in his mouth when he saw the name of his ship. The *Clarissa* had been lost with all hands. He stood on the pavement, dazed by the headline. People pushed by, telling him to step aside. He pressed the newspaper against the wall of the Clee Park and read the article. The names of the crew, his crew. Their ages and those they had left behind. Widows and orphans. He thought of Lenny Carter. His missus had lost her sons; now she had lost her husband. And it was all down to him.

He should have been on that ship. Perhaps it would have been better for all of them if he had. He turned to the left and walked into the snug of the Clee Park and ordered a pint. The first of many he was to drink that night.

* * *

Alec did not come home, and they ate supper and cleared it away, Dorcas dishing up a plate of food and covering it with another, keeping it warm in the low oven. Alfie had brought in the newspaper and handed it solemnly to Letty, who had sunk down in the nearest chair when she read of the loss of the *Clarissa*. The three women knew instantly why he'd not returned. Alec would blame himself, never mind that the ship had been hit by a mine. It could have happened to any trawler. But he should have been the skipper of it.

'Fate.' Norah rubbed her hand over Letty's shoulder, hoping to be of comfort, while Dorcas spread the newspaper over the kitchen table and read out the details. 'It was not his time.'

'He will be shattered by this,' Letty said. 'And I can't bear to think what those poor women must be feeling.' Though she was furious with him, she knew how hard this news would fall. He knew every one of the crew. Had sailed with them for months. Miss Sheldon would have spent the day knocking on doors of the bereaved and bearing bad news, offering help and comfort where it was needed. Letty always dreaded the day she might get such a call.

Long after the children had gone to bed, the three women

sat in vigil, watching the clock as it struck each hour. Norah took her leave of them at eleven, and at midnight Dorcas made Letty go to her bed, telling her she would wake her the minute Alec came home.

* * *

Dorcas spent the night in the chair and woke stiff and sore. Letty had left her bank paying-in book on the table and she opened the drawer of the dresser to tidy it away. In the drawer was a small blue box and she removed it, opened it, took out Alec's medal. For valour.

Where was he now? Her boy. Her lovely boy. She sat down, placed her fingers over the cold metal. Norah came in and Dorcas dabbed at her eyes with the tea towel. 'I have a bit of ash in my eye. The fire.' It was difficult to speak. She cleared her throat. Norah brought her a glass of water and she took it from her, not daring to look at the kindly face.

'I don't know what's gone on between Alec and Letty but they will sort it out.'

Dorcas shook her head. 'They won't. I hoped with all my heart she could find a way to forgive him, but he keeps making it harder for her.'

'These things have a way of sorting themselves out,' Norah soothed, placing a gentle hand to her shoulder.

If only it were so simple. Dorcas had grown to enjoy the other woman's company but if she knew that Alec had betrayed Letty, she would be devastated. And rightly so.

'A weaker woman would forgive him.' Dorcas returned the medal to the box and replaced it in the drawer. 'She would think she had no other choice, but not Letty.'

'Her strength is to be admired,' Norah said. 'She has a kind heart. She will find it in her to forgive.'

Dorcas wanted to believe her, knowing in her heart that it wasn't so simple. Nothing ever was. And Alec was making it worse with every day he drew breath.

'I can't blame the girl,' Dorcas said. 'She's been good to me. I didn't make it easy for her.'

'It can't have been easy for you either. Leaving your home behind, your friends.'

Dorcas felt ashamed of her sorrow when confronted with Norah's kindness. She couldn't imagine what sadness the woman carried in her heart. She had lost her husband, her home, her business, her belongings. Not once had she bemoaned her lot, only ever grateful that they had all welcomed her into the family. Dorcas sucked on her lip. 'That was my mistake. Dwelling on what I had lost. Not what I had gained.' It was so clear to see, looking backwards from where she stood now. It seemed so long ago. 'To be truthful, the lass frightened me. She was fearless. It only added to my fear. When Will died, then Robbie...' She couldn't speak, remembering her loss. And now here was Alec, throwing all the good in his life to the four winds, breaking her heart all over again. Norah folded her hand over hers and for a time they stayed there, with only the sound of the birds outside and the ticking of the clock inside. 'Alec was the reason I could keep going. I had no money other than what he brought in, and what I got braiding nets.' Dorcas sighed deeply. 'I was unkindly to the lass when she first wed.'

'You were grieving your loss, and they had a future,' Norah comforted. 'It must have been hard.'

Dorcas nodded. She'd been desperately lonely in those first few months, clinging to the old ways as her world rocked and crumbled. But the old ways were not the comfort they once were.

'I pray to God that she will forgive him.'

'In her own time, she will, Dorcas. Have a good heart. Letty will find her own way through this. I'm certain of it.'

41

On Monday afternoon, Arthur returned home in a state of agitation and Ruth knew there was only one reason for it. 'When did your father say he would add the money to the bank account?'

'He didn't. I asked for the money, and he told me I would have it. He doesn't keep large amounts at the house.'

'Did you express the urgency?'

'Not in so many words, Arthur. It was embarrassing enough asking for it in the first place. I was hardly in a position to make demands.' She wouldn't have done it anyway. They were in the situation because of Arthur's carelessness, not her own.

When the money had still not arrived by Thursday, Arthur's behaviour was increasingly erratic. He didn't come to the dinner table, making excuses to his parents, to Ruth. He cornered her in the drawing room when they were alone. 'There are three days to the end of the month. Don't you realise the severity of our situation?'

'It's not *our* situation, Arthur.'

He grabbed her wrist, pulled her to him and leered into her

face. The sound of tyres on the gravel stopped him and he released her. He went to the window, then turned to her.

'Your father has arrived.' He did not look as delighted as she thought he would. She went to join him. On the gravel outside the house was her father in his own car, another smaller car to the rear. She saw Evelyn get out of it, look about her. Her father walked to her and squeezed her hand, kissed her cheek. She could see the shared delight on their faces. Evelyn saw her at the window and waved. Her father smiled, pointed to the small car and suddenly Ruth knew why they had arrived separately. It appeared that Arthur had come to the same realisation.

'Damn! Damn the bloody man.'

She turned on him. 'That bloody man is my father.' Her kind and generous father. 'You told me to ask for a loan, for a car. My father has found his own way to solve the problem. But not the solution you had in mind.' She left him in the room and went outside to greet her father and Evelyn. A few minutes later, Arthur came to join them, slipping his arm about Ruth's waist. She flinched. He would be civil while they were present, but heaven only knew what would happen when they left.

Her father handed her the keys. 'It was Evelyn's idea. It's a gift, a selfish one of course. We shall see more of you this way and it will not inconvenience Arthur.'

'It is never an inconvenience.' Arthur was quick to defend himself.

'No, I'm sure it's not, Arthur. But it will leave you able to concentrate without the worry. And I know how expensive building houses can be. I can't expect you to do everything. It's our gift. Mine and Evelyn's.'

Mildred came out of the house and joined them. She was not impressed. 'Why any young woman would want to drive is beyond me.'

'Lots of women are driving these days, Mildred.' Evelyn was cheerful. 'There has been a ladies' race at Brooklands for more than a decade.'

Mildred twisted to Ruth. 'I hope you don't get that idea into your head.'

'I don't yet know how to drive, Mildred.' It was all very well her father bringing her the car, but she had only ever been a passenger.

'There's no time like the present.' Evelyn took out the crank handle, connected it to the front of the car and gave it a turn. The car spluttered to life.

'How unseemly,' Mildred said disdainfully. Evelyn ignored her. She opened the passenger door, got in.

'Driver's seat, Ruth.'

Her father was beaming. She looked to Arthur, his face a rictus, Mildred's barely concealed disapproval, and got in the car.

'Hands on the wheel.' Ruth did as instructed and Evelyn explained the basic mechanics of driving – the brake, the clutch, the accelerator. 'Now, darling, slowly release the brake.'

Ruth did so, nervously removing her foot from the clutch. She heard the engine engage and slowly and carefully they moved off down the drive. It was exhilarating to move under her own steam. When she returned, her father and Arthur applauded. Mildred was sour-faced but it was only as Ruth had expected. Arthur opened the door, helped her out of the car. She kissed her father, then Evelyn. 'Thank you so much for your kindness.'

When they were gone, she would face the consequences of their thoughtfulness, but somehow it didn't matter as much as she'd thought it would.

* * *

Arthur could barely conceal his anger over dinner. Ruth had made sure to stay in her mother-in-law's company, ignoring her comments as to the depravity of the world the arrival of the car had ignited, instead reliving the feeling of freedom that driving the car had given her. 'It was very generous of your father,' Cyril said.

Arthur stabbed at the beef. 'He beat me to it. I was waiting until Ruth's birthday to buy her a car.'

'Then he saved you the expense. I'm sure there will be other things to celebrate before long. Perhaps the patter of tiny feet?'

Ruth didn't comment. She couldn't eat, her appetite long gone, her stomach tighter with every glare Arthur sent her way.

When Arthur's parents had retired for the evening, Ruth remained in the drawing room. He was in a foul mood, and she was loath to go to her bedroom, knowing he would follow, afraid of how he would express his frustration. She felt safer down here. Arthur wouldn't try anything while the staff were about. His parents' rooms were directly above, and she wondered whether they were aware of Arthur's tantrums, for that's what they were. He filled a tumbler with Scotch and drank back a large mouthful. 'You know I wanted to buy you a car myself.' That was a revelation. He had expressed no such desire before. The idea of the car was merely a means to an end. It had slowly dawned on her that her marriage had been something similar. Her brother's deaths had left her vulnerable in more ways than one and in seeking the familiarity of the past she had compromised her own future.

'I didn't know that Father would go ahead and buy a car. He'd agreed to the loan.' Any delight she had felt at his gift had soon evaporated when she caught the expression on Arthur's face. She wondered that anyone else hadn't noticed.

'You should have insisted on a loan. That you wanted to choose your own car instead of having it chosen for you.'

'If I'd done that, Father would have guessed something was wrong.'

He poured another Scotch. 'You might as well have signed my death warrant.'

She thought his comment rather extreme. She'd had no evidence of the trouble he was in other than his word for it. 'Don't be so dramatic. I'm sure that—'

He spun round, his eyes wild. 'You think I say that light-heartedly?' He threw himself back into the leather armchair.

'If your life is in truly in danger…'

'And yours.'

'Surely your father would help? If it is indeed so drastic.'

'You're calling me a liar?' Spittle sprayed from his mouth.

'No, of course not. I just think you should at least ask him.'

Arthur laughed. 'And let my father have me beg.'

'You're his son.'

'You think that matters?'

'If you won't ask your father, then ask your mother. She'll do anything to protect you.' She'd suddenly had enough of his childish wailings. She thought of how brave Henry had been, not thinking of himself, only of doing his duty – as had so many others. 'You've brought this on yourself. It is not for me, *or* my father to sort it out. I'm sorry I asked him.' As she walked past his chair, he caught her arm.

'You wanted this. You're glad. You've never loved me.' She didn't answer him. He got up, turned her to face him. She looked into his eyes, despising his weakness. He shoved her away with force. 'You can't do anything right. You can't even get pregnant, for God's sake. What kind of woman are you?'

She started to walk away. She heard his intake of breath as he grabbed her again, forced her to the floor and kicked her. She put out her hand to get up and he stamped on her arm. She pulled it away, trying not to cry out as she held it to her breast. The pain made her feel nauseous.

He pulled her to her feet. 'Get up, get up, you snivelling bitch.'

She refused to cry, and she would not give him the satisfaction of seeing her afraid. It angered him more and he pushed her against the wall, gripping her by the chin. Her heart was beating hard against her ribs. He had his hand to her throat. She didn't move and they stood there for what seemed like an age, he panting heavily, Ruth hardly daring to breathe. Then he withdrew his hand, pulled her away from the wall and shoved her towards the credenza. She stifled a cry of pain as she fell to the floor once more. He walked back to the decanters and poured himself another drink.

'What does it matter. You won't have to put up with me much longer. If I don't get that money, it will all be over.'

* * *

She lay awake for most of the night, wondering what to do. If Arthur was in such trouble, surely his parents would want to help, no matter what mess he'd got himself in. What would Cyril and Mildred say of their boy? Cyril would be furious, disappointed, but so what. He had more than enough money to help him out of a hole. Mildred would want to protect him. Why didn't he ask her? Ought she to tell them herself? She had no idea how they would react, worse still how Arthur would react if she went behind his back to them, and she had no real idea of the scale of his dilemma. He was obviously in some sort of trouble, but was he truly in the danger he said he was, or was it just another way to extort money to feed his habit?

She remained in her room the following morning, hid her face when the maid came to make the fire. There was a livid purple mark about her throat where he had held her against the wall, bruises to the rest of her body. She thought he might have fractured her arm. When she dressed, she made a sling from one of her silk scarves to relieve some of the pain. When she ventured out of her room, she told Mildred she had fallen downstairs, aware of the irony that she'd told Arthur to tell the truth. She saw a flicker of something pass over her mother-in-law's face that made her think she had an idea of what was going on, but she didn't pass comment and Ruth knew she never would.

42

Alec drifted through the days, going from one pub to another, getting drink where he could, wanting to blot out the mess in his head. He couldn't go back to Letty, not like this. He went to the mission at Riby Square, hoping to get a bed for the night. It was warm inside and he could do with a bath, with fresh clothes. When the attendant at the desk wouldn't let him any further, he got hold of his shirt collar and dragged him over the counter. Someone else was at his back and he lashed out. Another caught his arm and pushed it up between his shoulder blades, pinning him over the desk. The superintendent, Miss Sheldon, came out from her office. Alec was shouting the odds. The man holding him drew him back so she could speak to him. 'Come, come, Mr Hardy,' she said firmly, but not without kindness. 'You know the rules better than any man. I can't let you in unless you're sober.'

'I-I-I ammm soooobah.' Why wouldn't his mouth work the way he wanted it to? He swayed on his feet, but the man held him tight. Were they on a ship? Was he back at sea? Nothing made sense. No sense at all.

'You've a good way to go before you're sober.' She said something to the man who was holding him, and he let him go. Alec staggered and Miss Sheldon caught him. She held his arm in a grip as firm as any man's and sat him down on one of the wooden chairs in the entrance hall. Somehow, he managed to lift his head and look at her. 'Try, for Letty's sake, if not your own. You're a better man than this, Alec.'

The rock in his throat almost choked him. She did not look away from him, but deep into his eyes, and he wanted to blubber like a baby on her shoulder. He wanted his mother, to be a boy again, to have someone tell him what to do and where to go, for the Lord only knew, he had no idea himself. He nodded, tears rolling down his cheeks. He wiped them away with a sweep of his sleeve. He managed to pull himself as upright as he could and staggered to the door. If word got back to Letty, she wouldn't want to show her face here. In all the years they'd lived in Grimsby, she'd volunteered at the mission, lending a hand where she could, whenever she could. She'd not judged the men by their misdeeds. But then she didn't love them, not like she loved him. Did she love him still? He didn't know how she could. He went out into the night, his head down, not knowing what to do next.

* * *

Alec had not returned home on Thursday, and by Friday Dorcas was sick with worry. She'd sat in the front room each night listening for footsteps in the darkness, the swaying gait of the fisherman. Letty might not have forgiven him, but the lass was worried. They all were. Dorcas would wring his daft neck when she found him, causing such upset. Couldn't the lad see that this was not the way to resolve things between man and wife? She'd seen too many men turn to drink to salve their nightmares. It was a hard life at sea, and it was a woman's job to keep a home worth coming back for. Letty was different; she was more than capable of providing for her family herself. She didn't *need* him, she never had, but Dorcas knew she'd loved him.

She began to walk the streets in the hope of finding him, her worry more than her shame as she called in at public house after public house in search of him. She only had to put her head in the door for the landlord or landlady to give a shake of their head to indicate he'd not been seen – or he'd told them not to tell. Either way, she had no news of him.

Letty was wiping the tables when she went back to the café on Friday afternoon. There were few customers. Behind the counter, Hilda and Polly were serving teas and butties to three of the chaps from Doig's. She removed her coat and replaced it with her apron, washing her hands and rubbing them briskly on the towel. A few tables filled up with men who had finished their shift and were in no hurry to go home. They sat with a newspaper and a mug of tea to pass the time. Dorcas had picked up a knife ready to slice bread rolls when a lad burst through the door. He slapped a pal on the back, leaned in and said something. There was a scrape of chairs as they got up. One of them fell to the floor and Letty went to set it upright.

'What's the rush?' she said as they made for the door.

'A body in the dock,' the lad called over his shoulder.

The older men remained where they were. They'd seen bodies enough, but Letty went after them. Dorcas dropped her knife and hurried out to the dockside, muttering prayers in her head. Men crowded about the body. Letty stood back, afraid, but Dorcas forced her way forward. The man was lifted upon a cart and God forgive her for the relief she felt when she saw that it wasn't her boy. She turned to Letty and saw that same relief written on Letty's face too, and the sight of it gave Dorcas hope that, somehow, the two of them could be as one again.

43

The days passed in a haze of drink. When Alec sobered and remembered the *Clarissa*, he found a way to drink again, waiting for someone to drop him a Wesley. There was always someone ready to chuck a bob or two his way. He'd done it himself many times, to men who were on their uppers, who couldn't get work. He drank until he was senseless and put out on the street by the landlord. When the pubs called time, he slept in back rooms, on floors, in alleys. He stank, he was unshaven, and he didn't care. As he walked he would think of Letty, picture her dear face, and see only Becky. He saw the *Black Prince* as it sank below the waves, Henry Evans, a boy, not much more than Alfie, dying of his wounds. The blood and the waste. The terrible bloody waste. He saw the *Artemis* and the men he had served alongside as they cleared the mines off the east coast. One blast and they were no more. He drank to drown the screams, to wash away the faces. He wanted sleep, and darkness, and oblivion. He slumped against the wall in an alley at the back of Orwell Street and slept. He heard men walk past him in the early hours, knowing it was the start of another day, and kept his face to the wall.

When he felt able, he got to his feet, using the wall to keep himself steady and stumbled forward. He knew he couldn't go on like this. He wanted it all to end but didn't know how. He looked to the mission and turned his back on it. He didn't know who he was any more; all he knew was the sea. Somehow or other he had to be back on the water. It was where he belonged. It was all he had left. He leaned against the wall, squinting against the low sun. A passer-by pushed coins into his hand. A half crown. Enough for a bottle of gin. Enough to forget the day. He went into the off-licence and ignored the pity on the shop-keeper's face as he handed over the bottle.

Hours later he walked down Gorton Street, the working day over for the men who walked towards him. It would be hours before the lumpers arrived to unload the catch ready for market, hours before the filleters would be back to gut and clean the fish. He passed the ice factory, the wagons rumbling over the gantry, the odd lump of ice falling around him, and made his way towards the wharf. Smoke drifted from trawlers at berth, the boilers kept going until they were ready to sail. Men moved about the decks: the night watch, men too old to fish but wanting to be on the water, even if they never left harbour. It would be warm and dry, and he might pass an hour or so with any one of them. But not this evening. Twilight. The sky was darkening and the moon sat halfway in the sky. He perched on a capstan, not feeling the cold, until the stars were visible, the gentle lap of the water on the wharf soothing. He couldn't remember when he'd last eaten anything other than the remnants of fish and chips someone else had cast aside. He got to walking again, stopped outside Hardy's café. Letty had been so proud, his mother too. They'd worked hard. They hadn't sat about moping. He shouldn't either. A chap came along with a cart and told him to move on. 'Don't even think about breaking in. Dorcas Hardy will have your guts for garters.'

He laughed. Then cried. Then emptied the bottle and tossed it aside. His head throbbed like the very devil and his feet hurt. His ankle had swollen. At some point he must have fallen. He slumped down against the wall at the side of Wiltshire's, rolled up his trouser leg. Looked down. His head swam and he leaned forward and vomited. He wiped it away with his hands, put his head back against the wall. And at last. Oblivion.

He awoke to someone shaking his shoulders. 'On your feet, Petty Officer Hardy.' The voice was familiar. He put his hand up to his face, the beam of an electric torch dancing over his cheek so as not to blind him. He saw a hand being held out to him, unsure whether to take it. 'Come on, Hardy. There's a good man.' He wanted to weep at the words. He was not a good man. He hesitated, but the hand remained steady. In the end he took it and was pulled to his feet. He squinted in the dim light as the man slung Alec's arm about his shoulders and took his weight. 'Let's get you somewhere warm and dry.'

* * *

Philip Proctor had heard the rumours. He couldn't think what had made a man like Hardy desert his ship, a man who had taken his duties seriously when they had sailed together on the *Black Prince*. After it was scuppered, they were allotted new vessels, but he'd not forgotten their time together. The two of them had brought Henry Evans's body home, had been at his grave the day he was buried. It must have been mightily important for Hardy to leave his post.

He put some of the stew he'd made earlier into a smaller pan, sliced some bread and slathered it with butter. When the stew was sufficiently warmed, he poured it into a pudding basin and set it before Alec. The man was a shadow. His cheeks drawn, his skin grey and unshaven. His hair, unruly at the best of times, was about his neck. He ate like a man starved.

'When you've had that, I'll get you a bowl of water. You can freshen yourself up. You'll feel better for it.'

Alec shrugged. 'It'll take more than a bowl of water.'

While he ate, Philip made a brew and sat down at the table with him. It was sad to see him like this, a broken man. But what was broken could be repaired, perhaps not enough to heal completely but that was down to the man. Philip knew Hardy was equal to it. He'd sat with many such men these last few years. Some wanted to talk out their nightmares; others just needed someone to sit with them. It was guilt mostly. That they had survived when so many had not. Tonight was not the night for talking; the man was exhausted. Philip had stoked the fire when they came in and it had taken hold and was burning strong. He told Alec to sit on the sofa.

'I'm soiled. Filthy.'

'The leather will wipe down.'

Alec hesitated, then sat down, stared at the fire. Philip stacked the dishes and placed them in the sink, made another brew. He pushed a mug into Alec's hand and the two of them sat in silence. Alec drained his mug and got up, placed it on the table.

'I should be going. Thanks for the grub, Proctor.'

'Sit down, man. Unless you're going home to Letty.'

Alec turned his back. Philip got up and put a hand to his shoulder. 'Stay. I'm glad of the company.' He felt Alec's posture weaken and said softly, 'Things will look brighter come the morning.' Alec sat down.

As the evening passed, Alec talked a little of trying to get work but nothing more. Philip did not mention the *Clarissa*. It was enough to break any man. Eventually, Alec's eyes grew heavy, and he fell to sleep. Philip pulled off his boots and pressed him to the sofa, covered him with a blanket. He couldn't see a man suffer and not reach out and try and save him. He was doing no more than Alec Hardy had done countless times before.

* * *

Alec had no idea how long he'd slept, confused as to where he found himself until he recalled Proctor taking him in hand. He sat up, pushing back the blanket and stretching. A sliver of light through a gap in the curtains told him it was morning. He called out but no one responded. He got to his feet and found a note on the table. Proctor had left fresh bread, a wrap of cheese and apples on the table and told him he would be back at one. He looked to the clock on the mantel and saw that it was after noon already. He ate an apple, the moisture filling his mouth. He had no idea what day of the week it was. He drew back the curtains and looked down onto the street. He could see the docks in the distance, the trains in the sidings, men going about their work.

He found a newspaper and saw that it was Wednesday. That was if it was yesterday's paper. News of the loss of the *Clarissa* had come eight days ago. He'd not been home since. He rubbed at his head, trying to recall where he had been, what he had done. He made himself coffee, ate the bread and cheese and when he'd finished took his plate to the sink, washed and dried what he'd used. On the draining board were jam jars and paint brushes.

Proctor came in with a parcel under this arm. 'Afternoon, skipper. Thought a few sausages might go down well.' He set the parcel down at the table. 'Good, you've eaten. I took the liberty of getting you a razor. And a change of clothes.'

Proctor got a bowl and put it on the table, poured some hot water into it, handed Alec a small mirror. He busied himself while Alec stripped and washed with flannel and soap. There was an easy familiarity that had been born of living at close quarters. They'd spent many an hour on deck wondering whether it might be their last. When he was freshened up, he cleared the table and poured the dirty water down the sink.

'I called in at Hardy's,' Proctor said, opening a newspaper and laying it on the table. Alec turned. 'To let your mother know you were safe.'

He nodded, grateful. 'And Letty.'

'She was relieved.'

Alec stared at him. 'She was?'

'You didn't think she would be?'

Alec shrugged.

'Want to talk about it?' Proctor opened a cupboard, pulled out a few potatoes and put them in a bowl, picked up a knife, handed it to Alec. Everything was neat and orderly as it was on the ship, stowed away for rough seas, for something loose could trip you up. Alec thought of the boy, of Becky.

'You do the spuds, and I'll take the onions.'

Alec hesitated.

'It will go no further.'

Alec picked up the knife, a potato, and began to take off the skin, brushing the soil away with his thumb. 'You remember the day the *Artemis* went down?'

Proctor nodded.

'I'd been yarning with the skipper only hours before. He'd been looking forward to being with his family for Christmas.'

Proctor picked up an onion.

'I heard their screams as the ship went down.' He paused, his recollection as clear as if it were yesterday. 'I got pissed. Trying to blot it out.'

Proctor raised an eyebrow.

'Not that it works. Nothing blots it out, does it?'

Proctor shook his head.

Alec continued. 'I left the other fellows and went to the beach. It was where I'd grown up as a lad.' He remembered the walk, the air on his face, the roll of the sea on the shingle. 'My father was lost in the waters off there, and my brother. I'd come to Grimsby to make a fresh start. With Letty. And Mother.' In front of him, the brown papery layers of the onion fell onto the table. Proctor pushed them away with the side of his hand. He did not look up. Alec continued. 'I couldn't take any more loss. I can't even recall how long I was there.' He took a deep breath, let it go. 'There was a lass...'

Proctor picked up another onion.

Alec picked up another potato. 'Becky. She was the lass I cast aside for Letty.' Regret and shame filled him as he recalled that night, those few minutes of recklessness. 'I don't need to say much else, do I.' He gave a small laugh. 'I could make an excuse, blame her. She came astride me. I didn't push her away.' It sickened him to think on it now. What he'd done. The consequences.

Proctor began slicing the onions. 'And Letty found out?'

Alec put down the knife. 'In the worst way possible.' He would never forget the look on her face. The pain he'd caused. But how could he have told her? 'Becky has a son. I believe he's mine.' It was hard to admit, even harder to deny. 'His age. His looks. It all fits.' Alec put down the knife, sank down onto the chair. 'I had no idea meself until last year. Letty needed to go home.'

'And you needed to go with her.'

Alec rubbed his hands over his face. 'I would have done anything to spare the lass the pain. Anything.'

'That's why you turned down the *Clarissa*?'

Alec nodded. It was the first time he'd been able to talk freely. With Dorcas and Letty, he was aware of the hurt and disappointment he'd caused them, the agonies. They couldn't keep it from their faces. Here, he didn't have to be alert to the sharp intakes of breath, the rising energy that meant their anger was too near the surface.

The vegetables prepared, Proctor took the pan of potatoes and filled it with water. He dropped the onions and some butter in a frying pan and opened the sausages from the cream butcher's paper and dropped them in with them. They began to spit, and he turned them with a wooden spoon. Alec took the ends of the newspaper with the peelings and wrapped them up, placed them in the waste bin by the sink. For some unfathomable reason, he felt like a great weight had been lifted from his shoulders. As they sat down to eat, Proctor passed him the salt.

'Well, what's your course, skipper?'

'I don't have one.'

'Then you'd better set one. Otherwise, you'll never get where you want to go.'

44

The following morning, Alec found Proctor at his easel in the room he used as a studio, his sleeves rolled back to his elbows, putting the final touches to a magnificent rendition of the Marshalls' new trawler. He'd seen it come into port. The crew on deck with their families as it came through the lock gates, bunting fixed to the fore and aft, the sound of cheers as it made its way into harbour. It was always a grand day when a new ship arrived to swell the ranks. There was a bed pushed against the wall, the linen and blankets neatly tucked as they were aboard a ship. A pine chest of drawers held his brush, a mirror and his notebook, a photograph or two that Alec assumed were of Proctor's parents.

'Beautiful morning,' Proctor said as Alec joined him. Light shafted through the window, setting his face in shadow.

'It is.' Alec looked about him as Proctor rummaged through his brushes. Canvases of varying sizes were propped against the walls of the room, some half-finished, others complete. Alec was curious. 'Mind if I take a look?'

'Not at all,' Proctor said, taking the cork from a bottle of turps and pouring some of it into a chipped mug. He swished his brush into it, wiped it on a rag that was tucked into his belt.

They were ships mostly, some of sail, others of steam, here and there a landscape, a seascape, the drama of huge waves and spume, a ship in trouble, a boat being rowed out to rescue. A large trunk was turned on its end and on top of it were piles of sketches. Each one bore the immense detail of life around the docks. The braiders, the herring girls, the auctioneers at the market, row upon row of fish in front and behind them. Men in their overalls, working men, all of them part of the industry that supported men who risked life and limb to bring home the catch.

They were resting on a black folder and Alec took it up, unfastened the ribbon. Each and every one of them was of a woman, her eyes unmistakable. The detail of her nose, her lips was so real he felt she could live and breathe. He turned. Proctor was wiping his hands with rags.

'Miss Evans.'

'Mrs Marshall,' Proctor corrected him. He'd never once mentioned how he felt about her to Alec, but there was evidence in every line, every softness of stroke.

'It was a bad day when she married that bugger.' Alec had watched him at the wedding breakfast, how he fawned over Ruth, and known instantly that she was the catch and not the other way around. He wondered that her father couldn't see it then, but now he had more of an understanding. Men do strange things when grief takes hold. 'Let thought she saw him on the night of the fire. Going next door.'

'With a woman?'

Alec shook his head. 'Gambling more like.' Proctor didn't let on what he knew, but he wasn't a man to miss a detail. 'You get to hear things. The men like a gossip to pass the time at sea. As you well know.' He replaced the folder, fastened the ribbon. 'You still see her?'

'Now and again. When I meet with Cyril or Arthur.'

'And she has no idea?'

Proctor sat on the bed. 'No. We wrote letters to each other, hundreds of them. Never once did she give the slightest hint. And she was already with Arthur.'

'If she had?'

Proctor smiled. 'I wouldn't be here sitting talking with you.' He rolled his sleeves down, fastened the buttons. 'Don't make the same mistake as I did, Alec. Don't leave it too late to speak to Letty. She loves you.'

'Aye, I reckon she does. But can she forgive me?'

* * *

Later that afternoon, Proctor had an appointment with the Marshalls at their offices on Wharncliffe Road. Alec was reading the newspaper. There was an item about the new mission being built and the generous donation from Marshall's. He sneered. Nothing was offered quietly; it was all for show. It was a ruddy shame that Ruth had to be part of it all. Letty had said so often enough.

He heard someone coming up the stairs, stopping now and again. He listened. There were more footsteps, another pause as someone hesitated outside the door. They knocked and when he opened the door, he discovered his mother, a parcel under her arm.

'I thought you might be in want of clean clothes.' She looked him up and down. 'Can I come in?' He stood back and she stepped forward, taking in the surroundings.

'How are you, Mother?'

She looked to him, her face pinched by worry, her expression a mixture of sadness and disappointment, and he couldn't bear it.

'I didn't want you walking around in rags.'

'As you can see, I've cleaned myself up.'

She nodded. He knew she was too full of emotion to speak.

'Tea?'

She sat down without replying. He was glad of something to do. While he boiled the water and got down two mugs, she sat looking about her at the paintings.

'You've made yourself something to eat?'

'We've been used to being on ship. We get by.'

'You'll not be coming home any time soon?' She couldn't hide her dismay.

'I'm not sure I'd be welcome.'

She screwed her mouth, stared at her hands.

'How's Letty, the kiddies?'

'Missing you. Stella believes you're at sea. She knows no different. Alfie is well aware of what's gone on. Not the lad, not Becky, but he's not so daft as to understand it's something terrible bad to keep you and Letty apart.' He put the tea in front of her. She held it in both hands, stared at it for a time. 'Come back, son. Thing's'll not mend like this.'

He had not seen her look so sorrowful in years, so deflated, but he couldn't go back, not yet. 'Does Letty know you're here?'

His mother didn't answer.

'If I could turn back time, I would. In a heartbeat.' He saw her eyes fill with tears, but she held them back. It wasn't only Letty's heart he'd broken. His mother had aged in the days since he last saw her and that was all his doing. He reached out and took her hand in his. The palm was rough with hard work, the upper soft with age. There had been too much sadness in her life; he'd not wanted to lay more at her feet. 'I'll find my way back, Mother. I'll set my compass and find my way home. I give you my promise.'

45

Alec had plenty of time to think over the days that followed. He enjoyed his chats with Proctor. Sometimes he watched him paint, others he walked around the docks watching the comings and goings. Pals offered to take him for a drink, but he turned them down. Many a time he stood outside Hardy's thinking of Letty and the kiddies, his mother. But he couldn't face them, not yet. Not until he had set his course. He didn't try for work, knowing there would be none. He had to sit this one out as best he could. His mother had brought some cash from their savings when she visited, and Proctor had loaned him a bob or two. Both would be paid back with interest. He still had money put by from the sale of the *Stella Maris*, though they had all dipped into it from time to time over the last four years, keeping things afloat. There was nowhere near enough to buy even a small ship outright, and no bank would lend him money, not now his reputation was in tatters. He'd been heading in the wrong direction for too long. Now he had to turn his ship around.

Proctor had been invited to dinner with Richard and Evelyn Evans. The Marshalls would be there, and Alec thought how excruciating it must be for him to sit with Ruth, with all the love he had for her and not be able to speak of it. His thoughts turned to Letty. The door was closed to Proctor, but he sensed the door back to Letty's heart might still be ajar. He walked along the wharf, watching as men loaded stores onto the trawlers. He saw many a man he knew and held up a hand in greeting. He was no longer ashamed to hold his head up. His conversations with Proctor had restored some of his dignity, his pride. They'd shared experiences that many others could not contemplate. They had survived. And he owed it to those who had not to live a good life. He stopped at the top of Henderson Street, remembering the night Letty had been caught up in the fire. He could have lost her then. He hadn't know how close he was to losing her altogether.

He walked down to the ruins of Parker's. The insurance money had still not been paid. He thought of Percy. Letty had loved him so. She had taken Alfie to stop him going to the orphanage in Hull. She had a big heart; could she find it in her heart to start again? To forgive him? He stepped inside the ruins of the shop, gutted and blackened. The debris had been cleared but there wasn't much left of what the Parkers had poured their hearts and souls into. He put his hand in his pocket, pulled out his lighter and went through to the back room, where he had sat many a time, yarning with the old boy. Things could be rebuilt. They would never be the same, but they could start again, if they had the will.

He heard a noise in the yard and went outside, saw a rat scurry across the charred wood. Something fell. He picked his way in the darkness, holding his lighter out to guide him. From the corner of his eye he saw a slight movement, then a man, crouched down low. He extinguished the flame. Whoever it was moved but Alec was ready for him. With one large stride he was on him and grabbed him by the collar, pressed his hand hard over his mouth. He was a scrawny bugger and it wouldn't take much to bring him down. 'Make a noise and I'll break your ruddy neck.' He pushed the man into a corner and held up his lighter to his face. 'Crowe. Why, you slimy little bastard.' The man's eyes were almost popping out of his head. If he was terrified, he bloody well should be, the trouble he'd caused. 'Where the bloody hell have you been?'

Crowe flinched at every word, held his hands up to his face. Alec could feel every tremble through his hand. He released his grip. He had nothing to fear from Crowe, but it seemed Crowe was in fear of something greater than Alec. 'It's about time you showed yourself. Perhaps now Letty and Mrs Parker can sort their business out. I'm surprised you've not been here sooner to sort your own mess out.'

Crowe cowered before him. 'What are you going to do with me?'

Alec laughed. 'Do with you?'

Crowe shrank back against the wall, his eyes darting, searching for anyone else that might be with Alec. 'You can't tell anyone you've seen me. You can't.' The man had lost his wits.

Alec tightened his grip once more. 'Now then, let's say we go somewhere quiet, and you can tell me all about it.'

* * *

By the time Alec and Crowe got to the flat, Proctor had returned. He was surprised when Alec pushed Crowe into the room. 'We have a guest, Mr Proctor; let me introduce Mr Crowe.' Crowe stumbled over his own feet. Proctor, ever the gentleman, held out his hand to the chair.

'Do take a seat, Mr Crowe.'

Alec smirked, shoved him into the chair. 'Now then, you little bastard. Where the hell have you been these past months?' He pressed his face up close, then drew back, his fists clenched and ready. 'Because of you, my Letty and Norah can't get the insurance money. Because of you, old man Parker died.' He knew it wasn't strictly true, but it had hurried it along. The fire had been accidental, Letty had told him that – but the result was the same. He'd caused endless suffering and Alec wanted to know why. Crowe was shaking violently, his hands across his face. Good – Alec wanted the bastard to be afraid. If he didn't want answers, he'd gladly have punched his lights out and dropped him in the river.

'I had to go.'

Proctor pulled Alec back and spoke quietly in his ear. 'You'll not find out anything if you don't let him speak.'

Alec stepped back, stood in front of the fire. Proctor gave the man a mug of water. Crowe's hands were shaking so much that water slopped over the side. He put it to his lips and gulped, coughing and spluttering, unable to swallow. He wiped his mouth with his sleeve.

Proctor took the mug from him. 'Why have you not come forward? Your absence has caused all manner of problems.' Alec wouldn't have put it that way, but Crowe's eyes flicked to Proctor, to Alec, then back again.

'I was in fear of my life. My wife and children…' The trembling came worse.

Proctor gave him more water. 'Calm yourself, my good man. There is no threat to you here.'

'Speak for yourself,' Alec muttered. Crowe looked to him. Proctor took the chair opposite their guest, relaxed back into it as if they were having a friendly chat. Crowe let out a long breath. Alec turned his back.

'I was in debt to' – Crowe swallowed – 'someone. I was told to get the Parkers out. I had wanted the shop for years.'

Alec turned. 'Aye, we know that.'

Proctor shot him a look. 'Go on,' he said to Crowe.

'I had given up. Mrs Hardy had made it unlikely the Parkers would sell.' That would have hurt, a mere woman scuppering his plans. 'The premises next door became available. I was loaned money to buy it.'

'And the loan became due?' Proctor suggested.

'Not exactly.' He was quiet, assessing what he was to say next.

Alec grew impatient. 'Come on, man. I haven't got all night.'

Crowe shook again. 'Marshalls wanted all three properties. Mine, Webster's and the Parkers'. I thought I could make a tidy profit from them. The shop was for storage. But that wasn't its true purpose, not when the Marshalls got involved. The properties on Henderson Street back onto their offices on Wharncliffe Road. They had a wall knocked through from Webster's.' Beads of sweat appeared on his forehead. 'Items could be taken in one door and exit through another without raising suspicion. It was concealed on both sides. In Webster's, what outwardly appears to be a safe leads through to Marshall's. They were able to bring things into the store and take them out onto a cart with no one any the wiser.'

'What sort of things?' Proctor asked.

'I don't know.'

'You bloody well do, and you'll tell me.' Alec lurched at Crowe but Proctor got between them.

'Stores. They falsify the stores on their ships. Leave the men short. Then sell them on again and skipper's profits are less.'

Alec had heard rumours, but the men needed work. They would put up with short stores; they would have no choice. They could grumble all they liked but Marshall's had the power and the men did their bidding if they wanted a pay packet at the end of a trip. 'Anything else?'

Crowe pressed his lips together.

'You might as well be hung for a sheep as a lamb,' Alec ventured.

'They had a thing going with one of the naval chaps during the war. Taking supplies of food and suchlike. They never went short of anything at Garth Hall.'

Proctor sat back in his chair. 'You have proof?'

Crowe nodded.

'Theft from the navy is theft from the crown,' Alec said. 'A hanging offence in time of war.'

'At any time,' Proctor qualified. Alec made an action as if to pull a noose. Crowe blanched in fear.

'So why did you risk coming back?'

'My wife and kiddies. I wanted to see them.'

Alec could understand that. He hadn't seen his kids for some time and though they were used to him being away, this was different. He forced himself to focus on Crowe. 'How are they getting on? Your shop is closed. I expect they are awaiting the insurance money as well?'

'Arthur Marshall sends them cash, as long as I stay away.'

'Does he know where you are?'

'He doesn't care as long as I'm not here.'

Alec felt fit to blow a gasket.

'You said you had proof,' Proctor ventured.

Crowe nodded. 'The wife has it in her safekeeping. I have the records from the goings-on. They thought they had burned in the fire, but I went back for them. They had been stored in safety. My own insurance, if you will. Arthur is a gambler.'

'That's no secret,' Alec said bitterly.

'He had... has,' Crowe corrected himself, 'large debts that his father has no knowledge of. When the fire started, he was in Webster's. He'd wagered his plot of land where his house is being built. And lost it. He was glad of the fire. Shackleton had taken his paper. He wanted five hundred pounds to get it back. Arthur could only manage to raise two. Shackleton has threatened to go to his father and expose him if he doesn't come up with the rest.'

'How do we know you're telling the truth?'

'I left the game to go next door to Parker's. The fire was an accident, I swear it. I wanted the Parkers out but not like that.' The man looked fit to weep but managed to keep control of himself. 'Marshall was glad of it. It's bought him time.'

Alec whistled through his teeth. He looked to Proctor.

'He wanted me out of the way. And I wasn't going to argue.' Crowe swallowed. 'The body in the docks. Stenning?'

Alec nodded.

'He was in the card game the night of the fire. The same will happen to me if they find out I've been hereabouts.' He wrung his hands. 'I need to be away before anyone sees me. If word gets back—'

'We can help you with that,' Proctor said. 'But you'll need to help us first.'

Crowe nodded. 'I have nothing to lose.'

'Only your life,' Alec reminded him.

* * *

Alec and Proctor decided between them on the best way forward. They had no idea who the Marshalls had under their thumb. They had made large donations to various charitable institutions and funded public buildings. Their connections were widespread, at every level of the local community. Any member of the police or legal profession could be in their favour, and so plans were made to take the case out of town. Proctor had a connection in Chester, a solicitor who had agreed to take on the case. Crowe remained at the flat with Proctor while Alec went to his missus and retrieved the paperwork. It was illuminating to discover the depths of the Marshalls' underhand dealings. When ships had been requisitioned by the navy for conversion as minesweepers or support vessels, the owners had been paid for the hire of them, or purchased outright. Marshalls had falsified the documents, ensuring themselves a good profit while men sacrificed their lives, and their livelihoods. Proctor was appalled when he saw the evidence, more so when he learned that a naval petty officer had lined his own pockets by diverting supplies to the Marshalls. It sickened him.

Having gone through all the paperwork, Alec and Proctor plotted their course. Proctor personally accompanied Crowe to safety, having assured him that his wife and children would be taken care of. Crowe's family followed soon after, Alec organising to have their furniture packed up and moved at the crack of dawn. Proctor's only concern was for Ruth. Neither she nor Arthur had attended the dinner at her father's the night Crowe was found, cancelling as Ruth was unwell.

'This will affect her, when it all comes to light. I would not hurt her for the world.'

'We don't have to do anything,' Alec offered. 'We can wash our hands of Crowe and let him face the music.'

Proctor shook his head. 'We can't let the Marshalls get away with it. If we do, we're no better than they are.'

While Proctor accompanied Crowe to Cheshire, Alec remained at the flat. It would take time for a case to be built against the Marshalls. It would be a grand day when their dealings were brought to light. He could wait long enough for that and play the long game. Crowe was the key and Alec needed him to stay alive, at least until he'd committed to paper what happened the night of the fire. Then the insurance would be sorted and Letty and Norah would get their payout. Perhaps things were not beyond rescue after all.

46

Ruth's arm had not healed by the following Thursday, but she refused to miss the guild, given it was the annual fundraising meeting. And Evelyn would be suspicious if she didn't turn up given that she now had the car. The bruises had mostly healed and a little dusting of powder and rouge concealed what remained of the bruise about her neck, a judiciously placed scarf hiding the rest. Mildred had tried to dissuade her, saying driving one-handed was far too dangerous. But she did not offer to help. Ruth was long past expecting any. She had removed her sling, not wanting to attract comment and have to tell more lies. It ached like the devil but if she raised it across her midriff while seated, she thought she might manage. Arthur's deadline had come and gone, and he was still alive, which made her think the threats to his life, and hers, had been a fabrication – though perhaps the net was closing in on him, for he appeared nervous and agitated, so much so that his mother thought a visit to the doctor was called for. Arthur had blamed pressure at work and problems with the builders, which Mildred had been happy to accept. Ruth despised his weakness, despised the way his mother accepted his explanation without question. Mildred avoided any unpleasantness in her life, ignoring it until it no doubt went away. She had seen Ruth's bruises and looked beyond them, not wanting to believe it was anything to do with her son.

The car had been driven to the stable and she made her way there, wondering herself how she could manage, but she at least had to try. She placed her bag on the passenger seat, picked up the crank and inserted it into the front of the car. It was awkward, her right arm totally useless, but she bent to turn it. The car spluttered and died. She tried again, tears of frustration pricking. She was about to give up when someone came up behind her. She tensed, forced back the tears. Had Mildred come to gloat?

'Let me, Mrs Marshall.' Ruth turned to find the maid. Her look left Ruth in no doubt that the girl knew what had been going on. Wordlessly, the maid took the crank from her and indicated that she get into the car. When she did so, the girl cranked the engine. It immediately came to life and as the maid stepped to one side, Ruth released the brake, and moved the car forward.

'Can you manage with one hand?' the maid shouted over the noise. Ruth had no doubt the girl would come with her if she asked, but she would probably pay for it with her job and Ruth didn't want to cause any more misery.

'I'm not sure. But I'm going to try.' She turned the wheel, grimaced.

The maid stepped onto the footplate. 'If you move to the passenger seat, ma'am, I'll do my best to get you where you need to be. I'm sure between us we can manage it.'

Ruth could have wept. The girl would be well aware of the consequences if Mildred saw her. Determined to make the meeting, Ruth moved her seat and began instructing the maid as only the week before Evelyn had instructed her. It was a slow and bumpy start but they had plenty of time – and Ruth was determined not to be beaten.

* * *

When Ruth arrived at the mission and walked to the meeting room, things were already underway. Evelyn twisted and smiled as Ruth took a seat on the back row next to Letty. 'I'm so glad you came,' Letty whispered, facing forward. 'We're on refreshments. We'll have chance to catch up.' Mrs Barton was chairing the meeting, reading out the apologies, specifically from Aunt Helen, who was attending a mayoral event with Uncle Jack and would join them at her earliest convenience.

At ten minutes before the hour, Letty and Ruth quietly got up and slipped through to the kitchen. They set out rows of cups and saucers, plated up biscuits and cakes and filled the milk jugs. Letty was too busy to notice that Ruth was struggling but she managed as best she could with her left hand. All was going well until Ruth filled the large metal teapot with boiling water. Her arm gave way as she carried it towards the hatch and the teapot clattered to the floor, sending sprays of scalding hot water all over her skirt, her legs. She cried out in pain. In the adjoining room, everything went quiet.

Letty sprang to her. 'We need to get cold water on it immediately.'

Ruth was close to tears. She couldn't allow Letty to see her legs. 'No, no, it will be fine. Please.' She looked to Letty.

Lucy Hewitt came to the hatch. 'Everything alright, Mrs Hardy, Mrs Marshall?'

'There has been an accident. Could someone take over?'

'Of course,' Lucy Hewitt said, her face full of her concern. 'Rosa and I will deal with it. You do what you have to do, ladies.'

Letty led Ruth to the small washroom off the kitchen, pulled the towel from the roller, ran cold water over it and passed it to Ruth, telling her to put it over her legs. 'You need to remove your stockings. The skin will blister. And I need to check your legs. We might need a doctor to see to it.'

'I can't. I...' She was at a loss as to how she could explain away the bruises on her legs.

'Ruth, you must.' Letty was aghast. Ruth was aware that not complying would be more suspicious. She tried to remove her stocking, hampered by not being able to use both hands. Her clumsiness worsened as she began to shake uncontrollably, mostly with pain, but also the knowledge that her injuries would be more than the addition of hot water. Seeing her struggle, Letty kneeled at her feet and began peeling down the stocking. As her bruises were revealed, Letty stopped and looked up to Ruth.

'I fell.' Ruth swallowed, her throat tight with fear. 'Down the stairs.' The bruises had turned an angry purple and yellowed at the edges. The skin had swollen and reddened with the hot water, but the evidence of Arthur's brutality had been revealed.

'Dear God.' Letty sat back on her heels.

'Please, don't let Evelyn know. She'll tell Father.'

'But, Ruth...'

She caught Letty's hand. 'Please.'

Letty nodded. 'Let me get Miss Sheldon. She will be discreet.'

Alone, Ruth toyed with the idea of leaving, the maid waiting for her in the car, but everything had begun to hurt, most of all her pride. Paralysed with fear, she waited for Letty to return.

* * *

Letty was appalled. The moment she'd caught sight of the bruises, she had known what was going on. She'd seen it among the women of Mariners Row and other shabby dwellings, women trapped by poverty, who had no option but to put up with a beating, for they had nowhere else to go. But to see it happen to a woman of Ruth's standing was shocking. She hurried to Miss Sheldon's office and, finding the door open, rapped once and went inside.

'Miss Sheldon. Could I trouble you to call the doctor? It's most urgent.'

'Which man?'

'Miss Ev... Mrs Marshall has been scalded by hot water. I have left her with a cold compress, but I think she would benefit from a doctor's opinion.' She hoped her look had conveyed her meaning.

'Should I call Mr Marshall?'

Letty shook her head. 'She would rather not. Not at this stage.'

Miss Sheldon held her gaze and no more words were needed. 'I'll get a man out to the surgery straight away.'

* * *

To Ruth's shame, it was Jeremy Howard who came to tend to her. The look of pity he gave her was too much to bear, and where she had managed to hold back the tears she could hold them no more. He turned to Letty. 'Could you get my sister?'

Evelyn smiled when she saw Ruth, oblivious to the extent of her injuries, which were concealed as Jeremy tended to her. 'I didn't know you were here, Jeremy. I hear Ruth spilled a cup of tea on herself.' Her brother stood back, exposing Ruth's injuries. He had fastened a sling about her arm and that had helped ease some of the pain, but she was more fearful of what would happen now that Evelyn was involved.

Her stepmother gasped, horrified when she saw Ruth's legs. 'What *has* he done to you?'

'You must not breathe a word of it to Father,' Ruth begged.

Evelyn squatted in front of her, pressed her hand to Ruth's face. It was soft and cool, and tender. 'Why ever not? He would want to know.' Her voice wavered with emotion. 'You must not conceal this from him. He loves you. We love you.'

'It's my fault. I'm not the wife he wants me to be.'

'Oh, darling. This is not your fault. None of it is.' Evelyn stared again at the bruises, clasped hold of Ruth's good hand. 'Would you expect your father, or your brothers, to have behaved in this way? What would you think of them, if they did? It is wrong. He has no right to treat you like this.' Tears were in her eyes and Ruth could not bear her pity. 'Was it the car?'

'No.'

'But that was part of it?'

Ruth did not answer.

'I had no idea that it had gone this far. I thought Arthur was merely controlling. If only you'd said something.'

Ruth looked at her. 'But what could I have said?'

Evelyn stroked her hair, kissed her forehead. 'Nothing, my darling, nothing.' She looked to her brother. 'I'm taking Ruth home.' Ruth flinched. Evelyn squeezed her hand. 'Home to Meadowvale House. Where she'll be safe. And loved.'

47

When Richard Evans had seen the state his daughter was in, he'd wept. Then he'd been furious. Ruth had become so distressed that Evelyn had taken him into his study to calm him while Mrs Murray tended to Ruth. She could not bear to see the pity on their faces. When she had protested that she should go home, Mrs Murray had all but broken down herself. She had made Ruth lie down on the sofa in the sitting room and brought her a glass of water. When Evelyn returned, Mrs Murray went to the kitchen to make her something to eat. Ruth heard her sob as she left the room. Evelyn brought the small chair to the sofa and sat facing Ruth, took hold of her hand.

'Where's Father?'

'On the telephone to Garth Hall.'

Ruth had felt the blood drain from her face.

Evelyn smoothed her fingers over Ruth's hand. 'Don't distress yourself. He is merely informing them that you will be staying with us tonight.'

'He hasn't said anything? About...' She glanced to her legs. Jeremy had given her something to numb the pain, but her legs throbbed where she'd been scalded. He had examined her only to reveal the bruises on her lower back. Evelyn had been enraged when she saw them. Letty had paled with horror. At that moment, Ruth had felt she might drown in her shame. When she'd arrived at Meadowvale House, Jeremy had asked Mrs Murray for a small stool or something similar that could be put over her legs to form a tent, ensuring the cloth did not touch her skin. He'd made her as comfortable as possible before leaving her to Evelyn's care.

'Nothing more,' Evelyn reassured her. 'I told him he needed to speak with you first. To know what *you* wanted to do.'

Ruth was grateful for her intervention. 'I couldn't face Arthur, or his parents. Not at the moment.'

Evelyn nodded her understanding. 'Do you love him?'

Ruth couldn't answer.

'I thought not.'

'I wanted to make him happy. To make Father happy. I thought if I was married, he wouldn't have to worry about me any more.' Marriage to Arthur had been presented as a good thing. And she had not wanted to be one of the million surplus women that the newspapers talked of. Women who would never know love, or tenderness. 'It doesn't happen all the time. He is always sorry afterwards.' Or he had been, until this latest episode. He'd not come to ask for her forgiveness as he usually did. There had been no flowers, no grand gestures.

Evelyn stopped her.

'Don't make excuses for his behaviour. It was wrong. In every way. When you love someone, you cherish them, and yes, you put their happiness above your own. But *this*.' She looked to the cage about Ruth's legs. 'This is not what you do to someone you love.'

* * *

Evelyn had arranged for a man to take the maid to Garth Hall and return Ruth's car to Meadowvale House. Less than hour later, Aunt Helen charged into the room.

'Mrs Barton said Ruth had been taken ill.'

She was appalled when Evelyn lifted the blanket and revealed the extent of Ruth's injuries.

'What on earth has happened?'

Evelyn told her.

Ruth's aunt was visibly distressed and her brother immediately went to her side, taking her from the room and into his study. Voices were raised and Evelyn got up and closed the door.

'I didn't want to cause trouble for anyone.'

'*You* haven't caused anything. Arthur is answerable for it all. And by God will he answer for it.'

Her aunt was red-eyed when she came to sit with Ruth, her father close behind her. Evelyn got up from the dining chair that had been drawn close to the sofa and Helen took her place.

'I have a mind to drag Cyril and Mildred down here so they can see for themselves what damage their son has done. God help me if I get hold of Arthur...'

'Please don't, Aunt. Not today. I don't want them here.' Ruth was finding it all too difficult, seeing those around her so upset, but she didn't have the strength to resist. Her father was still puce with rage.

Helen looked down at her hands. 'If for one moment I'd thought...' Her voice trembled with emotion, and she swallowed it back, lifted her head high.

'I didn't make him happy. I couldn't bear a child. He was disappointed.'

Aunt Helen couldn't hide her shock. Gently, she took Ruth's

hand in hers, gripped it as much as she dared, and leaned close to her niece.

'In all the years with your uncle he has never, not once, made me feel that our not being blessed with children was anything to do with me. He has never made me feel less than a woman for it, and I hope I have never made him feel less of a man. We are all played a different hand in life; we make of it what we will.' She smoothed her palm over Ruth's cheek. 'You are my child. I might not have given birth to you, but I love you as my own. Don't ever forget that.' She paused, overcome, composed herself. 'There are many ways to be a mother. I was lucky to be able to find out for myself, with you. Henry. Charles.' Tears slipped down her aunt's cheek and Ruth reached out to wipe them away.

* * *

That night Ruth slept in her old bed, her father and Evelyn taking it in turns to sit with her. Her father was haggard, barely able to conceal his fury. He had wanted to drive over to Garth Hall and have it out with Arthur, leave Cyril and Mildred in no doubt as to what kind of animal their son was. Ruth had begged him not to go and Evelyn had calmed him, asking him to agree to Ruth's wishes until she felt able to tell them more. It had been upsetting, and exhausting, recounting the horrors of the last few weeks, of Arthur's insistence that his life was in danger, as was hers. Her father had listened, his fist clenched, biting back his anger.

'There was plenty of money to finish the house. Has it all gone?'

'I don't know,' Ruth had admitted. 'Arthur dealt with everything. At first I saw it as his being protective. If ever I asked, he would tell me not to worry. If I pressed him, he would get angry, insist it was all in hand. In the end I didn't bother to ask, knowing he wouldn't give me a straight answer.'

'I'll kill him with my bare hands.'

'Please, Father. Don't upset yourself.'

'Upset myself—'

Evelyn had gone to him, said something so quietly Ruth couldn't hear. He'd stared out of the window, and she'd seen his shoulders drop. He'd turned, smiled at her, his eyes filled with sadness. 'I'll leave you with Evelyn. Cool my temper elsewhere, darling girl.' He'd planted a kiss on her forehead as he had done when she was a child, and she'd felt her heart swell with pain that she had caused him such distress.

* * *

Philip Proctor returned from Chester having secured lodgings for Gilbert Crowe and his family with the aid of the solicitor who was taking on his case. A barrister was in receipt of the incriminating documentation. In his learned opinion, the evidence against the Marshalls was damning. His advice was not to make a move until they had built a sound case. As such, they didn't want to alert the Marshalls of any investigation and give them the opportunity to build a defence – or dispose of any incriminating evidence that they themselves might be in possession of. Alec had appraised Philip of Ruth's situation when he arrived at the flat. Alec's mother had visited and told him of it. Philip knew of Letty and Ruth's friendship and thanked God for it. For who knew how long things might have gone on otherwise?

At Meadowvale House, Philip was greeted by Mrs Murray and shown into the sitting room. Through the French windows, he could see Ruth in the garden. She had an open book on her lap, Evelyn at her side. She lifted her face to the sun and Evelyn said something to her. If only he had spoken up all those years ago, he might have spared her this.

Richard Evans joined him; they shook hands. Richard asked him to take a seat. Philip told him of the Marshalls, of what had been discovered, and what might lie ahead. 'I had wanted to protect Ruth. Perhaps that will not be necessary now.'

'And Cyril is involved?'

'We have evidence to show that he was. Although Arthur's gambling debts are another matter. I fear he may have risked the money you gave to them as a wedding gift.'

Richard placed his hands on the mantel, leaned into the fire. 'He has. But I don't give a damn about the money.' His voice broke with emotion and he remained with his back to Philip. The door to the garden opened and Evelyn came into the room. The telephone rang out and Richard seemed glad to excuse himself as he went to answer it. Evelyn shook Philip's hand; hers was cold but her grip was firm.

'Philip. Good to see you. How are you?'

'Well, and yourself?'

'I'm fine.'

'Ruth?'

She turned to look out into the garden. 'Fragile. Finding herself at fault. I could kill the excuse for a man.'

'I visited Garth Hall many times. I had no idea.'

'She kept it from us all.' Evelyn looked to the garden. 'Why don't you go out to her? I'm sure she'll be glad to see a familiar face.'

As he stepped out and walked towards Ruth, she looked up from her book and smiled. She had a bloom to her cheeks but as he came closer the sadness in her eyes was unmistakeable.

'Philip.'

He motioned to the seat beside her. 'May I?'

She nodded. 'I was thinking of the time we sat sketching together. Do you remember?'

'How could I forget.' The day was imprinted on his heart. 'We went to the theatre afterwards. With your father and Henry.'

She smiled, remembering. 'It was a lovely day.'

He couldn't imagine how much her heart was hurting, and he yearned to be the one to heal it.

'There will be lovely days again.' He reached for her hand. This time he would not let her go.

48

It had been six weeks since Alec had learned of the loss of the *Clarissa*. Six weeks since he'd seen Letty and the children. His mother dropped by now and again but mostly she left him to sort himself out, hoping and praying that he would find a way back. Now that things had progressed with the case against the Marshalls, he felt able to make his move. He had a clean shirt and collar, his tie, a clean suit. Proctor slapped him on the back.

'Good luck, Hardy. I hope it all goes well.'

He stopped outside the Excel offices on Wharncliffe Road and took a breath, stepped inside and was shown into Evans's office. Richard Evans smiled when he saw him.

'You look well, Hardy. I had heard—'

'All true, Mr Evans,' Alec said.

Evans shook his head. 'I had heard from Philip Proctor that you were doing well.'

'He's been a good friend to me, sir.'

Evans nodded. 'And you to him by all accounts. Take a seat, Hardy.'

Alec did so. It gave him confidence to be offered a seat.

'What can I do for you?'

'I wanted work.'

'You know I can't give you skipper?'

'I do, Mr Evans. It wouldn't be fair on the men. But I am willing to start again, as deckie. Cook. Whatever you can offer me.' He didn't want to come over as weak. He wanted a chance, a helping hand as Proctor had offered to him.

'You have to prove yourself to them, not just me.'

'I have a lot of people to restore their faith in me, sir.'

Evans stared at his desk, shifted the paper and moved his pen. Alec hardly dared breathe.

'The *Valiant* is short of a deckhand. She sails tomorrow. If you're available?'

Alec had a lump in his throat. 'I am.' He got up. 'Thank you, Mr Evans, I won't let you down.' He reached out for Evans's hand across the desk.

The man took it in his and placed his other hand over the top of it. 'I know that, Hardy. You could have come here long before and asked in Henry's name. It would have been hard to deny you. To your credit you did not. A lesser man in your position would have.'

'You don't want to know why I turned down Hammond's ship, the *Clarissa*?'

Evans shook his head. 'You would have had your reasons.'

'The ship was lost with all hands.'

'It would have made no difference had you been on it. It was not your time.' Evans looked down at his hands. Was he thinking about his own boys who had gone in their prime? 'God spared you. You have been given another chance. Don't waste it, my boy.'

Back on the street, Alec looked up at the sky and thanked Henry Evans, for surely the lad had whispered in his father's ear.

He had work. It was a long road ahead, but he was on his way. Alec pulled his cap over his head and set off with a spring in his step. At last, he could set his course.

He called in at the flat to tell Proctor his good news and they celebrated with a brew and a biscuit. For the second time that morning, Proctor wished him luck before he left. He cut back down Orwell Street, past the public baths and Miss Sheldon's house. He'd not gone far when he heard a dog yelping in pain. He looked to see where it was coming from, decided it was the alley to his right. He crossed over the road, peered down it and saw the shadow of a man. He had a mongrel on a piece of string and was lashing out at it with a stick, the dog cowering, doing its damnedest to pull away from him. Even from a distance it was obvious there wasn't much meat on the scraggy little mutt. He strode down the alley, the sound of his boots echoing in his ears. 'Oi, yer nasty sod. What's the poor little beggar done to deserve that?'

The man turned. 'Nowt to do with you so keep yer neb out.' He raised the stick again. Alec sprang towards him and yanked it from his hands. It was the man's turn to cower.

'Like a bit of it yerself, would yer?' Alec challenged. The chap threw the rope at him.

'Have the little bastard, and much good it'll do yer,' he called as he hurried away. Alec turned his attention to the dog, the poor little runt shaking from nose to tail. It reminded him of Gilbert Crowe – things were ticking along on that front. Letty would have her insurance money soon enough. Things had taken a better turn today. He squatted on his haunches.

'Now then, little fella. I ain't going to hurt yer.' He patted the ground with the flat of his hand. 'You take your time. I've got all day. And all night if you must.' He fumbled in his trouser pockets and found a bit of biscuit. He held it out to the dog, who inched forward and took it from him. Alec touched the dog. It was a sorrowful sight; he couldn't just leave it. 'Best you come home with me. Letty might take pity on the pair of us.' He ruffled the dog's small head. 'Though I reckon you might have more chance than me at being allowed to stay.'

His mother had called that morning and told him Letty would be at home that afternoon. Dorcas was taking her shift at the café. He ran his finger around his collar, glanced down at the dog at his feet. He wondered whether to walk straight in – it was his home after all – or whether he should knock and wait. He opted for the latter.

Through the glass he saw someone coming towards the door. He knew it wasn't Letty. Norah beamed when she saw him. 'Good to see you, Alec. And looking so well.' She looked to the dog. 'Moral support?'

He smiled. 'Something like that.' She stepped back, allowing him to pass and he was strangely nervous, wondering how Letty would react. She was at the table, working on her accounts, her head bent over the ledgers. Billy had fallen asleep on the floor of the playpen and she had put her cardigan over him. He wanted to reach down and touch his son but didn't want to disturb him. His heart skipped a beat. She put down her pen, looked to him. She noticed the dog. At the same moment, Stella came in from the yard. She dropped her skipping rope on the floor and ran towards him. Alec let go of the dog and swept her into his arms, buried his face in her dress. He'd missed her so much. Missed all of them. Could he get any of it back again?

Stella clasped his head in her small hands and planted kisses on his cheek over and over again. The dog barked and she wriggled to be put down. 'Is it our dog?' She looked to her mother.

'It was being beaten,' Alec told her. 'I couldn't stand by.'

'No. You wouldn't.' Letty closed the book in front of her.

Norah came in with Stella's coat in her hands, already wearing her own. 'How about we take the dog for a walk?'

'Has it got a name?' Stella asked.

'I don't know,' Alec replied. 'I didn't ask the man.'

'Is it a girl or a boy?'

Alec checked. 'It's a girl. I suppose we ought to give her name. So she knows she belongs.'

Stella patted the dog's head, took hold of the piece of string.

'Can you think of something for me?'

'Nanny Norah, what do you think?'

'Let's talk about it while we walk.' Norah took hold of his daughter's other hand and led her away, Stella chattering ten to the dozen. When the front door closed behind them Letty got up. He wanted to hold her, bury his face in her hair, touch and taste her skin, kiss her, but held back, knowing he had to wait. How long he didn't know. It wasn't up to him.

'I came to tell you I have work.'

'I'm pleased.' She was tight-lipped.

He went on. 'Deckhand. Mr Evans took me on.'

Letty put the accounts book away on the dresser, placed the ink and pen in the drawer. She kept her back to him. 'And you're not too proud to start at the bottom?'

'I'm not too proud for anything.'

She gave a slight nod of her head.

'I was thinking of coming back home.'

She didn't reply. She was making him sweat, as he'd known she would. He hadn't thought for one minute that she would make it easy for him. But she hadn't turfed him out. She hadn't thrown anything. Yet. He was encouraged. She closed the drawer. He moved a step closer. She turned to face him.

'It'll be for the one night. I sail tomorrow afternoon.'

'Your mother will be pleased. Alfie will be glad to see you. The children have missed you.'

'I've missed them.' They'd been in his thoughts every day. 'And I missed you.' He wanted to touch her but was afraid; his hands hung loose at his side. 'I can't do anything to wipe away the past, Letty. If I could, Lord knows I would. All I'm asking is that you give me a chance.'

'You broke your mother's heart. You were her world, *are* her world. She held you above everyone.'

'It's your heart that concerns me.'

She was cool, calm.

'I didn't know what I was doing. I was in a state.'

'And that's what hurts most of all.' The pain in her eyes was still there but he couldn't look away, however uncomfortable it made him feel. He had to stay and listen. Listening healed; he knew that from his nights talking to Proctor. 'It wasn't just sex. You wanted comfort and she gave it.'

'It wasn't.' He wanted to explain, to make it right but he knew words were not enough and never would be. She went to the stove, took the kettle and filled it with water. It was what she did when she was angry, doing something, anything to stop her anger bursting forth. 'I can't ask you to forgive me, because I can't forgive myself.' He stood beside her, took the kettle from her and placed it on the stove. She remained where she was and he was overcome with such powerful love for her that he had to touch her, even if it was for one last time. He took hold of her hand. At first, she wouldn't look at him. He gently took hold of her chin and lifted it. 'I love you, Letty. I have only ever loved you as a man loves a woman. I was in a bad place.' She tried to pull away from him, but his grip was too strong. 'I will spend the rest of my life making it up to you.'

He didn't kiss her; he wasn't sure she wanted him to. She merely gave a nod of her head and he let her go.

'Better sit yourself down. I need to get on with the dinner.'

* * *

Stella bounced into the room when she returned, flinging the door wide, Norah at her heels. 'We're going to call the dog Tess. We practised calling her name in the park.' She undid the string from around the dog's neck and it immediately crawled under the table. Stella squatted in front her and rubbed her thumb over her fingers. 'Tess. Come on, Tess.' The dog crawled out on its belly and Stella took it gently about the neck, ruffling it and smoothing its patchy fur. 'She likes her name, Mother. Can we keep her?'

Letty sighed, shook her head, then smiled at her child. 'I'm sure we can find room for her, seeing as she's only small. As long as you and Alfie take her for walks, mind.' The delight on Stella's face was a picture and Alec heaved a sigh of relief.

'Thanks, Let. I was thinking of taking her to sea with me, if not.'

She looked at him from under her lashes. 'I think it'll be a while before you're given any concessions, don't you? Deckies don't hold much sway.'

* * *

A good hour later, Dorcas came home from the café. Norah was sitting in the armchair and Alec was laying the table, Letty at the stove. The back door was open, and she heard the children in the yard, a dog barking followed by squeals of delight. She looked to Letty, hoping the lass knew just how grateful she was, glad that her boy had come home at last.

* * *

That night it was the best feeling in the world to be lying in his own bed, next to his wife. He knew she wasn't asleep, and he was afraid to speak lest he spoil the little progress he'd made. She reached across for his hand, and he wanted to weep with the relief of it. 'I love you, Letty.'

'I know.'

'Could I kiss you goodnight?'

It was a long time before she answered him. He heard the clock strike the half hour in the room below, heard a horse and cart pass by in the street. He felt the movement of her head on the pillow as she turned to him. He turned too. He put his hand to her face, felt her tears, tears of his making. He kissed her cheek, then her mouth. She caught his hand.

'I don't know how we'll work it out, Alec. God knows you've hurt me. But I love you, and we'll find a way.'

49

At the end of the following week, Aunt Helen accompanied Evelyn, Ruth and her father to Garth Hall to collect her belongings. They would have done it in her absence, but Ruth had insisted she go; she had nothing to be ashamed of. She had not heard from Arthur, other than to learn that he had been set upon by some thugs, causing her father to comment that, 'We reap what we sow.'

Mildred came to meet them and Ruth was shocked to see the woman who had dominated this household somewhat shrunken by the events of the past few days. She was stiff-lipped as Ruth's aunt came to join them.

'Helen.'

'Mildred.'

'We've come to collect Ruth's belongings. Shall we go straight up?'

Mildred shifted uncomfortably. 'Surely it doesn't have to go this far. These young people can sort out their differences. Can't we do that, Ruth?'

'We're beyond that, Mildred. I trust Arthur has told you of his version of what's gone on. Of his gambling debts?'

Mildred stiffened. Aunt Helen was in no mood for negotiation and Mildred stepped back to let them pass.

Ruth felt for mother-in-law, her world crumbling about her. And worse to come. Her father had informed Ruth of the covert investigation on the Marshalls, of what Philip Proctor and Alec Hardy had uncovered. 'Thank God there are still good men in this world,' her father had said. She was quite sure Mildred had no idea of the extent of the situation. She ran her home and Cyril ran the business. A rude awakening was in store, but Ruth wouldn't breathe a word of it. Mildred had turned a blind eye to the goings-on under her own roof; Ruth would do the same.

* * *

The maid led them upstairs. Two trunks were open on the floor of Ruth's old room and they wasted no time in filling them. Ruth went through her clothing, taking only what she'd had before her marriage, the maid and Evelyn folding them, Aunt Helen staring out over the lawns. Ruth opened her jewellery box, and wasn't in the least surprised to find it empty.

'Arthur?'

Ruth nodded. 'He needed to get money somehow. He wouldn't care where it came from.'

She picked up her mother's handheld mirror, brush and comb. 'At least he didn't take these. It's all I really came for.' She handed them to the maid, who wrapped them in fine tissue.

'I was afraid you might have been dismissed for accompanying me last week.' It had been playing on her mind that Mildred might see fit to sack the maid. 'If you ever decide to leave, we would find work for you.'

'That's very kind of you, ma'am, but my family live in the village. I'm close to them here. It's important to me.'

'It is,' Ruth agreed, watching her aunt and Evelyn fold the last of her clothes into the trunk. When they were done, the three women went back downstairs and waited on the drive for them to be loaded into Aunt Helen's car. Her father had remained in his at Ruth's request, fearing he might lose his temper. Ruth had had enough of harsh words and raised voices, and Helen was more than any match for anything Mildred might say or do.

Her aunt made sure Ruth was comfortable in the rear of her father's car before walking to her own. Her father turned to her as Evelyn took her place beside him.

'Did you get everything?'

'Everything I wanted.'

Her father smiled, his first in days, and the two cars turned away from Garth Hall and made their way down to the road.

* * *

Philip Proctor called every day to update her father on the progress of the case against the Marshalls. An arrest was imminent. He did not leave without sitting with Ruth for a while, thoughtful as always. She had been sketching in the sitting room when he came to join her. She was delighted to find that on this occasion he had brought his own sketchpad and pencils, a portable paintbox and some brushes.

'Might I join you?'

'Of course.' She had been hoping he would. She went to the kitchen for a jam jar of water and when she returned he had adjusted the furniture, bringing two chairs side by side, a small table between them. She had been sketching a vase of roses, and he removed one, laid it on the table. Ruth admired the composition.

'That makes things more interesting,' she commented. 'It doesn't take much, does it? Just a small adjustment makes all the difference.'

The light from the window fell onto her face when he moved and for a moment she was blinded, Philip in silhouette. As he came close, she knocked the small table, sending the pencils onto the floor. She bent to pick them up and Philip rushed forward to do the same. Their fingers touched and Ruth felt a shot of electricity surge through her. She lifted her eyes to his, able to see clearly now. It was as if someone had opened a pocket in her brain, for at last she could see that Philip looked at her the way Evelyn looked at her father. How had she not noticed before? He pulled himself upright, held out the pencil. She got up to take it from him. 'Philip.' She waited for him to say something, afraid of what it all meant. Had she got it wrong again? She smiled, hesitant; her heart was beating louder than the grandfather clock in the corner. He opened his mouth to speak, closed it again. She caught her breath.

He took her hand, lifted it to his lips, drew her gently towards him, his arm about her waist. 'Oh, Ruth. You've been through so much. I don't want to rush you.' His expression was pained. 'I held back once before and lost you. I don't want to lose you again.'

She put her hand to his chest, could feel his heart beating beneath it, as loud and fast as her own and she smiled again, looked into his eyes, hoping he could see the love in them. And then he kissed her, and she knew there was no need to ask.

50

It took eight months for the restoration of Parker's Chandlery to be completed and ready to open for business. Once the insurance company had been in possession of Gilbert Crowe's affidavit, the payment to Norah and Letty had been released to their bank accounts. The turmoil and uncertainty triggered since the fire had finally come to an end, but that was not the best reason to rush headlong into putting things right. Not that they ever could be righted; they could only go forward. Norah was in her sixties. She wouldn't want to start again. Letty had urged her to make her choice on what she wanted to do with her portion of the money.

'You might want to use your and Percy's share to buy a house.'

'And rattle about it on my own?'

'I didn't want you to think you had to stay here, that you had to put it back into the shop.'

Norah had reached out and pressed her hand to Letty's arm. 'My dear girl, what else would I do with it?'

Thereafter, with Norah in agreement, Letty had taken care of everything, engaging the building firm and overseeing each stage of the rebuild and refurbishment. The blackened bricks were cleaned so well that they looked as they had when the Parkers first took it on almost forty years ago. Letty had been there each day, making sure that everything was going to plan. Occasionally, Norah came with her, emotional when she saw the shop that had been her and Percy's living, and home, for more than half her lifetime, rise from the ashes.

They went outside, their backs against the wall of the smoke-house opposite the shop, watching the signwriter at his work as he stood atop of his ladder. The front board had been painted black, the lettering of *Percy Parker – Ship's Outfitters* slowly appearing in gold across it. Just as it had been when Percy was alive. The mosaic tiles that spelled the name of Parker's in the doorway entrance had been damaged by the fire. What couldn't be restored had been replaced.

'I had thought you might want to change it,' Norah said. 'Perhaps call it Hardy's.'

Letty laughed. 'It wouldn't matter one jot what I changed it to; folk would always call it Parker's.'

Norah linked her arm in Letty's, drew her close. 'Percy would marvel at what you've done.'

The old man had not left Letty's thoughts while she worked to revive something that contained his very essence. 'What I've done, I've done for him. For you.' It had all progressed far better than she'd hoped. They were down to the last knockings. It had been touch and go whether it would all come together in time for the grand reopening of Parker's Chandlery and Café, the painters working well into the night. But they were almost there.

They had bought the premises next door to use for the café as Letty had always intended. Though for an entirely different purpose to the one she'd first imagined. Hilda and

Polly would run the one by Doig's, and Dorcas and Letty would run this one between them. Dorcas and Alec had invested in it, using money from the sale of the *Stella Maris*. When Letty had protested, Dorcas had stopped her. 'We're family, all of us. It's *our* legacy. For the future. For Alfie, Stella and Billy. And any who come after.' There was no mention of the child in Lowestoft. Dorcas had told Letty she had nothing to fear on that front. When Letty questioned her, Dorcas admitted that she'd visited Becky herself, while she and Alec had first been in Lowestoft. She'd gone to have it out with her and found the lass terrified lest her in-laws cut her and the child off. To them, the child was their son John's boy and would remain so. It was a lie worth keeping. Why should the child suffer?

The week before the opening, a parcel arrived, addressed to Letty. Inside it was an oil painting of the original Parker's that Philip Proctor had made from one of the many sketches he had done during his time in Grimsby. A gift to celebrate the reopening. A few days before the Marshalls were arrested and the scandal broke, Evelyn had taken Ruth down to Bournemouth, supposedly to convalesce. Philip had joined her a week later. They were living as man and wife until Ruth's divorce came through and they could make things legal. She was pregnant with their first child. Inside the parcel, Ruth had enclosed a letter and a photograph of herself and Philip smiling to the camera. Her friend was dressed simply, in what looked like an old pair of Philip's trousers, a shirt rolled up to the elbows, her hair bobbed short about her collar.

> *Your friendship has always meant a great deal to me, Letty. Philip and I wish you all every success and happiness with the reopening of Parker's.*

Happiness. It was such a hard thing to grasp, so difficult to hold on to.

The opening had been timed to coincide with Alec's two days ashore and they spent it together, working side by side. Last night, Alec had stocked the last of the shelves while Letty put the final touches to the display. At first it had been an uneasy peace, but somehow, over the last months they had found their way back to each other. Forgiving was easier than forgetting but it was the only way forward. Letty did her best not to look back; they were not headed in that direction. It hadn't been easy for him, starting again, but he had won the men's respect and when he returned to sea he would be back at the helm. She couldn't have been prouder of him if she'd tried – and neither could his mother. It had all worked out alright in the end.

That morning, all seven of them had left the house together, the children in their Sunday best, Alec in his suit. Norah had bought a new dress for the occasion, as had Dorcas, and Letty had treated herself to a new hat from Guy and Smith's in Victoria Street. The mayor, Jack Frampton, was going to do the official opening, the lady mayoress at his side. Helen Frampton had an eye for an interesting story, and it would give them good publicity when it appeared in the early edition of their newspaper. Not that they appeared to be in need of it, for over the last weeks so many friends, old and new, had stopped by to ask of progress. They'd derived great happiness sharing their memories of Percy, and Letty enjoyed going home and passing them on to Norah.

'He's not gone, is he, Letty? While we talk of him, he's still with us.'

Letty sensed him in the shop with her now as they readied to open the doors. She went through the doorway they had created to link the shop to the café.

Dorcas was behind the counter, giving instruction to Stella and Alfie, who were setting out a regiment of cups and saucers while she filled a glass dome with a pile of freshly made scones. 'Everything ready?' Letty asked.

Dorcas nodded. 'As we ever will be.'

* * *

The shop soon became crowded as friends brought flowers, or just themselves in support. Puggy and Wolfie took their old positions at the counter, sharing stories of the old days to anyone who cared to listen. Norah was overwhelmed as people came forward, some she hadn't seen in years. It filled Letty with joy to witness it.

'Mrs Hardy?'

Letty turned. 'Pearl.'

The girl smiled. 'I wanted to wish you well.'

Letty embraced her. 'I'm so glad you did,' she said, releasing her.

Dorcas came through, looking sheepish. Pearl tensed, sensing trouble, but Dorcas held out her hand. Pearl hesitated then took it. 'I owe you an apology, lass. Can you forgive me?'

Pearl blushed as they shook hands. 'There's nothing to forgive. I heard Mr Crowe stole a key. I was to blame for that.'

'You were kind. Trusting. Some people take advantage.'

'Letty did warn me.'

Letty shook her head. 'It wouldn't have made any difference, Pearl. Mr Crowe intended to cause mischief. If he hadn't taken a key, he would have found some other way to do it.'

'Anyway, I'm very sorry for my part in it,' Dorcas said. 'I hope you'll pop next door and have a piece of cake with me before you leave.' Pearl's eyebrows couldn't go any further up her forehead. Dorcas left as briskly as she had arrived and bustled back to take command of the café.

'Mrs Parker?' asked Pearl hesitantly, perhaps expecting more bad news.

'Why not ask her yourself.' Letty called across the shop. 'Norah, we have a visitor.'

Norah came over, squeezing past Puggy, who stood guard at the counter. Her face broke into a broad smile when she saw who it was.

'It's good to see you, Pearl.' She took the girl's hand in both of hers, clasping it tightly. 'And looking so well.'

Pearl blushed again, looked behind her, beckoned to a young man who was hovering by the front door. He came to her side, removed his hat and flattened down his curly ginger hair with the flat of his hand.

'Sidney, this is Mrs Parker and Mrs Hardy.'

'Sidney?' Letty was delighted. 'You found each other?'

'We did.' Pearl beamed. 'I never lost hope that we would.'

Her simple words choked Letty. Hope: it was such a fragile thing, but the girl had held steadfastly to it. 'You're a lesson to us all, Pearl.'

Pearl linked her arm through Sidney's. 'We're getting married at St Barnabas church on King Edward Street, the twenty-seventh of next month. You'll be very welcome. You, and Mr Hardy, and Norah. Mrs Hardy. I mean, the other Mrs Hardy.'

'I couldn't bear to miss it,' Letty told her, kissing her cheek. 'Why not ask the other Mrs Hardy yourself.'

Pearl raised her eyebrows.

Letty whispered in her ear, 'I think she might like to meet Sidney. Especially as she thought he didn't exist.'

Pearl laughed. Letty watched her usher Sidney through to

the café, and as she passed through the doorway she turned and winked at Letty.

At the end of the day, they were all tired, but in a good way. It had been a day of friends, of happiness, and hope for the future. Dorcas was in the kitchen at the back of the café washing the last of the dishes, Stella drying and Alfie putting away. They chatted as they worked, Stella regaling her grandmother with her antics of the day, Dorcas chiding her to pay attention and dry the saucers properly. Alfie caught her eye, and they shared a smile. Letty left them to it. Through the open doorway of the shop, she saw Alec out on the street, yarning with Puggy and Wolfie as they said their last goodbyes. She went through to the back room behind the counter.

Norah was resting in one of the chairs that faced the fireplace. Letty had replaced their old furniture with new, but it was the same as it always had been. Two easy chairs, one either side of the fire, a gateleg table pushed against one wall, two dining chairs, a chenille cloth, a vase of flowers. She'd done her best to recreate what they'd had, but some things could never be replaced. Norah looked up when she came to join her.

'It's been a good day.' She smiled. 'Percy would have been in his element.'

Letty sat in the other chair, Percy's chair. It was imperative that Norah have her own space to come to whenever she wanted. She would still live with them at Park Street, until she decided otherwise. Letty hoped that day would never come. Norah had been the bridge between her and Dorcas. It was because of Norah that Letty had stayed, had come to realise what was worth fighting for. Family. Higgledy-piggledy as it was.

'Are you alright, Norah?'

'I was thinking of all the days we had here. The years of struggle, the little triumphs of success. It was all worth it, Letty. I wouldn't swap a minute of it.' She stared into the empty fireplace. 'Percy wasn't perfect. No one is.' She looked to Letty. 'But I loved him, and I knew he loved me. In the end, that's all that matters. Love – and friends. That's the best measure of our days.'

They sat together in quiet companionship until Alec came through and put his head around the door. 'Mother is taking the children home. Would you like me to lock up?'

Norah looked to her. 'Just give me a moment and I'll join you.'

Letty followed Alec into the shop, ran her hand along the counter. It would take years for it to be worn smooth by customers. Forty years or more, but it was something to aim for. She looked about her. The shelves were all in order, the boots neatly paired, the tins of paint and varnish tidily stacked in pyramids. Just as they had always been – the same and yet different. She reached out for Alec's hand and took it in hers. He raised it to his lips and kissed it.

They waited on the street for Norah to join them. Further down, heading towards Fish Dock Road, Dorcas walked with the pram, Alfie at her side, Stella skipping ahead. Things changed all the time. Life was a constant ebb and flow, and trying to stop it was like trying to hold back the tide. All manner of things lurked below the surface; keeping afloat was not easy but somehow, they had managed to do it. Together. There was always someone ready to hold out a helping hand. The important thing was to take hold of it when it was offered. After a few minutes, Norah joined them. Letty put her key in the door and locked it.

'Back again tomorrow,' Letty said.

'And the day after, and the day after that, God willing,' Norah said, taking one last look at the frontage. Letty went to her, linked her arm in hers and the three of them made their way down Henderson Street and headed for home. No doubt there would be storms ahead, but together they would weather them. As Norah had said, love and friendship were the best measure of their days. Letty was lucky enough to have both.

* * *

MORE FROM TRACY BAINES

ACKNOWLEDGEMENTS

The book you have just read could not have been written without the help of a huge team of people. First and foremostly I'd like the thank my editor, Caroline Ridding, who helps me bring my muddled thoughts to order. To Becca and Shirley, who catch me where I've gone adrift. As always, any mistakes are my own.

To the amazing Boldwood team who make the book shine and get it into readers' hands.

To author Margaret Graham, and agents past and present, Vivien Green and Gaia Banks, and my Monday buddy, Helen Baggott.

Many people who have answered my numerous queries and assisted with research: Tom Smith, Martin Grant, Trevor Ekins, Dave Smith, Paul Fenwick, Steve Farrow and Paul Woolnough, Rachel Branson and Caroline Beeson Spence.

I only have to ask a question to tap into a huge wealth of information from various Facebook groups: Grimsby Memories, Cleethorpes Memories, Great Grimsby Fishing History, Grimsby Fish Docks Past and Present and Great Grimsby Retired Fishermen.

Boldwood ran a competition to name Alec's dog. So Tess arrived courtesy of Laura Hegarty in memory of her childhood dog.

I ran a little fun competition of my own to name Alec's ship, hosted by the fabulous Mel and Nick at The Rabbit Hutch Book

Shop on Freeman Street market. The name I chose was the *Clarissa* in honour of Margaret Swaby's mother who was a braider and worked on Grimsby Docks, and later at home when her children came along, just as Dorcas and so many other women did.

To the bloggers, reviewers, and fellow authors who give so generously of their time to get the word out about books, books, books!

To the fishermen and wives who have shared their stories over the years – John Meadows, Alfreda Evans, John Evans, Jim Evans, Ray and Janet Evans.

Thank you to you, the readers. I hope you enjoy this latest adventure.

And to my family, for all the love and strength they give me. And always have.

You can find more about my books on my website www.tracybaines.co.uk

ABOUT THE AUTHOR

Tracy Baines is the bestselling saga writer of The Seaside Girls series. She was born and brought up in Cleethorpes and spent her early years in the theatre world which inspired her writing.

Sign up to Tracy Baines's mailing list here for news, competitions and updates on future books.

Follow Tracy on social media:

x.com/tracyfbaines

facebook.com/tracybainesauthor

instagram.com/tracyfbaines

ALSO BY TRACY BAINES

Dockyard Girls

The Dockyard Girls

Trouble for The Dockyard Girls

Stormy Times for The Dockyard Girls

The Seaside Girls

The Seaside Girls

Hopes and Dreams for The Seaside Girls

A New Year for the Seaside Girls

The Seaside Girls Under Fire

www.ingramcontent.com/pod-product-compliance
Lightning Source LLC
La Vergne TN
LVHW030916080826
845145LV00013B/2916